Finding
COLIN FIRTH

Center Point
Large Print

Also by Mia March and available from
Center Point Large Print:

The Meryl Streep Movie Club

Finding COLIN FIRTH

MIA MARCH

CENTER POINT LARGE PRINT
THORNDIKE, MAINE

This Center Point Large Print edition
is published in the year 2013 by arrangement with
Gallery Books, a division of Simon & Schuster, Inc.

The text of this Large Print edition is unabridged.
In other aspects, this book may vary
from the original edition.
Printed in the United States of America
on permanent paper.
Set in 16-point Times New Roman type.

ISBN: 978-1-61173-902-2

Library of Congress Cataloging-in-Publication Data

March, Mia.
Finding Colin Firth / Mia March. — Center Point Large Print edition.
pages cm
ISBN 978-1-61173-902-2 (Library binding : alk. paper)
1. Motion picture locations—Maine—Fiction.
2. Firth, Colin, 1960– —Fiction. 3. Women journalists—Maine—Fiction.
4. Adoptees—Fiction. 5. Waitresses—Fiction.
6. Life change events—Fiction. 7. Maine—Fiction.
8. Large type books. I. Title.
PS3613.A7327F56 2013
813´.6—dc23
2013020263

For my beloved Max,
who made a mother out of me

"I cannot fix on the hour, or the spot, or the look, or the words, which laid the foundation. It is too long ago. I was in the middle before I knew that I had begun."
—Fitzwilliam Darcy, *Pride and Prejudice*

"I realize that when I met you at the Turkey Curry Buffet that I was unforgivably rude and wearing a reindeer jumper that my mother had given me the day before. But the thing is, um, what I'm trying to say, very inarticulately, is that, um, in fact, perhaps despite appearances, I like you. Very much."
—Mark Darcy, *Bridget Jones's Diary*

"I'm fully aware that if I were to change professions tomorrow, become an astronaut and be the first man to land on Mars, the headlines in the newspapers would read: 'Mr. Darcy Lands on Mars.'"
—Colin Firth

Chapter 1
BEA CRANE

The letter that would change Bea's life arrived while she was in the kitchen at Boston's Crazy Burger, working on four orders of Mt. Vesuvius specials—three patties stacked a foot tall and layered with caramelized onions, bacon, Swiss cheese, lettuce, tomato, sour pickles, and hot sauce. One of her new roommates, Nina, subletting for the summer in the dumpy three-bedroom apartment that Bea now shared with two strangers, poked her head in and said she'd signed for a certified envelope for Bea, and since she was coming to Crazy Burger for lunch, she brought it over.

"Certified? Who's it from?" Bea asked, taking a fast glance at the parcel as she scooped up the caramelized onions from the pan. Mmm. She'd been frying onions for three hours and still, the smell never got old.

Nina glanced at the upper left-hand corner of the envelope. "Return address says Baker Klein, Twelve State Street, Boston."

Bea shrugged. "Will you open it up and read the first few lines to me? I need both hands to finish this burger." Her manager, Barbara, would go nuts if she caught anyone but employees in the kitchen, but Bea was curious to know what the package was about, and Crazy Barbara, as the staff called her behind her back, was in her office, going over inventory.

"Sure," Nina said. She slit open the envelope, pulled out a letter, and read, "My darling Bea."

Bea froze, her hand paused on lettuce leaves. "What?" That was how her mother had always addressed the letters she'd written to Bea at college. "Turn it over—who's it from?"

"It says Mama."

Bea raised an eyebrow. "Well, since my mother died over a year ago, it's definitely not from her."

"It's handwritten, script," Nina said, "but it definitely says Mama."

That made no sense. But Bea's mother always signed her letters Mama. "You can just drop it on that chair, Nina. I'll finish this last burger and read it on my break. Thanks for bringing it over."

Bea was due for that much-needed fifteen-minute break; she'd been on shift at Crazy Burger since eleven and it was now close to two. She loved working at the popular burger joint in Boston's Back Bay, even if it was supposed to be temporary since she'd graduated from college a year ago and still hadn't found a teaching job, but her boss was driving her crazy. If Bea took sixteen minutes for her break, Barbara would dock her pay. The woman lived to dock pay. Last week, one of her Mt. Vesuvius burgers was randomly measured and discovered to be only eleven inches high; Bea's paycheck was cut short five bucks.

In between each layer of burger—three of them—Bea piled on the toppings, added an extra helping of hot sauce, put on the top bun, then measured it. Just shy of a foot, which meant she had to add more lettuce. Finally, she set it on a plate next to the three other Mt. Vesuvius burgers, plunked down a basket of onion rings and a basket of cheese fries, then rang the bell to alert the waitress to pick up. She called Manny, the other cook, in from his break, then took the manila envelope outside into the back alley. She lifted her face to the June sunshine. The breezy, warm day felt wonderful on her skin, in her hair, after she'd been cooped up in the small kitchen all afternoon.

She pulled out the contents of the envelope and her body went completely still. The letter was from her mother; there was no mistaking Cora Crane's handwriting. It was dated just over a year ago and attached to what looked like forms.

My darling Bea,

If you're reading this, I'm gone now. A year gone. I've kept something from you all your life, something I should have told you the moment you were placed in my arms when you were just a day old. I didn't give birth to you, Bea. Your father and I adopted you.

11

I'm not entirely sure why, but I was ashamed that I couldn't bear a child, something I wanted so desperately, something your father wanted so desperately. When the adoption agent placed you in my arms, you were mine. It was as though I had given birth to you, and I suppose I wanted to believe it myself. So your father—God rest his soul—and I made it so. We never breathed a word to you, never told you. And you grew up believing that you were born to us.

Now that I feel myself going, I can't bear to take this with me. But I can't bear to tell you with my final breaths, either, I can't do that to you. So I'll wait on this, for both of us. But you should know the truth because it is the truth.

How I wish I'd been brave enough to be honest from that first minute. To tell you how grateful I was, how you were mine before I even met you, from the second the adoption agent called with the news.

I hope you will forgive me, my darling girl. You are my daughter, and I love you with all my heart.

Mama

Bea pulled the letter from its heavy paper clip and looked at the forms. Adoption papers, dated twenty-two years ago, from the Helping Hands Adoption Agency in Brunswick, Maine.

Her hand shaking, Bea stuffed the letter and papers back inside the envelope, paced around the alley, then stopped, pulled out the letter, and read it again. The words, in black ink, started blending together. Should have told you. Adoption agent. Sorry. The truth is the truth. If it weren't for her mother's handwriting and the good stationery she'd used for all correspondence, Bea might have thought someone was playing a trick on her.

Adopted? What?

The letter and papers had been sent by a law firm Bea had never heard of; her mother had been long widowed and not well off, and when Cora Crane died last year, there was only the sparsely furnished year-round rental cottage far from the beach on Cape Cod to settle up. Bea had gone through the drawers and closets looking for every last precious memento of her mother, and if this letter had been in that house, she would have found it. Her mother had clearly arranged for Bea to hear the news well after she was gone, after the grief had subsided some.

She tried to imagine her mother, the sweetest person Bea had ever known, propped up in her hospice bed, writing that letter, in anguish, most likely. But another image kept coming: her mother, her father, twenty-two years ago, meeting Bea as a day-old newborn. "Here's your daughter," the adoption agent must have said. Or something like that.

Who the hell am I? Bea wondered. She thought of the framed photograph on her bedside table. It was her favorite family picture, taken when she was four, and Bea loved looking at it every night before she fell asleep and every morning when she woke up. Bea, sitting on her father's shoulders, her mother standing beside them, looking up at Bea and laughing, a tree ablaze with orange and red leaves behind them. Bea had been wearing the Batman cape she insisted on every day for months, and the red hat that her mother had made for her. Cora had saved those old favorites and now Bea kept them in a keepsake box in her closet. Another picture came to mind, one she kept on her desk in her room, of Bea and her mother at Bea's college graduation last May, just over a year ago, and just a few weeks before her mother had gotten very sick and diagnosed with ovarian cancer, as though she was holding on to watch Bea graduate. Two months later, her mother was gone.

Cora Crane, piano teacher with the patience of a saint, with the dark curls, bright blue eyes, and a smile for everyone, was her mother. Keith Crane, handsome construction worker who sang her an Irish song before bed every single night of her childhood until he'd died when she was nine, was her father. The Cranes had been wonderful, doting parents who'd made Bea feel loved every day of her life. If someone else had given birth to Bea, that didn't change anything.

But someone else had given birth to her. Who?

A hollow pressure started building in Bea's chest.

"Bea!" Her boss, Crazy Barbara, came charging outside, glaring at Bea. "What the hell are you doing? It's still lunch rush! Manny said you went out at least twenty minutes ago."

"I just got some very strange news," Bea said, her head spinning. "I need a few minutes."

"Well, unless someone died, you need to head back to work—now." Barbara started muttering under her breath. "Taking an extended break in the middle of lunch rush. Who does she think she is?"

"Actually," Bea said, barely able to think straight. There was no way she'd be able to get through the craze of orders. "I need to go home, Barbara. I just learned some weird news, and—"

"You either get back to work or you're fired. I'm sick to death of all these excuses—all day long, someone has a headache, someone's grand-mother's sick. Do your job or I'll find someone who actually earns their paycheck."

Bea had been working at Crazy Burger for three years, full-time since last summer, and was the best cook in the kitchen and the fastest. But nothing ever was good enough for Crazy Barbara. "You know what? I quit." She took off her apron, handed it to a for-once-speechless Barbara, and went back inside to collect her bag from her locker.

She shoved the letter in her bag and walked the half mile home in a daze, tripping over someone's backpack the minute she walked through the front door of her apartment in the four-story brick building. God, she hated living here this summer with strangers. She headed down the narrow hall, stepping on a pair of boxer-briefs, then unlocked her door and locked it behind her. She dropped her bag on the floor of her room and sat down on her bed, hugging her mother's old cross-stitched pillow to her chest. She didn't move for hours.

"Wow, Bea, your entire life has been a lie."

Slice of pizza en route to her mouth, Bea stared at Tommy Wonkowksi, star running back for the Beardsley College famed football team. A half hour ago, she'd been lying on her bed, staring at the ceiling, grappling with yesterday's bombshell, when her phone had rung: Tommy, at Poe's Pizzeria, asking if he'd gotten the time wrong for their date. She'd forced herself up and out the two blocks to the restaurant; she hadn't eaten since she'd gotten her mother's letter, hadn't left her room. But now, as she sat across from Tommy, she wished she'd canceled. With her universe tilted, she needed comforting and familiar, and Tommy Wonkowski was anything but. She wasn't even sure why she'd said yes to this first date, but it wasn't every day a hot jock asked Bea out. When they'd met last week at the university's Writing Center, where she had a part-time tutoring job (Bea had been helping him write a final paper for the freshman English class he was now bothering to take as a senior in summer session), she had been charmed by his good looks, his very differentness from her, and the fact that he towered over her. Bea was five feet ten, and Tommy made her feel kind of dainty for once.

"I wouldn't go that far," she said, wishing she'd never told him about the letter. But they'd run out of things to say to each other by the time the waitress had set down their large pizza, and she'd blurted out what was consuming her every waking thought as she'd shaken Parmesan cheese on a slice. *Guess what I just found out yesterday? Turns out I was adopted.*

But yes, it did sort of feel like her whole life had been a kind of lie. Friends, strangers—Bea herself—marveling over the years at how utterly different she was from both Cora and Keith Crane. They were dark-haired; Bea was blond. Her mother's eyes were startling blue, and her father's were hazel, yet Bea's were driftwood brown. Her parents were average height; she was an Amazon. She wasn't musical like her mother, nor mathematical like her father. They were both quiet introverts and she could talk and talk and talk. More than once, Bea could remember strangers, friends, looking at her and saying, "Where on earth did you come from?"

And her father responding, "Oh, my father is quite tall, almost six-two," and pictures of the late grandfather she'd never met reflecting that. Or her mother casually tossing off, "My mother— God rest her soul—had Bea's brown eyes, even though I have blue like my father's." And that was true too. She'd seen pictures of her maternal grandmother, who died when she was very young. Brown eyes, like Bea's.

It was as though I had given birth to you, and I suppose I wanted to believe it myself. So your father and I made it so.

"Holy crap, you must hate your mother now," Tommy said around a mouthful of pizza. "I mean, she lied to you your whole life about something so . . . what's the word?"

"Fundamental," Bea said through gritted teeth. How dare you suggest I'd ever hate my mother, you oversize blockhead, she wanted to shout. But once again, the image of Cora Crane, dying in that hospice bed, her hand holding Bea's with the last of her strength, was all she could think of. Her sweet mother. "I don't hate her at all. I never could, ever." Though if Bea let herself go there, as she couldn't help but do in the past twenty-four hours, she'd feel a strange anger that would build in her head and start her heart pounding, then give way to confusion that made her head spin and her heart just plain hurt. A fundamental truth *had* been withheld. But she couldn't be mad at her mother; she couldn't bear that. Her mother was gone. "She explained herself in the letter. And if you knew my mother—"

"Adopted mother."

She glared at him. "Actually, it's adoptive. But no, she's my mother. Just my mother. That she adopted me doesn't change that, Tommy."

He picked up a second slice and bit into it, gooey mozzarella cheese extending. "It kind of does, Bea. I mean, someone else gave birth to you."

Bea sat back, defeated. Someone else *had* given birth to her. Someone she hadn't known existed a day ago. Someone she couldn't even conjure up. There was no face, no hair color, no name. Last night, as her eyes were finally drifting closed at three o'clock, she imagined her birth mother to look exactly like herself, just . . . older. But how old? Had her birth mother been a teenager? A very poor older woman who couldn't feed an additional mouth?

On October 12, twenty-two years ago, someone had given birth to Bea and then had given her up for adoption. Why? What was her story? Who was she?

"Yes, Tommy, someone else gave birth to me," she told him, her appetite gone again. "But that just makes that person my birth mother."

"Just? There's no just about a birth mother." He chuckled and dug into his third slice of pizza, looking out the window at the busy Boston street as though Bea was proving to be the one who needed tutoring. He turned back to her. "Like, what if you're married and have a kid, and that kid is dying of some kind of horrible disease, and your blood and your husband's blood aren't a match. Your birth mother could save your kid's life. Man, that's epic. I mean, think about it."

But Bea didn't want to. Her parents were Cora and Keith Crane, la, la, la, hands over her ears. Still, the more she sat there, listening to Tommy Wonkowski tell her how she should feel about all this, the more she realized he was right about a lot of it.

For a week, Bea walked around Boston with the strange truth knocking around in her head. A week ago, she'd been one thing: the daughter of Cora and Keith Crane. End of story. Now she was something else. Adopted. She'd started as someone else's story. Ended someone's story, maybe. What was that story? She couldn't stop thinking about her birth parents. Who they were. Where she came from. What they looked like. And yes, Tommy Wonkowski, what their medical histories were.

She sat at her desk, her favorite novels, books of essays, a memoir about a teacher's first year, and her laptop making her feel stronger, more like herself. She stared at the manila envelope, lying right next to *To Kill a Mockingbird*, on which she'd written her senior thesis. She was supposed to be an English teacher by now, middle school or high school, teaching teenagers how to write strong essays, how to think critically about novels, why they should love the English language. But when her mother died last summer, Bea found herself floundering for months. She hadn't gotten a single interview for a teaching job at any of the private schools she'd applied to, and the publics all wanted her to be enrolled in a master's program for teacher education, which would mean more loans. A year later, here she was, not teaching, and still living with students. The only thing different was that she wasn't who she thought she was.

Bea stared at the photo of herself and her mother at her college graduation, willing herself to remember that she was still the same Bea Crane she was last week. Same memories, same mind, same heart, same soul, same dreams.

But she felt different in her bones, in her cells, as though they were buzzing with the electricity of the truth. She had been adopted. Another woman, another man, had brought her into this world.

Why did that have to change anything? Why did it matter so much? Why couldn't she just accept the truth and move on from it?

Because you're here alone, for one. Her two good girlfriends had left Boston upon graduation for first jobs. Her best friends from high school were scattered across the country and in Europe; everyone was off on their summer plans, except for Bea, who had nowhere to go, no home.

She felt caged and absolutely free at the same time. So this week she'd stalked around Boston, thinking of her parents with one breath, and this nameless, faceless birth mother with the next. Then she'd come back to her room and stare at the manila envelope until she'd open it and read the adoption papers again, which told her nothing.

Maybe if she did know something, just something to make this tenuous grasp on the words *birth mother* feel more . . . concrete.

"Damn it," she said, grabbing the envelope and sliding out the papers. Before she could stop herself, she picked up her cell phone and punched in the telephone number on the first page.

"Helping Hands Adoption Agency, may I help you?"

Bea sucked in a breath and explained the situation and that she just wanted to know if there were names. Most likely there would not be. Bea had done some reading and learned that most adoptions were closed, as hers had been according to the paperwork, but that sometimes birth mothers left their names and contact information in the adoption files. There were also registries birth parents and adoptees could sign up for. Bea would not be signing up for anything.

"Ah. Let me look in your file," the woman said. "Hold just a minute."

Bea held her breath. Make this difficult, Bea thought. No names. She wasn't ready for a name.

Why had she called? When the woman came back, Bea would tell her thank you for checking but she'd changed her mind, she wasn't ready to know anything about her birth parents.

"Bingo," the woman said. "Your birth mother called to update the file at her last address change just over a year ago. Her name is Veronica Russo and she lives in Boothbay Harbor, Maine."

Bea couldn't breathe.

"Do you need a minute?" the woman was saying. "I'll give you a minute, no worries." She did indeed wait a minute, and Bea's head was close to bursting when the woman said, "Honey, do you have a pen?"

Bea said she did. She picked up the silver Waterman that her mother had given her as a graduation present. She mechanically wrote down the address and telephone number the woman gave her. Home and cell.

"She even included her employment address and phone number," the woman continued. "The Best Little Diner in Boothbay."

Veronica Russo. Her birth mother had a name. She was a real person, living and breathing, and

23

she'd updated the file. She'd left every possible piece of contact information.

Her birth mother wanted to be found.

Bea thanked the woman and hung up. She shivered and grabbed her favorite sweater, her father's old off-white fisherman sweater that her mother had bought him while they were on their honeymoon in Ireland. It was the same sweater her father wore in her favorite picture, with Bea up on his shoulders. She put it on and hugged herself, wishing it smelled like her dad, like Ivory soap and Old Spice and safety, but her dad had been gone since Bea was nine. A long time. For the next eleven years, it was just Bea and her mom, both sets of grandparents long gone, both Cranes only children.

And then Bea lost her mother. She was alone.

She walked to the window seat and stared out at the rain sluicing down. *I have a birth mother. Her name is Veronica Russo. She lives in a place called Boothbay Harbor, Maine.*

She works in a diner called the Best Little Diner in Boothbay.

Which had a cute ring. A woman who worked in a diner like that couldn't be so bad, right? She was probably a waitress, one of those friendly types who called her customers "hon." Or maybe she'd fallen on hard times and was hard-bitten, a shell of a woman who set down eggs over easy and fish and chips with a depressive thud.

Maybe she was a short-order cook. That might explain Bea's ability to make an incredible hamburger, not that she could cook anything in her kitchenless room. This past year, between her jobs at Crazy Burger and the Writing Center, she had enough money to pay her rent. But now she would come up short for July, and the Writing Center was open only part-time for the summer sessions. Her last lousy paycheck, a half week's pay from Crazy Burger, wouldn't help much either.

She had nowhere to be, nowhere to go. But she had this name, and an address.

Bea could take a drive up to Maine, make herself walk into the Best Little Diner, sit at the counter and order a cup of coffee, and look at the name tags on the waitresses' aprons. She would be able to check out her birth mother from a very close distance. She could do that.

Yes. She would drive up, check out Veronica Russo, and if it seemed right to Bea, she would introduce herself. Not that she had any idea how to go about that. Maybe she'd leave a note in her mailbox, or just call. Then they'd meet some-where, for a walk or coffee. Bea would find out what she needed to know so she could stop wondering, speculating, driving herself crazy. Then she'd say thank you to Veronica Russo for the information and drive back home to Boston and start looking for a new place to live. And a new job. Maybe she had to let go of her dream of being a teacher. She'd come home once her past had been settled, and she'd figure out what the hell she was supposed to be doing with her life.

Home. As if there were one. This room was nothing more than a big closet. And her mother's rental cottage on Cape Cod, where she and her mom had moved after her father died, had long ago been sold by the owner. But that little white cottage had been the one place left on earth that had felt like home at Thanksgiving, Christmas, summer breaks, and at times when Bea was stressed or heartbroken or just needed her mama.

Now there were just memories and this old fisherman sweater. And a stranger named Veronica Russo, up in Maine. Waiting a long time to be found by Bea.

Chapter 2

VERONICA RUSSO

Only an idiot would attempt to make a pie—a special-ordered chocolate caramel cream Amore Pie—while watching *Pride and Prejudice.* Had she put in the vanilla? What about the salt? Damn Colin Firth and his pond-soaked white shirt. Veronica set down her measuring spoons on the flour-dusted counter and gave her full attention to the small TV next to the coffeemaker. God, she loved Colin Firth. Not just because he was so handsome either. This TV miniseries was at least fifteen years old, and Colin Firth had to be fifty now. He was still gorgeous. But it was more than that. Colin Firth was six feet two inches of hope. To Veronica, he represented what she'd been looking for her entire life and had never found and probably never would, at this point. Veronica was thirty-eight years old. Still not married.

If you wanted love, really wanted love, you'd have it, friends, even boyfriends, had said many times over the years. *There's something wrong with you,* her last beau had said before he'd stormed out on her for not agreeing to marry him. *Something wrong with the way your heart works.*

Maybe there was. No, Veronica knew it was true. And she knew why too. But now, at thirty-eight, friends were worrying about her ending up all alone, so she'd started saying what felt light-hearted but true at the same time, that she was holding out for a man who felt like Colin Firth to her. Her friend Shelley from the diner had known exactly what she meant. "I realize he's an actor playing roles, but I get it," Shelley had said. "Honest. Full of integrity. Conviction. Brimming with intelligence. Loyal. You just believe every-thing he says with that British accent of his—and can trust it."

All that and yes, he was so damned handsome that Veronica had lost track of her own Amore Pie, a pie she could make in her sleep. Her special elixir pies were in high demand ever since she'd been back in Boothbay Harbor—just over a year now. She'd grown up in Boothbay, but had bought a house in a different neighborhood than the one she'd lived in with her parents. It had been love at first sight for the lemon-yellow bungalow on Sea Road, and the day she'd moved in, while hanging the wooden blinds on her sliding glass door to her deck, she'd heard someone crying. She'd peered her head out the door to see her neighbor sitting on her back porch, wearing only a black negligee and black leather stilettos. Veronica had gone over and asked if she could help, and the woman blurted out that her marriage was over. Veronica had sat down, and within moments her neighbor, whose name was Frieda, shared the whole story, how she'd tried to entice her husband, who barely looked at her these days, home for lunch with exactly what she was going to do to him. But he'd said he'd brought last night's leftovers and would just have that.

"He'd rather have a cold meat loaf sandwich than me?" Frieda had cried to Veronica. "For months, I've been trying to entice him back to me, and nothing works." She broke down in a fresh round of tears.

Veronica had told Frieda that she was a baker and would make her a special pie to serve her husband for dessert that night. When she gave him his slice, she was to think about how much she loved him, wanted him. And just for good measure, she could run her hands up the back of his neck.

Well, that night, Frederick Mulverson had said he didn't know what came over him, but he was back. Frieda had Veronica's Amore Pie on standing order every Friday. One word to her friends and relatives, and Veronica's phone had started ringing with orders, just as it had in New Mexico. Amore Pies were her most requested.

She made upwards of twenty special pies a week. Plus two a day for the Best Little Diner in Boothbay, where she worked as a waitress. And nine pies a week for three local inns. But those—for the diner and the inns—were just her Happiness Pies, pies that tasted like summer vacation. She saved her special elixir pies for her clients around town, everything from Feel Better Pie, which came in all kinds of dietetic-friendly varieties, such as gluten free, dairy free, and even sugar free, to Confidence Pie, which involved Key limes.

What she couldn't seem to do was make a Colin Firth Pie for herself. She'd made Amore Pies for hundreds of clients that seemed to attract love to them. Sure, maybe it was mostly power of thought, but so what, since it worked. *You get what you believe* is what Veronica's grandmother used to say. At the thought of dear Renata Russo, who'd died just months before all the trouble had started when Veronica was sixteen, Veronica closed her eyes. She let herself remember what it was like when she'd had a family, when Veronica, her parents, and her grandmother would sit around the table in the house Veronica grew up in—just several miles away from here—and have big Italian dinners. Meatballs and so much linguini in her grandmother's homemade tomato sauce that it seemed to come from bottomless pots.

She missed those days, days that had ended on an April morning when Veronica was sixteen and blurted out over a pancake breakfast that she was pregnant. One minute, she'd had a family—minus her beloved grandmother. The next, Veronica had been sent away.

Why are you upsetting yourself by thinking

about all that? she asked herself as she turned her attention back to the TV and the Bennet sisters, Elizabeth and Jane, conspiring in their lovely white dresses about their love lives. But since she'd moved back to Boothbay Harbor, her past was all she could think about. It was why she'd come home, for heaven's sake. To face it. To stop . . . running.

She thought if she came home, if she faced her past, maybe her heart would start working the way it was supposed to. And maybe, maybe, maybe, the daughter she'd given up for adoption would contact her. Veronica had been living in New Mexico when that baby girl had turned eighteen, and Veronica had called the Helping Hands Adoption Agency and left her contact information, then did the same with the registry in Maine. She'd waited by the phone that day. And the next. But there was no call from a young woman asking if she was Veronica Russo, if she'd given birth to a baby girl on October 12 in 1991 in Boothbay Harbor, Maine. For weeks afterward, Veronica had kept her cell phone close, expecting a call any time. She wasn't sure why she'd believed her daughter would contact her on her eighteenth birthday, but she had believed it.

She'd started baking then, four years ago in New Mexico, pies that felt like hope. She'd never been much of a baker before, but she'd been watching a cooking show, a special on holiday pies, and Veronica had gone out and bought ingredients to make a pie from scratch. She loved the feel of flour in her fingers, the pale yellow sticks of cold butter, the texture of shortening, the whiteness of sugar and salt, the purity of water. Such simple ingredients for a piecrust, not that there was anything simple about making piecrust from scratch. But Veronica had persisted until she'd perfected her crusts, all kinds, depending on the pie. Just like that, she'd found what comforted her, what replaced lonely nights with work she loved in the kitchen. She loved baking pies. And her pies felt so special to her that when she made them for friends, she'd name them for the reason she was sharing them in the first place. For a heartbroken friend, Healing Pie. For a sick friend, Feel Better Pie. For a down-in-the-dumps friend, Happiness Pie. For the lovelorn, Amore Pie. For the worried, Confidence Pie. Her Hope Pies were popular too. One friend had wished that her boyfriend, on his second tour of combat duty, would come back from Afghanistan in one piece, and Veronica had baked her a salted caramel cheesecake pie that she put all her hope into and then told her friend to do the same while cutting the first slice. Her boyfriend had returned with only a broken leg. Her pies had worked their sweet magic on so many people that Veronica had developed quite a clientele. *How did it work?* they wanted to know. Either Veronica had a little bit of magic in her or it was all about prayer. And luck. Maybe some of each.

But Veronica had never bothered with a Colin Firth Pie in the hopes of bringing a man into her life whom she could finally love. All the magical pies in the world couldn't fix her messed-up heart. She wasn't capable of loving someone; kind as she was to others, she knew that. She'd loved once, so fiercely, and had been irreparably hurt. By her grandmother's death. By a sixteen-year-old boy. By her parents washing their hands of her. She'd tried to love; she'd tried damned hard. She'd had her share of boyfriends over the years. Some for a couple of years, some for just a few months—all kinds of men. From the cute short-order cook at the first diner that had hired her as a sixteen-year-old waitress in Florida, where she'd moved after giving birth; to the proud marine in New Mexico who'd announced he was tired of waiting for her to say yes, he was driving them to Las Vegas to get married that day whether she liked it or not. She'd tried to explain again, said they could have a wonderful, romantic weekend in Vegas without a wedding, without talk of marriage, but he'd figured she'd cave once they got to the wedding chapel. She hadn't caved. Furious and shouting that he'd had it with her and her inability to commit to him, he'd left her there, by the chapel, and driven away and she never saw him again. By the time she'd returned to New Mexico the next day, his few belongings were gone from the house he practically shared with her. Her heart had just never opened fully to him. It never had for anyone except Timothy Macintosh, a guy she'd spent the past twenty-two years trying not to think about.

It had been there, in front of the Little White Wedding Chapel, that Veronica had realized she had to go back to Boothbay Harbor. If she ever wanted to fix herself, she'd have to go back. Back to her hometown, where she'd been shunned and sent away, where she'd given birth to a baby girl she'd held for two minutes and then had to hand over. She believed if she came back, faced all those memories, her Hope Pie might work on her and her heart would suddenly open and that baby girl would make contact.

Veronica just wanted to know that the daughter she'd given up was all right. Sometimes Veronica thought if she could just know that, she could move on. Her jagged heart would piece together, and her life would change. Could change, anyway.

So she'd come home, uncomfortable as it had been. Come home and tried to face her demons right away. Before she'd even started looking for a house to buy in town, she'd driven by the house she'd grown up in, a white saltbox that new owners had painted blue. She'd pulled over and felt sick to her stomach and got away from there fast. But she'd driven by several times, and each time she'd had less of a reaction. Same for the house the Macintosh family had lived in, the brick cape where she and Timothy had spent so much time. She'd even walked in the woods where she and Timothy had set up her old Girl Scouts tent, where they'd talk for hours about dreams, about leaving Maine right after high school and taking a Greyhound bus to Florida, where it was always warm and never snowed. That old tent was where a child had been conceived.

She'd tried to face her past, but she was obviously doing something wrong—not facing the right things, maybe—because she felt as unsettled in Boothbay Harbor as she had the day she'd moved back a year ago. She didn't even know why. No one cared about what happened twenty-two years ago, except several folks who did remember her as the girl who'd gotten pregnant as a junior in high school, whose parents were so embarrassed they'd sent her away, sold their house and left town, left the state, leaving her behind to fend for herself. Two of those people who did remember had unfortunately signed up for Veronica's pie-making class that started Monday night—Penelope Von Blun and CeCe Allwood, who'd gone to school with her and now led perfect lives and fake-smiled at Veronica in town, then whispered behind her back. Veronica's pie classes were popular; she'd taught four so far, but she limited the class to five students so that she could give individual attention to each baker. Ironic, since she'd spent most of the past year trying not to pay any attention to Penelope or CeCe.

Fitzwilliam Darcy's face filled the TV screen. "If, however, your feelings have changed, I will have to tell you; you have bewitched me, body and soul, and I love, I love, I love you. I never wish to be parted from you from this day on," he was saying to Elizabeth, and Veronica felt something move in her chest the way she always did at this scene. God, he was intense. Intense with fierce love.

The doorbell rang, and Veronica pulled herself away from the kiss she'd been waiting the entire episode for. She wiped her flour-dusted hands on her apron, took one last glance at the TV, and went to the front door.

Officer Nick DeMarco and his daughter, who Veronica would guess to be about nine, maybe ten. Veronica always thought of him as Officer DeMarco, even though they'd gone to school together their whole lives. Well, until junior year, anyway. He'd been friendly with Timothy, the boy who everyone knew had gotten Veronica pregnant. So Veronica had kept her distance from Nick, who seemed to keep something of a distance from her, as well. He was out of his police blues, wearing jeans and a Boston Red Sox T-shirt. His daughter looked just like him. Same dark hair burnished with lighter brown, and dark brown eyes with long lashes. She had an elfin chin, though, and there was nothing elfin about Nick DeMarco.

"We're not late, are we?" Nick asked, peering in behind her. His daughter looked up at Veronica expectantly.

"Late for what?" Veronica asked.

"The pie class," he said.

Pie class? Nick DeMarco had definitely not registered for her class. If he had, even staring at Colin Firth for two hours the past four nights would not let her forget it. "Well, actually, you're early. My pie class starts Monday night. Right time, wrong day. But I don't have you on my registration list, do I?"

He winced. "I had your flyer in my back pocket for a week and kept meaning to call and then I figured we'd just show up."

The girl looked like she was about to cry. "We can take your class still, right?" she asked Veronica.

Oh hell. The class was full. She had six people already and really did prefer to limit each four-week session to five students. Otherwise, there wasn't enough of Veronica to go around and the class got too unwieldy. Too many elbows at the counters and table.

Officer DeMarco was staring at her, pleading with her to say yes, of course you can take my class, sweet girl.

"I happen to have a few slots open, so not a problem at all," she said to his daughter.

She watched the girl relax and wondered why learning to make pie—and perhaps one of Veronica's special pies—was so important to her.

"What's your name, honey?" Veronica asked.

"Leigh. Leigh DeMarco. I'm ten."

"Well, Leigh, you just turn up with your dad on Monday at six o'clock sharp and don't forget to bring an apron." One look from Nick told her that he didn't have an apron. "But if you don't have one or forget, I just so happen to have extras."

Leigh smiled and her whole face lit up.

"Is there a particular kind of pie you're interested in making?" Veronica asked Leigh. "I'm planning on teaching apple pie for the first class, but I'll have recipes for my special elixir pies available if anyone wants to work on one of those too."

The girl glanced sideways at her father, then at the ground. "Apple pie is fine. I had a slice at the diner last week. It was really good." It was obvious the girl had her mind set on a particular special pie but didn't want to say in front of her father.

"Ah, yes, my apple crumb Happiness Pie," Veronica said.

"I did feel happy when I was eating it," Leigh said, but her shoulders slumped.

Nick ruffled Leigh's hair. "Well, we won't take

up more of your time, Veronica. Sorry about the mix-up. We'll see you Monday at six, then."

He looked so uncomfortable that Veronica felt sorry for him. She was pretty good at reading people; it was how she earned her reputation with her pies. But Nick DeMarco was impenetrable beyond the obvious desire to leave. A cop requirement, most likely.

Just as Veronica turned the lock, the doorbell rang again.

This time, only Leigh DeMarco stood on the porch. Her father stood on the sidewalk. He held up a hand and Veronica nodded at him.

"Hi, hon," she said to Leigh.

"I remembered what kind of special pie I want to learn to make," Leigh whispered. "But I want to keep it secret, if that's okay."

"That's okay."

Leigh bit her lip and turned around, as if to make sure her father was out of hearing distance. "I want to make the kind of pie you made for Mrs. Buckman. She's my neighbor. She invited me in for a snack after school last week and gave me a slice of the pie. She told me you made it for her special. She said it would make me feel better too."

Veronica's heart squeezed. The pie she'd made for Annabeth Buckman was a Spirit Pie, a shoofly pie, the only kind that seemed to work for Veronica when she wanted to feel close to her grandmother. Shoofly pie was nothing special, just molasses and a crumbly brown sugar topping, and rarely seen these days, but Veronica loved it. Her grandmother had grown up making shoofly pie during her family's poorest times, and Renata Russo had said she'd be happy never to make a shoofly pie again as long as she lived and had access to fruit and good chocolate and other delectable ingredients. But one day, in those early weeks when Veronica had moved back to Boothbay Harbor and was so lonesome for her grandmother, she'd made a shoofly pie for the first time, and at the smell of the thick molasses and the crumb topping with its brown sugar, she felt like her grandmother was in the room. She felt her so close, felt her love, felt everything she'd say to Veronica now. God, how different life would have been had her grandmother been alive when Veronica had gotten pregnant. She would have kept the baby, most likely, instead of having to give her up for adoption. Her grandmother would have taken her in.

Focus on Leigh, she told herself, sucking in a quick breath.

"I know just the pie you mean, Leigh. It's my Spirit Pie—a shoofly pie. When you make it or eat it, you think about the person you want to feel close to. That's how it works. Shoofly pie got its name long ago because it's so sweet that it attracted flies while it cooled. So the bakers would say, shoo, fly! And it stuck."

"Shoofly pie," Leigh repeated. Then she nodded and turned to leave, then turned back again and said, "Thank you."

Her mother, Veronica realized. Leigh must want to feel her mother's presence. Veronica had heard that Nick DeMarco's wife had died in a boating accident almost two years ago.

Oh, Leigh, Veronica thought, watching her slip her hand into her father's as they started up Sea Road.

It would be no trouble at all to add the sweet girl to her class. Her father probably wouldn't last past the first session. They were likely "doing something together," and then he'd drop off Leigh at the next class and she wouldn't have to be in such close quarters, like her kitchen, with Nick DeMarco, who clearly remembered her from school and knew she'd gotten pregnant and then mysteriously disappeared. Back then everyone had known she'd been sent to Hope Home, a residence for pregnant teenagers on the outskirts of town. The few friends she'd had had told her that everyone was talking about it and that Timothy Macintosh was telling people he wasn't the father, that Veronica had slept around on him.

How did that still have the power to sting in the center of her chest? she wondered as she turned up the volume on the TV. Forget everything but *Pride and Prejudice* and Colin Firth's face, she told herself. After all, she had an Amore Pie to make, and she had to be in a certain frame of mind to make that pie. She'd finish watching *Pride and Prejudice*, ogle Colin Firth, and then she'd get to work.

Chapter 3

GEMMA HENDRICKS

Ever since Gemma had seen the pink plus sign on her home pregnancy test two days ago, she'd been in a full-blown panic. She'd kept the news to herself. The second she told Alexander, he'd grab her up in a crushing hug, swing her around the room, then call his family, order celebratory cigars by the truckload, and set the plan in motion that would slowly suck the life out of Gemma's soul.

Because she'd lost her job last week—a job she'd loved so much that she still got teary before she went to sleep every night—Gemma knew that Alexander, an assistant prosecutor, would use all his considerable skill to make his argument, the argument he'd been making for almost a year now: to get started on the three children he wanted, move to the same Westchester County town as his parents and brother's family, preferably equidistant between their two homes, and Gemma would be a stay-at-home mom, hosting playdates. "We're twenty-nine, for God's sake, Gemma," Alexander constantly said. "Married five years. We're grown-ups."

Gemma gripped the railing of their apartment balcony, high above the streets of Manhattan on the eighteenth floor. A minute ago, she'd been okay. She'd been sitting on her bed with her laptop, making final arrangements with her friend June about what time she'd arrive in Maine tonight for their mutual friend's wedding tomorrow night. Then ping, ping, ping. Seven e-mails from Alexander's mother. House listings in Dobbs Ferry, each annotated with Mona Hendricks's thoughts and feelings on every room, paint choices, landscaping, and a bit about the neighbors, since Mona had made it her business to scope them out in advance.

Good God. She'd been fine until that moment. Just knowing she was about to get in a car and drive to Maine for a girls' weekend, a weekend away from Alexander, who suffocated her (just wait until she told him she was pregnant; he'd be unbearable), Gemma had managed to calm herself, the panic abating a bit. Then the e-mails came from Mona, with a vision of the life Alexander would try to force her into, and Gemma had escaped to the balcony to gulp in air.

Oh no. Now the Bessells, who lived in the apartment next door, had come out onto their terrace with their infant, Jakey. Jakey-Wakey this, Jakey-Wakey that. Gemma heard the Bessells cooing at their baby all night long. "Jakey-Wakey needs his dipey-wipey changed!" Even at three in the morning, the Bessells always seemed thrilled to be awake and dealing with poop.

Lydia Bessell held up Jakey clad only in a

diaper, blowing raspberries on the baby's bare belly as John Bessell pretend-nibbled one tiny foot. Jacob gurgled his delight.

She full-out stared at them, trying to imagine herself with a baby, but she couldn't. She was meant to be a reporter, writing award-winning articles about life in a Brooklyn housing project, or about the effect of Hurricane Sandy on families on a particular block in Far Rockaway. She was supposed to be out there, getting the who, what, where, and why, and writing articles that generated hundreds of letters and comments. She was a reporter, had been a reporter from the moment she'd stepped into the school newspaper office as a high school freshman. It was all she'd ever wanted to do, find the truth, share people's real feelings, let readers know what was really happening out there from a personal perspective. But all her hard work, all the paying of dues, all the promotions, the writing around the clock to make insane deadlines—all that came down to being called into her boss's office last week at *New York Weekly*, a long-running, respected alternative newspaper where a byline meant something. She'd been let go. Let go with, "I'm so sorry, Gem, I fought for you, but times are tough, and upstairs said anyone who'd been on staff less than five years had to be first to go on this round of layoffs. Someone will snap you up fast, Gemma. You're the best."

Right. The best. The best wouldn't be let go, though, right? Alexander, to his credit, insisted "the best" had nothing to do with "upstairs" and their nutty decisions. Policy was stupid policy and he'd assured her any of the papers in the city would grab her up. Except they hadn't. "Not hiring, sorry" was the refrain she'd heard from five newspapers. But then Alexander had started saying that getting laid off was a blessing in disguise, that it was time to start a family, to move on to the next stage of their lives.

She wasn't even sure which had been more shocking—losing her job at *New York Weekly* or seeing the pink plus sign.

How had this happened? Gemma had taken her birth control pills like clockwork, at exactly seven o'clock every morning. Six weeks ago, she'd been prescribed an antibiotic for bronchitis, and when her doctor told her that antibiotics lessened the efficacy of birth control pills, she'd made Alexander use condoms, which elicited a deep sigh from her husband.

And now she was pregnant. One stupid condom that had torn. Whammo.

She wouldn't tell Alexander until she came up with a solid plan to present to him, one strong enough that she could refute any argument of his. For two days she'd been working on it. They'd stay in the city. They would not move to Westchester—let alone to the same town as the

46

overbearing Hendrickses. She'd send out a fresh batch of résumés to her second-choice news outlets. She'd find a great new job, work until the day before her due date, have the baby, then go back to work when the baby was three months old, a great day care or full-time nanny long arranged. She and Alexander would draw up a schedule of who would take off work for baby sick days and pediatrician appointments. For the past two days, when Gemma thought about it this way, she could at least breathe a bit easier, even if the part about the baby scared her to death. She had no idea how to be a mother, how to want to be a mother, how to want any part of motherhood.

But there was no way Alexander would say yes to any of her plan. For months now, all he talked about was wanting a completely different life: a baby, a house in the suburbs, a safe, sturdy car, like a Subaru, instead of their snazzy little Miata. According to Alexander Hendricks, they could be on their second child by now, like his brother, who had a two-year-old and another on the way. Alexander was sick to death of New York City— the crowds, the noise, the car alarms, the crazy cabdrivers, the subways. For the past six months, he'd been telling her "this isn't all about you, there are two of us in this marriage." She'd say the same back to him. Stalemate.

She glanced at her neighbor on her terrace, still blowing raspberries on little Jacob's belly. But suddenly Jacob's expression changed and his face got kind of red. Lydia laid him down on the padded chaise lounge and started moving his legs in bicycle formation. The baby stopped fussing.

How does she know what to do? Gemma wondered. Maybe it was as easy as Lydia always made it look. Maybe motherhood was about instinct.

But Gemma didn't have any maternal instincts. And Lydia Bessell was no help in Gemma's plan; the woman was a former Wall Street investment banker who wasn't planning on going back to work. The Bessells had already found their dream home in Tarrytown and were moving at summer's end. "See," Alexander would tell Gemma, since he knew she generally liked and respected Lydia. "Even Lydia gave up her three-hundred-thousand-dollar salary to be a stay-at-home mom in the burbs. It's the dream life, Gemma."

Once Alexander knew she was pregnant, he'd take over. He suffocated her now? She couldn't even imagine how bad it would get. The hovering, the nagging, the constant calls. Did you, are you sure you, don't forget to . . . The campaign for the life he wanted. Case closed.

"Gem, if you want to get to Maine before dark, you need to hit the road," Alexander called from his home office. "It's past eleven."

She absolutely did need to hit the road. Alone in a car for seven blessed hours. Heaven. She could think, formulate her plan, her arguments. She could figure out how she felt about being pregnant in the first place. Right now, all she had was one emotion: panic.

As Gemma turned to go back inside, her neighbor's mother, who visited practically every day, came out on the terrace. She beelined for the baby, scooping him up carefully in her arms and making more baby talk at him. Gemma's heart squeezed as it always did; she couldn't imagine ever sharing such a moment with her own mother, who was cold and kept to herself, always had. Even Alexander, who'd met some of the shadiest characters in his work as an assistant prosecutor for the state of New York, was taken aback by Gemma's mother's lack of warmth and social skills.

She went back inside the apartment and over to Alexander's makeshift office that he'd created and hated, two pressurized walls that reminded him on a daily basis he didn't have enough room and had to resort to fake walls. He was staring at his computer screen. For a moment she was startled, as she sometimes was when she looked at her husband, at how good looking he was—tall and muscular with all that sandy-blond hair and intelligent dark brown eyes that missed nothing.

She'd loved his overbearing ways when she'd first met him, loved how his family welcomed her on their third date as though they were already married, when Alexander had brought her over to meet the loud, opinionated Hendrickses. Unused to a happy, boisterous clan, she'd adored them all. During the first month they'd been dating, his mother had called her for her opinion on everything from what color shoes to wear with a brown dress to what she and Alexander's father should get Alexander for his birthday. Gemma loved being drawn in by the Hendrickses, loved every minute of how overbearing they were with their thoughts and opinions and family get-togethers during the week for no reason at all. Her own family life had been so lonely, her mother a French professor who spoke French most of the time at home despite Gemma and her sister never quite picking it up, and her father a businessman who traveled during the week. When her parents divorced when Gemma was eleven, Gemma was almost relieved, thinking the dead silences would end, that both parents would suddenly become warm and loving in their separate homes, but that hadn't been the case.

So yes, Gemma had been crazy about the warm, tell-me-your-every-thought Hendrickses. But a few years into their five-year marriage, it all got to be too much, and they wanted her to change, become more like them. When she and Alexander argued, he'd strike below the belt with what he knew would hurt the most: "You're acting like your mother, Gem."

She'd been so in love with him once—and she still loved him—but she was grateful to be getting away this weekend. The timing—at least on this—couldn't be better. Maybe a weekend apart would make him miss her, make him see her again as a separate person who had her own ideas, her own opinions, her own dream life that didn't include moving to Westchester and being a stay-at-home mother.

That panicky feeling returned, and Gemma reminded herself that in about seven hours, if traffic wasn't too bad, she'd be in Boothbay Harbor, sitting on that beautiful white wooden swing on the porch of the Three Captains' Inn with her old friend June, and her smart, insightful friend would help talk her through this. Thank God for girlfriends who owned beautiful old inns in Maine.

"I'm all set to go," she told him, eyeing his computer screen. Real estate listings.

"You look so tired," he said, studying her.

"Just worried about not being able to find a job—a job I really want. It's been keeping me up at night."

He stood up and hugged her. "Everything's going to be fine, Gem. You know why? Because I made an executive decision." He glanced at her, as if bracing for her reaction. "I put in an offer on a house in Dobbs Ferry. It's practically next door to my—"

Steam circled in her ears. "Wait a minute. What? You made an offer on a house? When you know I don't want to leave the city?"

"Gemma, something's got to change, and you're being really stubborn about this." He gave her the printouts. "This house is perfect for us and I didn't want to lose a shot at it. It's practically next door to my parents—that means when we have a baby, my mom can help out on a moment's notice. It's walkable to downtown. There are a few regional newspapers you can apply to for part-time work if you really insist on working. It's a good commute for me into the city. Just look at it, okay?"

Part-time work. If I insist on working. A shot of anger hit her in the gut. "You shouldn't have made an offer without talking to me, Alex."

"We've been talking for months now. Nothing ever changes. So we're just going to stay here because it's what you want? What about what I want?" He let out a frustrated breath. "I don't want to argue before you leave, Gem. Just take the listing and information with you," he said, handing her a sheaf of papers. "Just promise to look at them, okay?"

Fury gripped her. How dare he? "Promise me right now that you won't buy the house if your offer is accepted. Promise me, Alexander."

"I'll promise that if you promise to look—really look—at the information."

Let it go for now, she told herself. Just get in the

car and drive away. But before she could even think it through, she blurted out, "Alex, I'm going to stay up in Maine for the week instead of just the weekend. I think it'll do me some good."

He stared at her, then his expression softened. "Actually that's a good idea. All that fresh air, the beautiful cottages, the water. I think you'll see life in a small town is pretty great."

That wasn't what she'd meant at all. She glanced at her watch. "Like you said, I'd better hit the road if I want to get to Maine before dark."

He gave her that look, the look that said they weren't done talking about this, but they'd both been over this so many times that there was little left to say. Alexander had gotten the thing he needed to tip the scales in his favor; she'd gotten laid off and couldn't find another job. The pregnancy would send the scale plummeting down on his side. In a flash, she'd be in that house in Dobbs Ferry, her mother-in-law breathing down her neck, Alexander making to-do lists for her and creating feeding and napping schedules. Gemma pictured herself nine months pregnant, asking herself what the hell had happened to her life.

She got her suitcase, already packed, from the bedroom, wondering if she had to think about how heavy it was. She wouldn't drink at the wedding reception, of course. There were probably a hundred other little things she needed to know about how to live as a pregnant person.

Foods she couldn't eat, like Brie and Caesar dressing, she was pretty sure.

But this was Alexander Hendricks, who'd taken the morning from work to see her off, so, upset with her or not, of course he carried her suitcase down to the garage of their building and put it in the trunk of their car. Then he hugged her good-bye and reminded her to look at the listing. Only when she was on I-95 did she finally exhale.

The moment Gemma arrived in Boothbay Harbor, she relaxed. She hadn't been here in years, but she knew this place, it was inside her. Starting at age eleven, she'd spent a month every summer here with her father after her parents' inevitable divorce, running up and down the docks with her friends, getting crushes on boys, living for tans and new wave music. She'd always felt like a different person in Boothbay Harbor—carefree, lighthearted, happy, instead of tiptoeing around her mother back home on the Upper West Side of Manhattan, walking on eggshells for fear of saying something her mother would deem stupid. Here in this picture-postcard-perfect summer town, where you wore flip-flops all summer and your biggest problem was what kind of ice cream to choose, Gemma had always felt most herself. She'd even charmed the *Boothbay Regional Gazette* editor into allowing her a kid's column for the summers, polling people on the best fish and chips, who had the best ice cream, and favorite places to jump in the bay. Gemma smiled as she drove slowly through downtown, crowded with tourists, the harbor and the boats glittering just beyond. Yes, she could think here. She could never live in Boothbay Harbor year-round; she loved New York City with its grit and beauty and eight million stories, but she was very relieved to be here now.

Gemma lowered her car windows and breathed in the scent of summer, of the Atlantic, of nature. The bay shimmered in the late June sun as Gemma drove up Main Street with its one-of-a-kind shops, then turned onto Harbor Hill Road. The Three Captains' Inn came into view on its perch two winding streets above the harbor. Gemma loved the inn, a robin's egg–blue Victorian with white trim and a white porch swing, pots of flowers blooming everywhere.

She pulled up in the small parking lot beside the inn, her gaze on the woman on the porch swing. She held a baby on her lap and was swinging gently. A guest maybe. As Gemma carried her suitcase up the three steps the woman stood, put the baby in a baby swing on the porch, then slipped on a BabyBjörn and had the baby inside in under ten seconds. Gemma felt the usual rise of panic at how easily mothers seemed to do these things. There was so much to learn, so much to know.

The woman was smiling at her. "Gemma, right? I'm Isabel, June's sister."

Isabel, of course. Gemma had met the Nash sisters when she was eleven, the first summer she'd come to Boothbay Harbor with her dad. She and June Nash were the same age and had hit it off immediately, but Isabel was three years older and in a different orbit. "Isabel! Wow, you look fabulous. I've been in my own world and completely forgot that June said you'd gotten remarried and had a baby. Congratulations."

"Thanks. Her name's Allie. C'mon in and I'll get you settled. I manage the Three Captains'. June said she'd be by at seven to whisk you away for dinner."

Gemma followed Isabel inside the inn past an antique-filled foyer and into Isabel's office, unable to take her eyes off the baby. She was so beautiful, with lots of dark hair, blue eyes, and tiny bow lips. Gemma tried to imagine herself multitasking with a baby on her hip. She couldn't see it. "I'm a little early."

"No problem. We're happy to have you at the Three Captains'. You'll be in the Lighthouse Room, on the third floor. It's a single and small, but cozy with views of beautiful old trees. And like I tell all my guests, don't worry about hearing Allie cry in the middle of the night. I don't live at the inn, but we're very close by in town if there are any problems."

Gemma followed Isabel up the staircase to the third floor, which held two guest rooms and a full bathroom, since the Lighthouse Room didn't have a private bath. The room was just as Isabel had said, small but cozy. It held a full-size bed with a pretty scrolled headboard, a small antique bureau with an oval mirror above it, a round braided rug on the wide-planked wood floor, and a painting of the Portland Head Light lighthouse on the rocky cliffs of Maine. The one window looked out on the big backyard, trees as far as Gemma could see. Yes, she would be able to think here. It was perfect.

Isabel stopped by the door. "Oh, before I leave you to get settled, I wanted to let you know that we're officially starting up an old Three Captains' Inn Friday night tradition—Movie Night."

Gemma was glad to hear that. Two years ago, when June and Isabel's aunt Lolly, who'd left them the inn, had passed away from cancer, the sisters had put a hold on Movie Night. Every month they'd changed the theme. Romantic comedy. Food. Foreign. Meryl Streep. John Hughes. Dirty Harry, which always attracted the male guests, who usually passed on Movie Night. Gemma and Alexander had flown up for Lolly's funeral, but both had had to get back to work, and Gemma hadn't been able to spend much time with June.

Isabel shifted baby Allie to her hip and leaned

close to whisper. "It's Colin Firth month in honor of him coming to Boothbay Harbor to film scenes for his new movie. Three members of a Colin Firth fan club are in the room across from you, so hit the parlor a bit before nine to get a comfy seat. We're starting with *Bridget Jones's Diary.*"

Gemma's heart skipped a beat. "Colin Firth is here in Boothbay Harbor? I love him."

"Me too. I'm not sure if he's here yet—the fan club says there's no sign of him, but there have been supposed sightings. Big lights and trailers have been set up over by Frog Marsh."

Colin Firth. Here in Boothbay Harbor. Maybe Gemma could get a press pass from the *Boothbay Regional Gazette* and do a story on the effect of a movie set on a small tourist town, and score interviews with the stars. *You can take the girl out of the newspaper, but you can't take the newspaper out of the girl.*

Isabel left Gemma to settle in, and Gemma surprised herself by flopping down on her bed and staring out the window at the trees. She thought she'd lunge for her notebook to jot down ideas for the piece on the movie set to pitch to the *Gazette* on Sunday morning. She had to admit she was tired, though, in a way she'd never felt before. Pregnancy tired. And she was angry and frustrated that Alexander had put an offer in on that Dobbs Ferry house when he knew how she felt.

"Gemma!"

Gemma glanced up to find her dear friend June Nash in the doorway, her arms open for a hug. June, co-owner of the inn along with Isabel and their cousin Kat, who was away in France, looked as she always had—her beautiful long, auburn curly hair wild around her shoulders, and wearing a pretty cotton sundress. June had a nine-year-old son and had recently eloped in Las Vegas with her longtime love, Henry Books.

"Let's go to dinner and catch up. You hinted in your e-mails that you had something big to tell me."

"I sure do," Gemma said, two days of pent-up worries whooshing out of her. She'd finally share her news with someone. Someone who'd listen and help her work through the situation.

Dinner with June had been as good as an hour-long deep-tissue massage, except for the texts from Alexander. "Let me know you arrived safely. Don't forget to look at the information on the house." And a final one with a link to an article on how Dobbs Ferry, New York, was a great place to live. She'd texted back that she was here safe and sound and ignored the rest.

Over delicious steak fajitas at a Mexican restaurant, Gemma had told June everything. About the pink plus sign. About losing her job. About Alexander putting an offer in on a house near his overbearing family. About not being ready for motherhood—and definitely not being ready for the life Alexander was ready for. June had understood, just as Gemma had known she would. And since June was a mother, she gave Gemma an unscary introduction to Baby 101 and had stopped at the bookstore she and her husband owned for a book on pregnancy. June believed you didn't need instinct so much as love and commitment and a good book on what to expect when you were pregnant and during the first year.

"When do you think you'll tell Alexander you're pregnant?" June asked as they pulled back into the driveway of the Three Captains' Inn, with just minutes to spare for the start of Movie Night at nine.

Gemma bit her lip. "I'm not sure. I know I can't keep it secret much longer. It's too big. And I know it's unfair to keep it from him when it would make him so happy. But I just need to come to terms with it, what it means for me, us, before I tell him and get bombarded with what he wants, how he sees our future unfolding. We have such different ideas on what that is."

June leaned over and gave Gemma a hug. "You'll figure it out and you two will make it work for both of you."

Gemma wasn't so sure. On the long drive up, one thing she hadn't even thought of before came crashing down on her: who would hire her when she was pregnant? She'd have to disclose it at her interviews; it would be disingenuous not to. How would she ever get back what she'd had at *New York Weekly*? Alexander would realize this in a hot minute and argue her into that Dobbs Ferry house before she knew it. He'd make his case until she had no arguments of her own. And once she had the baby? He'd bombard her with articles about working mothers and bad nannies and reckless day cares. She would morph into a copy of Alexander's sister-in-law in no time.

When Gemma and June entered the parlor, it was packed with Movie Night attendees. Isabel and her elderly "helper," Pearl, who watered the plants, were sitting on the sofa with Isabel's sixteen-year-old stepdaughter, Alexa, who was very close to Isabel. The three members of the Colin Firth fan club, who wore "Happiness Is Colin Firth" T-shirts with his image on them, were on the love seat, and four others, including one man, were scattered around the large room on chairs. June went to get two more folding chairs and they sat down, a bowl of popcorn and a pitcher of iced tea on the antique table next to them.

The lights were turned off and Isabel slid the DVD of *Bridget Jones's Diary* into the player. Gemma had seen and adored the film when it first came out. A movie like that—warm and funny and true to life—was just what Gemma needed. That and the company of women. And popcorn.

"I had the biggest crush on Hugh Grant a bunch of years ago," Isabel said, sitting back down, a handful of popcorn on a napkin on her lap. "He's so great in this movie."

"For me, Colin Firth all the way," June said. "He's our generation's Cary Grant—that swoon-worthy older actor, tall, dark, and handsome, debonair but still very masculine and completely epitomizing everything a woman wants in a lifetime partner." June held up the DVD box of *Bridget Jones's Diary.* "Just look at how politely good looking he is. He's so British!"

The Colin Firth fan club rattled off a bunch of stats about Colin Firth. That he'd appeared in over fifty films and had a few in postproduction. That he'd been twice nominated for the Academy Award for Best Actor, for *A Single Man* and *The King's Speech*, winning for the latter. That as a young actor, he'd been involved with the actress Meg Tilly, with whom he had a son, and had lived with her in a remote Canadian town for years before resuming his acting career. And did everyone know that he'd been romantically linked to his costar in *Pride and Prejudice*, Jennifer Ehle, who appeared in *The King's Speech*? He was now married to a beautiful Italian woman named Livia with whom he had two children. And, if anyone wanted to know, he was a Virgo and six feet two.

The movie began so the fan club finally hushed up.

Renée Zellweger, an actress Gemma had loved since *Jerry Maguire*, appeared on-screen, woefully singing along at the top of her lungs to that old seventies ballad "All By Myself" in her pajamas. Gemma burst out laughing, as did everyone else. This was her, exactly how she felt, all by herself, her husband far away and as unconnected as if they weren't married at all, but the scene was hilarious, and Gemma felt herself loosening up inside. June had been right to suggest a movie—this movie.

Single in her thirties, bumbling but honest Bridget Jones swept Gemma out of herself to London, where Bridget, working as a publicist for a publishing company, has a huge crush on her boss, played by the always appealing Hugh Grant. Bridget's mother wants to set her up with a well-to-do lawyer named Mark Darcy, and they do meet at a Christmas party, he in a ridiculous sweater with a big moose on it, but she overhears him insult her, which is fine with her, since she's hardly interested in the smug jerk. She and cad Hugh Grant get involved, and when he tells her a big lie about Mark Darcy, she believes it and thinks even worse of him. Until the truth comes out . . . as does her own true feelings for him.

"No, I like you. Very much. Just as you are," June and Isabel repeated in unison after Colin Firth uttered those beautiful words in his gorgeous British accent.

Which was what everyone wanted, including Gemma's husband. "This is who I am," he'd said often over the past few months. "You knew that. You supposedly fell in love with that. Now you want me to be someone I never was."

The problem was that Gemma felt the same way.

"Think we'll get to see Colin Firth when he comes to film his scenes?" June asked when the credits started rolling. "I stopped by the set yesterday, but there's not much there. Just some guy with a clipboard who told me not to blab about the set and bombard the area with gawkers."

Isabel got up and began collecting the almost empty popcorn bowls. "That'll happen whether he likes it or not. For a glimpse of Colin Firth, even I'll brave the crowds."

"Me too," June said, stacking glasses and the pitcher of iced tea on the tray. "I loved him in *Pride and Prejudice.* That's when I first fell in love with him. *Bridget Jones's Diary* is loosely based on that book. I love that Colin Firth plays Darcy in both *Bridget Jones* and *P and P.*"

The three members of the Colin Firth fan club began listing every one of his movies, complete with costars and their opinions of the films, and that's when everyone else began heading their separate ways. Gemma went up to her tiny room on the third floor, changed into a tank top and her PJ pants, then slipped beneath the white and yellow quilt stitched with stars and moons. Her phone pinged. A text from Alexander: "Did you look at the information on the house?"

Gemma sighed and texted back: "Not yet," and that she was exhausted, then tried to will herself to sleep. But she couldn't stop thinking of Colin Firth telling Renée Zellweger that he liked her, very much, just as she was. She turned on the lamp on her bedside table and opened the book on pregnancy that June had given her, much preferring to read that than looking at the real estate listing.

Chapter 4
BEA

Bea pulled her car over on the shoulder of the road, by the huge green sign that read BOOTHBAY REGION. Her heart was beating too fast. For a moment she thought about turning around, just forgetting this whole thing. She'd almost turned around two and a half hours ago, at the sign reading WELCOME TO MAINE: THE WAY LIFE SHOULD BE at the Maine–New Hampshire border. The sign had loomed so large. *Keep going this way to meet your birth mother,* it might as well have read.

It had been three weeks since she'd received her mom's letter, and she wasn't even sure she wanted to be here to see her birth mother, let alone meet her. She had no idea what she wanted. Except for some kind of . . . closure. No, that wasn't the right word. Or maybe it was. Bea knew that sometimes, in order to get closure you had to open a door.

Such as sending away for her original birth certificate, which she'd received in the mail yesterday. Just the sight of "Name: Baby Girl Russo" made her tremble, as did the rest: "Mother's Name: Veronica Russo. Father's Name: Unknown. Time of birth: 7:22 p.m. Issued by: Coastal General Hospital, Boothbay Harbor, Maine."

She couldn't shake the feeling that she was someone else, that she'd started off life as someone else entirely, belonging to other people, a different family, in a different place. She had to find out who these people were, who Veronica Russo was.

She parked in a public lot and glanced at her little notebook: the Best Little Diner in Boothbay was on Main Street, the main drag she was on now. Bea glanced out her window. Boothbay Harbor was a coastal summer town, crowded with tourists walking along the narrow cobblestone and brick sidewalks, lined with shops and seafood restaurants, and hotels everywhere she looked.

She'd find a cheap motel for the night. She'd give herself a night here, maybe visit the hospital where she was born, walk around, think. Decide if she wanted to meet Veronica Russo. She could stick around town as long as she wanted since she had no home anymore. A few days ago, she'd gone back to the apartment to find one of the new roommates having sex in the living room. Bea had had it with this apartment, these strangers. The roommate had said her sister wanted to move in, and that was that. Now the money she'd been saving for July's rent could support her here for a while until she decided where to go next. And she could go anywhere, which was scary. The only place she wanted to go was Cape Cod, to her mother's little cottage. But that wasn't her mother's anymore. She'd have to throw a dart or apply to every school district in the United States and go where she got hired. For now, home was her car. Everything but her mother's furniture was in the trunk of her old Toyota—her clothes, her laptop and books, her parents' photo albums, the raggedy old stuffed Winnie the Pooh her father had given her on her sixth birthday. Her mother's furniture was in a cheap storage facility. When she landed somewhere, she'd get back her mother's belongings. She'd make a home as best she could.

Bea headed up bustling Main Street but didn't pass the diner or see it on the other side of the street, and she wasn't ready to. She turned onto a wide pier of souvenir shops and restaurants, the bay opening up in front of her. It was a Saturday in June, a gorgeous early evening, and the pier was packed with people, shopping, biting into lobster rolls, licking ice cream cones, drinking iced coffees, watching the boats. She passed couples, hand in hand, arms slung around each other, and felt a stab of pure envy. She wished she had someone to tell her everything would be okay, someone to be there if it wasn't okay. Her last boyfriend, someone she'd been dating for a few months, had flaked out on her when her mother had gotten sick; he hadn't even come to the funeral. She watched as a guy dipped his girlfriend for an impromptu romantic kiss; a few people clapped. Bea had never felt more wistful. Or alone.

She got herself a lemon ice from a cart vendor and stood in the sunshine, trying to orient herself, figure out where she was via the free shopper's map she'd picked up outside a store. She had no idea where the Best Little Diner was in relation to this pier. The diner was marked on the map; it was barely a quarter mile from where she stood.

Bea put the map away, her heart beating fast again. Just like that, with a snap of her fingers, and she could meet the birth mother she hadn't known existed until a few weeks ago. This was crazy. As was her sudden realization that any fortyish woman she passed could be Veronica Russo. That one, blond like Bea, in the pale yellow sundress and flip-flops, an outfit Bea might have chosen herself. She watched the woman check her phone, then look around the expanse of pier, as though she was waiting for someone. Bea's biological father, maybe. For all Bea knew, her birth parents had gotten married. Had always been married. Had other children, older or younger. Maybe both. Bea could have a sister. Twin brothers.

Bea sat down on a bench outside a weathered restaurant with a giant sign proclaiming THE BEST LOBSTER ROLLS IN BOOTHBAY. She had to stop this or she'd drive herself crazy. She'd spent three weeks wondering, speculating. How could she even begin to guess what her birth mother's circumstances were?

Veronica Russo could be the tall blonde jogging with a yellow lab beside her. Or perhaps Bea had inherited the blond from her biological father, and Veronica was the redhead who'd just walked away from the seafood shack's takeout window, biting into her lobster roll while gazing at a whale that had just made an appearance in the bay. *I have to know something about you, Veronica Russo,* she thought. *About my birth father. About my birth grandparents. I have to know who I was before the Cranes adopted me.*

Bea opened her backpack and pulled out her little red notebook. "Veronica Russo. Home: 225 Sea Road. Tel: 207 555-3235. Work: The Best Little Diner in Boothbay, 45 Main Street." According to the map, all she had to do was walk a bit up to Main and turn right.

Just go to the diner, she told herself. *Just go check her out.*

Bea couldn't pick her out right away. There were three waitresses, two the right age to be Veronica, and one no older than Bea. The one Bea's age was working the counter, so Bea took the empty seat that wrapped around the side by the door, giving her a view of the entire diner. The place was crowded; only one table was empty, and almost all the counter seats were filled.

She liked the diner. It was old-fashioned greasy spoon meets coastal Maine, with pale blue walls displaying the pricey work of local artists, and overstuffed chairs and love seats along with the more typical tables. The ceiling was covered in a lobster net with a giant wooden lobster caught inside. Near the counter where Bea sat was a bookshelf filled with books and a sign: READ ME.

Bea glanced at the two other waitresses and looked for name tags, but she wasn't that lucky. One was heading to a table with four plates balanced in her hands, and she was tall like Bea, but she didn't have Bea's blond hair; none of the waitresses did.

"Sorry it's taken me so long to even give you a menu," the young waitress said to Bea. She wore a gold nameplate necklace. Katie. "We're crazed right now, so I'm helping on the floor too."

"No problem." Bea ordered an iced coffee and the decadent-looking pie next to the carrot cake.

"Oh, that's fudge Happiness Pie and intensely good. One of our waitresses is a legend in this town for her pies." She headed to the coffee station, glancing around until her gaze landed on a woman coming out of a back room. "Oh, there you are, Veronica. I'm about to sell the last of your amazing fudge pie."

Bea froze.

Her birth mother. Standing not seven, eight feet away. Had Katie not gone to get Bea her coffee

72

and pie, Veronica's attention would still be on the area where Bea sat, and Veronica might have noticed Bea sitting there, white as her paper napkin and trembling. She closed her eyes and turned her head to look out the large picture window, telling herself to breathe.

My birth mother, she thought, turning to take another look. Veronica gave Katie a pleased smile, then went to the coffee station and filled a large takeout cup. She was no older than late thirties and tall, like Bea. Busty, unlike Bea. Her auburn hair cascaded just past her shoulders in soft waves. And her eyes were just like Bea's: driftwood brown and round. But Veronica Russo was beautiful in a lush, womanly way that Bea, who an ex liked to describe as looking like a farm girl, even though she'd grown up in Boston and Cape Cod, would never be. Still, there was something in the woman's expression that was like Bea's, something subtle.

She wore all white, a sparkly white tank top and white pants. And beaded sandals. Done with her shift, Bea figured.

You're a complete stranger, and yet my entire history comes from you, Bea wanted to shout. What is your story? What was your story?

Bea glanced at Veronica's hands as she added a packet of sugar to her coffee. No rings at all. So she wasn't married.

"Hey, darling," a man said, and Bea glanced

over to see a tall, skinny, half-balding redheaded guy wobbling in the doorway as though he was drunk, his foot stuck in the screen door. He was staring at Veronica. "Is today my lucky day? Gonna go out with me?"

Veronica cut him a sharp look. "Please stop asking me out. My answer is never going to change."

"She's breaking my heart!" he shouted, and mock stabbed himself in the chest, and those sitting around the front of the diner burst into laughter.

Bea watched Veronica shake her head good-naturedly and stir her coffee as the guy staggered away.

"Colin Firth's signing autographs at Harbor View Coffee!" a nasal voice called out from in front of the diner.

Colin Firth? The actor?

Veronica was out the door in a shot. Along with half of everyone in the diner.

Bea had the strongest urge to get up and follow her, but her body wouldn't listen to a single command. Except for her hand, shaking around her fork, she was frozen. She set down the fork, sucked in a breath, and thought about calling her good friend Caroline to tell her she'd seen her birth mother in the flesh, that she was beautiful, but Caroline was in Berlin for the summer.

Bea looked down at her untouched slice of pie, the gooey fudge, the flaky crust. Her biological mother had made this pie. She took a slow bite, letting herself savor it.

Bea wanted to chase after Veronica and throw some time-stop pixie dust on her so that she could surreptitiously study her every feature—the shape of her eyes, the line of her nose, the structure of her jawline—and look for herself in Veronica's face, her body, her mannerisms. Something to force her brain to accept that this was all true, that this woman, not Cora Crane, had given birth to her. That someone, a man whose name she didn't know, had fathered her. Who was he? Had they been in love? Was it a one-night stand? Something awful? Where did I come from, Bea wanted to know. Suddenly, she was itchy to learn Veronica's life story, Bea's own history. Who were her grandparents?

Who was Bea?

Bea put a ten-dollar bill on the table and raced out after Veronica.

Main Street was so crowded with tourists and bicyclists, a dog walker with the leashes of at least ten dogs, and a bunch of day campers walking toward her two by two, in neon yellow Happy Kids Day Camp T-shirts, that Bea couldn't see Veronica in any direction she looked. Harbor View Coffee was five shops down. Bea went in and looked around, but there was no sign of Veronica, let alone a British actor.

"If you've come looking for Colin Firth, he's not here," the barista called over, rolling her eyes. "Someone obviously thought it would be funny to send every woman in town rushing in here."

Bea saw a couple leave through the back door with their iced coffees, and she headed out to the small patio. No Veronica. A cobblestone path led to the street running perpendicular to Main, right along the harbor. Veronica must have gone out this way.

Okay, now what? She could come back tomorrow—and this time, perhaps she'd sit in Veronica's section. Bea headed toward the harbor and tried to think. She'd come to Boothbay to see the town, this place where she'd been born, where she'd begun as someone else's story. The plan was that when and if the time was right, she'd knock on her birth mother's door, either literally or figuratively.

It had felt right a moment ago. But what if she had caught up to Veronica? Would she have run up to her, tapped her on the shoulder, and said, "Uh, hi, my name is Bea Crane. You gave me up for adoption twenty-two years ago." It was clear Veronica wanted Bea to contact her; otherwise she wouldn't have updated the file. But maybe a call would be better, for both of them. A bit of distance, letting them both sit down and digest before actually meeting.

Yes, Bea would call, maybe tomorrow.

As Bea neared the harbor, even more crowded than the main shopping street, Veronica's features, her warm brown eyes, the straight, almost pointy nose, so like Bea's own, were all imprinted in her mind. Bea was so lost in thought that she started walking in no particular direction; she felt like she might tip over if she stopped.

Unless Veronica had stayed out of the sun her entire life, she was no more than late thirties. Bea would give her thirty-six or thirty-seven, which meant she'd had Bea as a teenager.

As Bea wound her way through the crowd of tourists, she imagined a very young Veronica walking these same streets, pregnant, scared, unsure what to do. Had Bea's birth father been supportive? Had he abandoned her? How had Veronica's mother, her own grandmother, handled it? Had Veronica been able to turn to her? Had she been shunned? Supported?

Bea let herself wander and speculate, until she realized she'd walked around the far side of the bay, away from the hustle of downtown. Up ahead by the side of a pond, she saw a bunch of people setting up huge black lights and huge black cameras, a long, beige trailer behind them. Looked like a film set—she'd come across a few of those in Boston and always hoped for a glimpse of a movie star, but she never saw anyone famous, though people around her claimed they had.

Maybe this was what the Colin Firth shout-out had been about. He must be in town to film a new movie. Bea headed over, needing a distraction from herself.

"Movie set, right?" she asked a tall, lanky guy in wire-rimmed glasses standing in front of the trailer. A laminated pass hanging down from around his neck read: TYLER ECHOLS, PA.

He was glancing down at a clipboard and either didn't hear her or chose not to answer.

A pretty teenage girl with long, dark hair sat a few feet away in a folding chair by the trailer. She had a book upside down on her lap, and if Bea wasn't mistaken, it was *To Kill a Mockingbird*. Bea would recognize that original cover from a mile away.

"I love that book," Bea said to her. "I wrote my senior thesis on it."

"I can't even get past the first paragraph," the girl said, fluttering the pages. "It's so boring. How am I supposed to write a paper on this book? It should be called 'To Kill a Boring Bird.'"

She had no idea what she was missing. "*To Kill a Mockingbird* is a brilliant reflection of its time— of the South, of racism, of right and wrong, of injustice, all through the eyes of a girl who learns a lot about life, her father, and herself. It's one of my top-ten favorite novels of all time."

The guy with the clipboard glanced at her, leaning one bent foot behind him against the trailer, then went back to checking things off on his clipboard.

The girl looked even more bored, but then brightened. "Could you write my paper?"

"Sorry, no," Bea said. "But give the novel a chance, okay?"

The girl rolled her eyes. "You sound like my brother," she said, upping her chin at the guy with the clipboard.

"So is this a movie set?" Bea asked the guy again, glancing at the cameras, then back to him.

He barely looked up. "Do us all a favor and don't go telling everyone we're here. The last thing we need is a huge crowd watching us position lights. There's no movie star here. That you can share."

Okay, Grumpy. "What's the movie? Colin Firth is starring, right?"

He shot her an impatient glare. "You're trespassing."

She seemed to be doing that today.

Chapter 5
VERONICA

Veronica had four plates, four coffees, four orange juices, and a basket of minibiscuits with apple butter on the heavy tray she carried over to table seven. It was Sunday morning, eight o'clock, and since the diner had opened at six thirty, she'd served what seemed like five hundred plates of eggs—from scrambled to omelets to over easy—home fries, bacon, and toast, maybe a thousand cups of coffee. And folks kept coming. A line had formed by the door, the counter was full, and every table was taken. The Best Little Diner in Boothbay lived up to its name and was one of the most popular eateries in town. Even the fish and chips rivaled the seafood joints, and that was saying something in a harbor town in Maine. And of course, when it came to pie, no one went anywhere else.

Of all the diners she'd worked in over the past twenty-two years, the Best Little Diner in Boothbay was her favorite. She loved how pretty it was, for one. The floors were wide-planked pumpkin originals dating back to the late 1800s, when it used to be a general store. Instead of standard vinyl seats for the booths, the seating was white painted wood (washable, of course) with soothing starfish-printed cushions. And the tables, twenty-five in total, were polished wood and round. When the diner slowed down at off times, she loved checking out the local artists' work on the walls. And the back room was a waitress's paradise of comfy recliners, a nice restroom, and even a lovely back alley to sneak out to for some fresh air. The diner's owner, Deirdre, had something of a secret flower garden out back, and Veronica often spent her breaks just standing amid the big pots of blue hydrangeas and breathing in the scent of roses.

"I see a table open right there, young lady," Veronica heard a familiar voice snap to the hostess. Oh no. Mrs. Buffleman, pointing, with her usual scowl, at the table that had just opened up in Veronica's section. Mrs. Buffleman was Veronica's old English teacher from junior year. Buffleman retired a few years ago and had breakfast practically every day at the diner; Veronica had long ago told the hostess to seat her in someone else's section, but sometimes, when it couldn't be helped, Buffleman ended up in hers, like today.

"Good morning, Mrs. Buffleman, Mr. Buffleman," Veronica said as she stopped at their table, coffeepot in hand. "Coffee this morning?"

Mrs. Buffleman studied her for a moment with her usual slight shake of her head, the shake of disappointment. When Veronica had had to drop out of high school, all her teachers had received a memo about why and that her last day would be at week's end. Mrs. Buffleman was the only teacher who'd brought up the subject with her. "Darn shame," she'd said to Veronica on her last day, when Veronica had been on the verge of tears since walking in the building that morning. Head shake. "What a waste." More head shaking. And Veronica, who hadn't thought she could possibly feel worse, had felt worse.

Veronica had never particularly liked Mrs. Buffleman, but the old battle-ax had given Veronica an A on every paper, and Veronica had earned A's on every exam. English had been her best subject, but it wasn't as if she'd planned on becoming a teacher or an editor of some kind anyway; Veronica had never known what she wanted to do. When she started baking four years ago, she thought about opening her own little pie diner, but that took a lot of money, to invest in it and to keep it up, and though Veronica had a nest egg socked away from twenty-two years of waitressing, low rents, and low overhead, she was afraid to spend it on something that might fail. It wasn't as though she had anyone else, like a life partner, to rely on for half the bills, half of retirement, and even then, if you did have a husband, you never knew what could happen. That little pie diner was nice to fantasize about, though.

"That's the gal who dropped out of high school because she got pregnant," she heard Buffleman whisper to her husband, for at least the hundredth time since Veronica had been back in town.

Veronica rolled her eyes, then groaned at the sight of Penelope Von Blun and her mother sitting at a table for two in Veronica's section. She'd have to add Penelope to the list of people not to put in her section. Penelope was one of the biggest snobs Veronica had ever met, and unfortunately, she'd signed up for Veronica's pie class, which started tomorrow night. Veronica was surprised the woman would deign to learn the art of making pies from Veronica, but she was pretty sure there was an ulterior motive involved. Penelope likely wanted to learn the secrets of making her own elixir pie so that she wouldn't have to give Veronica her business.

Penelope's whispering to her mother started the moment Veronica began walking over with her coffeepot. Veronica had no doubt what she was saying. *Remember the slutty girl who got pregnant my junior year and dropped out to go to Hope Home? That's her. Working at the diner. Guess we see how her life turned out.*

"Veronica!" Penelope said with fake brightness, and Veronica was struck by how different she looked than usual, toned down somehow, the hair less straight-ironed, the outfit more conservative, and just a couple of simple pieces of jewelry instead of gobs. "I'm so excited about pie class tomorrow night." She turned to her mother and said, "Veronica is known in town for special pies. Have you ever had one?"

"Oh, I don't go for that nonsense," her mother said with a dismissive wave of her hand. "Pies don't bring you love or cure cancer. Please."

The woman was such a stick in the mud that Veronica laughed. "Well, they sure do taste good."

"I know. I've had your pie here," the woman said without a smile. "Coffee please."

Veronica poured their coffee and took their orders. Penelope was having the fruit plate. Her mother ordered the most high-maintenance plate of substitutions Veronica had ever had the displeasure of writing down on her order pad. Two eggs, one over easy, the other sunny side up. Rye toast, extra light, but still warm, the butter on and melted. Home fries without a single charred piece of potato, which were Veronica's favorite kind, when the grill got ahold of the onions and the edges of the potatoes.

Sometimes, when she ran into people like Penelope or Buffleman—especially on the same day at the same time—she felt a small blast of that old shame. Nothing like when she was sixteen, of course, and newly pregnant, with people staring at her as though she had a sign around her neck. But just a frisson of that feeling that made her feel . . . uncomfortable. As if her life could have gone another way entirely if only she hadn't gotten knocked up. She'd be married, maybe. With two kids. And she'd have figured out what she wanted to do with her life. Discovered her pie-baking skills a lot earlier because she'd bake for school bake sales for her children. Maybe. Maybe not. Who the heck knew?

She glanced around at the counter, where Officer Nick DeMarco usually sat when he came in, which was pretty often. At least he wasn't here this morning. Too bad he hadn't been here yesterday, when she could have sicced him on that nudgy drunk Hugh Fledge, who wouldn't stop asking her out. She barely remembered Nick from high school, but she knew his face, recalled he was part of Timothy's crowd. Every time she looked at Nick, she felt exposed, as though he knew all sorts of things about her that weren't even true. She hated how that felt. And so she avoided him whenever she saw him at the diner or around town. But she wouldn't be able to avoid him tomorrow night at the class. She'd have to be extra polite too, because of his daughter.

Times like this, she wondered if coming back to Boothbay Harbor was a mistake, after all. If she'd ever really settle in and face anything of her past. Boothbay Harbor still didn't feel like home again, even a year later. And though she'd made some friends, Shelley, of course, right over there at table nineteen, explaining the difference between a

Western omelet and a country omelet, and had a lot of acquaintances, especially her clients, who seemed to rely on her as if she were a fortune-teller, Veronica felt . . . lonely. Lonely for something she wasn't even sure of. Was it love? A big group of close girlfriends, something Veronica had never had except for her seven months at Hope Home? Something was missing, that was all she knew.

People will come and go from your life for all kinds of acceptable and crappy reasons, her grandmother had always said in her saucy, straightforward style. *So you've got to be your own best friend, know who you are, and never let anyone tell you you're something you know you're not.*

Veronica had been thirteen when her grandmother had said all that, over a girl who'd told Veronica she couldn't be her friend anymore because her mother thought Veronica looked "too grown-up." She'd worn a C-cup bra in eighth grade, had a thin, curvy figure, and no matter how conservatively she'd dressed, the boys had come chasing. In ninth grade, girls—including Penelope—had started rumors about Veronica "sleeping around" when she hadn't so much as French-kissed a boy. The few boys she'd dated had made up stories about how far they'd gone, so Veronica had broken up with them. By sixteen, when she'd started dating Timothy

Macintosh, she'd had a reputation when she hadn't ever let a boy see her bra. Timothy had believed her too, said he thought she was beautiful and interesting and would never say a word about her to his friends. Girls had always kept their distance from her, so Timothy had become her first real best friend. Until a very cold April afternoon when she'd told him she was pregnant.

Bringing herself back to that day sent a fresh stab of pain to her chest. Maybe it would always hurt, even thirty years from now. Stop thinking about him, she ordered herself, calling out Penelope Von Blun's and her mother's order at the open window to the kitchen, which got an extended eye roll from Joe, the cook. She wished she could stop. But in the first few weeks of her return to Boothbay Harbor, she'd actually seen Timothy, from a distance in the supermarket, and she'd been unable to sleep well ever since, memories waking her up. She'd been so stunned to see him that she'd jumped back behind a display of bananas. She hadn't been sure, at first, if it was really him, but then she heard his laughter as he listened to something the woman with him had said. Veronica hadn't gotten a look at her, just the back of her head—a precisely cut bob—and an amazing figure. Timothy's arm had been around her, and he turned to look at something, and there was that profile, the strong, straight Roman nose. Veronica had almost started hyperventilating. It had been so unexpected. She didn't think he lived in town; she'd looked him up just so she'd know if she had to accept that she'd run into him in town, but there was no listing for him, and she hadn't seen him before or since that one time, so perhaps he was visiting relatives.

"Oh. My. God," Shelley said as she collected the discarded *Sunday Boothbay Regional Gazette* from one of her tables.

"What, Shel?" Veronica asked, coming over.

Shelley, a petite redhead in her late thirties like Veronica, with catlike amber-hazel eyes, was staring at a page of the newspaper. She held up the front section of the Life & People section. "This."

One glance at the front page and Veronica repeated Shelley's "Oh. My. God." A photo of Colin Firth, looking absolutely gorgeous in a tux, next to a brief article about the movie crew that had recently set up some equipment in Boothbay Harbor, near Frog Marsh, to film scenes of a new Colin Firth dramedy. Below the article was a call for extras.

Major motion picture seeks locals as extras. Apply on location at Frog Marsh between 4 and 6 Monday and Tuesday only. Bring a résumé and two photographs paper-clipped together, full-body and headshot, with name, phone, height, weight, and clothing size written in permanent marker on back.

So it was true. Colin Firth was coming to Boothbay Harbor—and could very well have been in Harbor View Coffee yesterday, despite the barista swearing on a stack of Bibles that Colin Firth had not been in the place. Perhaps he'd ducked out the back once word had gotten out that he was in there. The man had probably just wanted an iced coffee and a scone, for heaven's sake, not screaming fans bombarding him. Such as herself.

"Come by my house tonight and I'll take a bunch of pictures of you," Shelley said, ripping out the front page, folding it up and tucking it into the pocket of Veronica's apron.

"Pictures of me? For what?"

"So you can apply to be an extra!"

Veronica laughed. "Me? I work here. I bake a thousand pies a week. How could I possibly drop everything to work on a film set? I once read that extras are on call all day for as long as it takes to film the scenes on location. They sit around in a tent and read or chat until the director calls them to walk by wordlessly in the background or whatever." But still, just the thought of being an extra in a Colin Firth movie started an excitement inside her that Veronica hadn't felt in decades.

"Oh, you're applying," Shelley said, well aware of Veronica's love of Colin Firth. At least three times a month, Veronica invited Shelley over to watch a Colin Firth film, complete with fun drinks and appetizers and pie and discussion afterward about the film and why she adored Colin Firth so darn much. *Didn't we just see* Love Actually *a couple of months ago?* Shelley had asked when Veronica had told her she was planning to watch it, if Shelley wanted to join her. As if you could see *Love Actually* one too many times. "You've got money, Veronica. Your pie business will allow you to take off a few weeks, even a couple of months. You're going to miss the chance to be an extra in a Colin Firth movie in your own hometown?"

No, I'm not, Veronica thought, the image of Mr. Darcy walking soaking wet out of that pond coming to mind. There was no way she was missing this. She unfolded the newspaper page and stared at the photo of her heartthrob, then at the ad. She was smiling like an idiot.

Major motion picture seeks locals as extras. Good Lord, Veronica could be in the same airspace as Colin Firth. She could be an extra— why not? And Shelley was right; her pie business had been doing so well that she could easily take some time off from the diner.

Veronica in the same room as Colin Firth. She could look Mr. Darcy in the eye!

She'd be first in line to apply.

Which meant coming up with a résumé for the first time in her life, she realized, as she eyed the kitchen window counter and saw two of her orders were up. She headed over and filled her tray. Veronica had been a waitress at busy diners since she was sixteen and left Maine for Florida. All you needed for that job was to say you had experience and then show it on the floor and you were hired. Was she supposed to list every diner she'd worked from Florida to New Mexico to Maine for the past twenty-two years? She'd think it over later as she fulfilled her pie orders. If the movie people wanted locals, they wanted real people with local jobs, everyday people, not necessarily a résumé full of accomplishments. She'd tell the truth, go to Shelley's tonight and have her picture taken, and then she'd apply with fingers crossed.

She'd make herself a Hope Pie too. Salted caramel cheesecake. Just for good measure.

By four o'clock, Veronica's house was sparkling clean for tomorrow night's pie class, she had her recipes printed to hand out, and she'd written her résumé. On her cover sheet, she briefly described leaving Boothbay Harbor just months shy of her seventeenth birthday—but not why—and making her way, alone, to Florida, where she'd gotten a job in a diner, then a few years later heading slowly west, to Louisiana, Texas, New Mexico, and then back to Maine. She wrote a paragraph about working at the Best Little Diner, how she loved her regulars and enjoyed the tourists. She didn't know if that would be remotely interesting to whoever was in charge of hiring the extras. She went on Google and learned she wasn't off base about what extras did. Lots of sitting around and waiting. Apparently, there wasn't much about what made for a good extra, what would make her be chosen over anyone else. But if they wanted "real people," Veronica was as real as they got. According to the articles she read about extras, the one thing an extra wasn't supposed to do or be was star crazy, so she'd left off her enduring love of Colin Firth.

Veronica put away her laptop, made a neat pile of her recipes, and did a check of her cupboards, pantry, and refrigerator to make sure she had everything she needed for tomorrow's class. Enough flour, shortening, baking soda, and sugar, both white and brown. She'd have to replenish her salt supply, pick up eggs, sticks of butter, and a pound of apples and a few pints of blueberries. She added cherries, blackberries, bananas, Key limes, and chocolate to her list. She used her jar of molasses so infrequently that she didn't have to worry about coming up short for Leigh DeMarco's shoofly pie.

For the first class, she'd focus on good old apple pie—even though it wasn't apple season—and making piecrust from scratch, but if students wanted to make special elixir pies, they would be able to; Veronica had a professional oven that could handle many pies at once, and every possible kind of pie filling at the ready, from fresh fruit to good chocolate to coconut to custard.

Her phone rang. Hopefully it was Penelope Von Blun dropping out of class.

"Hello, Veronica speaking."

"I'd like to order a pie, a special pie." The voice was raspy, thirties, Veronica thought, and there was a tinge of anger, of bitterness, but also sadness.

"Sure. What kind would you like?" From the woman's tone, Veronica had the sense she'd order Amore Pie or maybe Feel Better Pie.

"The kind of pie that would get someone off someone else's mind. Do you make that kind?"

Her boyfriend or husband was having an affair. Or in love with someone else, Veronica thought, but that didn't seem quite it. Usually Veronica could tell so much by just a voice, but there was something complicated here that Veronica couldn't put her finger on. "Well, I'll need to clarify if you mean in a romantic sense or just someone you're trying to purge from your life."

"Maybe both," the woman said.

Cast-Out Pie. Veronica had made a few like that, just twice here in town and several times down in New Mexico. The first time, one of the busboys at the diner, an emotional wreck of a young man who cried while clearing the tables of any woman who had red hair, like the ex who'd broken his heart, had been on the verge of getting fired for all his crying. So Veronica had stayed late and found herself using peanut butter for its stick and coconut for its grit, figuring a lighter cream-based pie that felt airy couldn't dislodge and lift, whereas the heavier peanut butter and the texture of coconut could get in there, take those feelings of gloom and doom, and carry them away from the stomach, such a source of upset. She'd baked up her Cast-Out Pie and given the poor guy a slice the next morning while having a chat in the kitchen. She told him that he was stronger than he thought, that he was in control of his own destiny, his own future, and maybe it was time to let old hurts go. Maybe it was time to focus on the new. Reel off and cast in.

As he ate the slice of pie—he'd had one and a half slices, Veronica remembered—he told her that he did have a bit of a crush on Jenny, the dark-haired waitress with the big blue eyes, and maybe he'd ask her out. The Cast-Out Pie had been a success and so Veronica had stuck with the peanut butter and coconut.

"I call that Cast-Out Pie," Veronica said into the phone.

"It'll really work?" the woman asked, the voice suddenly more hopeful.

"I'll be honest—it's one of my special elixir pies that doesn't always do its job. I suppose you really, really, really have to want that person out of your heart for it to work. You have to be ready. If you're not, it doesn't seem to work. Some people are ready, they're there, but memories keep pulling them back. Others truly aren't ready to let go, even if it's self-destructive."

"Well, sometimes you don't always know what's best for you," the woman snapped.

Veronica had a feeling this person was not ready, that the pie wouldn't work. But the pain in the woman's voice had gotten under Veronica's skin. The woman was prickly. Prickly was a very uncomfortable way to be. Veronica wanted to help her.

"I'll tell you what," Veronica said. "When you pick up the pie, don't pay me. If it works, you can leave the money in my mailbox. Fair enough?"

The woman was quiet for a moment. "All right. Tomorrow then?"

Tomorrow? She had her résumé and cover letter to go back over, the little photo shoot at Shelley's tonight, and class to prepare for tomorrow. Plus, she was working the morning shift tomorrow and had to bake two special pies for clients after work and her own salted caramel cheesecake Hope Pie for herself. Tomorrow afternoon she'd need a good couple of hours to do some grocery shopping for her pie class and get everything set up.

And had the woman even said thank you for Veronica's offer not to pay if the Cast-Out Pie didn't work for her?

"Please," the woman said, and again, something in her voice seemed so desperate that Veronica couldn't say no.

Veronica breathed out a silent sigh. "If you come by around five p.m. tomorrow, I'll have your pie ready."

"Thank you," she said finally, and hung up.

For a full minute, Veronica couldn't shake the woman off, there had been something unsettling in her voice, something Veronica couldn't pinpoint. She couldn't get the woman's bitter voice off her mind. Then again, that would be very helpful in making a Cast-Out Pie.

Chapter 6
GEMMA

On Monday morning at nine thirty, Gemma left the office of Dr. Laura Bauer, OB/GYN, with a confirmation of pregnancy—a second positive urine test anyway—a prescription for prenatal vitamins, and a due date.

January 3. A New Year's baby.

The doctor had answered all of Gemma's questions about what foods she should avoid (deli meats, high-mercury fish, and Caesar dressing because of the raw eggs) and whether she could drink just one cup of coffee a day (she could). She'd been lucky to get the appointment; June had discreetly asked Isabel for the name of her OB, and thanks to a last-minute cancellation this morning, Gemma had herself an appointment. She'd get the results of the blood test in a few days, but the doc had told her that with two positive pregnancy tests, she was most definitely pregnant.

She touched her stomach, still relatively flat. When would it feel real? When the baby kicked for the first time, maybe. Her wedding ring glinted in the sunshine as she walked down Main Street. I'm pregnant, she said to herself. I'm having a baby. It was real, even if it didn't feel real yet.

Perhaps it was better for Gemma that it didn't feel real just yet. Part of her, the part that loved her husband like crazy, wanted to call him and share it with him, but every time she reached for her phone she stopped herself. The conversation would move from his jubilantly shouting "I'm going to be a father!" to his talking about the move to Westchester, to the Plan—for Gemma to be a stay-at-home mother and work part-time, if she "insisted," at the free weekly newspaper. The other night, June had said that sounded pretty darn good to her, from her perspective, and considering June had been a twenty-one-year-old college student who hadn't been able to locate the father of her baby, Gemma understood what June had meant. Gemma was lucky. She did have a doting husband. Too doting, maybe, but she was blessed. Still, was it wrong to want the career that meant so much to her? If she had to be pregnant now, couldn't she have both? A baby and a career?

A month ago, she'd been on assignment in a Brooklyn homeless shelter, sitting on a cot next to a single mother who had nowhere to go, no skills, and no way to work without leaving her two-year-old, who lay sleeping on the cot—alone. Gemma had been so touched by her story that she'd gotten the woman an interview at a day care center to be an aide, but the job had gone to someone else. Twenty-plus calls to day care centers later between the two of them, the woman had gotten herself hired and a slot for her daughter. Within two weeks, she'd be able to leave the shelter for her own small apartment. Gemma's feature story on three women at the shelter had elicited over a thousand comments on the *New York Weekly* website—some blasting her and the women for their circumstances, others full of empathy with talk of vicious cycles. This was what Gemma wanted to do—talk to people, tell their stories, some heartbreaking, some controversial, some just stories of everyday folks going through struggles like so many. She wanted to inform, start conversations. Alexander had once said he thought Gemma's drive to be a human interest reporter stemmed from her wanting people to be heard the way she herself hadn't felt heard as a child. Maybe so. Sometimes she thought Alexander understood her so well. Other times . . .

Perhaps she'd call him tonight and tell him the news. After her meeting with Claire Lomax at the *Boothbay Regional Gazette.* Gemma had gotten damned lucky by running into Claire Saturday at their mutual friend's wedding. As summer friends, the teenage Claire and Gemma would play reporter, interviewing people on the street and jotting down their answers in notebooks. Claire had always had a knack for coming up with the assignments; it was no surprise she was a big editor now at the well-read regional paper.

At their friend's wedding reception, Claire had

hugged Gemma as though they were close as ever, and they headed over to a table with their mini crab cakes and Stilton-stuffed grapes to catch up on their lives; they'd last seen each other at June's aunt's funeral two years ago. Gemma had been honest when she caught up with her friend, which had gotten Gemma congratulations on the pregnancy, sympathy about her issues with her husband and losing her beloved job, and an invitation to stop in this morning to discuss putting Gemma to work for the week. Claire, in a long-term relationship, related to everything Gemma had told her. Claire would give her a great assignment, a story she could put together in a few days, and just having the assignment, reporting from the field, researching, Gemma would feel stronger, feel like herself again. She'd be better equipped to make her case to Alexander when he started in about how it was a blessing in disguise that she'd been laid off.

As Gemma passed a shop called the Italian Bakery, she had a sudden craving for cannoli. She peered in the window at a plate lined with the delectable pastry. Just one, she told herself. She headed in and left with four, one for now, one for June, if she saw her later, one for Isabel at the inn, and one for tonight, when she'd be dreaming of cannoli. She sat down on a bench outside the shop and found her attention going to the passing mothers. And babies. They were everywhere suddenly. Strollers. Babies in soft carriers strapped to mothers' and fathers' chests. Or in elaborate backpack-like contraptions. One mother wore her baby in a sling across her torso.

They all had one thing in common, though. They all looked like they'd been doing it forever, this parenthood thing. Their faces were calm. The woman with the backpack stopped to window shop, another pushing a stroller paused to answer her phone, then went on pushing her stroller down the street as though taking care of a baby was no big deal. Gemma had to get a grip. Clearly, you could multitask. Clearly, she'd learn how to hold a baby and talk to someone at the same time. Mothers had been mothers since the dawn of time, for heaven's sake. She could learn. She could talk to Isabel, who managed the Three Captains' Inn, for advice on running a business and raising a baby. Isabel had a great nanny but she'd also said that June filled in for her often at the inn. Gemma's sister, older by five years, lived in California and they weren't close and never had been. Her sister ran cold, like their mother always had, and kept to herself.

She was struck with a memory of being alone in her apartment as a child, having no idea where her mother was, unable to find her, her father gone, as usual on a business trip. Gemma would go door-to-door in the apartment, looking for her mother, and if she came to a locked door, she knew she'd found her. Her mother had worked full-time as a professor, but she'd hired sitters to watch Gemma when she was young, and once she was old enough to be trusted with a key, Gemma would come home to an empty apartment, her sister busy with her own life. There had to be a happy medium, but heck if Gemma knew where or what it was. She just knew she'd never had that feeling friends had spoken about—the yearning to have a baby. Alexander often insisted it was because she was afraid, because of how she'd been raised, because she didn't have a warm and fuzzy mother. He also insisted she'd be a great mom, that she was loving and kind and full of compassion and commitment, and that was all you needed to be a great mother.

Gemma wasn't so sure about that, though. You needed something else. Something more than all that combined. You had to want to be a mother in the first place.

Out of nowhere, tears stung Gemma's eyes because it felt so awful to think such a thing, given that there was a life growing inside her. A life, a quarter inch long, with a pipe-shape heart just beginning to beat, according to the week-by-week pregnancy book she'd started reading Friday night. Her baby. Alexander's baby.

Gemma put her hands on her stomach, wondering if she'd feel a flutter. Still nothing. Are you a boy or girl? she said silently to her belly.

Will you have my straight light brown hair? Alexander's sandy blond? His brown eyes? My dark blue? She wouldn't mind if the baby inherited the Hendrickses' cleft chin. And, yes, their pull-you-in warmth. Complain as she did about them, Mona and Artie Hendricks would be fantastic grandparents, the kind a kid dreamed of, doting and spoiling and full of hugs and love.

A dog on a long leash came over and grabbed the cannoli out of Gemma's hand. She'd only had two bites. The owner was full of apologies and said she'd go right in and get Gemma another cannoli, but Gemma smiled and opened the box and said she had extras, so no worries, that the dog had done her a favor, anyway.

Thank goodness for cute, cannoli-swiping dogs to stop Gemma from thinking about her belly and how complicated her life—her head, really—seemed. She glanced at her watch. Time to head over to the *Gazette*. If she was lucky, Claire would assign her to cover the big story everyone in town was buzzing about—the film crew that had set up over by Frog Marsh this past weekend. Interviewing the wonderful Colin Firth, one of her favorite actors, perhaps over a cannoli in the Italian Bakery, would take her mind off just about everything. She'd be dying to ask him to repeat her favorite words ever uttered on screen—"I like you. Very much. Just as you are." But she wouldn't, of course.

And an interview with a major movie star, on her home turf—well, her summer home turf—could be her way back. The personal angle combined with a story and interview of a major A-list movie star? It was the kind of story that would get her back into her old boss's good graces. It very well might get her her job back.

A weight lifted off her head, heart, and shoulders, as she headed down Harbor Lane, one of her favorite side streets, with its cobblestone path, where the *Gazette* offices were located, just across from Books Brothers, on the second and third floors. She smiled at the Moon Tea Emporium, a fixture on Harbor Lane, where she and teenage June and Claire had often gone to feel more grown-up, ordering tea and tiny sandwiches. She'd also made good use of the fortune-teller next door. Gemma peered in the windows, practically covered by red velvet drapes, and could see Madame Periot sitting at a round table with a woman. Maybe Gemma would stop in later. Or maybe she didn't want to know her fortune. *You are confused and someone very close to you is getting impatient,* the middle-aged woman would say. Gemma would ask if she and Alexander would figure things out, find their happy medium, and Madame Periot would say yes, of course. She didn't need to fork over thirty-five bucks for that.

Gemma glanced at her watch. She still had fifteen minutes to kill before her interview, so she ducked into Books Brothers, where June worked as the manager. In the Local Maine Interest aisle, Gemma found June helping a man select a book about climbing Mt. Katahdin.

"Crazy morning and we've only been open since nine," June said, giving Gemma a kiss on the cheek once her customer had gone. "Feeling okay?"

"Something about the air up here and this town helps perk you up," Gemma said. "And guess where I'm headed—to see Claire at the *Gazette* about being assigned a story."

June smiled. "That's great!" Two customers vied for June's attention, so Gemma squeezed her hand and said she'd see her soon.

Gemma looked over the display of pretty notebooks and bought a new one to bring to her interview, then glanced at her watch. She still had ten minutes before she had to head over to the *Gazette* offices. She browsed the fiction shelves, then crossed over to nonfiction, lured by the sign that said BOOKS THAT MIGHT HELP YOU FIGURE IT OUT. Now there was a sign meant for her. An entire shelf was devoted to marriage. Relationships. And several books on divorce. Divorce. Gemma turned away, a heaviness dogging her again, and focused on the pregnancy section. This is who you are, she reminded herself. Pregnant. Not someone who's headed for divorce. Just someone who's pregnant. And has her entire life going in a different direction. She glanced at her watch. Time to go. Time to get that life back on track.

At ten o'clock, Gemma sat across Claire's big, scarred desk, feeling so hopeful again. Being here in the messy office of the loud newsroom in the center of town, the sound of keyboards clicking, of staff conversation, of editors yelling, and constant knocks on the door to interrupt Claire and ask for okays or sign-offs, made Gemma feel right at home. This was her territory, even if the offices of the *Gazette*—a daily paper—were an eighth of the size of the *New York Weekly*.

Gemma pulled out her new notebook, ready to jot down her assignment. "I thought you could assign me a piece about the movie set in town, the effect on the local economy, on morale, et cetera. I could interview Colin Firth, the other stars. I saw an ad for extras in the *Gazette* on Sunday— I could talk to the director about the hiring process, interview a few extras. There are so many interesting components."

Claire, tall and slender with poker-straight dark hair to her shoulders and narrow dark eyes, looked exactly like the angular teenage girl Gemma remembered. Claire took a sip of her coffee, and before she could say a word, someone knocked, then came in and shoved papers at Claire for her to sign. Claire, one of the most together women

Gemma had ever known—nothing frazzled her—scanned and signed, then turned her full attention to Gemma. "Actually, I've already got someone covering the movie set and all that, and I'll tell you—finding out when Colin Firth is actually arriving in town is proving impossible. But I asked you to come in because there is a story I'd like you to cover while you're here."

Yes! "Great," Gemma said. Her pen was poised to write. She sat up straight, any vestiges of her earlier pregnancy-related tiredness gone in a flash. She was on pure adrenaline right now.

Claire regarded her for a moment and took another sip of her coffee. "There's a home for pregnant teenagers on the outskirts of town. Hope Home's fiftieth anniversary is at the end of July, and I'd like to do a full-coverage story on the place—what the home provides, the girls there, past residents, a where-are-they-now type thing, what it was like to be a pregnant teen fifty years ago, twenty-five years ago, and today. I want statistics on all the angles, candid quotes, townspeople reflections, the whole shebang."

Gemma's heart sank. A story about pregnant teenagers? Pregnant anyones? This wasn't a subject Gemma wanted to focus on. The skin of her arms felt . . . tight. "Claire, I—"

Claire held up a hand. "Gemma, the fact that you're pregnant, and—well, I'll be honest—in a state of flux, not sure of anything, is the main reason why I want you doing this story. You—questions that you'll ask, the perspective that you have, or need—will bring something to the piece that none of my other reporters could right now."

Gemma sat back. "But—"

"Three thousand words. Front page of the Life & People section."

Three thousand words. Front page. That was big. Hope Home. Pregnant teenagers. Would she encounter a bunch of fifteen-year-olds who were giving their babies up for adoption? Keeping them? This assignment—from their stories to Hope Home's history and past residents, the adoptive parents, and the circle of it all—would be emotionally intense, to say the least. "You know I appreciate this opportunity, Claire. It's just . . . unexpected."

"Like most things," her friend said.

Gemma went back to the inn and took her laptop to the parlor, where Isabel had set up a noon tea for guests. It was so cozy that Gemma could stay in this sweet parlor with its overstuffed couches and chairs, mohair throws and soft pillows, forever. She helped herself to chamomile tea in a pretty cup and a small slice of the best Key lime pie Gemma had ever had, then got busy reading through the information on the Hope Home website.

The website was pretty basic, informative, but

gently written, about what the home provided—a safe haven for pregnant teenagers, room and board, counseling, a resident nurse, and help with adoptive services. "Since 1963" was written under the Hope Home logo. What had it been like to be a pregnant teenager, sent to a home, in 1963? Gemma pulled out her notebook and wrote some notes about research she needed to do today—statistics on the number of pregnant teenagers in the United States in the sixties and today, what percentage of babies given up for adoption were born to teenagers versus adult women. What percentage of pregnant teens kept their babies and what percentage put them up for adoption. As she jotted down questions, she found herself writing two full pages of notes.

Did they all want to keep their babies? Did some know right away that adoption was their answer? There were some harder questions that Gemma would delve into once she learned the basics, questions that even she didn't want to think about.

There was a photograph of the home on the main page of the website. It sure looked nice. A sprawling white farmhouse with a wraparound porch. And a plaque: BUILT IN 1883. There were flowerpots lining the porch, and under a huge shade tree were several chaise lounges in a semicircle. Group meetings, Gemma figured. She finished her tea and craved another piece of that incredible pie but forced herself to get off the gorgeous mahogany love seat, its soft cushion printed with glittery sea stars, like the quilt in her room.

Out on the porch, Gemma sat on the swing, pulled out her phone, and pressed in the number for Hope Home. Five minutes later, Gemma had a noon appointment with the director for an interview and a tour; the woman said she'd have to talk to a few of her residents to see if they'd like to participate in the article and share their stories, and she could discuss the possibility of giving contact information for former residents, both recent and from decades ago, at their meeting.

As Gemma opened her notebook to jot down more questions, her phone rang. Alexander.

"I'm on my way to court so just have a few minutes, but wanted to check in," he said. "All that fresh Maine air and small-town niceness make you want to move to Dobbs Ferry yet?"

He was relentless.

"I haven't had a chance to look at the listing yet, Alex. I have an assignment for the *Boothbay Gazette* and—"

"Gemma, you promised to look. You're being unfair. I almost got hit by a taxi this morning. I'm sick of this city. I want out."

"Alex, I really can't talk about this right now. I'm on assignment. And my time here is limited, so I have to do some research right now."

"Look, Gemma, I lost out on that house I put the

offer on because I underbid and then felt like I couldn't up the offer because you flipped out. We're moving. You don't have a job holding you to New York City. There's no reason to live there. We've been here since we graduated from high school, eleven years. Enough already."

She sighed. "For you, not for me."

"So I'll just be miserable, is that what you're saying?"

"No, I'm saying that I'd be more miserable in Dobbs Ferry. You wanted to live in New York, it was your dream. At least you have that. But if I moved to Dobbs Ferry, I'd be miserable. I'd feel like my soul was being sucked right out of me, every day. I wouldn't know who I was there, Alex."

New York City, where he'd gone to college and law school, had stopped being his dream long ago, though, and she knew it. When they'd been married about three years, they'd started having a good-natured argument about New York, Gemma listing its wonders, and Alex its many downsides, which Gemma barely ever noticed. She'd told him how as a kid, she'd take the elevator to the roof of her parents' fancy building on the Upper West Side and go out and stare at the twinkling lights, and she'd feel lit up by possibility, by how much was out there in the world for her to dream about, to hope for. When she was upset about her family life, which was often, she'd go up to the roof and fill herself up with all that wonder.

On the evening of her and Alex's third wedding anniversary, he'd told her he had a surprise for her, put a makeshift blindfold around her eyes, and then led her out of their apartment to the elevator. Only when he took the blindfold off did she realize they'd gone up and not down and were on the roof of their building. She'd gasped. He'd set up a table covered with a lace table-cloth, a bouquet of flowers, and two covered plates, which turned out to be his one specialty, chicken Parmesan over linguini. A space heater was plugged in since it was October and chilly at night, and his old boom box was playing their wedding song. "You're My Best Friend" by Queen.

He'd done all that for her, then sat her down, told her she was stunningly beautiful and he was grateful as hell that she was his wife, that as long as he had her, he would be happy anywhere. They ate and drank Champagne and had one slow dance in which they barely moved, then went downstairs and made love more passionately, more tenderly than Gemma could remember.

That was just two years ago. Her dear Alex, her best friend, her husband, had created that beautiful night for her. He'd been telling her that no matter what their marriage was like at the moment, full of arguments about where to live or when to start a family, their marriage would always be her New York City, her rock, her wonder, her possibilities. They would find a way.

Two years later, everything had gotten so terribly out of hand, so strained and tied in knots.

"You've never even given the suburbs a chance, Gemma," he barked into the phone. "You just claim to hate it because it's not New York and because you think you have any idea what it's like to live there. You have no idea."

Gemma closed her eyes, wishing she could wave a magic wand and just fix this. That Alex would want what she wanted. That she would want what he wanted. If only they could just agree.

They could go back and forth on this forever. Neither was wrong, but Dobbs Ferry was wrong for her—it would be the death of her. She knew that. But New York City had become the same for him. Maybe she was being as selfish as she thought he was being.

She said she had to go and heard his sigh, and pictured him, on the streets of New York City, grabbing a coffee on his way to court, taxicabs screeching by him, crowds of people, bus exhausts blowing in his face in the humid Manhattan air. For a moment, Gemma did feel selfish. If only she could find the middle ground, the answer for both of them.

She lifted her face to the sunshine and tried to

put the conversation out of her mind. June's Subaru turned into the drive, and she had her baby niece, Isabel's daughter, in the backseat in a rear-facing pink baby carrier. June waved and in moments had the baby in her arms, and again, Gemma tried to look at the baby and feel like most people seemed to feel when they looked at babies, a squeeze of the heart, an *awww,* an oh, can I hold her, smell her sweet baby smell, the yearning to have one of her own.

But Gemma felt none of that. All she felt was fear, deep inside.

She gave June a warm smile and then escaped in her car to Harbor View Coffee to work on her interview questions. But there was a Mommy and Me kind of get-together in the back, babies everywhere she looked. Maybe the universe was trying to tell her something. Gemma just wasn't sure what.

Chapter 7

BEA

Bea could barely turn around in the narrow shower of her crummy budget motel across the bay from downtown Boothbay Harbor. But at least the water was hot, the shampoo smelled good, and on the bathroom counter was a mini–hot plate, a mug, and a packet of instant coffee with nondairy creamer and sugar. Even more important, the motel was cheap. Bea had gotten her last half week's paycheck from Crazy Burger, but she'd spent a fortune on gas to drive up to Maine, and had already racked up two nights at the motel—with no idea when she'd be checking out. The motel—the cheapest she'd found in the middle of the summer in this bustling tourist town—was sixty-nine bucks a night. She could afford one more night, but even that would be pushing it. If she wanted to stick around for a week or two, get her bearings before she introduced herself to her birth mother, she'd have to get some kind of temporary job. Given that it was summer, she was sure one of the zillion restaurants needed kitchen help. After she visited the hospital, she'd look around for "Help Wanted" signs or check the local paper.

Bea blew dry her shoulder-length blond hair

with the tiny, tinny hair dryer attached to the wall, put on a little makeup—a little brown eyeliner and mascara and a quick swipe of pinky-red lip gloss—then headed back into the small room to get her bag. On the bedside table she'd put a photograph of herself and her mother at her graduation, to remind herself who she was, that this crazy deathbed secret didn't change the fact that she was Bea Crane, daughter of Cora and Keith Crane. They'd raised her, they'd loved her.

They'd lied to her.

Bea dropped down on the edge of the bed, that sick feeling hitting her in the stomach again whenever her thoughts went to that fact. Omission. And a big one. The past couple of nights, she'd lain in bed going over pieces of her childhood, instances when her parents might have told her the truth. Like when she'd had to do a second-grade class project called About My Family, complete with photographs and a few sentences about each family member, and a classmate had said: "You don't look anything like your mom or dad. Maybe you're a Martian."

By the time Bea was thirteen, she was three inches taller than her father, who was five feet seven.

Maybe once a certain amount of time passed and the words were never said—we adopted you, we chose you, we picked you—you couldn't just come out and say them when a kid was older, when it might be devastating to a seven-year-old, a twelve-year-old. Grow up with the knowledge from before your earliest memory and it was just a part of you. Bea supposed she could understand why her parents had never told her. They'd probably wanted to over the years, but once she'd gotten beyond a certain age, they just couldn't bring themselves to shatter her world, her identity, her image of herself.

When Bea felt angry about the omission, a word she preferred over *lie* in this case, she tried to remember that, that her parents had gotten themselves into a sticky situation they couldn't easily remedy.

Fortified by the coffee and the hot shower, she was ready to head over to Coastal General Hospital, where she'd been born. Or where she thought she had been born. Her original birth certificate listed place of birth as HHL, but it was signed by a doctor at Coastal General Hospital and issued from there. Perhaps HHL were the initials for which the labor and delivery ward or wing had been named. Bea grabbed her bag and headed out, and once again the brilliant blue sunshine, cotton-ball clouds, and breezy mid-seventies lifted her spirits. She'd found herself liking that she'd been born in this beautiful place, this beautiful state with its water and trees and fresh, clean air. Just two days in Boothbay Harbor, from Saturday afternoon to Monday morning, and it was already beginning to feel more familiar. But Veronica Russo loomed as strange in her mind as she had on Saturday when she'd gone to the diner. Her birth mother was a total stranger, connected to Bea in the most fundamental of ways. Bea couldn't wrap her mind around that one.

Coastal General Hospital was on the outskirts of Boothbay Harbor, a fifteen-minute drive along a stretch of rural highway. Bea had a love-hate relationship with hospitals. She'd said good-bye to her father in a hospital, though he'd been gone by the time he'd reached the ER. A heart attack—unknown heart condition—at forty-one. Bea shook her head at the thought, the memory of the look on her mother's face when Cora had gotten the call. "My husband is dead?" she'd said into the phone, her face full of such confusion, nine-year-old Bea standing just feet away, washing an apple in the sink. That had been her first experience with hospitals, and for a long time afterward, she couldn't pass a hospital without feeling sick to her stomach.

She'd said her final good-bye to her mother in a hospital, Cora barely able to move her hand in Bea's on that last day. Her mother's medical team had been top-notch and kind, and for a while the hospital had turned into a place of hope for Bea. Until there was no hope.

Bea walked up the stone path to the stately old

brick building, pushed through the revolving door, and asked the guy at the information desk for the labor and delivery ward. On the third floor, the elevator opened to a sign on the wall: THE MARTHA L. JOHNSON MATERNITY WING. No HHL there. Bea walked down a short hall, looking for the nurses' station, but stopped when she noticed the nursery. Beyond the glass wall were several babies wrapped in blankets with tiny caps on their heads. A nurse was picking up one red-faced angry baby who settled down along the nurse's arm.

She tried to imagine herself here, as one of these babies, her birth mother standing twenty-two years ago where Bea was now. Maybe Veronica Russo hadn't stood here. Maybe when you gave up your baby for adoption, you didn't stand staring at him or her in the bassinet. Had Cora and Keith Crane stood here? Or had the adoption agency arranged the transfer internally? Did it matter, anyway? Bea's chest felt tight, and she turned to leave, grateful for the nurse walking down the hall.

"Excuse me," Bea said to her, taking her birth certificate out of her bag and holding it up for the nurse. "Could you tell me what this HHL means?"

The nurse glanced at Bea's birth certificate, the original stamped with "Not For Legal Purposes" across the top. "Well, I know that HH stands for

121

Hope Home, but the L is throwing me. Let me go ask another nurse at the station."

"Hope Home?" Bea repeated, following her.

The woman turned to Bea. "It's a home not too far from here for pregnant teenagers."

Oh, Bea thought. Veronica had gone to a home? She wondered why she hadn't stayed at her parents' house, since they'd lived right in Boothbay Harbor. Had Veronica been sent away?

"The L stands for lot," another nurse explained, handing back Bea's birth certificate. "Every now and then, a Hope Home girl will go into labor and have her baby either in the home or en route to the hospital. HHL means the baby was born in Hope Home's parking lot."

"I was born in a parking lot?" Bea said. Of a home for teenage mothers. Just what is your story, Veronica Russo? she wondered.

"You were likely born in an ambulance dispatched to bring your birth mother here. But you started coming before it was safe to transport."

"I was born in a parking lot," Bea said again, but she was thinking less about herself and more about Veronica Russo, who must have been scared out of her mind.

Hope Home was twenty minutes in the opposite direction, on the other side of the peninsula and down a long, winding road that stretched for miles. A right turn down another long road led to nothing but trees. Finally, Bea found the marker, a white post that read 14 HILL CIRCLE. Another long dirt drive later, the house came into view. Bea was surprised; she'd expected an institutional-looking building. But a sign proclaiming HOPE HOME hung off the porch of a very pretty, sprawling white farmhouse with several padded rocking chairs and flower boxes everywhere. Big trees shaded the front yard. There was a group of empty chaise lounges in a semicircle under one shady tree. Under another was an enormously pregnant girl who looked all of thirteen, lying on a chaise and flipping through a magazine. Another very pregnant girl with beautiful long red hair was walking around the perimeter of the yard, earphones in her ears.

A few cars were parked alongside the house, stones marking spaces. Bea pulled in and wondered if she'd been born right here, in this spot.

As Bea walked around the front of the farmhouse, the pregnant girl who'd been reading *People* magazine pushed herself off the chaise and walked toward Bea. "Hi, are you pregnant?"

Now that the girl was closer, Bea could see she was a bit older than she'd first thought. Sixteen, seventeen maybe. Her long, light brown hair was in a French braid. "No. I was born here, actually."

"Oh. So what do you want?"

"I just wanted to look around. Maybe talk to a director or something?"

"Ask for Pauline." The girl glanced at her watch. "She's probably right at the desk when you walk in."

"Thanks." Bea smiled at the girl and headed up the steps. She pulled open the screen door. Padded benches lined the entry. Farther in, a woman sat at a white wooden desk with a bouquet of blue hydrangeas.

The woman looked up from the binder she'd been writing in. "Welcome, can I help you?"

Bea suddenly had marbles in her mouth. "I was born here twenty-two years ago. In the parking lot, apparently. I just thought I could look around. Maybe speak to someone about the place? Get some history."

The woman smiled. "Sure. I'm Leslie, assistant to Pauline Lee, the director of Hope Home. Pauline's in a meeting right now, but I'm happy to answer your questions if I can." She closed the binder and gestured at the chair facing the desk. Bea sat. "Parking lot, huh. Sometimes our residents go into labor so fast that we can't get them to the hospital in time. You were either born on a blanket right out on the grass or perhaps in an ambulance, depending on the timing."

Bea couldn't imagine anyone—the girl reading *People*, for instance—delivering her baby on the grass. Or in an ambulance, for that matter.

"Could you give me some information about Hope Home? I don't know a thing about it."

"Well, we open our doors to pregnant teenagers and young women through age twenty-one. Right now we have seven girls in residence. Last month we had two more. We provide a comfortable room, meals, education—whether keeping up with classes at school or GED preparation—and counseling in all regards: emotional well-being, decision making regarding the pregnancy, whatever that may be, and help with adoption services."

"That's wonderful," Bea said. "Everything under one roof." And the place did look homey, with its cottage decor and the flower boxes lining the windows.

Leslie nodded. "We're nonprofit and cover the costs of everything I mentioned. Medical care is not covered and handled via arrangements made with Coastal General. All prenatal care is handled there, but we do have a nurse on staff twenty-four seven."

"Were you working here twenty-two years ago?" Bea asked.

"No, I joined Hope Home two years ago. Pauline's been the director for almost ten years. We do have very strict privacy policies in place, so it's unlikely anyone who was here then would be able to answer certain questions."

Bea glanced out the window at the two pregnant

girls, who were now sitting on the porch swing. Her birth mother had been one of them twenty-two years ago. There was so much Bea wanted to ask this woman, but it was really only Veronica who could answer her questions.

"I could give you a brief tour, if you'd like," Leslie said. "It won't be exactly as it was twenty-two years ago, but the basics are the same."

Of course Bea wanted a tour, so she followed Leslie down the short hall to the dining room. "Three meals a day are served here. The dining room always has healthy snacks available for cravings too."

Next was the breathing room, then the counseling room, a classroom, the exercise room, a small library, then an empty resident room, which looked quite nice. The room wasn't big but had a white wooden bed with a stitched quilt and ruffly pillows, and a big braided blue and yellow rug was on the spotless wood floor. On the wall next to the white bureau was a quote from Eleanor Roosevelt. *No one can make you feel inferior without your consent.*

She wondered which room had been Veronica's. She imagined her sitting on the rocker, reading one of the books on pregnancy from the library. Or staring at the Eleanor Roosevelt quote. She was dying to know what Veronica's time here had been like.

She glanced down the hall out the window at the

two pregnant girls. They were on the porch now; the girl who'd greeted her was now French braiding the hair of the redhead. "Leslie, I hope it's not rude to ask this, but I'm wondering something. Do most girls come here because of the stigma of being pregnant teenagers?"

Leslie glanced out at the girls. "Yes. Sometimes it's to protect them from gossip and stress at home. Sometimes it's because we can provide round-the-clock care and education and a social factor. And sometimes, well, it's a matter of their having nowhere to go."

Meaning that they were kicked out of their homes?

Bea pictured Veronica's parents dropping her off here and driving away, dust flying up in their wake. She wondered what the story was.

"Well, I appreciated your time," Bea said. "I guess I just really wanted to see the place, and I have."

Leslie shook her hand. "I wish you luck in finding your answers, Bea." She smiled and sat back down at her desk, opening the binder.

When Bea stepped outside onto the porch, the redhead put down her *People* magazine, and the other girl took a bite of the turkey sandwich from a plate on her lap.

"So Kim said you were born here?" the redhead said. She wore square copper earrings with the name Jen imprinted on them.

"I was. In the parking lot apparently."

Her mouth dropped open. "In the parking lot?"

Maybe Bea shouldn't have said that. Damn it.

"In an ambulance, I mean. Parked here." At least that was what Bea assumed.

"Oh. Yesterday in prep class, the leader said that can happen, that you can go into labor fast and not make it to the hospital, but that between the resident nurse and the paramedics, everything would be fine."

Kim took a bite of her sandwich. "And by looking at her," she said, "clearly it was." She stared at Bea. "So you're, what—seeing where you were born?"

"Yeah. I'm thinking about connecting with my birth mother."

"Thinking?" Kim repeated, her face falling. "So you're not sure if you want to?"

"I didn't even know I was adopted until a few weeks ago," Bea rushed to explain for fear that she'd upset the girl. "It's all been kind of a shock. So I'm just trying to figure out how I feel."

The girls eyed each other.

"You just found out you were adopted?" Jen asked, her eyes both wide and angry. "Your adoptive parents never told you?"

Bea shook her head. "The longer they waited the more impossible it became, I suppose. Plus, my mother explained in a letter that she wanted to believe in her heart that she'd given birth to me. It's complicated."

"Complicated?" Jen said. "Try wrong. She totally cut your birth mother out of the picture."

"Jen," the other girl said, touching her arm.

"No," Jen snapped, pulling her arm away. "How dare she not have told you! Will the couple who adopt my baby not tell her she was adopted? Just pretend I don't exist?" She paced for a moment, and Bea felt her heart start to race. What the hell had she done? Why had she told these vulnerable girls her situation at all? They were teenagers. Pregnant teenagers. Oh, Bea, you idiot, she thought, her stomach flipping over.

"So are you going to look for your birth mother?" Kim asked, darting her eyes at her upset friend.

"Well, I'm here in town—this is where she lives. I'm not sure about meeting her. I just don't know anything."

"God, I hate this!" Jen shouted. "You don't even know if you want to meet the person who gave birth to you?"

"It's . . . complicated," Bea said. She needed to apologize to the girls for getting them upset— well, getting one of them upset—and get out of there.

"I hope my child comes looking for me one day," Kim said. "I mean, look at you. All pretty and healthy and nice. Who wouldn't want to know their baby turned out happy looking?"

"I wouldn't," Jen said, shooting her friend a glare. "I mean, I think it sucks that she doesn't even want to meet her own birth mother, but I don't think I want my child to come looking for me. How the hell am I supposed to get through every day knowing one day my doorbell is going to ring?"

"Isn't that kind of a contradiction, Jen?" Kim said gently. "Anyway, Larissa—she's the counselor here," she added, turning to Bea for a moment, then back to Jen. "She said you just live your life and make it a piece of you, and if you want to be found, you can give that information to the registry, and if you don't, you don't have to."

"I don't know what I want!" Jen yelled. "But I don't need to know that the baby I'm giving up is going to be a real person one day, wanting to find me. So get out of here!" she screamed at Bea.

"Jesus, Jen. I do want to know," Kim said, almost in a whisper. She turned to Bea. "I want to know every good thing about you. I want to know that one day my baby might love me anyway, even though I'm not keeping her. I want to know she might want to know me someday." She started crying.

"Now look what you did, idiot!" Jen said, and threw her sandwich at Bea.

Bea gasped as a slice of bread hit her on the

thigh and dropped to the ground, a piece of turkey and a little glob of mayonnaise sticking to Bea's jeans. A lettuce leaf landed on her foot. She shook it off, her leg trembling.

"I'm sorry," Bea said, her stomach twisting. "I'm sorry. I—"

The screen door squeaked open and three women came out, one of whom was Leslie, the director's assistant.

"Why do we have to listen to this crap?" Jen said to her, her face turning as red as her hair. "I don't want to know. Okay? I. Don't. Want. To. Know."

Kim started crying again and ran inside.

"I'm Pauline Lee," a tall, dark-haired woman said to Bea. "The director of Hope Home. I'm sorry, but I think it's best that you leave now," she added kindly. She sat down in the rocker next to Jen and put her arm around her shoulder.

Bea stifled back the sob that was pushing its way up her throat. She ran to her car.

The other woman who'd come out with Pauline and Leslie hurried over to Bea as she was about to get in her car. "I have tissues, if you want to wipe off that mayo," she said, handing Bea a pocket packet of Kleenex.

Bea took the tissues, tears stinging her eyes. "Thank you."

"I'm Gemma Hendricks," she said, her honey-colored hair shining in the bright sun. "I'm writing a story about Hope Home and was just finishing up a meeting with the director when we overheard the conversation you and the two girls were having. Pauline said she'd keep an ear on it, and I suppose she thought it had gone as far as the girls could handle."

"I feel horrible," Bea said, tears streaming down her cheeks. "I didn't mean to upset them. I didn't mean to say anything. One of the girls asked me why I was here, and I was honest, when I suppose I shouldn't have been. I should have realized they were vulnerable to what I might say." Bea shook her head and covered her face with her hands. "What the hell am I doing?"

Gemma touched Bea's arm. "I'm a reporter, and again, I'm working on a story about Hope Home, so I don't know if I'm the worst or the best person for you to talk to, but if you need an ear, even if it has to be off the record, I'm happy to listen."

"So you were in a meeting with the director?" Bea asked.

Gemma nodded. "Getting some history and basic information. I'm writing an article about Hope Home's fiftieth anniversary."

"Can you share some of the history with me?"

"Sure. It'll all be going in my article, so nothing I was told is confidential."

"What I tell you about my story might be, though," Bea said. "Not from my perspective. I mean from my birth mother's. She doesn't even know I'm in town."

"I'll be discreet. I won't even use your real name if that's your preference," Gemma assured her.

Her real name. It made Bea crazy to think that if Veronica Russo hadn't given her up, she'd have a different name entirely, a different life.

Bea had nowhere on earth to be, and maybe talking this whole thing out with someone would help her hear herself think. "Okay."

"Why don't we go have lunch?" Gemma said. "On me."

Twenty minutes later, Bea was sitting across from Gemma, a small black recorder on the table along with Gemma's notebook and pen, at a seafood restaurant, the events of the last three weeks pouring out of her. She told Gemma about her mother's deathbed confession, sent to her a year after her mother passed away. About calling the adoption agency. About her birth mother updating the file with every possible piece of contact information. About going to the diner to check out Veronica. Seeing her in person, a real, live, walking, breathing person. The woman who gave birth to her. Who held the answers to how she came about, who her birth father was, what Bea's history was.

"Wow," Gemma said, sitting back and putting down her iced tea, which she hadn't even taken a sip of. "That's some story. Can I share it in my article? What you've been through is so moving. I won't put in identifying details about your birth mother, such as where she works. Unless, of course, if I get her permission too."

"Well, how would that even come about?" Bea asked. "I'm not even sure I want to meet her. If I'm ready, I mean. I don't know anything."

"No worries," Gemma said. "I just mean if you do meet her, and if she'd like to share her story, her history. What a beautiful story of coming full circle it would be."

"I suppose," Bea said. "But I have no idea if she'd be interested in making her past public. I don't know anything about her. Except that she bakes a really good pie, apparently."

Suddenly a male voice boomed, "Hey, folks! Colin Firth is signing autographs and taking pictures on the pier right outside!"

At least twenty people jumped out of their seats and rushed outside or crowded by the windows. A minute later they were all back, shrugging and chatting about how he was nowhere to be seen.

"I'd know Colin Firth a mile away," Gemma said, peering out the window. "And I don't see him."

"That's so weird," Bea said. "On Saturday, when I was at the diner, someone called out a Colin Firth sighting too."

"Maybe he got wind of it and fled. I'd love to catch a glimpse of him, I admit," Gemma said.

"He's one of my favorite actors. 'I like you. Very much. Just as you are,'" she added in a British accent.

Bea laughed. *"Bridget Jones.* I love that movie. One of the last movies my mother and I saw together was *The King's Speech.* She was crazy about Colin Firth. We watched it in her room in the hospital on Netflix." Tears stung Bea's eyes. "She loved that movie so much. She'd seen it twice already but wanted to watch it again with me."

"Maybe not being able to say what you want to say, for whatever reason, resonated with her," Gemma said, her dark blue eyes full of compassion.

Bea almost gasped as she understood what Gemma was saying; she envisioned Colin Firth as King George VI, with his lifelong terrible stutter, thrust onto the throne and having to speak publicly to his people in order to assure them. "I'll bet it did. I didn't think of that."

"Well, you've had a lot to take in over the past few weeks," Gemma said, and Bea felt herself relax; it felt so good to talk to someone who was just plain kind. Granted, Gemma Hendricks was a reporter, and maybe all she was after here was the story, but Bea had a good feeling about Gemma. She seemed true blue.

Their lunch was served, fish and chips for Bea, and the crab cakes for Gemma. When the bill came, Bea offered to pay her share, even though it would hurt her wallet to do so, but Gemma insisted.

"I said it was my treat, and I meant it."

Relief flooded through Bea. "Actually, I really appreciate it. I'm staying at the cheapest motel in town, but I can't afford more than one more night. I'll have to find a job if I plan to stick around." But what was she even sticking around for? To decide if she wanted to meet her birth mother? She could do that from home.

Which was the problem. There was no home. Bea had nowhere to go, nowhere to be. She pictured her mother's old white rental cottage on Cape Cod, the cozy living room, the small, sweet bedroom she'd created for Bea for visits and summers. She saw her mother coming out to greet her in her cotton sundress and sandals, her hair in a loose bun, her face lit up with happiness that her girl was home for the summer. Cora Crane, her mother.

Bea glanced out the window and let out a deep breath. Suddenly, all she wanted was to really see Colin Firth out there on the pier, signing autographs and agreeing to photographs, her mother's King George VI, working so hard to be able to say what he wanted to say, what he needed to say, to his people. She wondered if her mother had tried in her own way, wishing she could come up with the words to make it less shocking—that she'd withheld the truth, that Bea had been adopted.

"Hey, you know what?" Gemma said, sipping her iced tea. "Yesterday I overheard the manager of the inn where I'm staying telling someone she's looking for kitchen and cleaning help, that she was offering room and board. It's the Three Captains' Inn, just a couple of streets up from the harbor. It's a gorgeous inn. After we're done here, why don't you go back to your motel and get changed so you don't smell like turkey and mayo, and then come over to the inn. I'll introduce you to Isabel and you two can set up a time to talk. Maybe you can just interview on the spot if she's not busy."

Bea felt herself brighten. "Kitchens are my thing. That would be great if it worked out. Looks like I owe you big now. For coming to my rescue at Hope Home, for lunch, for listening, and for this possible tip at the inn. You're like a fairy godmother."

Gemma laughed. "Now if only I could work the same magic on myself."

Chapter 8
VERONICA

Résumé and photographs in a manila envelope, Veronica headed out to Frog Marsh at three o'clock on Monday, figuring she'd be among the first in line to apply to be an extra in the Colin Firth movie. But there were at least a hundred people already there, holding their own manila envelopes. She recognized many folks from town and waved, sizing them up as her competition. Mostly everyone looked like what an extra was supposed to look like: a real person. Several women, though, were decked out and dolled up as though they were going out for New Year's Eve.

Veronica had spent an indulgent couple of hours face deep in her closet that morning, trying to settle on the right look. She'd realized she was going to wait on a line, fill out a form, and hand in her résumé and photographs, none of which required "a look," but you never knew who might be doing the collecting and what they were jotting down on your résumé after you turned it in. Trying too hard. Too old. Too young. Too much makeup. Too dull.

She'd made herself look everywomanish. The woman in the background, walking by, sitting at the next table in a restaurant, shopping at

Hannaford's supermarket, or cutting hair at the next station. Extras faded into the background. At five feet ten and slender, with a D-cup chest and thick, shiny auburn hair to her shoulders, Veronica had never been much of a fader, so she'd put on a pair of old jeans, a pale yellow peasant top, her comfortable clogs, swept her hair into a low ponytail, and then added her Best Little Diner in Boothbay apron, as though she were heading to work afterward. She wasn't, but how much more everywoman could a real-life waitress be? She was an old pro at walking around wordlessly with her coffeepot in the background of the Best Little Diner. Most times, all she had to do was lift up the pot with a glance at someone, who'd nod, and that was the entire conversation. She had this extra thing in the bag.

Her confidence had disappeared and returned every few seconds on the three-minute drive to Frog Marsh. She wanted this. Bad.

The set had grown since she'd last been here. Multiple trailers instead of just one. Three vans. Barricades stacked alongside one another. A long table was set up by one of the trailers, which Veronica learned belonged to the second assistant director. She knew this because as the line grew behind her to at least two hundred people, he came out of the trailer and said, "Peeps, listen up. My name is Patrick Ool. That's right, Ool. And yes, I've heard it all. Fool. Tool—a favorite with a certain PA—that's production assistant for those of you new to moviemaking. I'm the second assistant director on the film, which is as yet untitled. We're filming four scenes here in Boothbay Harbor, one in the Best Little Diner in Boothbay, two on the streets, and one on a cruise boat. We're looking to hire fifty to seventy-five extras—"

One in the Best Little Diner in Boothbay . . . Veronica glanced down at her apron and almost couldn't contain her smile. This just might be her lucky day. If Veronica could act like anything, it was like a waitress at the Best Little Diner in Boothbay. She supposed this meant the diner would be shut down for the filming days. The director or producer or whoever paid for these things must be paying Deirdre a small fortune.

"When's Colin Firth coming?" a woman near the front of the line shouted out. "That's all I really care about," she added with a laugh.

"You," Patrick Ool barked, pointing at the woman who called out. "You're banned from the set. Please leave."

"Wait, but—" she said.

A security guard, the biggest person Veronica had ever seen, was already next to the woman, ushering her away. Veronica felt sorry for the woman; you could see the tears shimmering in her eyes as she kept turning back.

"Sorry, folks," Patrick said. "I'm not a jerk, but

that was a good lesson. If you're here to get a glimpse of the stars of the film, leave now. If you're here because you think working as an extra on a major film sounds really interesting and like something you'd enjoy, please stay. Number one rule of working as an extra is that you don't talk to the stars. You don't bother them. You don't take pictures of them. You don't tell them you've loved them since blah, blah, blah. You just don't. If we're clear on that, and you're still standing here, great."

Well, so much for rushing Colin Firth the moment he appeared, not that he did appear; Veronica kept one eye on Patrick Ool and one eye on the trailers, hoping Colin would suddenly emerge with that dazzling smile.

She had to get hired. She had to. The more the second assistant director talked about what was required of an extra—their time, sitting around for hours, being dead quiet during filming, following directions from him—the bigger her hope grew.

Finally, the line inched up, and Veronica was next to meet the three people—two men, including Patrick Ool, and a woman—seated at a long table with a stack of résumés. The woman eyed Veronica's apron, took a Polaroid of her without even giving her the heads-up to smile, jotted something down on the back, then took Veronica's manila envelope and attached the Polaroid to it with a paper clip. With a thank-you and "we'll be in touch," Veronica was dismissed and Patrick Ool called out, "Next."

It all happened so fast that Veronica hadn't even thought to ask questions, but luckily the woman in line behind her had, and Veronica overheard Patrick Ool say that selected applicants would be notified in the next few days. Tonight, if she wasn't all pied out after her class, she'd make herself that salted caramel Hope Pie and have a huge slice.

The Cast-Off Pie for Veronica's newest client was all boxed up with Veronica's signature red velvet ribbon and waiting on the kitchen counter. Veronica glanced at her watch. Five forty. The woman asked for a special rush pie and then was late picking it up? Nervy. In twenty minutes, Veronica would have a kitchen full of students for the first pie class.

Making the Cast-Off Pie had been an unexpected blessing earlier this afternoon. Measuring out the thick peanut butter and mixing in the shredded coconut and chocolate chips, making the graham cracker crust, had let her take her mind off tonight—having students like snobby former classmate Penelope Von Blun, who never let her forget who she once was: the high school junior who'd gotten pregnant and sent away, and Officer Nick DeMarco, who always made her feel unsettled, perhaps because he represented

Timothy to her in a way and brought back how Veronica had once—and never since—felt: deeply in love. Both people would be in her kitchen, the place that had long been her refuge. While making the pie, she'd focused on what she wanted to cast off from her own heart, her own mind: feeling less than, feeling ashamed, feeling sorry that she'd gotten herself into a situation at age sixteen that had had such incredible consequences—a baby taken away. A love destroyed. A family torn apart. Veronica, alone. She found herself putting all that into the pie, those negative feelings, but instead of feeling better, her heart felt heavier.

As she'd told her client, Cast-Off Pie didn't always work. Then again, she hadn't been making the pie for herself. The recipient would make the pie her own; that was how it worked, how it had always worked.

Veronica took a final glance around her kitchen, making sure everything was ready for class. She'd set up pie stations at the big center island, rolling pins and labeled canisters of ingredients for six people. Two students had called this morning to drop out; one forgot her knitting class started this week at the library, and another could barely get the words out that she was sick because she was coughing so violently. That made six students. Tonight they'd make a traditional apple pie, working on it together, unless anyone, such as Nick DeMarco's daughter, wanted to make a special pie. Since Veronica had been teaching the class, she always handed out recipes for the special pies, as most people preferred to make them at home once they learned the basics of pie making and saw that it wasn't so hard at all.

The doorbell rang. Either a very late client or an early student.

Veronica didn't recognize the woman at the door, and she knew all her students by sight. For a moment, the woman stared at Veronica, and she realized she had seen her around town a couple of times over the past few months. She was in her midthirties, with shoulder-length, swirly, high-lighted blond hair and a dressy outfit, and she wore serious makeup, reminding Veronica of the way the Real Housewives of TV tended to style themselves. Veronica tried to imagine the Real Housewives of Maine, running around in fleece and L.L.Bean duck boots.

"I'm here for the special pie we discussed," the woman finally said, hostility radiating from her. "You said it was called Cast-Off Pie." She was dressed in such feminine, airy clothing at odds with her anger—a pale lavender silky tank top with ruffles down the front, off-white pants, and high-heeled mules. She wore a lot of gold jewelry too, including a wedding ring.

Her husband was having an affair? Veronica was no psychic, but she knew, somehow, that that wasn't the case.

"I have it boxed up and ready to go," Veronica said. "Why don't you come in and I'll go get it." Veronica extended her hand. "Veronica Russo."

The woman hesitated for a split second, making Veronica curious. What was up? "Beth," was all she said in response.

As Veronica headed into the kitchen to get the pie, she sensed Beth staring holes into her back, shooting daggers, maybe. Her hostility didn't seem truly focused on Veronica, though; there was something complicated at work here. When she returned with the pie, Veronica said, "Do I know you from somewhere? I think I've seen you around town a couple of times, maybe."

"I don't think so," Beth said, taking the pie. "So if the pie does its job, I just leave the fee in your mailbox, right? Fifteen dollars?"

"Yes. And if it doesn't work, you don't owe me a thing."

"Well, we'll see, then," Beth said, offering Veronica a tight smile before turning and walking out the door, past two women coming up the walk.

Even if Veronica wanted to think about strange Beth, her first two students had arrived. And they were a lot friendlier too. A pair of sisters in aprons, Isabel and June Nash, who owned the Three Captains' Inn, which had Veronica on standing order for two pies a week. Veronica liked both sisters, but she didn't know them well. She was several years older than Isabel, who'd called her months ago to rave about her pie at the diner and to ask her to bake for the inn. Isabel had had a baby just six months ago, but you'd never know it from her perfect figure and how elegant she looked, even in jeans and a T-shirt. Veronica was at least ten years older than June, who had the most gorgeous wild curly auburn hair, secured tonight in a bun with chopsticks. June worked in Veronica's favorite bookstore and had a very polite son.

"I'm determined to learn how to make my own piecrust without it turning all crumbly or getting all wet," Isabel said. "Every time I try, it's a disaster."

"You should have tasted the banana cream pie I made for a bake sale for Charlie's school last year," June said. "I think I forgot the sugar entirely. Someone bought a slice, then came back to the table and asked for their money back!"

Veronica laughed. "That'll never happen again, I promise."

Next to arrive was Penelope Von Blun, who announced that her friend CeCe couldn't take the class after all because of a conflict with something. Once again, Veronica was struck that Penelope looked different. For the past few weeks, she seemed . . . toned down. Her shoulder-length dark hair, which was usually flat-ironed to model perfection, was natural and wavy. The makeup was minimal. And without her usual fashionista wardrobe, she looked kind of like everyone else, like someone who lived in Maine instead of New York City. She'd always worn gobs of jewelry, but lately, Veronica noticed she wore only a gold heart locket around her neck and her wedding ring. A "make-under" instead of a makeover, really. Veronica wondered what it was about. Penelope Von Blun had had the same flashy, expensive style since middle school. But instead of pushing past Veronica and making snide comments about what Veronica was wearing or how small her house was, Penelope offered everyone a huge smile, complimented Veronica's foyer painting of wildflowers and her earrings, then chatted up the Nash sisters and told them she'd heard "fabulous" things about their inn. This was a new and improved Penelope.

As Isabel and June chatted with Penelope, Nick DeMarco and his daughter, Leigh, arrived.

Nick knew everyone, of course. Between patrolling around town and writing tickets for speeding and expired registration stickers, Nick DeMarco and the other cops in town stood out. Women usually fawned over him, since he was good looking and widowed, and though Isabel and June were warm and friendly, especially to Leigh, they certainly weren't fawning. Penelope was very friendly to him but not flirtatious. And Veronica, the only single woman in the house, focused her attention on his daughter instead of Nick.

Just when Veronica thought Penelope couldn't possibly get any warmer or fuzzier—or less snooty—she shone her attention on young Leigh DeMarco, asking her all about her summer camp, then shook Nick's hand and told him that it was thanks to hardworking police officers like him that Boothbay Harbor was such a safe and wonderful place to live. Veronica had no idea why Penelope Von Blun had turned . . . nice, but it was a welcome change.

"So, let's head into the kitchen and get started," Veronica said, leading the way. It'll be just the five of you, a perfect number for a pie class."

"I love this kitchen," Isabel said, glancing around the large room.

Veronica did too. The moment she'd seen the yellow bungalow, she'd known it was the right house for her, but when she stepped into the kitchen, she couldn't believe her luck. A big country kitchen with painted white cabinets, lots of counter space, and original wood floors, the room was made for baking pies. Veronica had painted the walls a very pale blue and had a professional oven installed, but otherwise, she hadn't had to renovate much at all. A back door opened to a small deck overlooking a tiny yard and Veronica's container garden. She didn't have much of a green thumb but liked to see flowers when she looked out the window.

The group gathered around the island, checking

out the canisters and picking up the rolling pins.

"Tonight we'll make a traditional apple pie," Veronica said. "I know some of you might be interested in learning to make my special elixir pies. I have the most requested recipes printed out, so if you'd like any of them, just let me know. If anyone would like to instead make a special pie, you can do that too and be off on your own, asking for help as you need it."

"Apple pie for us, right, Leigh?" Nick asked his daughter.

Leigh glanced at the floor, then at Veronica. "Actually, I'm making a special pie. Shoofly pie."

"I think I remember my great-grandmother making that when I was a kid," Nick said, smiling at his daughter, then Veronica.

"Shoofly pie," Isabel said. "My aunt Lolly used to love that! It's molasses, isn't it? She had such a sweet tooth."

Veronica nodded. "Molasses and brown sugar crumb topping. I love it, but you don't see it made much these days."

"What kind of elixir pie is that?" June asked, picking up a canister of baking soda and peeking in through the plastic top.

Leigh DeMarco was staring at her feet.

"It's what I call a Spirit Pie," Veronica said. "It can help you feel close to someone you lost."

For a split second, it was as though everyone in the room held their breath. Nick was nodding,

150

slowly, and taking his daughter's hand, and Leigh looked like she wanted to run out the back door, but she didn't. June and Isabel glanced at each other and were silent. And Penelope seemed subdued.

"I miss my mom," Leigh said, staring at her sneakers, but Veronica could see she was holding back tears. "Mrs. Buckman, she's our neighbor," she added, glancing up at her dad, then around the room. "She had one of Veronica's Spirit Pies and said she felt like her mother was right in the room with her."

"Sometimes I feel that way at the inn," Isabel said. "I'll be in the foyer, putting brochures on the sideboard, and all of a sudden, I'll feel the presence of my mom and dad. A few weeks ago, I was in the kitchen, whipping up an Irish breakfast for guests, and for the briefest moment, it was as though my aunt Lolly and uncle Ted were with me, telling me I was doing a good job. Doesn't happen often enough."

"If I could eat a slice of delicious pie that would help me feel their presence," June said, "I'd have a great excuse to eat the whole pie."

Veronica smiled. "That's the good thing about shoofly pie. It's so sweet you can probably only eat one slice. When I make it, and then sit with my tea and have a piece, I do feel my grandmother with me. It's the most comforting thing."

"So why don't we all make a shoofly pie instead

of apple pie," Leigh said. "We can all have a slice and we can all get to feel close to who we want." She shuffled through the recipes on the island and pulled out the one for shoofly pie.

Penelope turned to Veronica. "Will it work on someone who's not dead? You said it helps you feel closer to someone. Will it work if they're alive?"

"I think so," Veronica said. "You just think about that person while you're working on the pie, while you're having a piece, and it should help. Shoofly pie instead of apple?" Veronica said to the class, looking at each student.

Everyone nodded, except Nick. Leigh was staring up at him. "You can tell Mommy you're sorry, Dad," she said.

Once again, it was as though the air stopped circulating.

Nick took a deep breath and put his hand on his daughter's shoulder, but looked away, his dark eyes once again unreadable. Whoa. Everyone was politely looking at the canisters of ingredients and printouts of recipes on the island, trying to give him—and Leigh—a little privacy.

Nick kept his gaze on the recipe for shoofly pie that Leigh handed him.

"Okay, shoofly pie it is," Veronica said quickly. "If you didn't bring an apron, grab one from the pegs by the door, and let's get started."

As Veronica tied her apron around her back, she

glanced at Nick, who looked as though he wanted to be anywhere but here.

Veronica held up a color printout of the last shoofly pie she'd made, a couple of weeks ago, to celebrate what would have been her grandmother's eighty-fourth birthday. Veronica's parents hadn't made a fuss over birthdays, but Renata Russo always had. "Shoofly pie. It's very simple to make, but the most important ingredient will come from you, from the heart. While you're pouring or stirring or mixing or even just waiting for the pie to bake, you just think about the person you want to feel close to, and then when you're having the pie, you think about that person some more, and you'll likely feel them with you."

"If only everything were that easy," Penelope said with a sigh.

Veronica smiled at her. "I didn't say it was easy. Just that it seems to work." She turned to Leigh. "Leigh, why don't you read out the list of ingredients while I go print out more copies of this recipe so everyone can have one."

Leigh smiled and took the paper and began reading as Veronica headed into her small office off the living room. "For the crust," Leigh was saying. "Flour, sugar, kosher salt . . ."

Veronica came back into the kitchen and handed out the recipes. "Thanks, Leigh. The first thing we'll do is make our pie dough because we want to let it chill in the refrigerator for thirty minutes."

The tension seemed to seep out of everyone as they all got to work, Leigh adding the flour to the bowl of the food processor, Nick pouring in the sugar, and Penelope the salt. Veronica asked Leigh to pulse a few times, then had Isabel add the diced butter, and June the shortening.

"Now, some folks make their piecrusts with either just butter or just shortening," Veronica said, "depending on the pie, but my grandmother used both shortening and butter for her crusts, so I do too." Veronica added a little cold water to the mix, then explained how to dust the counter so that the dough wouldn't stick and how to roll the dough into a ball. "We want to be careful not to work the dough too much or it might get tough."

"Everyone says making piecrust is so difficult," Isabel said. "But this was easy."

Penelope wiped her flour-dusted hands on her apron. "I'm so glad I signed up for this class. I think I'm going to bake a few pies a week for the senior citizens center."

Okay, Veronica really liked this new, nice Penelope. "Now, let's wrap the dough in plastic and let it chill for thirty minutes while we work on the filling."

"Wait, I wasn't really thinking about my mom while I was adding the flour to the bowl," Leigh said, her face crumpling. "Now the pie won't work for me."

"No worries," Veronica said, aware of Nick's

eyes on her. "Remember, I make Spirit Pies for other people. They sit down with their pies and think about who they want to feel close to. So it works if you make the pie or if you don't. But in our case, since we're making the pie, we'll each think about who we want to feel close to as we're making the filling."

Leigh brightened. Nick looked uncomfortable. Penelope seemed relieved. Isabel and June were the only two that seemed to be enjoying themselves. Because they're at peace with their losses, with their grief, Veronica understood.

Veronica assigned everyone an ingredient for the filling. "Now, as you pour your ingredient into the mixing bowl, think about the person you want to feel close to—you can just picture them, think of a memory, anything that reminds you of them, and close your eyes."

Veronica watched Leigh dump in the baking soda as slowly as she could, her expression a combination of happiness, sorrow, and determination. Nick added the brown sugar so fast Veronica almost missed it. Isabel put in the butter, and Veronica showed Leigh how to whisk it together, then June poured in the egg. Penelope stood before the bowl and, as she added the vanilla extract, she closed her eyes for a moment as though she was praying, and Veronica couldn't help but wonder whom she was thinking about. Perhaps she'd offended a friend or a relative and was hoping to be forgiven. Leigh poured the molasses and whisked it again.

"I feel her hand around mine!" Leigh yelped, glancing around. "I feel my mom's hand!" She stood very still and started to cry, and Nick put his arm around her.

"Leigh? Are you okay?" he asked.

"I felt her hand around mine," she said again, and even though she was crying, her face held an almost joyous wonder.

Nick squeezed her shoulder and kissed the top of her head, but he was looking out the window.

Veronica added the boiling water to smooth out the filling, startling herself for a moment because it wasn't her grandmother's sweet face that came to mind.

It was the baby girl she'd given up for adoption. Veronica had only held her for two minutes, and in those two minutes, Veronica had fantasized about breaking out of the ambulance, where it had been parked at Hope Home, and making a run for it with the baby. But as she'd looked at that beautiful little face, the three-quarters-closed eyes and wisps of blond hair, just like Timothy's, she was reminded that she had nowhere to go and no way to provide for her child. Her parents had disowned her. Her boyfriend had insisted it wasn't his baby. And her grandmother, the only person who'd ever been her rock, was almost a year gone by then. With no support from anyone, how could Veronica hope to support a child, emotionally and financially? When the EMT guy gently took the baby back to tend to her, Veronica had squeezed her eyes shut and turned her face away, reminding herself over and over that the baby wasn't hers, really hers, and that she was doing the right thing, the best thing for the baby.

The right thing. How many times had she heard that phrase, over and over and over. Not from the staff at Hope Home, who knew better than to throw around platitudes that weren't necessarily true. But from strangers. Visiting parents. Anyone she told her story to. *You're doing the right thing. You did the right thing.*

I did the only thing I could do, Veronica had thought then.

Over the years, she rarely tried to imagine what her daughter looked like. At birth, the hair might have been Timothy's, but the face was Veronica's. The eyes, even just a quarter opened, were Veronica's. Same with the nose. Maybe the chin and something about the shape of the face were Timothy's. Veronica liked kids fine, but she tended to keep her distance. Playgrounds made Veronica feel unsettled. Parents walking hand in hand made her feel like she'd once had something and then didn't, not lost exactly, but just gone. Veronica went to the sink, ostensibly to wash her hands, but really to close her eyes for a moment and let this feeling pass. But it didn't pass. The baby's face came to mind again, the feel of that tiny weight in her arms, against her chest. She felt it now, as though she were right back in that ambulance.

Since she'd been back in Boothbay Harbor this past year, she'd had strange dreams about Hope Home and the night she gave birth, quite unexpectedly, in the ambulance. The baby had started coming and that was that; there was no time to get her to the hospital safely, and the EMT guy with the kind face had delivered the baby. Veronica had been having odd bits of dreams, pieces of experience, but she never let herself think too much about the baby girl or where she might be or what she really might look like. It was too painful, and Veronica had learned at sixteen how to tamp those thoughts down so she didn't fall apart. Maybe these sudden thoughts about the baby while making the pie were about all those bits coming together. Maybe subconsciously, she did always think about the baby.

"I don't know about the rest of you, but I didn't feel anything," Penelope said, worrying her lower lip.

"I'm not sure that I felt my parents' presence," Isabel said, "but I did think about a memory I haven't thought about in a long time, a really good memory."

"I did too," June said to her sister. "The seven of us—you and me, Mom and Dad, and Aunt Lolly and Uncle Ted and cousin Kat. Christmas at the inn when we were really little, and that stray cat Lolly took in unraveled all the garland from the tree and then got her nails caught and brought the whole tree down."

Leigh laughed. "Was your aunt mad?"

"She was at first," Isabel said. "But our uncle Ted was laughing so hard because the cat finally found his way out of the tree and had garland around his tail. That cat lived a good long life as the inn mascot."

"Daddy, who were you thinking about?" Leigh asked.

All eyes turned to Nick. "My grandfather," he said quickly, and Veronica had a feeling he hadn't been thinking about anyone in particular. "You would have loved Great-grandpa DeMarco."

Leigh smiled. "Will you show me pictures when we get home?"

Nick nodded, and she put her hand in his.

The filling for the shoofly pie was done, and now it was time to take the piecrust out of the refrigerator and roll it out. Everyone gathered around the island as Veronica demonstrated, and then she gave the rolling pin to Nick, who looked as if he needed something to do. Once the pie tin was laid out and the pie filled, Veronica got them started on the crumb topping, just some brown sugar, flour, cold butter, and salt.

"Can I talk to you privately?" Penelope said to

Veronica as she watched over Leigh gently breaking the mixture into a crumbly texture.

"Sure," Veronica said. "Everyone, I'll be back in a few minutes. Leigh, just keep doing what you're doing."

Veronica led the way to her office and shut the door behind Penelope for privacy.

"It didn't work for me," Penelope said. "What am I doing wrong?"

"Were you thinking about the person you want to feel close to?" Veronica asked. "I know you said this was a living person."

"Yes." She closed her eyes for a second, then opened them, frustration and anger evident. "I don't know. I'm not thinking about her so much as I'm thinking about what I want to happen. Does that make sense?"

"I thought you said you wanted to feel closer to this person."

Penelope pushed a swatch of her wavy brown hair behind her ear. The diamond ring above her diamond-encrusted wedding band was the biggest one Veronica had ever seen. "I just want this person to like me. That's all."

Okay, this was weird and Veronica had no idea what Penelope was getting at or what she could possibly be talking about. "Well, do you like this person?"

"I don't know, to be honest. But I need her to like me. I thought I could take your class and learn to make one of your special pies that I hear people talk about all the time. Hope Pie or whatever. But when Leigh brought up the Spirit Pie, I thought maybe it would work for this too. I don't believe in this nonsense, Veronica. But I'm not religious and outside of a genie coming along and granting me my greatest wish, I'm stuck and will try anything."

"Stuck wanting something that you're worried won't happen because you're not sure this person likes you?"

"Yes. Exactly."

Veronica had no idea of the particulars, but there was true desperation in Penelope's eyes.

"I'll give you my recipe for my Hope Pie," Veronica said. "Maybe that'll help. Make it at home and put all the force of your wish into it. I'm planning to make one later for myself."

Penelope glanced at her, as though surprised Veronica could want something. "I'll try it."

"Is this why you took the class? For the recipe?"

"Among other reasons," Penelope said.

"Veronica," Leigh called. "The oven dinged. Preheating is done."

"Coming!" Veronica called back.

"Let's go put the pie in the oven," she said to Penelope. "I'll be spending the remaining class time going over techniques, and each student will work independently on a piecrust. You can try again at the feeling you're after with this person."

Penelope nodded and looked away. There was defeat in her face now.

"And Penelope, if you need to, you can call me. For whatever reason."

Penelope glanced at her. "Thank you. I appreciate that."

A few minutes later, the brown sugar crumb topping was over the pie and it was in the oven, and everyone was making their own piecrusts as practice. The class was going well. Nick and Leigh were laughing about the dusting of flour on Nick's cheek and in Leigh's hair. June and Isabel were chatting away about family memories. And Penelope was forming her dough into a ball, much too roughly, as though she were trying to force the feeling again, forge a bond where maybe none existed. Veronica reminded her to be gentle or the dough would be too tough. And then again, out of nowhere, Veronica felt the strangest sensation of a tiny weight in her arms.

Chapter 9
GEMMA

Gemma sat on the porch swing of the Three Captains' Inn with her laptop, typing up her notes from her visit to Hope Home earlier that day. She had about ten minutes left before Bea would arrive for the introduction to Isabel about the job in the kitchen. Gemma was glad she'd recorded her interview with Pauline Lee and had taken notes; there was so much to digest, and each answer she got from Pauline had elicited more questions. Of the seven residents at Hope Home right now, one was keeping her baby, four were going the adoption route, including the two girls whose conversation with Bea had spiraled out of control, and two were undecided, including a newly pregnant seventeen-year-old with a college scholarship who was considering terminating the pregnancy.

The seven girls at Hope Home came from all over; two girls were from New York, four others from the New England states, including one from right here in Boothbay Harbor, and one came all the way from Georgia. According to Pauline Lee, none of the girls had intended to become pregnant. Two girls, caught up in the moment, had been assured when their partners said they would "pull out," so they "had nothing to worry about." Another used no birth control at all, having heard that a woman could only get pregnant at a certain time of the month, and she was sure it wasn't that time for her. Two others were careless with remembering to take their birth control pills. And two others had reported that their partners had used condoms, but that they had broken.

Gemma could attest to a broken condom causing an unexpected pregnancy.

She'd lost her own virginity at sixteen to her high school boyfriend, a cute, driven fellow reporter on the school newspaper who'd unfortunately taken "getting the story at all costs" to new heights and become very unpopular. They'd been a couple for over a year when Gemma had had enough of his relentless determination to put the story above people's feelings; that was a line Gemma had never—and would never—cross as a reporter.

She'd asked her boss at *New York Weekly* if that was the real reason she'd made the list of those being let go, and he'd hemmed and hawed and said most of the time, in the types of stories she covered, people came first anyway. But there had been a time when Gemma was expected to hound a woman who'd recently lost her soldier son for reaction to a controversy surrounding his death, and Gemma had refused. Another newspaper had gotten the shot of the grieving, angry woman, who'd refused to talk to reporters anyway. But Gemma's refusal to bother the woman had been noted.

There were questions she didn't want to ask for the article on Hope Home either. Questions she wouldn't ask, ones that were too personal and no one's business. There was a line, and Gemma tended to know what it was. Her high school beau hadn't believed in that line, and her admiration of him had turned to disdain.

And if she'd gotten pregnant then? If the condom had broken at sixteen instead of at twenty-nine? What would she have done?

She didn't know. But the thought that went through her mind was: There but for the grace of God go I.

Because you were having sex in the first place, she heard her older sister say, as though Anna were sitting right next to her. Once, when Gemma was sixteen and worried that she might be pregnant because her period was almost a week late, Anna, home from college for Christmas break, had said almost exactly that. *If you weren't having sex, you wouldn't have to worry about being pregnant. Don't do the thing, and you won't be the thing. It's that simple.*

Nothing was really ever so simple, Gemma thought. Absolutes, maybe. But not emotions.

Gemma's phone rang and she grabbed for it, hopeful that it was the director of Hope Home.

Pauline had promised to ask a few of the residents if they'd be willing to speak to Gemma to be interviewed and quoted in her article.

But it wasn't the director. It was Mona Hendricks, her mother-in-law. Gemma sighed and answered. She could picture fifty-six-year-old Mona, with her curly brown bob and multicolored reading glasses on a beaded chain around her neck, working on an elaborate recipe like beef bourguignon in her kitchen, which was bigger than Gemma's living room.

"Gemma, what's this I hear about you staying up in Maine for the week?" Mona asked. "Is there trouble between you and Alex?"

Did all mothers-in-law ask such nosy, personal questions?

"I came up for a wedding and since I lost my job, I figured I'd extend my visit with my girlfriends. I don't get to see them much."

"Well, you won't get to see Alexander much three hundred miles away either," she said. "When are you coming home—I want to make an appointment with a Realtor I've heard great things about. There are two new houses on the market I think would be perfect for you and Alexander. One is a Colonial with—"

"Mona, I'm sorry to cut you short, but my friend just arrived, so I need to go. Talk soon. Bye." It was a waste of Gemma's breath to remind Mona that she didn't want to leave New York City. Mona didn't hear her, didn't care how she felt. All the Hendrickses thought she was wrong and selfish for wanting to stay in the city.

Gemma might have felt guilty for practically hanging up on her mother-in-law, but Bea had indeed pulled into the driveway. She'd changed out of her jeans and T-shirt into a pretty cotton dress and ballet flats, her light blond hair pulled back into a ponytail. There was something about Bea that made Gemma feel protective. Bea was all alone in the world and was dealing with an emotionally heavy situation. While Bea had been telling Gemma her story, about receiving the deathbed confession letter—a year later—from her late mother, Gemma wondered how she'd feel if she'd received a letter like that. *I didn't give birth to you. We adopted you.* But there was a big difference between Bea's mother, whom Bea had described as mother of the year, twenty-one years strong, and Gemma's mother, who Gemma was pretty sure suffered from some kind of dissociative disorder. Gemma would read that letter, addressed to herself, and want to think ah, yes, now it makes sense, no wonder, she wasn't really my mother. But motherhood didn't work like that—that much Gemma was sure of. Motherhood wasn't about who gave birth to you, who adopted you, who raised you. It was about love, commitment, responsibility. It was about being there. About wanting to be there.

It's not that I don't want to be there, she directed toward her belly. It's just that . . . I don't seem to want this—motherhood—the way I want my career back. I know that's awful. Because I'm going to be a mother in seven and a half months.

You sound like Mom, she blasted herself, and again felt that icy squeeze in her heart.

"Hey," Bea said as she came up the steps. "I can't thank you enough for offering to introduce me to the inn manager. I don't know if it'll work out, since I don't know how long I can promise to stay."

"Well, let's go find Isabel. I let her know that I met someone who might be perfect for the kitchen job, and she said to just come find her when you arrived. I'll cross my fingers for you."

They found Isabel, her baby strapped to her chest, refilling maps and brochures on the sideboard in the foyer. She extended her hand to Bea and introduced herself and baby Allie.

Gemma stared at the baby, again trying to imagine herself multitasking like this with a baby strapped to her chest. How did Isabel make it look so easy when it couldn't be?

Isabel shook Bea's hand. "My interview consists of you whipping me up a traditional American breakfast, then cleaning up," Isabel said. "I should have told Gemma to tell you not to dress up for the interview—ratty old clothes would have done fine."

Gemma almost laughed. Bea could have shown up in her turkey sandwich–encrusted jeans and been properly dressed for the interview.

"Gemma," Isabel said, "I know this is a lot to ask, but we'll just need about a half hour—would you mind watching Allie for me?"

Gemma froze. Watch the baby? She was shocked that Isabel trusted her in the first place. Granted, Gemma was considered a family friend who had known the Nash sisters since they were kids, but what in the world made Isabel think Gemma knew how to hold a baby, let alone change a diaper? Maybe the baby wouldn't poop in the next half hour.

"Won't be more than thirty minutes," Isabel said. "Trust me, if Bea takes half that long to make scrambled eggs and toast, she's in trouble," she added, winking at Bea.

Gemma eyed the baby, face out to the world with her big blue eyes and chubby cheeks. She was just sitting there, looking quite curious, not crying, not making strange noises. Gemma could do this for a half hour. She should be able to do this. It would be a good practice run.

"No problem," she said to Isabel.

"You can take her in the backyard. Her swing is out there, and her diaper bag with everything you might need is right next to it. She's been fed and changed very recently, so I think she'll be content to just be held or rock in the swing."

"Okay," Gemma said. *I can do this. I will be doing this in seven months. I can do this.*

Isabel lifted the baby out of the BabyBjörn and handed her to Gemma. Just like that, the baby was in Gemma's arms, Gemma shifting her so that she had a good grip on her. She was so light!

I'm doing this, she thought. She'd avoided holding her own niece, Alexander's brother's daughter, until she was a year old. Gemma had finally held her when she'd been foisted in her arms when her sister-in-law had needed to use the bathroom, and her husband was on grilling duty. She'd been so uncomfortable until Mona had plucked the baby from her arms.

Bea smiled at Gemma and followed Isabel into the kitchen, and just like that, Gemma was left alone with the baby. She glanced down at Allie's profile, her tiny nose, the big cheeks. She was so pretty. Gemma walked down the short hall to another small sitting room and a library, where sliding glass doors led to the backyard, fenced on all sides. The yard was big and went back far, with huge trees and a small boulder at the far end. On the patio were chaise lounges and umbrellas, and Allie's swing was next to one of the chairs. Gemma sat down, the baby sitting on her lap, and Gemma gave her a little bounce.

This was going okay. This wasn't so bad.

Gemma glanced along the windows until she

found the kitchen and saw Bea at work at the counter, Isabel sitting at the table, talking.

"I'm going to have a baby," Gemma whispered to Allie. "In January, I'll have a baby just like you."

Fear gripped her again. It was one thing to watch a baby for a half hour and give her back. It was another to be responsible for a baby for the next eighteen years. For the rest of her life, Gemma amended.

Allie began . . . fussing seemed the right word. Gemma stood and shifted her in her arms, rocking back and forth a bit the way she'd seen her sister-in-law do. Allie calmed down, but then got fidgety.

"Maybe you want to be in your swing," Gemma said, setting Allie down in the swing. Yes, that seemed to do the trick. Gemma pushed the on switch, and the pale yellow and white swing gently swung back and forth.

Gemma's phone rang again, and she wasn't sure she should answer it, since she was babysitting, but she saw mothers and caregivers talking on the phone all the time as she passed them on the streets and playgrounds, and Allie was safely ensconced in the swing.

Gemma pulled her phone from her pocket. Pauline Lee, the director of Hope Home.

"One of our residents has expressed interest in talking to you for the article," Pauline said.

"Chloe Martin. She's seventeen, five months pregnant, and planning to keep her baby."

Seventeen and keeping her baby. At seventeen, Gemma's biggest worry was about getting into the college of her choice. Chloe Martin's life would be completely different.

"Is there a particular time that works best for me to come interview her?" Gemma asked.

"If you're free tomorrow at noon, that works for her."

"That's perfect," Gemma said.

It was Monday, barely seven o'clock, and time-wise, for the article, Gemma was right on track. Given all the information Pauline had provided, the pictures she'd taken with her phone camera, Bea's story, and now a resident's, she was right on schedule. Hopefully tomorrow and Wednesday she'd be able to interview past residents and perhaps an adoptive mother. She could have the piece written and sent to Claire at the *Gazette* by Friday morning, when Alexander expected her to head home to New York.

She did miss her husband. And granted, it was only Monday. But Gemma was not looking forward to leaving Boothbay Harbor. She felt so . . . herself here. Safe. Far, far away from her husband's opinions and so in tune with her own. He wasn't hounding her the way she thought he might; he texted instead of calling, letting her have this time to herself. She leaned back on a chaise lounge, one eye on Allie, and let herself relax, the late June sunshine still abundant in the sky.

Allie began fussing in the swing. Gemma pushed the off button and scooped Allie up, but she was starting to cry. Oh no. Now what? Gemma bounced her, but she started crying harder, and her face was turning red.

The baby was squirming and crying hard. A couple who'd come out onto the patio were staring at Gemma.

How long had it been since she'd come out? Twenty minutes? Maybe she'd peek in and see if Isabel and Bea were finishing up? She didn't want to interrupt the interview, especially an "interactive" one.

The baby screamed louder. Isabel's face appeared at the window, and in moments she was coming toward Gemma. Gemma felt like an incompetent moron. She couldn't handle a crying baby? She couldn't do this for thirty minutes.

She'd confirmed what she already knew. She wasn't cut out for this.

"What's wrong, sweetcheeks?" Isabel said to Allie, taking her from Gemma. The baby continued to cry, which, Gemma had to admit, made her feel a little better. "Gas in the tummy? Teething? Let's go try your favorite teething ring." She smiled at Gemma. "Thanks for watching her. I forgot to mention she's teething up a storm right now. Oh, and by the way, your friend Bea knows her way around a stove. Her scrambled eggs rivaled my aunt Lolly's, and that's saying something. I was called to the front door to sign for a package, came back, and she'd even cleaned everything up in the time I was gone. I'll check her references, but I'll tell you, I owe you, Gemma."

The baby was just teething. Gemma wasn't the worst caretaker on earth. And Isabel wasn't annoyed at her for not being able to handle Allie. Add Bea getting the job—if her references checked out—and Gemma would say today had gone from crazy to pretty darn okay.

At noon the next day, Gemma arrived at Hope Home for her interview with seventeen-year-old Chloe Martin. She recognized Jen and Kim, the pregnant girls whom Bea had been talking to yesterday. They were lying on the chaises under a tree, each reading a book on pregnancy. Another girl, who wasn't yet showing, was doing some yoga moves. Gemma headed in and found Pauline at the front desk.

Pauline stood up. "Hi, Gemma, Chloe is waiting for you in her room. I'll introduce you."

The director led Gemma to an open door down the hall. A girl who looked to be around five months pregnant sat on one of the two beds in the room. There were at least ten posters above her bed. One Direction. Vincent Van Gogh's *Starry Night*. Justin Bieber. Chloe was pretty, with silky brown hair to her shoulders, and hazel eyes.

"You can sit there if you want," Chloe said, pointing at the chair of the desk near her bed. An identical desk was across the room near the other bed.

"I appreciate your interest in letting me interview you for my article. If you don't want me to use your name, I can change it to protect your identity. If there's anything you tell me, and you realize now or later that you don't want me to write about it, you just tell me, okay? And I'll take it out."

"Okay," Chloe said. "That sounds good."

"Is it all right if I record our interview?" Gemma asked.

Chloe nodded and leaned against the wall, her legs straight out in front of her. She held a throw pillow to her stomach, embroidered with "I love you."

Gemma put her recorder on the desk and pressed play, then got out her notebook and pen. "Pauline told me you're keeping your baby. Can you tell me about making that decision?"

Chloe put her hand on her belly. "I always knew I'd keep him—I don't know if it's a boy or a girl, but something just tells me it's a boy. I'm going to name him Finn."

"Finn, I like that name." Gemma hadn't even

considered names yet. The thought hadn't even occurred to her. Because the baby doesn't feel real yet, she reminded herself. Because you haven't accepted reality.

Chloe smiled. "Me too. It's not after anyone."

"Can you tell me about the father of the baby?"

Her face lit up. "Dylan. He's my boyfriend. He's stood by me when no one else has. My parents think I'm ruining my life. My mom said she'd be a good grandmother and she'd babysit on occasion but that if I was making this choice, it would have to be whole hog, that I couldn't rely on her to raise this baby for me."

Gemma couldn't stop focusing on how young Chloe was. Seventeen. And about to be a mother in four months. "Where will you live after you give birth?"

"I've already got a job lined up. An elderly lady who lives around the corner from us down in Massachusetts and needs a live-in caregiver hired me. There's a small studio apartment attached to her house, and I'll get room and board and a small salary. My boyfriend and I will get married when I turn eighteen, and then Vivian said he can move in too. He's finishing high school and I'm getting my GED."

Gemma hoped with all her heart that this would all happen. "Why did you come to Hope Home, Chloe?"

Chloe glanced away for a moment and gripped

the pillow tighter. "My mother made it clear that if I was insisting on having the baby, I'd have to do this on my own, she wasn't going to make this easy on me. She researched homes for pregnant teenagers and there was a spot open, so here I am."

"What do you think about this kind of 'tough-love' approach?"

Chloe shrugged. "I'm getting through it is all I know. I'd rather be home than here, especially because Dylan can only visit me on weekends for only a whole Saturday. It's okay here, though."

The home did seem like a warm, inviting place for these girls. "How did you feel when you found out you were pregnant?"

"Scared. But I love Dylan, and I can't imagine giving our baby up. I know most of the girls here are but I just can't."

That had to be a big topic of conversation among the residents. "Does that affect your relationship with them?"

Chloe shrugged again. "Some think I'm making a huge mistake, that at seventeen I won't know how to be a good mother, that I'm not giving my baby his best possible shot at life. But I think I'll be a good mother. Everyone says I'm kidding myself, that I don't know anything about what I'll be facing."

"Do you feel ready to be a mother?"

"I know I'll take care of him. I'm not some irresponsible loser. I've been reading some of the books on baby care. But you know what? The reason I'm not really scared?"

Gemma leaned close.

"I love the little guy like crazy already," Chloe said.

Gemma sat back. She talked to her stomach sometimes, but again, the baby still didn't feel real. Maybe once it did, Gemma would feel a bit like Chloe felt.

"Do you have kids?" Chloe asked, looking at Gemma's wedding ring.

"No, but I'll tell you a secret. I'm pregnant. Just seven weeks. I haven't told anyone but a girl-friend. Even my husband doesn't know yet. I'm waiting for the blood test confirmation."

Her doctor had told her the blood test results would be in by tomorrow or Thursday at the latest. She'd get the positive results, and there would be no excuse for her not to pick up the phone and tell Alexander. It would be wrong not to tell him.

She'd get the results and then she'd tell him. She'd go over her plan before she called, lay it out for him, how she saw their future. But he'd steamroll her, she knew it.

"You're so lucky," Chloe said. "You're married, you've lived life, you have a career. It must feel like a real blessing. God, I wish I were in your position. I'm so jealous."

Gemma sat back on the chair, the breath knocked out of her for a moment.

Chapter 10

BEA

On Wednesday morning, Bea woke up in her little room at the Three Captains' Inn, her bed much more comfortable than at the super-budget motel. On the second floor, a former large utility closet had been transformed into a cozy room with a small arched window out of a fairy tale, pale cabbage rose wallpaper and a full-size bed with a beautiful wrought iron headboard and a soft old quilt embroidered with seashells. There was also a small dresser with a round mirror above it, a soft rug, and a painting of a distant lighthouse. Bea could live without a private bathroom; there was a large bathroom right across the hall that no one used because the other three second-floor rooms had private baths. And Gemma's room was just upstairs on the third floor, a tiny one like Bea's, across from the honeymoon suite, which was now taken over by three very serious Colin Firth fans.

Bea had moved in late last night, just a day after the interview with Isabel. Her boss at the Writing Center and Bea's old boss at Crazy Burger—not Crazy Barbara—had apparently given Bea glowing references. She was starting work this morning, which was perfect because she had very little money left. She was responsible for cooking the guests' breakfast, leaving the order taking and schmoozing to Isabel. After breakfast, she'd clean up the dining room and kitchen, tidy up the common rooms and patio, and keep a running list of what grocery items the inn was running short on. Her workday began at six and ended at eleven, and for that, she received a room, free breakfast, use of the kitchen for all other meals, and a small salary. The inn was beautiful and cozy and so close to downtown. After what had happened Monday afternoon at Hope Home, Bea had felt so adrift, so unsure of what the hell she was doing here, but thanks to Gemma, Bea now had some grounding. Even better, Isabel said she was okay with Bea's inability to commit to the entire summer. July fourth was booked solid, the week before and after, and Isabel had said as long as Bea could promise to stay until mid-July, she could have the job.

Of course, now that she felt more grounded, she felt a bit more ready to contact her birth mother. Maybe today was the day. She could call her, they could meet for lunch or something like that, and since Bea was staying in town for a few weeks, they could have coffee now and again, so that Veronica wouldn't have to feel obligated to spill out her entire life story in one hour-long first meeting. Unless she wanted to, of course.

At least, that was how Bea envisioned it would go. They'd meet for lunch and talk. Bea would ask about Veronica's life, about her family. She'd ask who her biological father was and if Veronica thought he'd be open to contact. Then their lunch would be over, and they'd go their separate ways. But now that she was here, with a place to stay and a job, she could meet with Veronica a few more times, and perhaps they could get to know each other a little.

The sun was just starting to rise. Bea got out of bed and moved over to the narrow chair wedged by the beautiful little window and looked out at the breaking dawn over the huge oak trees. She loved this room. On the small dresser, she'd put her two favorite family photographs next to the collection of pretty seashells that were here when she'd arrived. She moved to the dresser and picked up the photo of herself as a four-year-old with her parents. "You are my parents, no matter what," Bea whispered, setting the picture down and picking up a seashell, which reminded her of her father. Keith Crane had loved the ocean, and had told Bea when she was very small that if she had a question she couldn't figure out the answer to, all she had to do was find a seashell, big or small, hold it up to her ear, and listen.

"Do I ask it the question?" seven-year-old Bea had asked.

"Nope. No need," her dad had said. "The question is already inside you. You just have to hold the shell to your ear and listen. Really listen."

She remembered beach trips over the years when she'd find a shell and hold it to her ear, silently asking her burning questions. Will I make friends in my class? Does he like me back? Does my dad watch over me? She'd listen hard, and the shell itself never said anything, but as she pressed it against her ear, hearing the whoosh, she'd know the answers to her questions. Much later, Bea would learn the answer depended on what she believed deep down. Sometimes shells had no answer for her. Sometimes they confirmed the worst. Sometimes they offered hope. But Bea had been asking her burning questions to seashells for as long as she could remember.

Bea held the shell to her ear. "Should I call Veronica Russo after my shift today and introduce myself?" she asked.

Bea thought it was time. She'd arrived in Boothbay Harbor on Friday and now it was almost a week later. She'd struck gold on seeing Veronica in the diner the day she'd arrived, but she hadn't been back to the Best Little Diner in Boothbay; the thought of returning had made her feel both oddly exposed and like a stalker of sorts.

She listened. There was a whoosh. And then the answer, coming from inside her. Yes.

There were five guest rooms at the Three Captains' Inn. The three on the second floor, and two on the third floor. Breakfast was served between seven o'clock and eight thirty for the current twelve guests. At seven on the dot, Bea's first orders came in for the Osprey and Seashell Rooms—four various egg dishes, including a bacon and Swiss omelet, which was exactly what she'd made herself before her shift had started, a bagel with cream cheese, two bowls of cereal and a plate of sausage links for the kids, and two fruit plates. By seven forty-five, the dining room was in full swing, guests leaving, guests arriving, and Bea was in dynamo mode, scrambling eggs and flipping pancakes like an old pro. As Isabel had come into the kitchen with the orders, she'd commented more than once how impressed she was at Bea's cooking skills and shared the compliments she'd gotten from her guests. After having her burgers measured and pay docked for every slight infraction at Crazy Burger, Bea was thrilled.

At eight thirty, she made crepes for the newlywed stragglers in the Bluebird Room, a couple in their late twenties who took their plates out to the backyard and fed each other bites. Bea watched them through the window as she began rinsing dishes for the dishwasher, smiling at how lovey-dovey they were.

Gemma came down in the nick of time for a hot breakfast, and when Isabel brought in her order, Bea made sure her omelet was perfection. Gemma had done her a huge favor. She was a little curious about the woman. Gemma had a warm, pretty face, and when she smiled, her entire face lit up, but something seemed to be troubling her just under the surface. Or maybe Bea was imagining it. Bea had noticed Gemma twisting her wedding ring a couple of times, and when she'd come in the dining room to clear the final tables, she found Gemma sipping her herbal tea and staring out the window a bit forlornly, and again she wondered what Gemma's story was. Gemma's husband wasn't with her at the inn, unless Bea just hadn't seen him. But then Gemma had gone off on an interview, the lovebirds cleared out of the yard, and just like that, the breakfast rush was over.

After the dishes were cleaned, dried, and put away, and the kitchen left spotless, Bea cleaned the dining room tables and swept and mopped the floor, then headed out to the patio to straighten the chaises and collect coffee mugs. She grabbed messy newspapers and neatened them, adding them to the basket just inside the door. In the parlor, Bea refilled coffee cups and sliced up lemons for iced tea for a few guests, collected more mugs and teacups, took the pie, bagels, and muffins that Isabel set up in the parlor for morning stragglers, and put everything away.

By ten o'clock, the inn's common rooms were spotless, so Bea just hung around, making herself useful as needed. Straightening the maps and brochures on the table in the foyer. Cleaning up a trail of sand from the kids. She went through the refrigerator and pantry, making a list of what Isabel would need to restock. Eleven o'clock. Quitting time. Bea liked her duties. She wasn't cooped up in the kitchen the entire time; she got to mingle among the guests in the parlor and backyard, chatting about where they were from. And she'd surprised herself a few times by being able to answer questions about where certain landmarks were. A few days of walking around Boothbay Harbor, trying to get this place—in which she'd been born—inside her, and she'd learned more than she realized.

She had a phone call to make. Up in her room, she got out her notebook and her phone, sucked in a deep breath, and pushed in Veronica's number. *Hi, my name is Bea Crane,* she practiced in her head. *I was born on October twelfth, twenty-two years ago. I'd like to meet you, if you're interested. You can reach me at this number. I'm staying at the Three Captains' Inn.*

Answering machine. "Hello, you've reached Veronica Russo. I'm unable to answer your call right now, but if you leave a message, I'll return your call as soon as possible." Beep.

Damn. Bea hung up, her heart beating a mile a minute. She could call back, leave a message. That would give Veronica a moment too, instead of being bombarded with the call and Bea at the other end all at once.

But when she picked up the phone, she found herself unable to press the numbers. She needed to do this in person. She needed to go see her, to not draw this out anymore. Bea changed out of her work clothes and back into her interview dress, which was just a pale yellow cotton dress with cap sleeves, a little something more than just jeans and a T-shirt, but nothing fancy. She put on her sandals and headed out, her heart beating too fast again.

Bea walked the half mile to Veronica Russo's house. She'd driven past it at least ten times since she'd been in town, and the sight of it, a cute lemon-yellow cottage with glossy white shutters and flower boxes on the windowsills, started her heart going crazy again.

But there wasn't a car in the driveway, and the house didn't have a garage. Veronica was likely at work, and Bea had a feeling she'd gone to her house as a stalling tactic. Bea would never be ready for this, it would never feel right, so she might as well get it over with now.

Just in case Veronica was home, Bea walked up the path to the front door. Bea rang the bell and waited, but she knew Veronica wasn't here, that the door wouldn't open.

She could go to the diner. She could introduce herself, then tell Veronica that perhaps they could chat on Veronica's break. She wants to meet you,

Bea reminded herself. She drove back to the inn and parked there, then walked down the two long, winding streets to Main Street and over to the diner.

She glanced in the big front windows and didn't see Veronica, but maybe she was in the back. It was in between breakfast and lunch, not very crowded. Bea pulled open the door, her heart beating, her hope rising.

This was it.

She'd sit in Veronica's section, and when she came to hand her a menu or ask her if she could get her something to drink, Bea would come right out with it.

My name is Bea Crane. I'm sorry for just showing up like this, but I don't really know how to do this, and I felt funny leaving a message. I was born on October twelfth. Twenty-two years ago.

It would be a start.

Bea glanced around for Veronica to determine what section was hers, but she didn't see her. Maybe her shift started later? She'd ask a waitress if Veronica was working today.

She went to the counter. The young waitress who'd served her the day she'd arrived was refilling a woman's coffee. Bea waited until she came over.

"Menu?" she asked.

"Actually, I just want to know if Veronica Russo was working today."

"Lucky stiff got hired as an extra on the Colin Firth movie—made first cut too. Instead of delivering eggs and burgers all day, she'll be hobnobbing with the stars."

An extra on the Colin Firth movie? That was unexpected.

Now what? Maybe she could find out where they were filming today. Equipment was still out by Frog Marsh. She'd start there. A friend of Bea's from college had been an extra on a romantic comedy once, and she'd said the extras mainly sat around for hours until they were called. Perhaps Veronica was just sitting on a blanket, reading a book or staring into space.

She had in her mind to do this and couldn't see putting it off any longer.

Three huge beige tents, trailers, lights, cameras, and barricades were set up by the pond now. There were barricades in front of the tent and a guard sitting beside it with a plate of chicken wings on his lap and one wing in his mouth. The guy she'd met the night she'd arrived came out of a trailer beside the tent, eyes on his clipboard.

"Filming today?" she asked him from the other side of the barricade. It was the grumpy production assistant. Tyler Echols. The girl reading *To Kill a Mockingbird* wasn't around this time.

He didn't look up from his clipboard. "I'm not at liberty to discuss."

So officious. "Can you tell me where the extras are?"

This time he did look at her. With irritation in his eyes. "Are you an extra?"

"No, but I know someone who is, and—"

He went back to his clipboard. "You'll need to stay behind that barricade, then."

"Can you just tell me where the—" Bea began.

Tyler rolled his eyes and walked away, disappearing into the crew coming and going. Who needs you, anyway, she shot at him silently, then weaved her way through the crowd watching from behind the long barricades, straining their necks to spot anyone famous. She eyed signs on the tents for the word *extras*. Bingo. The one at the far right. Ten minutes later, as she crossed the barrier to peer inside it, Tyler Echols was back, pointing beyond it, then at the big guy sitting in a chair and devouring chicken wings, paying more attention to them than to anything else.

She moved behind the barricade. The grump grimaced at her and went back to his clipboard. She turned to the woman beside her. "I guess they're filming today?"

"Test footage, apparently," she said. "For lighting and whatnot."

Bea strained to look at the group of people lining up at a table on the far side of the extras tent. Food. Bagels and tubs of cream cheese, cold cuts, cookies. She looked for Veronica but there were so many people milling inside the tent. Bea saw the grump with the clipboard chewing out some guy who looked like he wanted to punch him, and she headed around the other side, where two new trailers were now, surrounded by barricades and guarded by a large man balancing a plate of scrambled eggs and home fries on his lap.

She waited until he was looking down at his plate, then leaped over the barricade. If she could just get to the other side, where the tent flap was wide, she could peer in. Maybe she'd catch Veronica just sitting or eating breakfast and Bea could ask to speak to her.

"God, you don't give up, do you? I assure you, Colin Firth is not here. He's what, more than twice your age? Go take your daddy issues to a therapist."

Bea whirled around and there was Tyler Echols. "I'm not here to stalk Colin Firth! Someone I know is an extra, and—"

"Ah, so you're stalking an ex who dumped you. I get it. You have one second to get behind that barricade and stay there or I'll personally call the police and have you arrested for trespassing. I take stalkers seriously when it comes to my actors—and my extras. Two days ago, some lunatic woman threw a cup of orange juice at Christopher Cade just so something she drank touched him. Another fan rushed him and grabbed his balls. So leave now."

Okay, fine, she got it. He had a job to do. But he was so dismissive. She glanced at his badge: "Tyler Echols, PA." PA—production assistant? "Look, I have no idea who Christopher Cade is. I have zero interest in the movie stars. I—"

He pulled out his phone. "This is me dialing the local police."

The guy was impossible! "I'm here because my birth mother is an extra on this film and I'm just hoping to watch and decide if I want to introduce myself and—"

God, what the hell was wrong with her? Did she just blurt all that out? She let out a deep breath and stared at her feet.

Tyler made a sound that sounded like a snort, but tucked his phone back in his pocket. "You're lucky, then. My rules will save you the trouble."

"The trouble of what?"

He glanced at his clipboard and checked something off. "My sister is adopted—she's sixteen and was obsessed with finding her birth mother, thought it would solve all her problems with grades and the jerk boys she goes for. I spent months trying to track down her birth mother for her. I finally got her name and location—which cost me thousands of dollars, by the way—and if I could do it all over again, I'd save the three thousand."

"Sorry, Tyler, but you seem incredibly easy to disappoint. And you don't know my situation."

He ignored that. "Yeah, well, the lady wasn't interested in meeting my sister. In the end, all she wanted was money. Maddy—my sister—is still screwed up over the whole thing. So, really, I'm doing you a favor." He pointed to the barricades. "Either stay on the other side or I'll call that guy." He pointed to the big man in the chair.

"Yeah, he's really paying attention," she said, as the man popped a bunch of home fries into his mouth. But at least she'd been downgraded from the local police. "And anyway, my situation is very different."

"I'm just saying you should proceed with caution. Reality and fantasy are two very different things."

Bea's stomach twisted.

A man, in his late twenties, with messy dark brown hair and gorgeous blue eyes, came up behind Tyler. "Problem here?" he asked Bea. His badge read PATRICK OOL, SAD. "This brute bothering you?"

"He's just incredibly bossy," Bea said. "I know one of the extras and wanted to watch her work, that's all. I'm not here to bother the stars, I swear."

"What's your name?" Patrick asked.

"Bea Crane."

Patrick smiled at her. "Well, Bea Crane, you can watch all you want." He put a badge around her neck with "Guest" written in black letters. "I'm the second assistant director on this film, and if this guy bothers you, you tell me." His cell rang. "Be right there. Don't touch anything," he barked into the phone, then pocketed it and sighed. "Fire after fire," he said to Bea. "Hope we run into each other again," he added, holding her gaze.

Bea watched him rush away, then shot Tyler something of a triumphant smile.

Tyler rolled his eyes. "He's a notorious womanizer, by the way."

"That you being realistic again?" she asked.

"Screw up your life in every aspect. Not like I care."

He stalked off, and Bea shook her head, wondering what the heck his problem was. But she wasn't about to give Tyler Echols, PA, too much thought; she was free to be here with her guest pass and walked right past the guard with a wave, which he returned. From this side of the tent, she could see inside. At least fifty people were sitting or standing by the food table.

Then she saw her.

Veronica was sitting on a folding chair, a muffin on a little round plastic plate on her lap, talking to the woman next to her, her expression animated. She seemed lit up, glowing from within.

She was right there. Bea's birth mother.

She could walk right in. Introduce herself.

Except maybe she'd come off as a little bit nuts for "stalking" Veronica on the film set. Working as an extra was obviously something special to

Veronica, given how happy she looked, and Bea would just throw a huge monkey wrench into it. *Oh hi, I know you're working on the movie here in town, but here I am suddenly—the daughter you gave up for adoption!*

Crap. Bea would just call her tonight. She'd call, giving them both space—for Bea to put the phone down and calm her beating heart, and for Veronica to digest that her birth daughter had made contact. If Bea got the machine, she'd leave a message.

Bea was about to leave when Patrick Ool walked up to her.

"Sorry about Tyler giving you a hard time," Patrick said. "I appreciate how seriously he takes his job, but sometimes, he takes it a bit too seriously. Anyway, I'm just going to say this outright, Bea. I met you ten minutes ago, and I can't stop thinking of your face."

Bea blushed. The guy wasn't traditionally good looking, but there was something about him, something . . . sexy, and he was staring at Bea as though she were drop-dead beautiful. She had to admit, it did nice things for her ego.

"Has that ever happened to you?" he said. "Where you meet someone and you just wish you could go off on a walk with them or sit across a table with a cup of coffee and just talk?"

She smiled. "It's happening now."

He smiled back at her. He had one dimple, she realized. And those gorgeous blue eyes. "Can I take you to dinner tomorrow night? It'll have to be early, since we're wrapping for dinner at five, and I'll need to be back to check the dailies at seven. But a good start, I think."

"Agreed," Bea said.

"Tomorrow at five, then. Where should I pick you up?"

Just like that, Bea had a date with a good-looking second assistant director named Patrick.

Chapter 11
VERONICA

Veronica loved being on the set, loved sitting in this big tent marked EXTRAS HOLDING PEN. Even if yesterday and most of today, she and her fellow extras had done a lot of sitting around and waiting . . . for not much of anything. She'd spent most of her time chatting with the people sitting near her—whispering over mutual admiration of Colin Firth—thinking up new pie recipes, and wondering how her students had fared with making their own shoofly pies. Since Monday night, two days now, she'd thought about calling each student to ask if they'd made the shoofly pie at home with the recipe she'd handed out. But that had felt intrusive to Veronica with this particular bunch, with the uncomfortable Nick DeMarco, who, his daughter thought, might want to say "sorry" to her mother. And ten-year-old Leigh, who'd lost her mom so young, with so much hope in her sweet face. Veronica couldn't imagine calling the formerly snooty Penelope, of the cryptic trouble, though she wouldn't be surprised if she got a call from Penelope. And Veronica didn't know Isabel, who felt like a client first and a student second, or her sister, June, well enough to get personal, so she'd just decided to wait until next Monday night for the answers to her questions.

She still couldn't believe the universe had cut her this lucky break of being chosen to be an extra. Late Monday night, long after her students had gone home and she'd cleaned up the kitchen, her cell phone had rung with the Call. An excitement, a feeling she hadn't experienced since she was a young teenager, had burst inside her; she felt it in her toes, along her spine, the nape of her neck, a firecracker going off inside her and catching her by surprise. She'd wanted to be an extra on the Colin Firth movie, yes. But she hadn't realized how much she wanted it. Perhaps she hadn't let herself want something that bad in a long time. It was a bit of an escape. A chance to lay eyes on Colin Firth—and to have a crush on an actor felt luxuriant to Veronica, a self-indulgence she'd allow herself.

Just like that, she was an extra, something that had been a twinkle in her friend Shelley's eye at the diner just days ago. Her boss was thrilled for Veronica and told her to come back to work whenever the fairy-tale experience was over. It did feel a bit like a fairy tale, watching all these productive-looking people rushing around past the tent with their clipboards and iPhones, hauling equipment and calling for meetings. The extras had been instructed to come in regular clothes they'd wear on a routine morning, so Veronica had opted for her uniform, which got a "fabulous!" from the wardrobe manager, who'd checked over every single extra and sent many to the small tent next door to change. In the big white tent with her yesterday and today were around forty people, several of whom were reading books with titles such as *Break into Acting!* and *How to Make It in Hollywood.* She and another extra had made a list of every Colin Firth film they could think of, and when Veronica looked up Colin Firth's profile on IMDb, she'd been surprised to discover he'd been in over fifty films, with a few in production. Veronica planned to watch a movie a night. A Colin Firth marathon sounded heavenly after a long day of dreaming about seeing him in the flesh. If he was here in town, he wasn't on the set. She'd kept an eagle eye out and so did several other women sitting near her, who made sure to keep their Colinmania on the down low in case Patrick Ool was walking around with his intolerance for star stalkers.

Yesterday, she and around thirty others had arrived at eight o'clock in the morning for some lighting work, and then filming was expected to begin today, but an actress had hurt her knee early this afternoon, and filming had been pushed back again and then again.

Now it was nearing four o'clock, and finally, Patrick Ool came into the tent and informed them shooting was a go. Yes! The extras sitting around

Veronica sat up with excitement. Patrick explained the scene again: the female star, a beautiful actress whose name Veronica kept forgetting, was standing in the nearby pasture of wildflowers with her selfish mother, who was trying to talk her out of her misgivings about her upcoming wedding to her supposedly perfect man, who was not Colin Firth. The mother was played by an actress Veronica had seen many times before. Patrick had gone over the rules—no talking to the stars. No talking, period. And no photographs.

Veronica and the forty or so extras walked out to the barricade labeled "Extras Wait Here." Patrick Ool placed about ten of them around the scene, some on the path between the pond and the pasture, some in the pasture, sitting down to a picnic, two walking dogs. Veronica was to walk by when the mother said her first line and look nowhere in particular, checking her watch once. The woman behind her was to carry a brown paper grocery bag. A man was to wave at someone in the distance. Most others were to just walk by at a normal pace.

Patrick called "Get ready, people," and again, that burst of excitement lit up in Veronica. She was so close to the two actresses, standing just inside the pasture, that she could see the worry lines on the mother's forehead and see how exquisitely beautiful the younger actress truly was.

The director called action, and Veronica waited until the mother said her first line before walking by, looking nowhere in particular as instructed. But just as Veronica had passed, the mother pointed her finger in the woman's face with such disdain, such anger in her expression, and it shook loose a memory that made Veronica's hands tremble. She walked as naturally as she could, checked her watch, as she'd been told, then ambled off to the side, out of camera range, and realized she was actually shaking. Good God. What was wrong with her? One finger point and she was a mess?

She rarely let herself think about her parents, her mother's cruelty. But as she stood on the other side of the barricade, suddenly feeling so alone amid so many people milling about and watching the scene being shot, she felt lost in the memory, of her own mother sticking her finger in sixteen-year-old Veronica's face, in much the same jabbing way, after Veronica had blurted out that she was pregnant.

She wouldn't let herself remember that conversation. Not here, not now, especially. Being here on the set, being a part of this magic felt a little bit like Christmas. But the truth was that twenty-two years after that finger jabbing, those cruel words, the pain of that memory was as vivid as ever.

She closed her eyes tight against it, but so many different words, sentences she'd never forget, from her mother, from Timothy, jumbled in her mind. Focus on the scene, she told herself. A movie is being filmed in front of your eyes. You could see Colin Firth tomorrow for all you know! But she couldn't stop seeing her mother's face, the anger, the shame. This was the new normal now, now that she was back home. Hadn't she come to face her past? But how would remembering how cruelly her parents had treated her help her? How could those thoughts do anything but sting, remind her that except for her friends, she had no family?

She'd have to learn to deal with her memories, somehow, someway. She was back home now, and memories were everywhere. She was grateful when Patrick called out to the extras, "Great job, people," and to let them know they were dismissed for the day and expected back at eight o'clock the next morning to reshoot that scene two different ways.

Two different ways. Countless takes, perhaps. She'd have to get over that finger jab fast if she wanted to be part of this movie.

As she left the tent and slipped on her cardigan against the breeze, she heard footsteps behind her.

"Va-va-voomica," a man's voice said, then chuckled as though his nickname for her was adorable. "I came down here to check out the film set and saw you in that big tent. How about we go for a drink? You can fill me in on the life of an extra."

Ugh. The pest, Hugh Fledge. Just pretend you didn't hear him and dash away, she told herself. And judging from the slight slurring of his words, he'd clearly already had that drink. She quickened her pace.

"You won't be able to resist my charm and good looks for long," he called out on a laugh just as she rounded the corner.

Forever wouldn't be long enough. Would he ever stop bugging her?

Hugh Fledge wasn't much of a distraction from her thoughts, though. She had avoided walking past the pier where she and Timothy Macintosh had kissed many times. However, her memories trailed her all the way home.

Veronica tended not to think about anything but pie and its mission when she was baking, so when she got home, she set to work on an Amore Pie for her neighbor's friend, thinking only of Colin Firth telling Elizabeth Bennet that he loved her and couldn't pinpoint when she'd captured his heart: "I was in the middle before I knew that I had begun." Oh, Mr. Darcy, she thought as she finished forming the dough into a ball, not surprised that she could recall so many lines from the movie. Tonight she'd watch *Love Actually* for perhaps the tenth time, even if it was a Christmas movie. It was exactly the kind of movie she needed.

The phone rang and Veronica grabbed it, a dusting of flour on the receiver.

It was Beth. The client who'd ordered the Cast-Out Pie.

"It didn't work," Beth said. "I should have known it was just bullshit."

Whoa. The woman's voice was so angry, but Veronica heard something else in it: pain.

Give her a little slack, Veronica told herself. "Did you think about casting this person from your heart while you were eating the pie?"

"I'm not the one who's casting someone out. It's someone else who has to get someone out of his goddamned head."

There it was. Perhaps her husband *was* having an affair. Veronica had never been married, but she could certainly understand the pain that would cause. "Ah."

"I just wanted you to know it's bullshit," Beth said, her anger rising. "I'm not paying."

"That was the deal, so that's fine. I'm sorry it didn't work for you."

"Yeah, you're sorry." Beth slammed the phone down.

What the hell was that about?

She was in no mood to make Amore Pie with that woman's anger and frustration still so heavy in her mind. She'd give herself the thirty minutes for the dough to chill, let the tension ease out of her, then conjure up Colin Firth walking out of that pond, his white shirt dripping wet. Hear him tell Elizabeth Bennet how he felt about her. *My feelings will not be repressed. You must allow me to tell you how ardently I admire and love you.*

She'd put the dough in the refrigerator and was just adding the chocolate to a mixing bowl when her doorbell rang. She glanced at the clock on the wall. Seven o'clock. Had she forgotten a client was picking up a pie? She doubted it. She had nothing but time to think the past two days in the extras tent. Her Amore Pie client—the shy gal who worked part-time behind the circulation desk at the library—wasn't due to pick up the pie from her neighbor until tomorrow morning.

Veronica wiped her hands on her apron, checked off chocolate on her recipe so that she'd remember what she was up to, then went to her front door.

Nick DeMarco.

She froze for a split second, the way she always did when she saw him. Whether he was up close and personal, standing a foot in front of her, like now, like two nights ago in her kitchen, or around town, as he patrolled the streets on foot or in his police car, she froze for the slightest moment. She'd grown up with him but didn't remember him clearly at all, other than he'd been a fringe friend of Timothy's. When she'd been hired at the diner a year ago, Nick would come in, as he sometimes did, for breakfast or lunch, say his hellos, that it was nice to see her again, and then he'd keep a distance. Or maybe she was imagining it. She hadn't been sure if he knew who she was because he made it his business to know who was in town, or because he remembered her as the junior who'd gotten knocked up by his friend—or said she had—and then mysteriously disappeared. Unlike some other patrons at the diner, he wasn't a flirt, didn't stare at her, and she couldn't read him at all. Which made her even more aware of him.

"I'm sorry to just barge in on you like this," he said. "I wanted to let you know that Leigh and I won't be taking your class anymore."

She looked at him, hoping to read something in his expression, but he had his usual poker face. Cop face. If this was a time or schedule conflict, he would have called. But he'd come to the door, which meant there was something else going on here.

"Was the shoofly pie just too upsetting for Leigh?" Veronica asked. "I know she's only ten and perhaps I overstep—"

"It's not—" he began, then leaned his head back and sucked in a breath. He shook his head slightly.

There went the poker face. She opened the door wide. "Come in. I'm working on a pie—Amore— right now. We can talk in the kitchen."

He was in uniform and took off his police hat,

which she set on the counter next to her bowl of apples. He brushed back his dark brown wavy hair with his hand. Despite how big her kitchen was, how tall she herself was, Nick was six feet two, maybe six three, and muscular, and he overwhelmed the space. Overwhelmed her; no easy feat.

She moved to the island counter and added the eggs and brown sugar and cornstarch, whisking them together. She glanced at Nick, standing on the opposite side of the counter. He looked uncomfortable, so she thought it best not to rush him.

"The pie is working too well for her, actually," he said. "She had three slices of the pie since Monday's class, and she says every time she even forks a piece, she feels her mother with her, can smell her perfume, feels the wool of her favorite red sweater."

She stopped whisking. "Well, then that's good, isn't it?"

"Her grandparents—her mother's parents—think it's some kind of voodoo nonsense and don't like it. They don't like me, really."

Veronica looked at him and he glanced away, out the window.

"I assume it's not voodoo nonsense," he said. "Just power of suggestion. Just pie, actually."

She smiled. "Yes. It is just pie. With some prayers and wishes and hopes baked in. The elixir pies seem to work for people because of the spark of hope in their names—Feel Better Pie, Amore Pie, Spirit Pie."

He leaned against the refrigerator, letting his head drop back. "Got a pie to make sure you don't lose your kid?" he said, his voice breaking a bit. He turned around and faced the window, jamming his hands into his pockets.

"Nick? What's going on?"

He turned back to her, looking between her and the floor. "Leigh's grandparents think she might be better off with them. If she lived with them, they say, she wouldn't have to go to an aftercare program at school. She'd come home off the school bus to a waiting, loving grandmother instead of a single father with unpredictable hours, an unpredictable job. They think she needs a maternal influence, specifically her grandmother's. The thought of my marrying again makes them sick. Any time I have so much as a date they seem to know about it." He turned toward her. "What the hell am I doing? I came here to tell you we wouldn't be back to your class and now I'm blurting out my life story."

"I'm glad you explained," she said. "Leigh is such a sweet girl, and the shoofly pie really seemed to comfort her. That's all it is. Comfort."

"I know. What's crazy is that when she asked if we could take the class, I thought, perfect, her grandparents will like this—good, clean fun for a father and daughter to do together. How wholesome." He rolled his eyes. "Instead, my former mother-in-law called me at work today, screaming up a storm about this 'voodoo pie nonsense' Leigh's been talking about, and again said she was thinking of filing for custody."

"That's serious," Veronica said. "Is she just upset or do you think she really will?"

He shrugged. "I don't know if she just needs reassurance or if she's really going to file the papers. I'm going out of my mind. I don't even know why I'm telling you all this. I'm just trying to explain why we won't be back Monday. I can't give the woman ammunition."

"I understand," she said. "I feel bad that this caused a problem. It's really just about comfort. That's all."

He crossed the kitchen, leaning against the counter and looking out the window again. "I was in the process of filing for divorce when the accident happened. Our marriage was falling apart and things weren't good between us. My wife— she was having an affair. I found out and it was the last straw. But then she died, and my former in-laws, who didn't know about the affair, have hated me ever since. I'm sure they think I initiated the divorce because I was the one sleeping around."

"Oh, Nick, I'm so sorry."

"Leigh is staying at their house tonight. This has got me so worked up I don't even want to go home. Just makes me think of what it'll be like if they try to take her away from me."

"You can help me make this pie," Veronica said, gesturing at her mixing bowl. She'd give up on the Amore Pie for the moment; worry and stress and threat of custody battles didn't make for a good love pie for a hopeful client. "Just a plain chocolate pudding Happiness Pie for you to take home. No voodoo nonsense."

He nodded, offering something of a smile.

"You can grab the dough from the refrigerator," she told him, wondering if he even remembered her. He never brought up high school. Maybe he recognized her as someone who'd gone to his school and that was it. Maybe he didn't even know she was the girl who'd been Timothy's girlfriend, the girl who'd "accused" him of getting her pregnant. She'd bet anything he did know, though. "It's been chilling long enough."

He seemed grateful to have something to do. He got out the dough and spread some flour on the surface, then began rolling it.

"You were paying attention in class, I see," she said.

"I always pay attention. Job requirement."

Yes, indeed, he knew exactly who she was. "I'll bet. How about some coffee."

"I could use a strong cup," he said, continuing to roll the dough.

Veronica stepped away to the coffeemaker, glad

to turn her back to him for a moment. God. This was unexpected. She added an extra half scoop of Sumatra to the filter, noticing that her hands felt trembly, not like during the movie shoot, more shaky, as though she weren't on solid ground.

"You clearly love your daughter," she said. She hadn't meant to say that out loud; she'd been thinking it, but it just came out.

He nodded. "I do. More than anything. But her grandparents are right about some stuff. I can't be there when she gets home from school. I do have a job that puts my life in danger when I'm her only living parent. I do suck at cooking."

"You know how to roll out a piecrust," she said.

He smiled. "Thanks to you, I do."

The piecrust was ready to be filled, but a few minutes later, after he'd drank half his coffee, he said he should be going.

"I need to go for a long walk and process all this, think," he said. "Maybe I can take a rain check on a slice of the chocolate pie."

"Sure," she said.

Just like that, he was gone.

Veronica couldn't stop thinking about him. She felt for him, obviously. But there was something else going on here, something unexpected, an attraction to Nick DeMarco that she wouldn't let rise to the surface.

She sat on the window seat in her kitchen,

looking out at the backyard and sipping the coffee she'd made for them. His half-finished cup was still on the island counter, where he'd left it before he'd gone, in quite a hurry, as though he couldn't wait to get away. He probably felt as though he'd said too much.

It was just past eight, and dusk was finally beginning to fall. No matter how she tried to move her thoughts away from Nick, to the pie she still had to bake, to packing her bag for tomorrow's long day in the holding pen, to going over her schedule to make sure she knew what pies she'd need to bake tomorrow night, she couldn't get Nick off her mind. Had he always been so attractive? He was tall and well built, yes, with that dark, wavy hair and deep brown eyes, and he had a great jawline with a slight cleft, but she'd never much paid attention to him as a man before; he'd always represented something else to her: her very distant past. Timothy. A life she barely felt connected to yet couldn't get away from this past year. Her own doing.

Her doorbell rang, and she startled at the sight of his police hat on the counter next to the bowl of apples. She hadn't even noticed he'd left it behind. And Veronica usually noticed everything.

She assumed it was him and went to the door with the hat in her hand to save him from having to come in and wait for her to get it; he clearly

212

needed some time and space, and she'd give it to him.

She opened the door and there he stood.

"I usually don't go around leaving my hat in people's kitchens," he said with a brief smile.

"I—"

The phone rang, and Veronica ignored it, letting her answering machine pick it up. She was about to offer Nick the other half of his coffee in a travel cup when a woman's voice began leaving a message.

"Hello, Veronica?" the melodic voice said into her machine. "My name is Bea Crane. I was born on October twelfth, 1991, in Boothbay Harbor, Maine. I'm here in Boothbay Harbor, staying at the Three Captains' Inn. I'd like to meet you, if you're open to that. You can reach me on my cell at 207-555-1656. Bye for now." Click.

Veronica went still, heard herself let out a strange sound, and dropped the hat on the floor. She stood there, in some kind of daze, aware that Nick was kneeling at her feet, picking up the hat and staring at her. Then he was leading her to a chair in her living room and helping her sit down.

"Veronica? Are you all right?"

Her hand flew to her mouth. The baby. Her baby. The daughter she'd given up for adoption.

She'd called.

Veronica started crying and stood up, then sat down, then stood up.

Nick stood beside her. "Veronica?"

"I—" she began, but words wouldn't come. She stood there, sobbing, and then felt arms, strong arms, around her. She let herself slump into them and cried, unable to stop, unable to speak. Finally, she began sucking in air and calming down. "It's—it's . . ."

"The child you placed for adoption?" He sat in the chair next to hers. "What she said, and the birthdate . . . I just put two and two together."

She closed her eyed and nodded. She hadn't been wrong that he remembered. "I've always updated the file at the adoption agency so she'd be able to find me when and if she wanted. I've been waiting for this day since she turned eighteen. She's twenty-two now. I can't believe it."

"I should go, give you some privacy to call her back."

"Actually, I think I'm glad I'm not alone right now. It's such a shock. I guess I lost some hope that I'd ever hear from her." Bea Crane. Her baby was named Bea Crane. Her voice was lovely. She sounded so polite and kind. Tears started stinging the backs of Veronica's eyes again.

Nick went into the kitchen and returned with the box of tissues she kept on the counter. He handed her a tissue and sat back down. "Can I get you a glass of water? Anything?"

She shook her head. "You and . . . Timothy were friends back then, right?" she blurted out. She sucked in a breath. She hadn't even meant to ask.

He nodded. "He is the father?"

"Yes. I know he told everyone he wasn't. But he definitely was. There was no one but him. I had quite a reputation for a girl who was a virgin before I met him." She shook her head. "All in the past."

"To tell you the truth, I feel a bit like that now with my in-laws. They think I'm this terrible jerk when it couldn't be farther from the truth. And now I'm letting them push me around? Over pie?"

He was giving her an out, to change the subject, to tell him to go. But she was glad he was here, strangely enough. The connection to her past, to Timothy even, seemed more of a comfort than anything else. She'd always been so alone with thoughts of that very lonely, confusing time when she'd been sixteen. When she'd had the baby, alone in an ambulance with an EMT who'd been thankfully very kindhearted. She'd been alone with the memory of handing that baby back and never laying eyes on her again. Twenty-two years was a long time to be alone with those thoughts.

"At sixteen I let everyone push me around, I guess," she said. "I didn't know how to stand up for myself, how to make people believe me."

"I try hard to teach my daughter that she has to believe in herself, that that's how it works. You believe in yourself, and to hell what anyone thinks."

She nodded. "You're a good father, Nick. Her grandparents must know that."

"Sometimes people see what they want."

That was terribly true, Veronica thought.

"For the past twenty-two years—actually, from the day I was sent away to Hope Home, I kind of shut my eyes to everything. I tried so hard not to think about what I'd left behind—my parents, who wanted nothing to do with me. The boyfriend I'd lost, like that," she said, with a snap of her fingers. "The future I envisioned for myself. Back then, I couldn't imagine what it would be like to have something so vital in the back of my mind, always there, something that had changed my life yet wasn't a part of it going forward. I had to tamp everything down so it wouldn't feel real."

"Did it work?"

"Too well," she said. "I've spent so much time trying not to feel anything."

He looked at her for a long moment. "But now here your daughter is, very real, asking to meet you."

"It feels wrong to think of her as my daughter. I didn't raise her. I wasn't her family."

He squeezed her hand.

Veronica bit her lip. "I could pick up the phone right now and in a second I'll be talking to her. To Bea Crane. I can't believe it. I wonder who she is, what she's like, what she looks like."

"Are you going to call her back tonight?"

216

Suddenly she didn't know. She couldn't actually imagine just picking up the phone and calling Bea back. She wasn't sure she could handle it. "I just want to sit with it for a bit. It's more shocking than I thought it would be."

He stood up. "I'll let you have your privacy then. I need to get going, return the squad car. Maybe Leigh and I will be here Monday for the pie class. I don't know. I don't know what the hell I'm supposed to do."

"Do what feels right," she said. "Actually," she added, "do what you need to do."

"You too," he said, and then was gone again.

Two hours later, Veronica sat at the kitchen table, looking from the landline phone she'd pulled over to anywhere else. She wasn't ready to make this call. At first she'd planned to call Bea from her bedroom, thinking she'd feel safe and comfortable reclining on her bed against the array of soft pillows and all her familiar things and keepsakes, but she'd realized she needed to be in her kitchen, among her pie plates and the faint smell of chocolate and caramel in the air. A fresh mug of coffee sat untouched in front of her, next to the phone.

Bea Crane. Here, in Boothbay Harbor.

She'd known Bea Crane for nine months and two minutes, and now here she was, no longer that six-pound weight she'd held against her chest, but a grown woman of twenty-two. She tried to envision Bea—did she look like Veronica? Like Timothy? A combination of both? She had no doubt Bea was tall; Veronica was five feet ten, and Timothy was over six feet. She wondered if Bea had gotten Timothy's fine, thick, light blond hair, that beautiful fine-spun hair all the Macintoshes had had.

She's going to ask about him too, Veronica knew. Was she supposed to tell Bea the truth about everything? How she'd been treated by her family? By Bea's biological father? That she had no idea where Timothy Macintosh or his family was now? Veronica could give her own brief history, of course, but she couldn't imagine telling a curious twenty-two-year-old the more painful circumstances of her birth. She would tell Bea that she'd been sixteen and she'd placed her for adoption to give her the best possible life. That was true after all, and that was what she'd tell Bea. Veronica didn't have to tell her what her mother had said, what her mother had called her. Or how Timothy had screamed at her and walked away. She wouldn't tell Bea any of that.

She stared at the phone.

They would talk. A bit of small talk. They would meet for coffee or lunch or dinner. They'd talk about their lives. Bea would probably want to know her medical history, and Veronica could provide that, what she knew, of course. But then

218

what? What would they talk about? They would be like strangers with the most fundamental thing connecting them.

Just call her back already, Veronica told herself, picking up the receiver, but her hand started trembling and she waited. She found herself wishing Nick hadn't left; he'd encourage her to press in the numbers, top off her coffee, tell her to go ahead.

She'd memorized the phone number. She pressed it in, slowly.

It rang twice. Then: "Veronica?"

She sucked in a breath and went still. "Yes. Hello."

Silence for a second, and then, "Hello."

Okay, they were both nervous. "I'm glad you called," Veronica said. "I was hoping you'd call."

"The adoption agency said you updated the file every time you moved, so I felt comfortable calling." Bea's voice, the cadence, was so different from Veronica's. "I'm glad you're glad." Silence. "Oh God, I sound like an idiot already."

Veronica laughed. "No. Not at all. I'm as nervous as you are."

Silence.

"I've been waiting for this day for a very long time," Veronica said. "Hoping to meet you again, know that you were okay." *I wasn't supposed to think about you. I told myself not to. My friends at Hope Home told me not to, that it was the only way to get through. But as much as I locked down memories of you, I've thought about you every day. If you were happy. If your parents were loving.*

On your birthday, every year, sometimes I'd be unable to get out of bed, but then I'd think of you blowing out the candles on your birthday cake, and I'd feel better . . .

"I am okay."

"Good," Veronica said. "That's what I wanted to know most of all."

"Should we meet?" Bea asked.

Veronica felt her heart swell, and tears pricked her eyes. "I'd like that."

"I'm just not sure how this is supposed to go," Bea said, "how it's supposed to feel. I don't know anything," she added, and her voice sounded so strained.

Given how nervous Bea sounded, perhaps she would feel more comfortable coming over to Veronica's house, getting an outward glimpse of who she was, instead of sitting in a neutral coffee shop or restaurant, aware of people at nearby tables listening to their conversation. Veronica could set up a nice tea for the two of them and bake a pie, a Happiness Pie.

"I'd much rather come to your house," Bea said when Veronica gave her the choice.

Again, Veronica tried to picture Bea. Would she look like a younger version of herself? Would she share some of Veronica's traits? Her likes and dislikes? She didn't know all that much about the ways of nature versus nurture, but she figured that at the least, Bea would look something like her. Veronica had been a waitress more than half of her life; except for her pie baking, she didn't even know what she might excel at, what she wasn't much good at. She couldn't hit a tennis ball, and she was no math wiz, but she read a lot, could spend every night watching a movie, and she did like to travel. God, she'd bore Bea to death tomorrow with who she was.

"Tomorrow, evening? I won't be home until around six or seven o'clock. I could make dinner, or if you'll have already eaten, I can make a pie."

Bea was silent for a few seconds. "I have early dinner plans, but I figure I could be over by eight, if that works."

"Eight o'clock tomorrow night, it is."

And just like that, the baby girl she'd held against her chest for less than two minutes on an October night would be knocking on her door tomorrow.

Chapter 12

GEMMA

The tap on her door at the Three Captains' Inn startled Gemma. She glanced up from her laptop on the small desk by the sun-filled window to the clock: it was just past nine in the morning. She got up reluctantly; she'd been working from the moment she'd woken up two hours ago and hadn't even been down to breakfast, but was on a good roll. The first few paragraphs of her article on Hope Home, its history, some statistics then and now, were done, opening up to the long middle of the piece, which would focus on human interest—past residents, current residents. True stories.

Gemma stretched her arms above her head on the way to the door. When she opened it, Bea Crane stood there, looking like she might burst.

"I did it," Bea said. "I called my birth mother last night. We're meeting tonight at her house." She lifted her hands in front of her. "I'm shaking."

Gemma squeezed Bea's hand. With Bea's blond hair pulled into a ponytail, her pretty face free of makeup, she looked so young. "What was the call like? Oh, gosh—I must sound like the nosy reporter here. I'm asking as a friend. Remember to just say this is off the record, and everything you tell me will be private."

"Use whatever you want for your article," Bea said. "Except for Veronica's name, of course. Though for all I know, she'd be happy to talk to you and give her perspective."

"That would be so great if she would," Gemma said. "Of course, I don't expect you to show up at her house and say, 'Nice to meet you. Want to repeat all of this to a reporter writing an article on Hope Home?'"

Bea smiled. "Definitely not. But I will bring it up. She should know I'm talking to a reporter about her, even if her name isn't used."

Gemma hoped Bea's birth mother would be open to talking to her for the article. The dual perspectives of a birth mother from Hope Home, and the daughter she placed for adoption making contact, a first meeting—it would add so much to the article. But Bea and her birth mother were meeting for the first time tonight—Gemma wouldn't expect to talk to Veronica, if at all, for days. It all depended on what kind of person Veronica was, how open to sharing her story she was.

"If you need someone to talk to, as a friend, just knock or call, okay? Even if you just need a little reassurance before you head over to her house tonight."

"I appreciate that," Bea said. "I'd better get back to work—the kids from the Osprey Room had a little oatmeal-flinging war in the dining room."

She smiled and then dashed down the stairs.

Gemma closed the door, her thoughts whirling about the meeting Bea and Veronica would have, the emotion that would be in that room tonight. Bea's story was so heart tugging. If Gemma could get her birth mother's side for the article . . .

Gemma grabbed her phone and called Claire, her editor at the *Gazette*, and explained that she might have the opportunity to talk with a birth mother and her birth daughter who were reuniting, get both their perspectives, and maybe she should take an extra couple of weeks for the article since Claire didn't officially need it until mid-July.

"No problem on the time," Claire said. "I really don't need it until July eighteenth to run it the Sunday before the fiftieth anniversary, which is July thirtieth. So take your time. I'd rather have a really full, knockout piece, and perspectives like the ones you're getting are exactly what I had in mind."

Perfect, Gemma thought, sentences of her article forming themselves in her mind. She'd really have the time now to develop her story, go deep, write the heck out if it.

She was supposed to go home tomorrow, but she'd just given herself an extra couple of weeks here, she realized. *Because I don't want to go home*.

She stood before the mirror hanging outside her

closet door and put her hand on her stomach, turning to the side to see if her stomach looked even a bit rounder. Not yet. But she was definitely pregnant; a letter from her doctor confirming the positive blood test had arrived yesterday afternoon.

She took in her slightly pale complexion, the bit of shadow under her dark blue eyes, which might be from working so intensely the past few days. Her light brown hair, falling straight to her shoulders, seemed thicker, though, unless she was imagining it. More luxuriant, somehow. And her nails were longer. Her nails were never this long.

You're so lucky, she heard seventeen-year-old Chloe Martin echo in her head.

It had been just over a week since she'd seen that plus sign on the pregnancy test. A week that she'd kept the news a secret from Alexander. But she still wasn't ready to tell him. Another couple of weeks to finish the article, turn it in, and then she'd be ready to go home. Already, just a few days in full-out reporter mode, conducting interviews, doing research, and writing, she felt more like her old self—and she was a bit more used to the idea of being pregnant. In two more weeks, she'd be much more confident, have stronger legs to stand on when she told Alexander the news.

She picked up the phone and pressed in the number of his cell phone. She wouldn't mention the pregnancy yet, but she did have to tell him she wouldn't be coming home tomorrow, after all.

"Two more weeks?" he repeated after a deadly silence. "What the hell is going on, Gemma?"

"I just want to go more in depth with the article. I might have a chance to interview the birth mother of one of my sources. It'll round—"

"Gemma, you were going to Maine for a weekend. Then it turned into a week. Now it's three weeks."

"I'm just—"

"Are you saying you need a break from us? If that's what this is, Gemma, just say so. Don't make it about an article for some small-town paper."

I need a break from you, she said silently, closing her eyes.

"Neither the article nor the newspaper is small to me, Alex. Why can't you understand how important my career is to me?"

"Jesus, Gemma, what career? You were laid off. There's no job. You have no career at the moment. You're chasing some fluff piece for a summer tourist-town newspaper that gave you a column when you were eleven. Please. If you're leaving me, just say so. But don't leave me hanging while you 'sort out your feelings' and interview teenagers over ice cream."

God, he could be infuriating. She paced around the small room, her heart beating too fast. Calm down, Gemma, she told herself. Just calm down. Look at this from his perspective. He wants what he wants just as much as you want what you want. "Alex, I'm just trying to . . ." Find my way through this new normal, she finished silently, one hand on her stomach again. Find myself in this.

"Just trying to what?" he barked. "What the hell are you trying to do besides screw things up between us? I want to know what the hell is—"

"I'm pregnant!" she shouted, then started to cry.

Oh God.

There was silence for a moment. "What? Gemma—what?"

"I'm pregnant, Alex." She could barely believe she'd said the words aloud to him.

"Are you sure?" he asked, the tone of his voice changing—dramatically. Instead of anger, there was . . . wonder.

"Two positive pregnancy tests and positive blood test results yesterday."

"Oh my God, Gemma. This is amazing! We're going to have a baby! Wait a minute," he said, the voice changing again, growing hesitant. "How long have you known?"

"I took the first pregnancy test last Wednesday. It was positive. I was so shocked—as you can imagine. I thought maybe my cycle was off because of the stress of losing my job. I only took the test to rule out the craziest reason why my period would be late. We'd used a backup plan when I was on those antibiotics." She closed her eyes and sat down on the edge of her bed. "But there it was, a pink plus sign."

He was quiet again for a long few seconds. "Gemma, you've known you were pregnant for a week and didn't tell me? You left for Maine and didn't tell me? What the hell, Gemma?"

"It's a loaded topic, Alex."

"Loaded?" he repeated, his voice full of disdain. "So you're not happy about it? Is that what this is all about?"

"I don't know."

"You don't know," he repeated. Flatly. "And were you going to tell me during this call if it hadn't just come out?"

"I don't know that either. I don't know anything except that I don't want to move to Dobbs Ferry and live next door to your parents. I don't want a part-time job at the local paper if I insist—as you called it—on working. I don't want this life you're trying so damned hard to force me into."

"Well, guess what, Gemma, you're pregnant. It's not about you anymore."

"Who the hell is it about?"

"The baby. Me. Us. Our marriage, our family."

She suddenly felt very, very tired. "I don't know how I feel about any of this, Alex. I need time to—"

"Gemma, you're not fifteen and pregnant like

one of the girls you're interviewing. You're a grown woman. Act like it."

"I'm going now, Alex. I need to go."

Click.

She dropped her head in her hands and cried.

Gemma checked the address of the woman she was due to interview in three minutes. Caitlin Auerman, 33 Banyon Road. The small white cape halfway down the street with the tricycle and Big Wheels out front was the place.

The director of Hope Home had called Gemma as she'd been out on Main Street, needing to be alone in a crowd. The conversation with Alexander had drained her, and she couldn't stay cooped up in her small room. She'd gotten an herbal iced tea and a bagel with cream cheese and was sitting on a bench, trying to calm herself down and eat a few bites, when Pauline Lee had called with the news that a woman who'd lived at Hope Home fifteen years ago, as a fifteen-year-old, and had placed her baby for adoption was interested in speaking with Gemma for the article, but only had a two-hour window. Gemma had been grateful for somewhere to go, to have something to focus on besides her marriage.

Gemma pressed the doorbell, and a woman who could only be described as weary opened the door. She looked like she hadn't slept well—or perhaps in days. There was a baby swing in the living room, and lots of kid paraphernalia around the room.

"You must be Gemma Hendricks," she said. "I'm Caitlin Auerman. I forgot to mention to the Hope Home director that I have to insist on anonymity—that you won't use my name in the article. Hope Home was good to me, and I have only positive things to say about it, but if I'm going to be truthful about how my life has been since, I don't want my real name used."

"I can assure you I won't use your name. I'll make up a name and use your real age and time frame that you were at Hope Home, but I can assure you I'll protect your identity. I appreciate your willingness to sit down with me."

Caitlin led Gemma into the living room, full of toys, and they sat down on the sofa. Gemma pulled out her recorder and her notebook, and the woman started talking before Gemma could even get out her pen and ask a question.

"Everyone said: you'll ruin your life if you have a baby at fifteen," Caitlin said. "You have your whole life in front of you. Put the baby up for adoption. It's the right thing. For both of you. On and on. I even agreed to go live at Hope Home so that no one in town would know I was pregnant, so that it would stay a family secret. Well, here I am, thirty years old, and I did everything everybody told me to do—I went to college. I went to law school. I got all the 'see, you listened to us, and now look at you.' Well, fifteen years later, I have three kids under ten, I can forget about my career, and I can't even hear myself think ninety percent of the time. I'm not saying I could have achieved everything I did with a baby at fifteen—who knows, maybe I could have. I just know that it all added up to me sitting at home with three kids, a husband who's never home, and a career that's basically over. Why the hell did I work so hard? To be treated like the invisible woman at my husband's business functions? I'm suddenly a stay-at-home mother so I have nothing of value to say? I hate this."

This will be me, Gemma thought, her head spinning for a few seconds. I don't want this to be me. Focus on the interview, she reminded herself. "Can I ask a personal question?"

Caitlin let out a harsh laugh. "I think I've made it clear you can."

"Did you plan to get pregnant with your first child?"

Caitlin shook her head. "It was an accident. Twins. I wasn't really ready, but I was excited. I thought I could do it all, be superwoman, even though everyone said it was impossible. I thought I could work full-time and be a great mom and take cooking classes and learn to speak Italian and take yoga. Boy, was I in for a rude awakening."

"So you had a plan, but life didn't go accordingly?" Gemma didn't want to hear the answer. Clearly, Caitlin had had a big plan, big plans for herself.

"Exactly. One of the twins was sick a lot with ear infections, and the other would wake up every couple of hours, and my husband would argue with me endlessly about quitting the firm and staying home with the boys. I know it sounds awful, but I didn't want to. I loved my job, loved the office environment, getting all dressed up every day. I didn't want to stay home with the twins, as much as I loved them."

"But then both worlds started suffering," Gemma said, more statement than question.

"Exactly. Home and work. My marriage was a wreck. I blamed my husband for not helping more; he blamed me for being selfish and not agreeing to quit when we could swing it financially if we were careful. The pressure won and I quit, and suddenly I had three kids and had been out of the game so long I couldn't see ever finding my way back to who I used to be."

Who I used to be. That was exactly what Gemma was afraid of: waking up one day and wondering what had happened to the person she used to be.

"I know I'm not that woman," Caitlin said. "I'm not twenty-five and childless and a rising young associate. But sometimes I hate who I am now. That my life feels like it's not my own. That's how I felt at fifteen and pregnant. Like my life wasn't my own. It wasn't." She shook her head. "Maybe it's just me, though. I know two other attorneys at my old firm who have two kids and manage to put in their hours and be great moms. They make it work. I couldn't."

Gemma also could think of several working mothers who seemed to have great balance—exactly what she was hoping to achieve. "I really appreciate your being so open and honest. I think many women will be able to relate to how you feel." Not Gemma's sister-in-law, who'd had a very similar experience to Caitlin's, minus the pregnancy at fifteen. Lisa Hendricks gave up a high-powered job to stay home with her baby and loved her life, every moment of it. *I was meant to be a mother,* Lisa said all the time. *My whole life has been leading me to this,* she'd say, wiping her toddler's runny nose while patting her seven-months-pregnant belly.

"Do you have kids?" Caitlin asked Gemma.

"Not yet."

Caitlin nodded. "I didn't think so. You don't look exhausted enough."

Gemma smiled, but she wanted to cry.

"You remind me so much of who I used to be," Caitlin said. "Here you are, conducting an interview, writing for the paper. Living your life, the one you probably imagined when you were a teenager."

The sound of a car pulling into the driveway had

Caitlin leaping up to peer out the window. "It's my mother with the baby." She glanced at her watch. "She's a half hour early coming back. Lana must be fussing up a storm."

Gemma stood up. "I won't keep you then. Thank you so much for your time, Caitlin. And I just want to say—maybe you can find a happy medium for yourself."

The front door opened, and an older woman came in, carrying a beautiful baby, who was indeed fussing up a storm. "She's been crying nonstop."

Caitlin took the baby and bounced her a bit. "Right," she said to Gemma with a roll of her eyes. "A happy medium."

Gemma thought she might ask Caitlin's mother a few questions about what it was like fifteen years ago when her daughter had been a teenage resident of Hope Home, but the woman was already rushing out the door, calling over her shoulder that she'd call Caitlin later.

"I can't even sit down to a half-hour interview," Caitlin said, shaking her head. "There is no happy medium."

Gemma wished she knew what to say to make the woman's resentment, the way she looked at her life, abate some. But what she'd said hit so close to home that all Gemma could do was wish Caitlin well. She'd send her a little something tomorrow, maybe a gift certificate to a restaurant in town where she and her husband could go if her mother or a sitter would watch the kids. Something to take her away from her life for a little bit.

Why was it this way for some women and not others? she wondered, thinking of herself and Caitlin in one dreary category and women like her sister-in-law, and her neighbor in New York City, Lydia Bessell, in the other. Mindset? You chose this or that because of this or that, though sometimes, of course, you had no choice whatsoever, and then there you were, in your life. There was another category, though. Mothers with full-time jobs who made their lives work—because they had to, because they wanted to. Gemma would be in that category. She would, she assured herself. Despite how much Caitlin had wanted her life to work. Everyone was different.

Gemma didn't even have a job. Or a baby yet. She had no idea what she was talking about, how anything would be. And that might be the scariest part of all.

After a long day of research and two more interviews—one with a current resident of Hope Home and another with a woman who'd adopted a baby from a Hope Home resident five years ago, Gemma arrived back at the inn at around five o'clock, desperate for a hot bubble bath and the new chapter of *Your Pregnancy This Week*.

A man sat on the porch swing, and from the

distance of the driveway he looked so much like Alexander that for a moment, her heart swelled with such longing for her husband that she had to draw in breath. Despite everything happening between them right now, she missed him. She wished she could turn to him with all her fears, her worries, the way she'd always been able to. But she couldn't in this case.

I do love you, Alexander, she thought. I do. So much. I just wish—

The man on the porch stood up. It *was* Alexander.

Gemma gasped as he came toward her without a word and wrapped his arms around her. She fell against him, holding him tight, so relieved to have him standing right here. Just let everything fall away and let your husband hold you, she told herself.

"I should have known you'd fly up here," she said. "My head is in so many different places that I didn't think of it."

"No kidding." He offered a half smile and put his arm around her and they walked up the short stone path to the steps.

"We're having a baby," he whispered.

"I'm scared to death."

"I'm not," he said.

She led him into the inn, quiet on a sunny late afternoon. They headed up the stairs to the third floor, and Gemma unlocked her door.

The two of them barely fit in the room together. She drank in the sight of him; with all their arguing, she'd forgotten how attracted she was to Alex, how easily his face, his body, could overwhelm her. In her frame of mind and exhausted, she'd have to be careful around him. She needed a hot bath and her husband's strong arms—but she couldn't let him strong-arm her.

She closed the door behind him. "I can learn how to be a mother, I know that. But I can't learn how to want what you want. I don't want to move to the suburbs and be a stay-at-home mother. It's wonderful for those who do want that, and yes, I get that it's a blessing that we can afford it in the first place. But I want to be a reporter. I want to work on exactly the kind of stories I'm working on now. Tonight, a birth mother is meeting the daughter she gave up for adoption twenty-two years ago."

He put her hand on her stomach. "I don't see why you can't do this from Westchester, then. You'll work part-time at the local paper. If you're assigned this story here, why not there?"

I'm not moving to Westchester to live next door to your family, dammit! "I don't want to leave the city." The local newspaper might not hire her, anyway, she full well knew.

He shook his head and sat down on the edge of the bed. "Well, I do, Gem. And I'm not raising this baby in the city. I won't."

"Well, I won't move to Westchester."

"You're so selfish!" he snapped.

"Did you come here to scream at me?"

He dropped his head back and let out a frustrated breath. "How are we going to work this out?"

She sat down beside him and took his hand, and he closed it tight around hers. "I don't know. I just know that I want to stay here for the next couple of weeks and work on this story. I want to get used to being pregnant, come to terms with it. It's completely unexpected."

"Come to terms with it?" He shook his head. "Do you know how lucky we are?"

Why couldn't he understand?

He sighed. "Fine, come to terms with it, if that's what you have to do. If that's what it takes to make you see that moving to Dobbs Ferry is in all our best interest. We'll have my family right there for support, babysitting, community. The neighborhoods I'm interested in are full of young families like us. We'll fit right in."

"But I won't."

He closed his eyes in frustration. "I don't know how you can stand this tiny room. Why not get a bigger room?"

"June gave me the dear-old-friend discount on this single," she said. "The regular rooms go for almost two hundred a night, and I didn't want to take a room away from a full-paying guest. And I like this room. It's cozy. Isabel, June's older sister, manages the inn and she's been great to me."

"I miss you, Gem."

Tears filled her eyes. "I miss you too."

He sat on the bed, leaning against the headboard, and pulled her back against his chest, wrapping his arms around her. "We'll figure it out."

How, though? Gemma wondered, Caitlin Auerman's weary face flashing in her mind.

Chapter 13
BEA

In a romantic little Mexican restaurant on a pier, Bea sat across from Patrick, the tall, dark, and intelligent second assistant director on the Colin Firth film, listening to him tell a hilarious story about an A-list movie star he'd once worked with, without mentioning names. She liked that he didn't name-drop or talk behind the actors' backs. She liked that he'd said some of the biggest movie stars were among the nicest people he'd ever met. She liked the way he listened intently to her, the warmth in his expression. She liked him. He was twenty-eight, from Seattle, and his dream was to direct interesting documentaries. He'd been around the world on various film shoots, but he wasn't full of himself at all. And the more Bea looked at him, the hotter he got. He was exactly her height—at five feet ten, Bea rarely wore heels or she'd tower over most people—with narrow blue eyes, freckles, and sexy dark, wavy hair. He'd picked her up at the inn right on time, and they'd walked to the colorful restaurant, where he'd made a reservation, though at five o'clock it hadn't been necessary.

After the waiter left with their orders, he asked her to tell him all about herself, and she wanted to blurt out that in less than three hours she'd be meeting her birth mother for the first time ever, but instead she found herself telling him about her mother's death and losing sight of her own dreams to be a teacher, and that maybe getting fired from her crutch job at Crazy Burger had been a blessing in disguise.

"What brought you to Boothbay Harbor, Maine?" he asked, swiping a tortilla chip through the excellent dish of salsa between them.

She explained about the letter from her mother. The weeks she'd spent walking around Boston, going back and forth about looking up her birth mother. And then finally deciding to drive up to Maine to check her out. "I won't name names, either, but the reason I've been hanging around the film set is because my birth mother—who I'm meeting for the first time later tonight—is one of the extras. I found out she was working on the film and just wanted to look around."

He raised his margarita glass to her. "I admire what you're doing, Bea. That takes guts. All of it. Especially after getting hit with such a whopper of a letter like that. Have you gotten a little more used to it all?"

"I guess. Sometimes it feels like it can't possibly be true, but then I take out my mom's letter and reread it, and I know it is true."

"I'm doubly sorry that Tyler—the production assistant—was giving you a hard time yesterday.

But then again, if he hadn't been, I might not have overheard you guys arguing and I might not have seen you at all. I'm pretty glad I did."

She smiled. "Me too."

When their entrées arrived—enchiladas suizas for Bea, and steak fajitas for Patrick—they talked about everything and anything, from movies they both liked and hated, to books, to places they'd traveled—he had Bea beat there—and the weirdest foods they'd tried. Bea told him about having to measure her Mt. Vesuvius burgers to make sure they were exactly one foot tall, and he told her about filming on location near the volcano in Italy. They talked so easily, so naturally, and Bea found herself laughing for what felt like the first time in a month. Maybe months.

After dinner, they had coffee and split a basket of cinnamon churros, then headed out to the back deck overlooking the bay, where they both tried to pick up a crab from the touch tank, but they'd been bested by an eight-year-old who picked it up without getting pinched.

As they were leaving, Bea told him she'd walk him back to the set, since her birth mother's house was nearby and she was due over there soon. "I can't believe I'll be face-to-face with her, talking to her, in less than an hour."

"I'd love to hear how it went," Patrick said. "Tomorrow is nuts, all day, but maybe you can come by my trailer around one o'clock on Saturday for a quick lunch on the set. I can impress you with the craft services table."

Bea smiled. "I'd like that."

He smiled back and took her hand, the comfort of it, the warmth, startling her. Yup, she liked this guy.

As they approached the trailers, which had grown much busier since yesterday with people milling about and rushing around, a man's voice called out, "Hey, people, Colin Firth is signing autographs in front of O'Donald's Pub!"

A swarm of people ran toward the little pub, but the only person standing in front of it was an elderly woman who was feeding two seagulls from her bakery bag. She let out a yelp at the crowd racing toward her, and a man came out of the pub—also not Colin Firth—and jumped in between her and the storming mass. "Watch it, people," he shouted. "Don't run the lady down."

"Is Colin Firth in there?" a woman asked.

"The only Colin in O'Donald's Pub is my drunk uncle visiting from Scotland," the man said. "What's this nonsense?"

Bea looked back at the guy who'd called out the Colin Firth sighting. Tall and very skinny and quite possibly a little bit drunk, the forty-something man, who had a huge smile on his face, looked like the one who'd asked out Veronica at the diner. "Is he just yelling out random Colin

Firth appearances to make people run around like crazy?"

Patrick glanced at him. "He must be, because Colin Firth is not even in the country. He's not due here on set for at least a few days, maybe more."

Bea barely had time to thank Patrick for dinner before three different staffers rushed to him with various emergencies.

"Until Saturday, then," he said, giving her a very quick and sweet kiss on the lips.

She smiled. "Until Saturday." She watched him hurry toward the field of wildflowers, where a group of people were crowding around one of the cameras.

Bea heard a loud snort, and then a familiar voice said, "Don't say I didn't warn you."

She turned around to find Tyler Echols sitting on a director's chair next to his teenage sister, Maddy, who had *To Kill a Mockingbird* open on her lap but was looking everywhere except at the book.

"I don't even know you," Bea said. What was with this guy?

"Oh, hey, are you the one who knows everything about this book?" Tyler's sister said to Bea, holding up *To Kill a Mockingbird.* "Do you know who this Boo guy is?"

Bea smiled at her. "Boo Radley. He's the town recluse in Maycomb. Because no one ever sees him, but everyone knows he's been holed up in his family house from childhood, they come to all sorts of conclusions about him. Wrong conclusions. Boo ends up saving the day for the kids. His characterization has a lot to say about the harm of gossip, the harm of assumptions."

Maddy sat up. "Really? I hate gossip. A few months ago, someone started a rumor about this girl at my school and she never came back after spring break. Maybe I'll read a little more to get to the parts about him."

Bea smiled. "It's a great book. Honestly. The whole thing."

"Omigod, is that Christopher Cade over there?" Maddy said, staring at the tall, handsome actor on the field, surrounded by people with headsets and clipboards.

"More reading, less star staring," Tyler told his sister, pushing his wire-rimmed glasses up on the bridge of his nose.

Maddy rolled her eyes at him. "I already have his autograph anyway." She went back to the book but stole peeks of the very good-looking twenty-something actor every few minutes.

Tyler had gone back to pretending Bea wasn't standing a foot in front of him, so she glanced at her watch. She might as well start walking over to Veronica's.

"Good luck with the book," she said to Maddy, ignoring Tyler, and headed toward the harbor, her heart fluttering in her chest.

● ● ●

Bea stood on Veronica Russo's little porch, staring at the red front door, at the doorbell, which she still hadn't rung.

She glanced up at the sky and closed her eyes, thinking of her mother. She wondered how Cora Crane would feel about her standing at her birth mother's door, about to ring the bell, about to meet the woman whom Cora had spent so many years hiding via omission. Her mother must have realized Bea would seek out her birth mother; she couldn't suddenly have this truth sprung on her at age twenty-two and not do anything with it. She'd have gone crazy otherwise, wondering, speculating, imagining, turning the truth over and over in her mind. It was right that she was here. Yes, Cora Crane had kept that truth a secret, but in the end, she wanted Bea to know. Where it took Bea was up to Bea. She knew her mother had accepted that while she wrote the letter. Cora had needed peace. She touched the tiny gold heart locket necklace she never took off—her mother had given it to her for her sixteenth birthday—and now it felt as though her mother were here with her.

I love you, mama, she said silently up at the sky, dusk just beginning to darken the blue.

She pressed in the doorbell and held her breath.

The door opened and there was Veronica Russo, who gasped and covered her mouth with her hand.

Veronica looked at Bea for the longest time. "Oh my goodness, oh my goodness," she said, tears coming to her eyes. "It's so nice to meet you, Bea. I don't think I've ever meant that phrase more in my entire life."

Bea smiled. "I'm glad to meet you too."

Bea tried not to stare, but she couldn't help herself. She wasn't a carbon copy of Veronica, but she saw enough of herself in her face, in her height, that she began looking for the details—the straight, almost pointy nose, the slightly too big mouth, the texture of the almost straight hair with its wave, if not the color. Veronica was beautiful. She wore a lavender shirt embroidered with silver along the neck, a white skirt with a flouncy hem, and low-heeled sandals. A few gold bangles were on one wrist, a bracelet watch on the other.

Bea had spent a good half hour pawing through the makeshift closet in her room, trying to decide what was appropriate to wear for a first date and for meeting your birth mother for the first time. She'd gone with her white skinny jeans and a silky yellow tank top.

Veronica ushered Bea into the living room, where a big square tray was set up on the coffee table, holding a pie, an ornate teapot, and cups. "Why don't we sit on the sofa," she said, gesturing for Bea to sit.

They sat on opposite edges, clasping and unclasping their hands. Bea put her hands underneath her thighs and glanced around the room. Cozy, homey. The sofa was plush velvet ecru with lots of colorful throw pillows, a matching love seat perpendicular. A crowded bookcase took up one wall, and a stone fireplace another. It was easier for Bea to look around than to stare at Veronica, which was what she wanted to do. Stare.

"I'll be honest," Bea said. "I'm at an advantage here because the adoption agency, where I got your contact information, told me where you worked. So I went to the Best Little Diner last Saturday, when I first arrived in town. I just wanted to see you from a distance, if that makes sense."

Veronica seemed startled, but she said, "It does. I'm sure I would have done the same thing." She picked up the teapot. "Tea?"

Bea nodded and Veronica poured, and Bea noticed that Veronica's hands were a bit shaky. Bea added a little cream and a sugar cube, and lifted the pretty cup to her lips just to have something to do with her own shaky hands. The smell of the Earl Grey was soothing.

When Bea looked up, Veronica was staring at her, but then she glanced away. "You can look," Bea said. "I got to stare at you when I went to the diner. You're more familiar to me than I am to you, physically, anyway."

"You have my eyes," Veronica said. "And height, of course."

"The hair is my father's?"

Veronica seemed to stiffen, unless Bea was reading into it. "Yes," she said, glancing away.

No elaboration. Did she not want to talk about him? Had their relationship ended back when Veronica was pregnant? Had he stayed by her side through the pregnancy but stress tore them apart? Bea was so curious, but she sensed she should stick to Veronica herself right now, especially for the first meeting.

Bea took a sip of tea. "There's so much I want to ask you, I hardly know where to begin. Can you tell me how old you were when I was born?"

"Sixteen. I turned seventeen just a month later." Veronica set out two small plates on the coffee table. "Pie? It's chocolate fudge."

She doesn't want to talk about herself, Bea realized. Bea sensed that Veronica would answer her questions, but her body language, the stiffness of her shoulders, her tight expression, made it obvious that talking about this wasn't easy.

"I'd love some pie," Bea said. "I had your chocolate fudge pie at the diner the day I was there. That's how I found out which waitress was you. One of the waitresses called to you by name and said your pies were to die for."

Veronica smiled. "I'm kind of known for my pies in town."

"I can understand why," Bea said, taking a bite. "Delicious."

Okay, I don't want to make small talk about pies, Bea thought. I want to know who you are. Who you were. Where I came from—and why.

"Is Russo Italian?" Bea asked, figuring she'd stick to the reasonably neutral to start.

"Yes. My father's family came from northern Italy, Verona, à la *Romeo and Juliet*. My mother's family was Scottish."

"And my biological father's family?" she asked.

"Scottish too," Veronica said. "I remember that because it was something we had in common. We were partnered on an ancestry project in high school. That's how we started seeing each other."

Italian and Scottish. Not a drop of Irish, as she'd always thought, like both Cranes. With her light blond hair, pale brown eyes, and pale complexion, Bea was often thought to be Scandinavian.

"How long were you dating?" Bea asked.

Veronica picked up her tea and took a sip. "Not long. Six months."

"Were you in love?"

"I thought so," Veronica said. "I was, anyway."

Bea waited for her to elaborate, but Veronica gave Bea a tight smile and took another sip of tea.

Bea took a bite of her pie, then put her fork down. "How did your parents take the news? About your pregnancy, I mean."

"Well, it wasn't ideal," Veronica said. "So they reacted the way many parents might."

"They were upset?"

251

She nodded. "I was sixteen and my life as a typical high school junior was suddenly interrupted. They had a hard time with that. My parents had expectations for me, that I'd make them proud, go to college, build a career, get married, have children—in that order."

"And my birth father," Bea said, unable to stop herself from trying again. "Was he upset too?"

Veronica topped off her tea, even though her cup was practically full. She was stalling for time. "He was pretty shocked," she finally said.

"Do you have a photograph of him?" Bea asked.

Veronica put down her teacup so quickly that Bea figured if she hadn't, she might have dropped it. "I do. Just one. I kept it in a keepsake box, and there was one time during the pregnancy that I took out the picture and looked at it. And then I turned it over and put it on the bottom of the box and never touched it again."

Bea bit her lip. She wouldn't ask to see it right now. "He must have hurt you pretty bad, then."

"Well, that's in the past," she said too brightly.

"Veronica, can I ask you something?" She seemed to be bracing herself. "Are you not saying too much about what life was like for you back then because it's painful to talk about? Or to protect me, maybe? To spare my feelings?"

"Maybe a little of both, but mostly the latter. This is your history, after all. And you've come all the way here to learn about it, where you come from. I'd like to give you the basics without the unnecessary gritty details."

The gritty details were truth, though. And Bea wanted truth. Not sidestepping, not omission. Not anymore.

"I can handle it," Bea said. She'd buried both her parents. She'd discovered—at twenty-two—that she'd been adopted. She could handle just about anything.

Veronica nodded. "It's not easy for me to talk about my past, mainly because I don't talk about it ever. I kind of had to put a lock and key on the subject twenty-two years ago or else I'd have gone crazy."

"Because it was so painful?"

"My parents didn't handle the news well. Your biological father didn't either. And I was sent to a home for pregnant teenagers, where I didn't have a single visitor in the seven and a half months I was there. Even that is a bit hard for me to say—I guess because I hate the idea of you having this in your head. That these blood relations of yours weren't exactly . . . supportive."

"You didn't have anyone?"

Veronica shook her head. "I had an amazing grandmother—my father's mother, Renata Russo. But she passed before I found out I was pregnant. She would have saved my life back then."

"Would you have kept me, do you think, if your grandmother had been alive?"

Veronica took a deep breath. "Maybe. I really don't know for sure."

"It's crazy for me to think that I might have had a completely different life, a completely different childhood. A different mother."

Veronica seemed relieved that the focus had switched from herself to Bea. She shifted her body slightly more toward Bea. "Did you used to think about that a lot as you were growing up?"

"Actually, I didn't know I was adopted until a month ago. My parents never told me. My father died when I was nine, and my mother died last year. She'd arranged to have a deathbed confession letter sent to me a year after her death. She wanted me to know the truth she was unable to bring herself to tell me when she was alive."

Veronica was staring at her. "Wow. That must have been some shock."

"It was," Bea said.

"What was your mom like?" Veronica asked.

"The best. The absolute best."

Veronica smiled. "Good." Tears shimmered in her eyes. "That's what I always hoped, all these years. That you were somewhere safe and wonderful with loving parents."

Bea's parents' faces flashed into her mind, the picture of the three of them when Bea was four, she up on her dad's shoulders, her mother smiling up at Bea. God, how she missed them.

And yes, she had been somewhere safe and

wonderful with loving parents all those years.

Bea stood up suddenly, wanting to leave. This was crazy, all of it. What was she doing here with this . . . stranger? And Veronica Russo was a stranger. A total stranger. Cora Crane was my mother. Keith Crane was my father. *That's all I need to know.*

Why couldn't her mother have left well enough alone? Bea wondered, that hollow pressure forming in her chest again. Bea would have gone on not knowing, blissfully ignorant that she was a different person entirely. That she was Italian and Scottish and not a bit Irish. That she'd come into this world because of the woman standing a foot in front of her.

She needed fresh air. A break. She needed to digest all this privately, not that she'd learned that much. She just knew that her skin felt . . . tight.

Veronica stood up too. "Are you all right?"

"I should get going," she said.

"I hope I didn't scare you away. Say too much. Or too little. I want to answer your questions. I just don't want to overwhelm you."

"With the truth?" Bea asked.

"Yes."

"That way of thinking kept me from knowing I'd been adopted in the first place," Bea said—too harshly, she realized. "Maybe if I'd always known, this would be a little easier. I would have had my entire life to lead me here one day." Suddenly she didn't want to have gone on blissfully ignorant. She had no idea what she thought. What she felt. She just knew she needed air. She needed to leave.

"I understand, Bea."

Bea hated the concern in her eyes. You're a stranger, Bea wanted to shout. A total stranger.

"When you're ready," Veronica said, "if you want, I'd like to meet again. I'd love to learn more about you."

Bea tried to smile but she felt so jumpy and uncomfortable. "I'll call." She sounded like one of those noncommittal guys after a so-so date. "Thank you for the pie," she added, grabbed her bag, and headed toward the door. Veronica opened the door for her, and she hurried out, aware that Veronica was staring after her.

Oh, darn, she thought as she was about to say good-bye and then flee. She'd forgotten to tell Veronica about the Hope Home article. "I almost forgot. I found out about Hope Home from my original birth certificate, and when I went for a visit a few days ago, I met a reporter who's writing a big article about the home's fiftieth anniversary. I told her my story and didn't give your name on the record, of course. But I wanted you to know that I did talk to her. She's staying at the same inn I am. She got me a temporary job there, and it comes with a room."

Veronica's eyes widened. "So you'll be staying in town for a while, then?"

"For a couple of weeks," Bea said. Was Veronica happy about that? Worried?

"I appreciate that you didn't give the reporter the okay to use my name. I'm pretty well known in town because I work at such a popular diner and because of my pie business too, but I'm a pretty private person. I'm not sure I'd want my personal history in the paper."

"Are you upset that I let her interview me?"

"No, not at all."

"I think she's especially interested in the here and now where we're concerned," Bea said. "I know she'd love to talk to you too."

"I'm not sure I'm up for that," Veronica said.

"I can understand that. Well, good-bye then."

"Good-bye," Veronica said, and Bea could see tears shimmering in her eyes again, which she was trying hard not to show.

Chapter 14
VERONICA

Veronica shut the door behind Bea, half wanting to go running after her and hug her tight and ask her to come back, half wanting to never have to answer another of Bea's questions.

Bea looked so much like Veronica and Timothy. She had Timothy's blond hair, and there was something about the shape of her face and the general expression that were all Timothy Macintosh, but the features were Veronica's. The round, pale brown eyes. The straight, pointy nose. Wide mouth. She had the hint of a cleft in her chin, like Timothy. She was tall, like both of them. Fine boned, like Veronica.

You have my nose, Veronica had thought over and over while she'd been sitting so close to Bea, trying not to stare. And my mouth. I see myself in your face.

Every time Bea smiled, which hadn't been often, she saw her own smile, with Timothy's long, even, white teeth.

She sat back down on the sofa, staring at Bea's teacup, the faintest bit of berry-colored lipstick on the rim.

The phone rang, and Veronica would have ignored it, but it might be Bea.

It was Nick DeMarco. Relief unwound the tight muscles of her shoulders.

"Just checking in," he said. "I know you were meeting with your birth daughter tonight."

Veronica burst into tears. She couldn't stop. She sat there, clutching the phone and crying, unable to speak.

"Veronica, I'm coming over. Just hang on."

She hung up the phone and buried her face in her hands. You're just overwhelmed, is all, she told herself.

She went into the bathroom for a tissue and dabbed under her eyes, but when she looked in the mirror, all she could think about was how much Bea looked like her, that the young woman who'd been sitting on her sofa fifteen minutes ago was the same six-pound weight Veronica had held against her chest in the ambulance twenty-two years ago.

The doorbell rang, and when Veronica opened the door, the sight of Nick, in jeans and a dark green Henley T-shirt, almost obliterated all other thought. The look in his eyes—concern, curiosity . . . interest, Veronica thought—was everything she needed right now. She did have friends, and she did open up to Shelley often, but she mostly kept to herself and never talked about the baby she'd given up for adoption or her travels the past twenty-two years. But Nick knew; he knew her from high school. He knew Bea had called her. He knew they'd met for the first time tonight. And here he was, standing on her doorstep, strong shoulders and all.

She couldn't remember the last time she had strong shoulders to lean on, and she was overtaken by the need for him to pull her into his arms and just hold her. He wouldn't of course, that would be crazy, but she wanted him to—and that scared her. She relied on no one.

"The two of you got together tonight?" he asked.

She nodded and stepped aside for him to come in. "I could use some coffee. Maybe a glass of wine."

"I'll have whatever you're having," he said. "Leigh's on a sleepover tonight at her friend's and will be going to school straight from their house, so I don't have to rush back."

"How are things with her grandparents?" she asked as she led the way into the kitchen.

"They call Leigh every day—sometimes I think more to check up on me than because they want to hear that she has double-digit multiplication homework. God forbid she didn't have eggs for breakfast—I'd never hear the end of it. And when she told them she was going on a sleepover tonight after having stayed at their house last night? They assume I pushed her into the sleepover so I could have 'women over.'"

"Oh, Nick, I'm so sorry you have to deal with all

that pressure. I figure it's hard enough to raise a girl on your own."

"Tell you the truth, it's not that hard. Mostly because Leigh's a great kid, but things are great at home. We have a routine, we have a great relationship. I give her what she needs, I'm there for her. But because I'm not her mother, because of the trouble between us when her mother died, I've been the enemy for two years, and now they're keeping a list of my infractions."

"Because of a Pop-Tart for breakfast? Or whatever wasn't 'eggs'?"

"She had a bowl of Cheerios and a glass of orange juice and that was too skimpy for them."

In the cabinet Veronica found a bottle of wine that Shelley had given her last Christmas. She wasn't much of a drinker, but she'd love some red wine right now. "I think we could both use a glass of this."

He sat down at the round table by the window, and Veronica was struck by how the moonlight filtering through the curtains rested on his dark hair, on his green shirt. "Anyway, forget my crazy life. Tell me about meeting your birth daughter."

"She's exquisite," Veronica said, handing him his glass of wine as she sat down across from him. "Lovely. She seems very intelligent, polite, kind. She had no idea she was adopted until just a month ago. She found out in a deathbed confession letter."

He raised his eyebrows. "Are both her parents gone?"

She nodded. "I can't imagine how shocking that letter must have been. She must have started questioning everything she knew about herself."

"She must have had a lot of questions for you."

"I had no idea how hard it would be to answer those questions, though. I don't want to tell her how awful it was back then, how my parents treated me, how her father treated me, how completely alone I was."

He took a slug of the wine and looked down at the table, then up at her. This time, she could read his expression: compassion. "Sixteen years old. You must have been so scared."

She also took a sip of wine. "I was. Sometimes, when I look back on that time, I don't know how I got through it."

He shook his head and was quiet for a moment. "I remember Timothy telling us—a group of his friends—that his girlfriend was saying he'd gotten her pregnant and that there was no way it was true. I wasn't sure what to think then."

She felt that old familiar stirring of shame, of embarrassment in her gut. "Because of my reputation?"

"Because Timothy was my friend and I didn't know you at all. He never brought you around us."

Veronica nodded. "He used to tell me he didn't want me to hang out with his friends because he hated what they thought they knew about me, he hated my reputation. He said he was never able to change it, make anyone think he was seeing me because he really liked me, not because I'd 'go all the way.'"

"I wasn't all that close with him; I was more a friend of a few of his close friends, but I remember how everyone would talk crap to him about getting lucky. God, I'm sorry, Veronica."

"Well, then I got pregnant and confirmed everyone's opinion of me. The slut got knocked up. I thought he'd stand by me, tell everyone that he was the only guy I'd ever been with, but I think he was so shocked, scared maybe, that he wanted to believe the worst so he could walk away, pretend it didn't involve him."

"So he told everyone he wasn't the father, that he used condoms, that it couldn't be his."

Veronica nodded. "I never saw or heard from him again. Not a word. The day after I told him I was pregnant, I was sent away, to Hope Home, the home for pregnant teenagers on the outskirts of Boothbay Harbor. My parents washed their hands of me—they even filed emancipation papers on my behalf. And then after I had the baby, I left the state. How can I tell Bea all this?"

"The truth is the truth, isn't it?"

Veronica shrugged and looked away. "When she was sitting right next to me, all I could think of was that she'd been that six-pound baby girl I got to hold for two minutes. Completely innocent, having nothing—and everything—to do with how she was brought into the world. I don't want her to know the truth. Even if she says she wants it."

"You're a good person, Veronica," he said, reaching for her hand and holding it. "I'm sorry I didn't know you back in high school. I'm sorry I wasn't your friend."

She started to cry again, and he was beside her in seconds, lifting her out of the chair and wrapping his arms around her, after all.

He held her for barely fifteen seconds, but it felt like forever—in a good way. She could smell his soap, the faint scent of laundry detergent, and the feel of his arms around her was better than anything she could have imagined.

She backed away, afraid that he'd kiss her when she couldn't handle it; the idea of it scared her so much that she moved across the room and turned her back to him. Thirty-eight years old and unable to act normal in front of a man. God.

"Should I go?" he asked, leaning against the counter, his hands in his pockets.

She turned around. "No. I'm just . . ."

"Overwhelmed?"

She nodded. "Exactly that, yes."

"Meeting your daughter is monumental, Veronica."

Yes. And so is being in your arms like that.

"My head feels like it's going to explode," she said.

"If you're all talked out, we can just watch a movie."

He'd surprised her. "That's exactly what I am. All talked out."

"That's two for two on reading you," he said.

He didn't seem to be flirting; there was gravitas in his expression. Compassion again. She hadn't been able to read him before, and it was unnerving that he was so good at reading her.

"A movie sounds perfect. Take us both out of our lives for a couple of hours." She thought about the film she had on deck for tonight. "Have you ever seen *A Single Man*? About a British professor grieving over the loss of his partner in the early 1960s? I missed it when it first came out, but now that I'm an extra on the Colin Firth movie shooting here in town, I plan to watch every one of his films. He was nominated for an Oscar for this role."

"I had no idea you were an extra for the movie. That's great. What's it like?"

She told him about mostly sitting around for two days, and how yesterday they'd started filming a scene in the meadow. "My job was to walk and check my watch at the same time, and I almost messed that up." She didn't have to mention the finger jabbing. She was glad to be finished with heavy conversation and memories.

"Well, let's celebrate your new gig by watching *A Single Man*, then. I haven't seen it."

And so fifteen minutes later, they sat in the living room, watching the opening credits of *A Single Man*, a slice of blackberry pie on a plate in front of him and two cups of coffee on the table. If anyone had told her a few weeks ago that one night in late June, she'd meet her birth daughter, tell Nick DeMarco her life story down to the last detail, then watch a movie with him, his feet up on the ottoman, his arm stretched out across the back of her sofa, his fingers brushing her own shoulder, she would have laughed. Now here they were.

"This pie is insanely good," he said, his fork cutting through another bite. "Is this one of your special kinds?"

"It's just plain old Happiness Pie."

"Nothing plain or old about happiness."

She smiled at him, a weight lifting off her shoulders—why, she wasn't sure. She just knew that she never wanted him to leave this room. As long as he didn't touch her or try to kiss her, that was. Yet, anyway.

Chapter 15

GEMMA

The morning light streaming in through the filmy curtains on the window in her room at the Three Captains' Inn woke Gemma, and she was surprised to find Alex in bed beside her. A full week away from him and she'd gotten used to hogging the center of the bed and the blanket. She'd gotten used to him not being there. And lately, yes, his not being there was a good thing. But the sight of him lying there, facing away from her, his broad, tanned back, the way his thick sandy-blond hair curled behind his ear, was still familiar and comforting.

They'd argued all night long, getting nowhere. They'd gone out to dinner, for Chinese food, since she was craving sesame chicken and fried dumplings, and she'd laid out her plan to him. She would find a great new job as a reporter, despite disclosing her pregnancy. She would work until the last minute, then take maternity leave. During her leave, they would line up a loving nanny with impeccable references, then she would return to work on schedule. They would alternate taking off for when the baby was sick or had an appointment with the pediatrician. Both of them would take off for in-school teacher conferences, concerts, and various holiday celebrations. She would not, under any circumstances, become like Caitlin Auerman, she'd added to herself.

"Absolutely not," he'd said after a long, hard stare.

"Yet my plan is exactly what you're planning to do, isn't it? Except you won't be taking maternity leave—no need, right? And I'll be your nanny, won't I? I'll be the one staying home with the baby. I'll be the one taking the baby to doctor's appointments."

"For God's sake, Gemma, you're not going to be the damned nanny. You're going to be the mother. Get that through your head."

"But your life doesn't change at all."

"Yes, it does. I'll be solely responsible for taking financial care of our family. I'll be a father. My entire life is going to change. How dare you say it won't?"

"You're not giving up everything you want. Why can't you see this?"

"Gemma, what are you giving up? You don't have a job. The timing couldn't be more perfect."

She'd known he would say exactly this.

"So if the roles were reversed," she said, "if it were you who'd lost your job, you'd be fine with staying home with the baby, being a stay-at-home dad, your entire life revolving around the baby instead of prosecuting criminals, pursuing justice, making a difference in the world."

"Gemma, you're pregnant. You don't have a job. You've sent out a bunch of résumés and haven't gotten a call back. How easily do you think you'd get your dream job when you have to disclose at an interview that you're pregnant?"

"Can we just eat," she said, stabbing her fork in a dumpling. She was surprised she didn't lose her appetite.

"Gem, I love you. We're going to have a baby. Aren't you happy about that at all? We're having a baby."

She put her fork down, tears stinging her eyes. "I'm not going to be a good mother anyway," she whispered. "I don't have a maternal bone in my body."

He reached across the table and took both her hands. "You do so. You're incredibly loving and kind and generous. You have a huge heart, Gem. You're going to be a great mother."

"I don't know where you get that faith from," she said, and as usual, that faith buoyed her up some, made her feel better. "Do you really think I'd be a good mother?"

"You will be a great mother. No doubt."

Now, the memory of how relieved she'd been to hear him say it, to hear in his voice how much he believed it, made her spoon against him in bed, her cheek against his warm shoulder. She wondered if he could be right, if she could work at it, develop maternal instincts. Maybe once you had the baby, hormones and biological impulses took over. She would love her baby, that much she knew. Maybe love was three-quarters of the battle, the big motivator.

He turned around to face her, lying on his side, and the streaming sunlight lit his hair. "How are you feeling, Gem? Tired?"

"Actually, I feel pretty good. I'm really looking forward to today's plans. I've got three interviews scheduled. One with a teenager who's giving her baby up for adoption, and two with residents of Boothbay Harbor who have strong opinions on Hope Home and the effect they feel the home has on the town. One woman thinks that a home for pregnant teenagers encourages teenagers to get pregnant, encourages a false sense of protectiveness. Another feels there should be a center in every county in the state." She was hoping to meet with at least one former resident of Hope Home who had lived there in the sixties or seventies, and Pauline was working on arranging interviews.

"I see you're in full reporter mode," Alex said. "But I meant how you're feeling physically. Don't you have anything to say about being pregnant? How it feels? Whether you think it's a boy or a girl? Names you've been thinking about? You've had a whole week to think, remember?"

"I've spent the week getting used to the idea of being pregnant at all. Not thinking names."

He leaned up on one elbow. "I'm thinking

Alexander Jr. if it's a boy. Gemma Jr. if it's a girl."

She raised an eyebrow. "Really? Gemma Jr.?"

He trailed a finger down her cheek. "I'd love a mini Gemma. With your beautiful face and that whip-smart mind."

She almost started to cry. "Why do you love me so much, Alex?"

"Because I do. And we're going to work through this. Somehow."

Somehow. Somehow they'd have to.

She kissed him, hard, and felt his hands travel under the blanket onto her stomach, then up, slowly, to her breasts.

"They're bigger," he said, wriggling his eyebrows at her.

"Oh, that's romantic."

He laughed and pulled the blanket over their heads, shifting himself on top of her, and somehow Gemma forgot all about interviews and baby names and the world.

After a fabulous breakfast of country omelets that Bea whipped up for them, Gemma walked Alex to his rental car in the driveway. She'd been dying to sneak into the kitchen to ask Bea how last night had gone with meeting her birth mother, but the dining room was packed with guests, and she knew Bea would be crazed in the kitchen. She'd find her after Alex left.

He lifted his face to the beautiful late June

sunshine. "The air up here is amazing. So fresh and clean. I'm not thrilled we're living three hundred miles apart, especially now that you're pregnant, but at least you're in a picture-postcard town. And maybe this place really will help you see things my way a little bit. Suburban life, slower pace, no killer taxis, everyone knows your name, playgrounds everywhere you look, pre-schools that cost less than a house."

"You're not supposed to be telling me your evil plan to get me to embrace moving to Westchester, Alex."

He smiled. "I just want us both to be happy. I don't know how we're going to work that out. But it's what I want."

"Me too."

He hugged her and kissed her good-bye, reminded her to take her prenatal vitamins and to stay away from Caesar dressing and unpasteurized cheeses, and then he was gone, the silver car turning on Main Street and disappearing out of sight.

By five o'clock, Gemma was exhausted and wanted to crawl right back into her comfortable bed at the inn, but she remembered Alex wouldn't be there to give her a massage—both back and foot. Suddenly, she didn't care about having the bed to herself and avoiding talk of suburbs and preschools. She'd forgotten how wonderful he could be, how much she could count on him, how good he could make her feel. But she had no idea how they could find a happy medium. Without her moving to Dobbs Ferry. Next door to Mona Hendricks.

She sat on the porch swing, resting her head against the rim and staring up at the beautiful puffs of clouds in the blue sky.

"Ready to go?"

Gemma sat up, glad to see her friend June standing in front of her car in the driveway, and her adorable nine-year-old son, Charlie, waving to Gemma from the backseat. Gemma grinned at him and waved back. They were headed to a birthday party for June's husband, Henry, at the bookstore they owned. A night off from working on the article, from thinking about her life, was just what she needed, and then later tonight was Movie Night again at the inn at nine o'clock.

Gemma loved Books Brothers, with its red canoe handle on the door. The moment you opened the door, you left the world behind. Low jazz played, and the rows of gleaming walnut bookshelves, overstuffed chairs and sofas, and the interesting artifacts and old books on shelves high up on the walls, made you want to stay and explore all day. By the checkout desk there were café tables, and a side table always held coffee canisters, milk and sugar, plus a plate of sample goodies. Now, for the party, that table held various bottles of wine and Champagne and juices, and a gorgeous buffet of appetizers. Gemma was about to grab two tiny pigs in a blanket when she remembered Alex saying hot dogs were full of nitrates and off-limits for the pregnancy. She went for the mini quiche Lorraine instead.

The party was crowded; Henry Books, June's husband, was a beloved fixture in town, even if he was on the quiet side and left managing the store to June, who loved her job. Gemma loved their story; almost ten years ago, Henry had employed June as a twenty-one-year-old who'd dropped out of college when she discovered she was pregnant, the father, a guy she'd had a whirlwind two-day love affair with, unable to be located. Apparently, Henry, ten years June's senior, had loved her from afar for years, but two years ago, after finally learning that her son's father had passed away long ago, June was ready to say good-bye to the past she'd held on to and open her heart to Henry. They lived on a big houseboat docked in the back of the store, and if only Gemma didn't get incredibly seasick every time she stepped on a boat, she might have loved staying with the Nash-Books family instead of at the inn.

Gemma watched them now, her dear old friend June with the long, curly auburn hair that Gemma had always coveted, speaking to her son with such love, such tenderness in her expression, as Charlie told a funny story about something that had happened at day camp. Henry was belly laughing and then scooped up Charlie and swung him around, accidentally bumping Isabel in the butt. Isabel whirled around and started tickling Charlie all over. They made family look so . . . inviting, reminding her of how she'd felt about the Hendricks clan before their warmth turned into suffocation. The Nash sisters weren't overbearing in the slightest, though. Gemma tried to picture herself and Alexander walking with their toddler holding their hands, and swinging him with an upsy-daisy. But she couldn't see it, couldn't see any of it. Any time she tried to imagine herself with a baby, she felt a heavy pressure in her chest.

"Stop being so demanding!" her mother would snap at her if she tried to tell her about something that had happened at school, or if she asked why her mother hadn't come to a chorus concert. "I have a full-time job, Gemma. You'll understand when you're an adult."

What she understood, now that she was an adult, was that she was just like her mother, no matter what Alexander said about her supposed big heart. If she had such a big heart, why would her job—a job she no longer had—come first? Why was her career more important to her than starting a family? Why wasn't she rejoicing in being pregnant, talking to her baby as she lay in bed at night?

Why wasn't she thinking of baby names?

Because you're scared. Scared of everything. Losing who you are. Not being able to do both— be the investigative reporter and a mother. Snapping at your little child for asking a question, for wanting more of you.

Gemma's chest began to constrict and she turned away, pouring herself a glass of cranberry juice and trying to stop her brain from going places she didn't want it to go. Focus on the party, she told herself. Look around for Claire, who was here somewhere.

But Gemma's attention focused on six-month-old Allie in the arms of Isabel's husband, Griffin. Theirs had also been a relationship that had taken work and compromise. Griffin, a divorced veterinarian, had met Isabel two years ago, when he and his daughters had been guests at the inn, the fourteen-year-old daughter angry at the world, and Isabel dealing with the end of her own marriage. Isabel hadn't thought she had what it took to be a mother either, but she wanted a family, wanted children, wanted a baby. She'd embraced stepmotherhood from the get-go, and now, with her own baby, Isabel seemed like the perfect mother to Gemma, the kind Gemma wished she could be. She watched Allie stretch out her arms for her mama, saw Isabel's eyes light up, watched how she took the baby with such joy, cuddling her against her pretty blue dress. Griffin put his arm around Isabel, and they both stared in happy wonder at their daughter.

This was how it was supposed to be. Maybe it really did just happen; maybe you could have no maternal instincts, no baby fever, no interest in motherhood, at the moment, anyway, but you had a baby, you looked at your baby's face, and you fell in love. Maybe that was how it was. Gemma sure hoped so. Because right now, she still didn't even feel pregnant. No flutter. Certainly no kicking yet, though her doctor and her *Your Pregnancy This Week* book had said that would come later on in the second trimester. It was helpful to Gemma to know that Isabel managed to work full-time at the inn, though granted, she had her baby at work most of that time. Gemma couldn't exactly bring her infant to a busy newsroom, tending to her baby with one hand while typing with the other.

We'll make it work. Somehow . . .

There was a big commotion, and Gemma saw that June and Isabel's cousin, Kat, who'd been living in France and working as a pastry chef for the past couple of years, had arrived with her long-term boyfriend, Oliver. According to June, they'd gotten engaged a couple of years ago, but Kat had broken it off to follow her dreams to leave her hometown and study baking in Paris. Kat and Oliver were holding hands and clearly very much in love. Kat, tall and blond and pretty, looked a lot like Oliver, also tall and blond. They kissed, and Gemma caught the lingering look they'd given each other.

Kat and Oliver had managed to make it work too, Gemma thought, swiping a mini potato and cheese pierogi from the buffet. She'd wanted one thing, he'd wanted another, and they'd made it work. Kat had left the country, of course, and broken off their engagement. But they were together.

Gemma had left the state. And there would be no breaking of anything—especially not vows. She and Alexander loved each other—that was not in question. And they both wanted the other to be happy—while being happy themselves. They both wanted this to work, and it would.

Gemma just couldn't see how.

Chapter 16

BEA

A few minutes before nine o'clock on Friday, Bea headed into the parlor of the Three Captains' Inn for Movie Night. Isabel was there, and June, and there was Gemma, sitting on the love seat and waving Bea over to the empty spot next to her. Bea hurried over before one of the members of the Colin Firth fan club could beat her to it. Bea had never been so glad for a familiar, friendly face. She'd spent last night tossing and turning for hours after her meeting with Veronica, and all day today she'd wandered around aimlessly, trying to figure out what she was uptight about.

What seemed to be bothering Bea the most was that going forward, she didn't know what she was supposed to do with Veronica Russo. Who was she to Bea? Last night, at Veronica's house, she was overcome with the notion that Veronica was a stranger. But she was hardly a stranger. For God's sake, she'd given birth to Bea. But now what? She'd get her biological father's contact information from Veronica, if she had it—or at least a place to start, since there were a few Macintoshes listed in the Boothbay Harbor phone book, and then what? Were she and Veronica supposed to be friends?

"Did you turn your phone off or something? I tried to call you a few times," Gemma said. "I'd love to hear how your evening went with your birth mother."

"It went . . . okay," Bea whispered back. "She's very nice. But it was a little strained for both of us. I told her that you were writing an article on Hope Home and would love to interview her, but she said she wasn't up for that."

"That's okay," Gemma said. "And thanks for asking her." She leaned closer. "Another reason I called is because Isabel mentioned that the Colin Firth movie we're watching is *Then She Found Me*. It's about a birth mother trying to connect with the daughter she gave up for adoption. I wanted to prepare you in advance. I saw it when it first came out in theaters, and it's a wonderful movie. But it might hit close to home."

"Maybe I'll learn something useful," Bea said, touched that Gemma had tried to call her.

Isabel and June, handing out popcorn around the room, introduced their cousin, Kat, who was visiting for the weekend. Kat was holding two bowls of popcorn, one with her arm against her chest, and Bea jumped up to help.

"Perfect—that one's for you guys on the love seat," Kat said. "Everyone have popcorn?" she asked, glancing around the room.

The Colin Firth fan club, three best friends from Rhode Island who were wearing their "Happiness

Is Colin Firth" T-shirts again, had taken over the big white sofa; three other guests, one of whom had the pickiest breakfast order that Bea had ever seen—hold the "this," add the "that"—were in overstuffed chairs; and Isabel, June, Kat, and Isabel's sweet elderly helper, Pearl, were on the padded folding chairs. Bea offered her seat to Pearl, but she said the chair was better for her back.

"I love that you're doing Movie Night again," Kat said to Isabel. "I feel like my mom is watching with us."

Isabel had told Bea that her aunt Lolly, Kat's mother, had left the three of them the inn when she'd died two years ago. Movie Night had been an inn tradition for years, and when Lolly had passed away, it had been Meryl Streep month, in honor of Lolly's favorite actress. Lolly had raised Isabel, June, and Kat after the death of her husband and the Nash sisters' parents in a car accident, and to the women, Movie Night and Lolly were synonymous.

June squeezed Kat's hand.

"I'll bet she is," Isabel said, standing up with the DVD and heading over to the console table. "Okay, everyone get ready for *Then She Found Me*, starring our Colin Firth, who has yet to make an appearance in town, unfortunately, and the wonderful Helen Hunt, Bette Midler, and Matthew Broderick."

Isabel shut off the lights, and Bea took a handful of popcorn. So much for leaving her thoughts behind and being swept away by a movie, but as she'd said to Gemma, maybe she would learn something, get some perspective.

Bea watched as Helen Hunt, who played a thirty-nine-year-old teacher in New York City, had her husband—Matthew Broderick—walk out her door the day before her mother dies. Then Helen's biological mother, played by a pushy Bette Midler, appears in her life, insistent on getting to know her, and Helen is resistant. She'd had a mother. Bette is a bit on the obnoxious side and makes up crazy stories about her father being Steve McQueen. When Helen gets involved with a student's father, played by Colin Firth, she starts to calm down, finding herself actually feeling happy. But then she realizes she's pregnant, a longtime dream, from a one-night stand with her own estranged husband, and she has to figure out all the pieces of her life.

"You okay?" Gemma whispered.

"Yeah," Bea whispered back. "Veronica's not pushy like Bette Midler at all. I told her I needed some time to process everything, and she hasn't called. Bette would have been at my door this morning. She'd be here now, pushing you out of the way."

Gemma smiled.

Bea wondered if Veronica felt like Bette did, if

she wanted Bea in her life, wanted to be close. Maybe she too needed some distance from Bea's questions about her biological father, about Veronica's parents.

Bea loved a scene in which Colin Firth attends a party for Bette Midler with Helen Hunt. She loved how protective he was of Helen, how clearly enamored with her he was. She was glad she had a date with Patrick tomorrow afternoon. Just a little something fun and sweet and romantic for her to have to herself.

But the more she watched, the more she realized that Veronica and Bette had something very much in common: the same hopeful look in their eyes.

Another evening of tossing and turning. Bea's alarm went off at five thirty on Saturday morning, and she felt awful. She'd been unable to stop thinking of Bette Midler, on her knees, begging for a chance, promising to do whatever Helen Hunt wanted. Maybe Bea had rushed out of Veronica's house too soon.

She trudged into the shower, which helped, then got dressed and slogged down the stairs to the kitchen, making omelets and waffles and today's special, blueberry pancakes. She cleaned the dining room tables, then swept and mopped the floor, imagining Veronica waiting by the phone, wondering if Bea would call back. With that hopeful expression.

They'd met on Thursday night. It was now Saturday.

She was so tired and just wanted to fling herself in bed for a good hour's nap, but before she could, she grabbed her phone and called Veronica.

"Veronica, it's Bea."

"I'm so glad you called."

Bea had done the right thing. She could hear the relief in Veronica's voice. "I thought maybe we could get together again. Dinner tomorrow night, if you're free?"

"I'd love to get together, Bea. But rather than have dinner, I'd like to take you on a tour."

"A tour? You mean of Boothbay Harbor?" Bea had already seen all the sights. She'd even taken a whale cruise around the bay. She didn't want to *ooh* and *aah* over lighthouses. She wanted to know the where, what, why, and how of her birth.

"A tour of my life when I was sixteen," Veronica said. "We'll start at the high school and end at the Greyhound bus station."

Bea's heart skipped a beat.

Two hours later, Bea was sitting inside the empty crew trailer on the movie set, still parked by Frog Marsh, waiting for Patrick for their lunch date, when the door burst open.

"I'm not going back, so don't waste your breath," Maddy Echols snapped to someone behind her.

Tyler, her brother. The grumpy production assistant.

He stared at Bea. "What are you doing in here?"

"Meeting Patrick for lunch."

He rolled his eyes, then turned to his sister, who'd stormed in and sat down on a narrow bench. "Maddy, you are going back. You want to take sophomore English when you're a junior?"

She pushed her long hair behind her shoulders. "Leave me alone. I can't understand a word of the stupid book. I'm not reading it."

"I bought you the CliffsNotes to help you."

"So now I have to read that too?" she shouted.

He threw up his hands. "Fine, fail the class. Fail high school. Drop out."

Bea realized she was watching them as though she were at a tennis match. Both spoke in the same rapid-fire way. They looked nothing alike, of course; Maddy was petite, with wavy, dark brown hair and huge hazel-green eyes, and Tyler was tall and angular, with that mop of sandy-blond hair. She'd give Tyler twenty-three, maybe twenty-four. He had a dimple in his left cheek, which she probably hadn't noticed before because he never smiled. But the chewing on the inside of his cheek brought it out. He cared about his sister, that was obvious.

"I don't mean to eavesdrop," Bea said, "but since I'm sitting right here . . . I assume you're talking about *To Kill a Mockingbird* again?"

Maddy turned to her. "You mean 'To Kill a Boring Bird.'"

That got her Tyler's trademark eye roll. "It's a great book," he told his sister. "One of my favorites."

"Like we're so similar," Maddy muttered.

"Maddy, I graduated from college—Beardsley—last year with an English degree," Bea said. "I'm planning to be an English teacher. Middle school or high school. I've read *To Kill a Mockingbird* at least five times since I was a sophomore in high school, and like I said, I wrote my senior thesis on it. I could help you, talk you through the themes of the book or whatever's giving you trouble."

Tyler was watching her, she knew.

"You're in summer school, I presume," Bea said to Maddy.

"And if she doesn't pass the class by reading the book and writing an essay with a grade of B minus or better," Tyler said, staring hard at his sister, "she fails and will have to take sophomore English again when she's a junior in the fall. Then she'll end up short of English credits to graduate."

"So what?" Maddy said. "It's not like I'm necessarily going to college. I don't need to read 'To Kill a Stupid Bird' in order to backpack around Italy."

"I backpacked around Italy the summer I graduated from high school," Bea said. "I had the most amazing time."

Maddy's face lit up. "Really? I'm obsessed with Rome. I want to see the Colosseum, throw coins in the Trevi Fountain. See the statues of angels. And the Sistine Chapel."

"If you pass this class, I'll take you," Tyler said, gritting his teeth.

The girl stared at him. "Seriously?"

"Seriously. You pass the class and I'll take you to Italy. You'll see the Sistine Chapel."

She wanted that trip, Bea could see. Bad. Bad enough to pass the class.

"You can help me?" Maddy said to Bea.

"We don't even know her," Tyler said, clearly mimicking Bea from the other day. Though it was true.

"I'm staying in town for the next few weeks. At the Three Captains' Inn. I tutor at Beardsley during the school year, so I'm experienced. Here's my ID from the Writing Center." She took it from her wallet and handed it to him.

He studied it, then handed it back to her. "Maddy, can you wait for me outside for a second?"

Now that Italy was on the table, Maddy jumped at his request.

When the door closed behind her, he said, "How much do you charge?"

"If I wasn't broke, I'd offer to do it for free," she said. "But I'm working for my room and minimum wage at the inn, so I really could use some extra cash. Fifty bucks an hour."

"Fifty bucks? Jesus." He moved aside the little curtain at a window and peered out at Maddie, who had her compact out and was reapplying her gooey lip gloss. He let the curtain drop. "Fine. But I want you to work with her in the library—not our om's house or here. I want her to take this seriously."

"Okay. The library it is."

He pushed his wire-rimmed glasses up on his nose. "The class ends in three weeks. I'm thinking once a week for an hour should be fine."

"So you're from Boothbay Harbor?" she asked.

"Two towns over," he said, as though giving personal information was a hardship for him. "The high school's regional."

The door pounded. "Hello, I'm sweating out here," Maddy shouted.

"One sec," he called out. "When can you start?"

"Whenever you want."

"How's Wednesday? I take her out to dinner every Wednesday night so I know it works for both our schedules."

Fifty bucks would buy a nice outfit at the consignment shop for the dinner cruise Patrick told her he wanted to take her on sometime soon.

"Meet her at the Boothbay Harbor library at five," Tyler said. "Will that work?"

She nodded, and he stepped toward the door, then turned back to her.

"Don't bring up the birth mother thing," he said. "She'll get angry and distracted."

"Okay."

He headed for the door, then turned back. "Did you meet yours yet?"

"I don't really want to talk about it with you," she said.

He stared at her, then shrugged and went down the step.

Patrick had time only for a twenty-minute lunch, but Bea didn't mind. It was fun to eat in the air-conditioned trailer, watch the occasional assistant come in, then dart out when it was clear this was a private lunch. Over Italian subs, he told her about production schedules and call sheets, which listed where and when the actors had to show up. He explained he was something of a backstage manager, making sure everything was as it should be for filming the scene.

She liked him. A lot. He was good looking and smart and responsible for quite a bit on this film. He asked right away how meeting her biological mother was, and when she told him she'd rather talk about him, he still tried to keep the conversation about her. She told him more about losing her way last year, after her mother's death, and that she planned to apply to a hundred schools if she had to for a job as an English teacher. He said he thought it was noble, that teachers should make more money. She liked the way he looked at her, his intelligent blue eyes full of interest, respect . . . desire for her.

He was called away to douse yet another fire, as he put it, but not before he kissed her on the lips. "The next few days are going to be crazy all day, but maybe you could come by my hotel Tuesday night. For a late dinner around eight? I won't be back till right before then, and have to get up at the crack of dawn, but I'd love to sit on my balcony with you and have some great room-service fancy dinner and just talk. And I mean that—just talk. This isn't some ploy to get you in bed. Not that I don't think you're incredibly beautiful, Bea."

She smiled, and he kissed her good-bye, a sweet kiss on the lips. This was perfect. Now she'd have something exciting to look forward to, especially if Veronica's "tour" was too much, too hard to take in. And Bea was sure that it would be.

Chapter 17
VERONICA

Veronica sat in her car in the driveway of the Three Captains' Inn at noon on Sunday, reminding herself that she was here as much to deliver three pies as she was to pick up Bea for the tour of her life. She got the pies out of her trunk, her monthly invoice for June in an envelope taped to the top box. The box labeled blueberry reminded her of Nick; he'd mentioned that Leigh had caught a bad cold on Friday, and Veronica had baked a special Feel Better Pie—blueberry—and brought it over Friday evening. Nick's house was a white clapboard cottage not too far from downtown. Leigh had been propped up on the sofa, watching *How to Train Your Dragon*, and she'd invited Veronica to come watch with them, but Nick hadn't seconded the invitation. Veronica wasn't sure if two movies in two nights with her would be one too many, or if maybe their evening together on Thursday had been a bit too unexpected. He'd left soon after *A Single Man* had ended, giving her a squeeze of the hand when she'd expected a kiss. Not that she'd been ready for a kiss from Nick DeMarco—talk about loaded—but if she was honest with herself, she wanted him to want to kiss her. She wanted him to want her.

Because he represented her past? Because she hadn't been accepted back then? Because the one guy who had accepted her—someone Nick had been friends with—had turned around and betrayed her? Or maybe it was much scarier than any of those reasons. Maybe she just . . . liked Nick.

Boxes of pies in her hands, she headed up the pretty stone path to the porch of the inn. For almost a year now she'd been making weekly deliveries of her pies to the Three Captains', and the beautiful Victorian was as familiar as her own house, but now her birth daughter was inside. Waiting for her in the parlor to go on a tour of Veronica's life at age sixteen.

This was your idea, she reminded herself, placing the pies on the table inside the foyer, where she always left them for Isabel. She went into the parlor, but Bea wasn't there yet. The inn smelled wonderful, the hint of bacon and warm bread in the air. From where she sat on the love seat, she saw Bea appear at the landing of the stairwell, in a pale pink tank top and jeans, and Veronica stood up as Bea came into the room.

"So you're responsible for how good it smells in here?" Veronica asked as they headed toward the front door. She was surprised she could make small talk right now.

"If I do say so myself—yes. And the dining room has been closed since ten o'clock too—

brunch hours for Sunday. Everyone wanted bacon this morning—I must have fried up five pounds. If you smell bread, it's Isabel's doing—she's taking bread-baking lessons from the owner of the Italian bakery. Hot crusty Italian bread with butter? Nothing better."

"She's taking my pie class too," Veronica said as she opened the passenger door of her car for Bea. "With all her new skills, she may put me out of business."

"Your pies are a big hit at the inn, especially at tea time. Isabel says no one could ever come close to touching your pies. I wanted to tell her that Veronica Russo, pie maven, is my biological mother, but I know you probably want to keep that private."

Veronica hated how tight her expression must seem. Why did she want to keep it a secret? A holdover from how her parents had made her feel? From how her one trip into town, at seven months pregnant, had made her feel? Ashamed. Dirty. Damaged. The whispers and stares of people she knew, of strangers, had been unbearable.

Bea buckled her seat belt. "Are you sure you really want to take me on this tour? If it's too much for you, I'll understand."

"It will be too much for me," Veronica said. "And that's probably a good thing. I came back to Boothbay Harbor to face my past, to stop running from it. But being here alone hasn't been enough—I've kept a year of my life balled up inside me, locked up tight. I need to . . . let myself remember."

Veronica drove the short distance to the high school, which was located far down Main Street. She passed it all the time but rarely let herself look at the building. She'd hated who she'd been there, how she'd felt in those halls and classrooms. Only for five brief months, when she'd been Timothy Macintosh's girlfriend, had none of that mattered. She'd walked the halls with her head high, and for the first time, she'd felt as though nothing could touch her, hurt her.

She pulled into the parking lot and stared up at the school. "When I look back on it now, it seems crazy that I was in love with Timothy after just a few months of dating, but you know how it is when you're sixteen. The weight of a day feels like a month, everything happens so fast and with such intensity."

Bea nodded. "I'm embarrassed to say it's still like that for me."

"You have his smile," Veronica said. "My mouth, but his smile. I loved his face so much I could just stare at him for hours. He had light blond hair, exactly like yours, and the most beautiful hazel eyes. He was a bit of a rebel but not a troublemaker. He wore a beat-up black leather jacket that smelled like his soap, and if it was remotely chilly, he'd give it to me. I used to love wearing that jacket."

"His name was Timothy Macintosh, you said?"

She nodded. "Everyone was always so surprised by the quiet guy in the leather jacket with his head down suddenly raising his hand to ask intelligent questions or give right answers. I had such a crush on him, and when he asked me out, I said no at first. I was so used to being asked out because of my reputation—because of the lies spread about me, first by a group of mean girls who didn't like the way the popular boys were following me around, and then by the boys who made up stories about sleeping with me. And I told him so. I told him off, actually—it was the first time I'd ever done that, stood up like that. But he insisted he liked me for me and that he wouldn't even try to kiss me for a month if I went out with him."

"Did you hold him to that?"

"I sure did. But he didn't try. We spent so much time together that first month too. He didn't try once."

Bea smiled. "I love that."

"Me too," Veronica said, lost in the sweet memory for a moment. "We had such honest conversations—about how we felt, about school, our teachers, our parents, the world, government, everything. He came from a rougher background than I did, and I cared so much about him that I wanted to take him away from all that by just loving him with all my might."

"Did you?"

"For five months, I did. And then I found out I was pregnant." She started the car and drove the three miles to the house she'd grown up in, pulling over across the street. "See that blue house, number forty-nine? That's where I grew up. My period was late, over a week, and I was shaking when I took the pregnancy test. I was so scared when that plus sign appeared. I told myself it couldn't be true—we'd used condoms. But I took another one later in the day, and it was positive too. It took me two days to work up the nerve to tell my mother. I was so afraid to say the words out loud. But then while my parents and I were having pancakes one morning, I blurted it out."

Bea was staring from the house to Veronica. "And they didn't take it very well."

"Understatement of the year. I'll never forget the expression on my mother's face," Veronica said, the memory so vivid that as she repeated her mother's words, verbatim, to Bea, it was as if she was reliving it right now.

"Your grandmother is rolling over in her grave right now," her mother had screamed, her father just shaking his head and muttering, "How could you be so stupid, so careless?" Over and over.

Veronica had wished with everything inside her that her grandmother was still here, that she could tell her everything. She knew her grandmother would have wrapped her arms around Veronica, told her everything would be okay, that they'd get through this, that they were Russos, and Russos were strong.

All she had was her mother, pointing her finger in Veronica's face and saying, "This makes you trash. No better than Maura's trashy daughter who got pregnant and now has a toddler at seventeen. And I won't stand for it."

Veronica had stood there, shocked.

"Just what the goddamned hell is everyone going to think?" her mother had said, shaking her head. "Goddammit." And she reached out and slapped Veronica across the face.

Veronica winced as though her mother had slapped her right now.

"Oh, Veronica," Bea said.

"I ran—to the one place that felt safe: my and Timothy's 'spot.'" Veronica started the car and drove back to Main Street, not too far from the high school, and parked across the street from Seagull Lane, a brick alleyway leading to the bay. The place where she and Timothy had kissed, finally, for the first time. Their meeting spot.

The place where she'd told him she was pregnant.

"I found a pay phone and called him," Veronica said, "barely able to speak for the sobs coming from so deep inside me. He'd rushed to meet me—right there," she added, pointing to the alleyway. "And I was so scared to tell him. Despite how close we were, all we'd talked about, the plans we made to run away together after high school, I was afraid to say the words. His mother had gotten pregnant at sixteen, and she had a hard life because of it, and I knew he'd be very upset at the news."

"What did he say?" Bea asked.

"He didn't say anything for the longest moment. Then he told me it couldn't possibly be his baby. He said a lot of other things." She closed her eyes for a second. "But it was his. Couldn't possibly be anyone else's. I was so shocked, so hurt, then I went back home, in a daze, and my mother told me to pack my bags, that there was a spot for me at Hope Home. I was gone the next day."

"The next day," Bea repeated. "I can't believe how fast it all happened. I can't imagine what you were going through."

Veronica drove the five miles to Hope Home, the long dirt driveway and pretty white farmhouse with its porch swing still so familiar. There had still been some snow on the ground when she'd arrived as a sixteen-year-old in early April. "This was actually a bright spot. I lived here for seven months."

Veronica told Bea what it was like back then at Hope Home, how some girls had been sent away because their families were embarrassed to have a pregnant teenage daughter, but that most parents visited every week with care packages full of treats and L.L.Bean sweaters and books about pregnancy and what was happening in your body, even though the Hope Home library was full of them. And those girls had gone back home after their babies were born and adopted, stories made up about two semesters away as foreign exchange students.

She explained how no one had visited her in the seven months she'd been there. How her mother had called twice—once, her voice strained, to see if she needed anything, and another time to let her know the family dog had died. Even after that, when her mother had clearly wanted Veronica to feel worse than she already did, Veronica had hoped she'd call again, but she hadn't. And any time Veronica called home, no one picked up or returned her calls. So she'd eventually stopped calling.

"Oh God," Bea said, and Veronica was aware that Bea was trying to catch her eye. "You must have been so lonely."

Veronica kept her gaze on the white farmhouse, on the swing. "Well, to tell you the truth, my parents always made me feel lonely, even before I got pregnant. They were always on the cool side, difficult to get to know, very proper, impersonal. My mother found someone just like herself in my father. They even brought up the idea for me to get emancipated so that they wouldn't be held liable in any way."

Bea shook her head. "But you had friends at Hope Home?"

Veronica nodded. "Some of the girls didn't get along all the time, but generally we did. The staff was wonderful."

"Good," Bea said. "I'm very glad to hear that. You went into labor at Hope Home but I started coming while you were in the ambulance?"

"I was screaming my head off—in so much pain, scared out of my mind—but the EMT guy who delivered you was great to me. He said there wouldn't be time to get to the hospital, and he coached me through the whole thing. Then suddenly, there you were. I got to hold you for two minutes, and then he took you to clean you up."

"What about on the way to the hospital?" Bea asked. "Were you able to hold me again?"

"The social worker who accompanied us said safety regulations prohibited it and that besides, it wouldn't be a good idea."

"So you wanted to?"

Veronica sucked in a breath. "Yeah."

Bea was quiet for a moment. "Did you ever consider keeping me?"

Veronica didn't answer; she drove off again, this time to Coastal General Hospital. She parked in the main lot, and they both glanced up at the stately brick building. "I had fantasies about it. Of running away with you. But I was sixteen and had nowhere to go, no family, nothing. And the social workers were very good at their jobs, reassuring me that I was doing the best thing for you, that I was being selfless and not selfish."

"So what happened after I was born? Did you ever get to see me again?"

Veronica glanced away. She didn't like these questions. "Just once. On my way out of the hospital. Even though I was told I shouldn't look, that it might be too painful, for my last memory to be of leaving you. And that nurse was right. Even thinking about how I'd held you those two minutes in the ambulance was enough to do me in. So I learned to close it all off. After a while, I had trouble even conjuring it up at all."

Bea was quiet for a moment. "So after you left the hospital, then what?"

"I went back to Hope Home to pack my things for the trip to Florida. And before I left, I called the adoption agency and left my name for the file and said I'd call to update when I found a place to live. I felt like if I didn't leave my name, one day it would feel like it never happened at all, that I didn't give birth to a baby girl. But on the way to Florida, I ended up working damned hard to make myself feel exactly that way—like it didn't happen."

"I can understand that," Bea said. "After all you'd gone through. How did you make it on your own in Florida? How did you even get there? You weren't even seventeen."

This was easier to talk about. She started the car again, driving to the Greyhound bus station in Wiscasset. "I was an emancipated minor at that point, thanks to my parents preparing the paperwork for me. I had around six hundred dollars saved from my part-time job, so I asked for a ride to here and bought a one-way ticket to Florida."

"Why Florida?"

Veronica explained that Florida was about an old dream of her grandmother's, where there were no blizzards and lots of orange groves. Even though Veronica loved winter, loved snow, she'd always thought the hot and sunny orange-filled dream sounded magical. Once there, she lied about her age, got a waitressing job, something familiar, and found a nice female roommate in an apartment complex with palm trees and a pool. She'd stayed in Florida for a year, had a boyfriend or two, no one she'd loved, and certainly no one she'd tell her story to. When one of her boyfriends accused her of cheating on him, something Veronica had never done in her life, it had reminded her of Timothy and she'd packed up again. By then she'd been almost eighteen and wouldn't have to lie about her age. Things would get easier. She'd headed west, crossing the south, staying for months at a time in various towns until she'd hear about someplace and pack up. She'd stayed in New Mexico the longest, but then her former beau had ditched her in Las Vegas when she wouldn't marry him, and she'd known she had to come back home if she ever hoped to fix herself.

"I half expect you to drive us to Florida right now," Bea said, smiling.

Veronica smiled back.

"Did you talk to your mom again?"

"I tried over the years, calling on her birthday, my father's birthday. Christmas. But the conversations were stilted. No matter how many years passed, they couldn't forgive me, couldn't move on." Veronica drove the fifteen minutes back to her house, parking in front of it. "Then I moved here."

Just before she'd moved to Boothbay Harbor she'd called her mother to let her know she was moving back home, that she was hoping to put her past to rest. Her plan had been to finally do what she should have done long ago: give up on her mother the way her mother had given up on her. Of course, the moment she'd heard her mother's voice, she still longed for her, for something to change. But it hadn't. In twenty-two years, Veronica had come to understand something about limitations, that sometimes, even when you needed them most, the people you loved couldn't rise to the occasion. Not wouldn't. Couldn't. Her mother's response to her call: "I think too much time has gone by, Veronica, but I wish you well," and Veronica had hung up, the breath knocked out of her. Good Lord, it was no wonder she was the way she was. With a heart that didn't work right.

"I'll drop you back at the inn," Veronica said. She was spent. Even more so than she thought she'd be.

When they pulled up to the Three Captains', Bea said, "Thank you for all that. I wanted to know, and though some of it wasn't easy to hear, I'm glad I know the truth. Are you all right?"

"I'll be fine. How about you?"

Bea nodded. "I'll be okay. I just need to digest it all. I have a date, so that'll help. I guess I should mention that I'm dating someone who works on the film. Patrick Ool. He seems like a great guy. We've only gone out once."

The two worlds entwining seemed strange. "Oh yes, I know Patrick. He's in charge of the extras. I don't really know him, but he treats us very well, makes sure we know what we're doing and that we're comfortable."

"I haven't told him that you're my birth mother," Bea said. "I mean, I've told him that meeting my birth mother is the whole reason I'm in town and that you're an extra on the movie, but I didn't mention your name. I'll absolutely keep your privacy."

"Thanks. I don't know if it matters, but like I said, I haven't shared the fact that I gave up a baby for adoption with many people, so I do like the idea of keeping that private."

She was so exhausted. Why didn't she feel better? Why didn't facing her past this way, going back over everything, make her suddenly open up inside?

She glanced at Bea, whose expression had changed. Did it bother Bea that Veronica wanted to keep it private? Veronica had spent so long keeping her past to herself, not talking about it, keeping it locked up tight. "Bea? Did I say something to upset you?"

"I'm just thinking about my mother. About all the times she might have told me—when I was two, three, four years old. She wanted to wipe all that away, pretend the adoption never happened. She made it so for herself—and for me."

Veronica wanted to say something, about how love and hope and need could sometimes make you do—or not do—what you knew you should. Sometimes to protect others. Sometimes to protect yourself. But she didn't dare say anything about Bea's mother, the woman who'd raised her. And all she really knew about Cora Crane was that she'd done a beautiful job as a mother, raising the wonderful young woman who'd just been on a tour of Veronica's life at sixteen.

"Now what?" Bea said. "I mean, I'm not even sure what we're supposed to be, who we are to each other."

"We're a part of each other's history."

"I guess that doesn't necessarily have anything to do with the future, though."

It was a statement and not a question, Veronica noticed, her heart constricting.

Bea bit her lip and got out of the car. "Thank you for today, Veronica," she said through the open passenger window. "I know it had to be very hard on you."

Doesn't necessarily have anything to do with the future . . . So was that it? Would she never hear from Bea again? "It was worth it."

Bea sucked in a breath. "I just don't know how I'm supposed to feel about you. I'd better get going. Thank you again for today," she said, then hurried into the inn.

I know how I feel about you, Veronica thought, watching Bea disappear through the front door. How I've always felt about you, since the moment you were placed on my chest as a newborn.

Veronica loved Bea, always had. And she knew then that that was what she'd been unable to face all these years.

After half a day on the movie set on Monday, Patrick Ool, whom Veronica could not look at without thinking of Bea, dismissed the extras because of a lighting issue. She was glad to leave; she felt a bit claustrophobic in the tent with the crowd and white material and her thoughts closing in on her. On the way home, she stopped at the farmers' market for peaches for tonight's pie class, and stocked up on strawberries and Key limes for special pies she needed to make this week.

At home, she placed the peaches she'd bought in two big bowls on the island counter, but even the beautiful, fresh peaches, one of Veronica's favorite summer fruits, couldn't shake the unsettled feeling lodged in Veronica's chest, in her heart.

I'm not sure what we're supposed to be, how I'm supposed to feel about you.

It was complicated. And not.

Would she never hear from Bea again? Had Bea found what she'd come for, answers to her questions, a person to put to the reality of the words *birth mother,* and now she'd leave, no interest in forging a relationship?

She understood Bea's problem; she wasn't sure what they were supposed to be to each other either. They were not mother and daughter. They were not . . . friends. They were connected in a biological, fundamental way, though. Perhaps Bea would decide biology did not a relationship make. But for Veronica, Bea had never been about biology and birth. She'd always been about the future—a future Veronica hadn't been able to be part of.

The doorbell rang, and Veronica hoped it would be Nick and Leigh. He hadn't called to say if he was coming or not, and with a kitchen full of students, she wouldn't be able to talk to him about her personal life, anyway, but the sight of him would help. She wished that was only because he was so attractive to her, but it went further than that. What she was beginning to feel for Nick DeMarco felt a lot like need.

When she opened the door, Nick and Leigh stood on the porch, Leigh carrying a pie wrapped in plastic. Thank you, Veronica whispered silently to the universe.

"I made you a chocolate pudding pie," Leigh said, holding out both her hands. "It doesn't do anything. It's just good. Or, at least I hope it is. I made one yesterday too, but I forgot the vanilla, I think. I remembered everything this time."

Veronica smiled and took the pie. "I love chocolate pudding pie, and I'm touched you made this for me. Thank you."

She was aware of Nick watching her, and his face, his body, his presence, had its usual effect. She felt a combination of relief, happiness, and something fluttery in her stomach, like butterflies or good nervousness.

"Leigh, if you want to head into the kitchen and choose your apron and start reading over the recipe on the island counter, go right ahead. We're making peach pie tonight. I'm putting you in charge of measuring out the dry and wet ingredients."

"I love peaches!" Leigh said, disappearing into the kitchen.

Veronica closed the door behind Nick. "I'm glad you two are here."

"I thought about not coming," he said. "But then I remembered that when you let people try to control you, to dictate how you should live, you've given up. I might be a little afraid of Leigh's grandparents, I admit it, but I'm not afraid of pie."

She smiled and wanted to hug him. Luckily, the phone rang, keeping her from making possibly unwanted displays of affection, and she went into the kitchen to answer it. It was Isabel, reporting that neither she nor June could make it to class; June, her husband, Henry, and their son, Charlie, all had bad colds, and Isabel was playing nursemaid at their houseboat.

The doorbell rang, and there was Penelope, once again looking toned down, less brassy, less showy. She was petite and thin as always, but the mass of expensive jewelry was gone. She wore a simple gold cross around her neck. Her clothes were more conservative. And her perfectly highlighted hair wasn't flat-ironed to model perfection as usual, but instead seemed . . . natural. Also once again, Penelope was as friendly as could be, complimenting Leigh on her T-shirt and hair, telling Nick he was doing a fine job keeping the citizens of Boothbay Harbor safe, and thanking

Veronica for offering "such a fun and informative pie class."

With her three students around the center island, they set to work on the peach pie, Nick and Penelope on slicing, and Leigh on measuring out the dry and liquid ingredients. Unless Veronica was imagining things, Penelope kept staring at her. When Veronica would glance over, Penelope would smile fast, then shift her eyes away. Veronica had long ago given up on wondering what was going on in Penelope Von Blun's mind. Back in high school, Penelope had ignored her completely; she hadn't been mean to her, she simply pretended Veronica didn't exist. But over the past year, if Veronica saw her around town, or in the diner, like the other day, Penelope would stare at Veronica, or whisper to her mother. Maybe those days were over.

"Mmm, this smells so good," Leigh said, closing her eyes and inhaling over her mixing bowl, the smell of peaches, nutmeg, vanilla, and brown sugar fragrant in the air.

Penelope poured the filling into the crust, and Nick laid the top crust over the pie, then pressed the edges together. When the pie went into the oven, Veronica spent fifteen minutes talking about piecrust again, how technique was the most important part of making the crust, the not overworking, the not kneading, and then they practiced making lattice tops because Leigh wanted to, even though their peach pie didn't require a lattice top.

"So, did everyone's shoofly pie work?" Leigh asked, dipping her finger against the sides of the bowl and licking the bit remaining. "Mine did. But I'm not supposed to talk about it. Oops," she said, putting her hand over her mouth.

"You can talk about whatever you want," Nick said. "I'm glad the pie works for you. I'm glad for whatever makes you feel close to your mother."

"Grandma thinks it's voodoo nonsense, though," Leigh said. "I told her what we put in the pie, every ingredient, and even though there's nothing black-magicky about anything in the pie, she still said it was the idea, not the ingredients."

"I think it's like prayer," Penelope said suddenly. She'd been a bit quiet for the past forty-five minutes. "It's just about comfort, that's all."

"Did it work for you?" Leigh asked Penelope.

"I don't know," Penelope said, and she looked very sad for a second.

The timer dinged, and Veronica had Nick pull out the oven rack so that Penelope could make three slashes in the top of the pie. Then they turned down the temperature of the oven and the pie went back in for another thirty minutes.

"What about you, Veronica?" Leigh said. "Did having the shoofly pie help you feel closer to your grandmother?"

"It always does," Veronica said. "Even just

looking at shoofly pie, that crumbly brown sugar topping, makes me think of Renata Russo. I can smell her Shalimar perfume as though she's right next to me. I can hear her voice, stories she used to tell me about when she was a girl and learned to bake pies. I can feel her with me, and it's like Penelope said—it's pure comfort."

"That's how I felt every time I ate my shoofly pie," Leigh said. "Like my mom was right there with me. Sometimes it just felt like she was in me, though. That's just as good."

"It sure is," Nick said, running his hand down his daughter's pretty brown hair.

A half hour later, the pie came out and they waited as long as they could for it to cool, and then Nick served a slice to everyone. Everyone declared it delicious, and Veronica divided the leftovers between the DeMarcos and Penelope. At eight thirty, the class was over, and Nick said he'd better get his little pastry chef home to bed, that she had camp the next morning. Veronica didn't want them to leave. She liked having Nick in her house, in her kitchen, and she adored Leigh.

"Talk to you soon," Nick said, his gaze lingering on her for a moment.

As she stood by the open door, watching Nick and Leigh walk to his car, Veronica realized that Penelope wasn't behind them.

Veronica found her in the kitchen, sweeping the

floor. "Oh, Penelope, that's thoughtful, but I'll do that."

Penelope put the broom back in its wedge of space by the back door, then went to the sink, wet a paper towel, and began wiping down the island counter. "You lived at Hope Home back when you were in high school, right?"

If Penelope Von Blun was cleaning, ostensibly even, this wasn't about bringing up Veronica's past as a pregnant sixteen-year-old. This was about Penelope. Veronica sensed this conversation called for tea, and she added water to the kettle and set it to boil. "Yes, for seven months."

"Did . . . any of you girls talk about the kind of parents you wanted to adopt your babies?"

Ah. Now Veronica had an idea what this was about.

"Most of us had closed adoptions, so it's not like we could pick and choose, but we talked about it, of course."

Penelope scrubbed at a clean expanse of counter. "And what was it that all of you seemed to want in adoptive parents?"

"Well, we wanted the parents to be loving and kind. Lacking in bad tempers, like some of our fathers."

"What else?" There was desperation in Penelope's voice.

Veronica shut off the burner and poured the water over Earl Grey tea leaves in the teapot.

"That's it, really. Loving seemed to be the key word."

Penelope stopped scrubbing. "But how would you know if someone was loving. I mean, you'd have to really get to know them, right? It's not something you can just tell from a few brief meetings."

"You can generally tell someone's disposition right away, though, don't you agree?"

Penelope looked like she was about to cry. She flung the balled-up paper towel on the counter. "My husband and I have tried for years to get pregnant. And now I'm thirty-eight and my chances are slimmer and slimmer. So we decided to look into adoption, and I know there are so many couples hoping for a baby—we were told it could take a long time. But then a girl from Hope Home chose us. I can't tell you how happy I was, maybe happier than I've been in my entire life. But now she might be unchoosing us. She likes my husband, but says she's not sure I'm the right mother for her baby, after all." She turned away and covered her face with her hands.

Oh dear. "Why did she choose you and your husband in the first place?"

Penelope looked up at Veronica. "To be honest? Because we're wealthy. The girl comes from the wrong side of the tracks, had a rough, impoverished childhood—she's still a child—and it's very important to her that her baby be raised with

316

wealth, that he or she never want for anything—whether breakfast or an iPhone. It's important to her, and she wants a wealthy, Catholic family from Boothbay Harbor only. So we finally fit the bill for a birth mother. But then she met us, and I tried to be what she wanted, but the more time we spent with her, the more dissatisfied with me she seemed to get."

Veronica poured two cups of tea and gestured for Penelope to sit. "What do you think her issue is?"

"My husband says I'm coming across as forced, that I need to be myself. But I know what kind of image I project—snobby. I'm trying to change that."

I noticed, Veronica thought. But it can't be fake.

Penelope added cream and a sugar cube to her tea. "I know I'm not the friendliest person there ever was. And maybe I have a reputation of being snobby. But I'd love this baby with all my heart—and my heart is big, Veronica. I might not show it to everyone, but my husband knows it. And my mother. My sister too—I'd do anything for my family. And this baby, this precious angel I want to love and raise and share my life with—I'll be the most loving mother. I know that more than I've ever known anything."

"You need to tell her this, Penelope. You need to say it just like you said it here. You need to tell her from here," Veronica said, touching her chest. "It needs to be more than words to her. She needs to hear you mean it."

"I've tried—three times. She doesn't like me." Tears shimmered in Penelope's eyes.

"I think you should go see her. Just you. The real you, not this toned-down false you. You in all your real Penelope Von Blun glory. Tell her, from the heart, what this baby means to you. How you want to raise her. Tell her why you'll raise her baby better than anyone else could. Tell her everything you think about every night before you fall asleep. That's usually where the truth is."

Penelope nodded, then reached over and pulled Veronica into a hug. "Maybe I should take home a recipe for your Hope Pie."

Veronica went over to her pie binder and took out a recipe for salted caramel cheesecake pie. "I don't think you'll even need an elixir pie, Penelope. I feel your hope in waves."

Close to eleven o'clock that night, Veronica was sitting on the edge of her bed, rubbing lilac-scented lotion into her dry elbows, when her phone rang. Nick? Penelope, maybe?

"Hello?"

Bea. Veronica was so surprised to hear her voice that she almost dropped the receiver. After brief hellos and some talk about today's unusually hot weather and how it wasn't great for pie baking,

Bea said, "I've been thinking, and I would like to contact Timothy Macintosh."

"I expected that you'd want to." Veronica wondered what would happen when Bea did call him. How he'd respond.

"Do you have a place for me to start? I did a search for Macintosh in the area, and there are quite a few. No Timothy Macintosh, though."

"I know someone who might have his current address. I'll call you right back." Veronica hung up, a strange pressure pressing on her chest. She called Nick, and he did have Timothy's address. He lived in Wiscasset, just fifteen minutes away, in the same town where Veronica and Bea had been yesterday during their brief stop at the bus station. Nick had run into him last Christmas while shopping in Best Buy, and Timothy had handed him his card. He was a boat mechanic.

A boat mechanic. Living just fifteen minutes away.

Veronica sucked in a breath and called Bea back and told her what Nick knew. Her stomach churned.

"Thank you, Veronica," Bea said, and Veronica couldn't get off the phone fast enough.

She went upstairs to her closet, to the back, where her hope chest was. She'd kept things she'd brought with her to Hope Home, and things she'd saved, move after move, over the past twenty-two years. She reached into the bottom and dug out the picture of Timothy Macintosh and looked at it. Sixteen-year-old Timothy was standing in their spot, wearing that leather jacket, his hands in his jeans pockets, a sweet smile on his face.

It didn't hurt like Veronica thought it always would, perhaps because of all the opening up she'd done. God, Bea looked a lot like him. She was walking proof that she was his daughter.

Veronica put the photograph in a small manila envelope and wrote Bea's name on it, then added a note: "Thought you might want to have this. Timothy Macintosh, March 1991."

She'd walk it over to the inn in the morning and leave it in the mailbox. That settled, she slipped into bed and had a feeling she'd sleep pretty well tonight.

Chapter 18

GEMMA

After a long morning of research and interviews, including a heart-tugging breakfast with a woman who'd given her baby up for adoption back in 1963, the year Hope Home opened, and a poignant hour spent with a pregnant fifteen-year-old who would only let her baby be adopted by a wealthy, local couple, yet was having trouble finding a loving enough set of "filthy rich" prospective parents, Gemma stopped by the movie set. She hoped to catch a glimpse of Colin Firth and talk her way into an interview. Her editor at the *Gazette* had said that she'd assigned a reporter to cover the movie being shot in town, but that didn't mean Gemma couldn't try to score an interview with the actor herself. Now that she was almost done with her research, she'd be ready to write the long middle section of her article over the next couple of days, and then she'd be done. She'd have to give up the ID card that Claire had made up for her. She'd have to go back to being unemployed.

She'd have to go home and face her future.

But an interview with Colin Firth could be her ticket to a job. A one-on-one with an A-list movie star. An Oscar winner. A handsome Englishman whom everyone respected. It would add a bit of cachet to her clips—and just might get her her dream job. Maybe even her job back at *New York Weekly*. And once she was employed again as a reporter, Alex would have to accept her plan to stay in the city.

Except he hated the city now. And making him stay wasn't fair to him.

"Hey, everyone! Colin Firth is signing autographs in the Best Little Diner!" a man called out, and a big crowd rushed toward the harbor and up to Main Street. Gemma was embarrassed by how quickly she took off for the diner; she cut through a brick alleyway that she remembered from her teenage summer days and raced into the diner, out of breath, a crowd hot on her heels. The diner was busy even at eleven in the morning, and Gemma glanced all around, hoping to spot him and get to him before anyone else could. *Excuse me, Mr. Firth,* she'd say, *I'd love to treat you to dessert, perhaps a slice of that delicious-looking blackberry pie on the counter, if I might ask you a few questions for the* Gazette. But there was no sign of him in the diner. Not in the booths, not at the counter, not flattened against the wall, trying to escape detection while he awaited his coffee.

"Well, where is he?" a woman shouted, pushing past Gemma.

A waitress was refilling the little sugar bowl at the next table. "Where's who?"

"Colin Firth. Someone said he was in here, signing autographs."

The waitress, a short redhead in her early forties, raised an eyebrow. "This again? If Colin Firth were in here, do you think I'd be arranging packets of fake sugar? Or would I be a puddle on the floor?"

"She's just saying that," another woman yelled, racing around to look in the bathroom—including the men's. "He's probably hiding in the kitchen!"

"He's not, I swear," the waitress called out. "If you're not here to eat, beat it."

Maybe Gemma could catch him coming or going from the set, she thought as she left the diner with a large herbal iced tea. She'd recently seen two of his films, *Bridget Jones's Diary* and *Then She Found Me*, and she'd seen a few others over the past few years—*The King's Speech*, *Love Actually*, and *Mamma Mia!* After she worked on her Hope Home article tonight, she'd watch one of his more recent films and sketch out ideas for how to frame the story. Oscar winner arrives in small town Maine. Mr. Darcy comes to town. An Englishman in Boothbay Harbor. Perhaps he'd share what sights he'd taken in while in Maine, if he had, and Gemma could frame it as a bit of a travel piece too. And by a fan girl, of course. She adored Colin Firth and had no doubt she'd be that puddle on the floor herself while standing just inches from him, listening to him talk in that beautiful accent of his. Her mind was whirling with ideas as she neared Frog Marsh, where the number of trailers had quadrupled, and Gemma's phone rang just as she pulled out her little notebook to jot down ideas. Her mother-in-law's name flashed across her screen. Oh no.

"Gemma, just what on God's green earth do you think you're doing?" Mona Hendricks asked, her voice full of judgmental anger.

Gemma rolled her eyes. Had Alex told her she was pregnant? Granted, they hadn't talked about telling or not telling people at this early stage, but the later Mona knew, the better. "I don't know what you mean, Mona."

"You know perfectly well what I mean. You're pregnant and running around Maine for three weeks? You're giving Alexander a hard time about moving to Dobbs Ferry?"

Good Lord. Had he sicced his mother on her?

"Oh, he tried to make it out like it didn't matter to him. He said you two might end up staying in the city because you feel so strongly. Just how goddamned selfish can you be?"

"Excuse me, Mona, but why isn't Alexander selfish for wanting to move to Westchester when I want to stay in the city?"

"Don't be daft. You know perfectly well why. You're pregnant. You're bringing a life into this world. It's not about you."

Like son, like mother. Alexander had said that same thing.

"Mona, this is between me and Alexander." *Don't let loose on her. Just get her off the phone. Don't add to your problems.*

"This is a family issue. We're all here in Dobbs Ferry. And now that you're expecting, the three of you belong here too. Think of the baby if your own husband doesn't matter to you."

"I have to go, Mona," she said. "Good-bye."

Anger bubbled in Gemma's stomach. How dare she! *Think of the baby if your own husband doesn't matter to you.*

She had to get an interview with Colin Firth. She had to.

After an hour of fruitless calls to find out when Colin Firth was due to arrive in town—even the guy Bea was dating, the second assistant director on the film, wasn't sure because of scheduling conflicts, according to Bea—Gemma got to work on her article about Hope Home. She couldn't stop thinking about Lizzie Donner, the fifteen-year-old pregnant resident who was insistent that her baby be adopted by a wealthy family from Boothbay Harbor, where she herself had been raised in poverty. Gemma's heart had gone out to the girl as she'd shared her story. Lizzie had thought she'd found the perfect prospective adoptive parents—very wealthy, Catholic like herself, lived in Boothbay Harbor in a mansion on the water, but every time she met with the couple, she found she didn't like the wife. *I want my baby to have everything she'll ever dream of,* Lizzie had said. *I thought that was the most important thing. But the wife is so phony and fake—how could she be a good mother to my baby?* Gemma left out that last line as her hands flew over the keyboard of her laptop. She'd promised Lizzie she'd only write the gist of what was important to Lizzie and not disparage anyone, especially since Lizzie hadn't written off that couple just yet. Gemma thought about her own mother—not fake, but just cold. Her parents were very well off, but money and vacations and expensive summer camps certainly hadn't made anyone happy.

Gemma moved on to the paragraph about Lindsey Tate, a New Hampshire woman who'd adopted a baby whose birth mother had been a Hope Home resident thirty years ago. She was looking back at her notes about Lindsey when a strange pain began in her stomach, like menstrual cramps. She put her hand to her stomach and stood up, thinking she'd been hunched over her laptop too much. But the pain intensified. Gemma walked around her room, as much as the small space would allow, and the pain got so bad she doubled over. What was this?

Was she losing the baby?

She opened her door and braced herself against

the doorjamb, the pain getting worse in her abdomen. "Isabel?" she called out, startled by the desperate wail in her voice. Please be here.

"Gemma?" Bea called from upstairs. "Are you all right?"

"I'm having really bad pains in my abdomen," Gemma said, barely able to get the words out.

Bea rushed down the stairs, and in moments she was back with Isabel.

"I'm pregnant," Gemma said. "Just nine weeks. The pain is really intense."

Isabel's eyes widened. "I'm taking you over to Coastal General. Bea, can you cover the inn?"

"Of course. Anything you need."

Gemma could barely stand straight up as Isabel helped her down the stairs. What was happening? She walked doubled over in pain to Isabel's car, the cramping pain unrelenting.

"Honey, listen. I don't want you to worry about anything," Isabel said as she backed out of the driveway. "When I was in the early stages of pregnancy, I also had some severe abdominal pain, and it turned out to be nothing. The ER will likely do an ultrasound and just check you over. Don't worry."

But Gemma was worrying. She'd never felt cramps this bad. "Am I losing the baby?"

Isabel sped up, her knuckles white on the steering wheel. Gemma doubled over, rocking a bit up and down. "We're here." She pulled up to the Emergency entrance and called out, "My friend is nine weeks pregnant and having severe abdominal pains!"

In moments Gemma was in a wheelchair and being pushed through the automatic doors into the ER. Before she knew it she was lying on a cot, two nurses hovering to take her vitals and insert an IV of fluids. Breathe, she told herself. The pain began to lessen some. A doctor came over and introduced himself as the attending OB and explained that he was going to spread some cold, jellylike substance on her belly for the ultra-sound.

"Okay, there's the heartbeat," he said, and Gemma glanced up at the screen, her hand over her mouth. "I'm not quite sure what caused the pain, but it seems to have abated, and the baby is fine."

Gemma couldn't stop staring at the flashing heartbeat, at the fetus right there on the monitor. A part of her, a part of Alexander. For the first time, she felt connected to the life growing inside her. She was really going to have a baby.

A baby she would have been devastated to lose, especially without having had the chance to feel something—and she didn't mean a flutter. She meant connection. The stirrings of love.

A nurse helped wipe off the jelly from her stomach, and then told her to lie and rest there for thirty minutes before she'd come to discharge her.

She stared up at the ceiling, overtaken by something that felt a lot like wonder. Mixed with cold fear.

Gemma had been instructed to take it easy for the evening, but a walk didn't seem like much exertion. She found herself drawn to the playground on Main Street, always full of children climbing over the fairy-tale-character structures and being pushed on the swings. She was hoping that after the scare, her perspective would be different, that she'd suddenly have all these warm and fuzzy feelings, that the elusive maternal instinct would suddenly settle into her bones, her bloodstream, and she'd be a different person altogether.

But as she watched two toddlers packing sand in buckets in the sandbox, she felt . . . nothing much at all. No rush of *oh, how adorable, I wish I had one of those.*

There was only the same fear. That she wasn't up to the task, that she'd fail as a stay-at-home mother even with all day to practice her new life.

For reasons she wasn't even clear on, Gemma pulled out her phone and pressed in her mother's telephone number.

"Gemma, how lovely to hear from you."

How formal. "Mom, I wanted to ask you a question. Did you plan your pregnancy with Anna or was she an accident?"

"What kind of question is that?"

"I'm just curious. I know your career is very important to you, so I wondered if you planned getting pregnant or not."

"I did plan it. And five years later, I was ready for a second baby—you. What's this all about?"

She hadn't expected that. She'd always figured both pregnancies had been surprises. But her mother had planned the "interruption" to her life and career. "I'm pregnant. I'm due in January. I guess I'm just thinking about how I'm going to handle everything."

"There's no need to be all dramatic about it, Gemma. You'll hire a well-vetted nanny and you'll do what you need to do. I'm surprised at the news, though. I thought you wanted to focus on your career for a few more years yet. You're not even thirty. I was thirty-four when Lisa was born. Thirty-nine with you."

God, is this what she sounded like to Alexander? Probably. Where were the congratulations? Where was the "I'm going to be a grandmother"? What did you expect? she reminded herself. Your mother suddenly being different when you're not?

Except Gemma was different now—if just a little.

"Well, I'm pregnant now."

"Yes, indeed!" her mother said, finally injecting a note of excitement in her voice. "And congratulations. If you're thinking of names already, you can consider Frederick, after my father."

"Actually, Alex likes Alexander Jr. or Gemma Jr."

Silence. "Are you kidding? I never know when you're kidding."

"I'm not sure," Gemma said, smiling to herself. She was amazed that the sweetness of the memory of Alexander trailing a finger over her cheek while suggesting Gemma Jr. as a name, telling her she was beautiful and whip-smart, overrode her mother's flat, cold demeanor. "Well, I just wanted you to know the news. I'd better get going."

When she hung up, it wasn't with the usual hole in her heart, wishing that her mother were different, though, yes, it would be nice. Her mother was who she was. Gemma was who she was. Alexander was who he was. All she knew was that she felt fuller where there used to be empty space, and not anywhere near her belly, either. Was it the pregnancy? Not wanting it, then almost losing it and realizing that she did feel something for the little burst of life inside her? Maybe it was these past weeks, working on a story about women, about family, about pregnancy, about interruption, about hope, about despair, about dreams—a story that had ensnared her, heart, soul, and mind.

Chapter 19

BEA

"I can understand how you feel," Patrick said as he sat down across from Bea at the little round table on the balcony of his hotel. Even the view of the lit-up harbor, the incredible dinner he'd ordered them from room service, and her attractive date couldn't get Bea's mind off all Veronica had told her, showed her.

Bea sipped her wine, her appetite for her grilled salmon gone. "But was it mean of me to say it to her? That I don't know what she's supposed to mean to me?"

She was so damned confused. Last night when she'd called Veronica for Timothy's contact information, Veronica had sounded so strained. But this morning, she found an envelope with her name on it slipped under her door. Inside there was a photograph and a note. Her biological father. *Thought you might want to have this. Timothy Macintosh, March 1991.*

Bea had stared at the picture for a long time. She looked a lot like the teenage boy standing there in the leather jacket. But despite how long she looked at it, she felt no connection to the person in the picture at all. Probably because of all Veronica had told her. Timothy Macintosh had never felt any connection to her. But Veronica had.

Bea hadn't done anything with that contact information. The piece of paper on which she'd jotted down his name and address and telephone number lay under one of the seashells on her dresser in her room at the inn. Last night, when she'd hung up with Veronica, she'd picked up a shell and asked it her burning question: Should I call Timothy Macintosh?

There was the usual whoosh, but nothing else. No yes. No no. Just . . . nothing. She'd wait a couple of days and let it all settle inside her—that she had his address and phone number, that she could contact him when she was ready.

"This relationship is new to both of you," Patrick said, taking the last bite of his swordfish. "It's okay to have some speed bumps. To figure things out, how you feel, what you're comfortable with. For both of you."

Bea nodded. That made sense. There was no rush, and she couldn't feel something out of nothing. She would have to feel her way with Veronica. Just as Veronica would need to do the same with her.

Patrick stood up and moved behind her, and she felt warm, strong hands massaging her shoulders.

"Thank you for talking me through it," she said. "And thank you for dinner. It was great. The whole evening was great."

"You're welcome. And I had a great time too." He sat back down and scooched his chair closer to her. "Tomorrow's insanely busy at the set, and we're going to be setting up shop at a diner in town for a few days, but maybe you could come by around five to say hi? I don't want the whole day to go by without seeing you."

"I'd love to, but I've got a tutoring gig at five. With Tyler's sister, Maddy."

"Tyler Echols, the PA?" he asked. Was that concern on his face?

Bea nodded. "He's paying me fifty bucks an hour. I can definitely use it."

"I probably shouldn't say anything," Patrick said. "But given what you're going through with your own birth mother . . ."

Bea stared at him. "What are you talking about?"

Patrick seemed to be weighing whether or not he should tell her. "Look, I don't know Tyler too well and maybe I misheard him, but I don't think so. About a month ago when we were filming in New York, I overheard him talking to another PA buddy of his about a documentary film he did an internship on, about adoption. Anyway, Tyler was telling this guy that his sister was adopted and that he found her birth mother for her—and shook her up for money. He was just out of college and broke and figured she'd feel guilty and give him whatever he wanted to arrange a meeting between them. To his credit, he did seem to have real interest in helping his sister, but I got the sense he figured he'd kill two birds with one stone, you know? Set up contact—and line his pockets."

"God," Bea said. "That's vile."

"If he wasn't so good at his job, I'd fire him. And who knows—maybe he was just talking smack. I don't know. But I just figured I'd tell you in case he tries to get out of paying you for tutoring his sister."

She'd be on red alert. "I appreciate it. Duly warned. So did he get money out of the birth mother?" She remembered Tyler saying the experience was disappointing, so clearly not. And no wonder Tyler had said not to bring up the subject with his sister. Maybe they were both grifters. Or maybe his sister didn't know what Tyler had tried to do.

"I don't know," Patrick said. "Just make sure he pays you fair and square, okay?"

"Okay," she said, liking that someone cared. She missed that, someone looking out for her.

She'd give the tutoring one session and get a feel for Maddy. If she seemed shady, Bea would quit. But she wouldn't spite Maddy just because her brother was a class-A jerk.

"I love this view," Patrick said, and this time, his face and the lights and the boats worked their magic. They sipped their wine, and then he took hers and put it down and kissed her.

All thoughts of birth mothers and birth fathers and shady production assistants went out of her head; she could only think about Patrick's lips, the beautiful sensations running up and down her spine. How long had it been since she'd been kissed? Almost a year. Too long.

His hand went to the zipper of her jeans.

She covered his hand. "I really like you, Patrick. But let's take this a little slower, okay? In fact, I should get going. But thank you for tonight."

"You sure I can't convince you to stay?" he asked, running a hand down her back.

"I should go," she said. "See you soon?"

"Can't be soon enough," he said, and gave her a kiss good-bye to remember.

Maddy Echols was ten minutes late for her first tutoring session. Bea would give her twenty minutes, then leave. She sat at a square table in the Quiet Room of the Boothbay Harbor library, trying not to think about what she'd learned about Tyler—and possibly Maddy. Shaking down Maddy's biological mother for money? Could it be true? Tyler did seem to care about Maddy, but he'd also shown himself to be a jerk who couldn't bother to be civil.

A minute later, Maddy poked her head in, and Bea could see she was annoyed that Bea was there.

"You were hoping I'd given up on you, huh?" Bea asked.

Maddy smiled. "Kinda."

"Well, I need the money. And you need to pass this class. So sit your tush down and let's talk *To Kill a Mockingbird.*"

Maddy noisily sighed, dropped her backpack on the table, and sat down.

"You have to write an essay?" Bea asked.

Maddy nodded. "I have to pick one of four quotations from the book that supposedly means something to me and write a five-page typed essay on what the quote means, using more quotes from the book, at least five." She started writing her name in pen on her palm.

Bea halted the pen. "Let's see the four quotes."

"I already picked one, actually. That was the easy part."

"That's great. Read it to me." If she'd chosen a quote, Bea's job wouldn't be as difficult as she'd feared. Often the students she tutored at the Writing Center didn't look at the assignment until they were forced to by her.

Maddy pulled a sheet of paper from her binder. "This is from Atticus Finch. I think he's the father of the kid who narrates the book? Okay, here it is. 'I wanted you to see what real courage is, instead of getting the idea that courage is a man with a gun in his hand. It's when you know you're licked before you begin, but you begin anyway and see it through no matter what.' It's the longest quote of the four and I totally get it."

Bea was encouraged. "Tell me what it means to you, since that's part of the assignment—to choose a quote that means something to you."

"Well, when I first read all the quotes, I was, like, boring, boring, *bor-ing*. And then I got to this one, and it reminded me of something that happened last year."

"Can you tell me about it?" Bea asked.

Maddy bit her lip and looked away, glancing at Bea every now and then. "I'm adopted, and my brother—Tyler—helped me look up my birth mother, but she wrote back that she didn't want contact and that it was her right and please not to contact her again. But I wrote her another letter anyway, telling her I just wanted to maybe see her once and see if I looked like her." Maddy's eyes started getting watery. "So when I read that quote, that's what I thought of. I was totally licked before I began, but I wrote her again anyway because I had to."

It took everything in Bea not to reach out and hug this girl.

"She wrote back again to say sorry, she didn't want contact and that was final," Maddy said, "but she enclosed a picture of herself. Want to see it?"

"Sure," Bea said, trying to imagine herself—at fifteen, no less—getting that kind of response from Veronica. How disappointing—crushing— that must have been for Maddy.

Maddy handed her the picture. The woman looked rough around the edges.

"I was adopted too," Bea said. "In fact, the whole reason I'm in Boothbay Harbor is because I came to meet my own biological mother."

Maddy's jaw almost dropped open. "Seriously? What happened?"

"Well, she seems like a wonderful person, but I just don't know who she's supposed to be in my life. We got together twice, she answered all my burning questions—and then some—and now I just don't know where we go from here. I've backed away, I guess."

"I can't relate at all. I can't imagine not wanting my birth mother in my life, especially if she's nice. You're so lucky."

Bea reached over and squeezed Maddy's hand.

"Since you're still here, though," Maddy said, "maybe the quote applies to you too."

"What do you mean?"

"Well, you're the one who kind of got licked by your own self—being unsure, I mean. But you're still here. It's not like you went back home."

Bea smiled. "I think you might be onto something there. I give you an A plus," she added, and Maddy beamed at her. "Have you read more of the book? What that quote—which you understand very well—means in the book is really, really interesting. Heartbreaking, but interesting."

"I can't get past the second page. Like I care

about the details of the town? It's so boring."

"Well, those details help explain what life was like then, when the book takes place. It would be like you explaining your life here in Maine to someone a hundred years from now."

"What was it like then?"

Bea gave Maddy a quick lesson on the 1930s and the Depression, on what race relations were like in the South. "Then comes Atticus Finch, a very honest, honorable lawyer, a widow with two young kids, whose job it is to defend an African-American man accused of raping a white woman. No one thinks the black man deserves a trial to begin with. They just think he's guilty and should hang. Atticus knows a jury won't believe his word over hers."

"So . . . that's what the quote means—the lawyer knows he is going to lose but he defends the guy anyway?"

Bea nodded. "And against a lot of ill will in town too. He ends up opening a lot of people's eyes. But most of all, he teaches his children something very, very important."

"What?"

"I want you to find out for yourself," Bea said. "You know, since we're alone in here, I'm gonna shut the door and read the first chapter to you. When you go home tonight, you read the next two chapters. Then the next two the following night. Keep doing that, two chapters a night, and we'll discuss what you're up to at our next session."

"Okay," Maddy said, and Bea knew she had her. The girl's ears were open.

Tyler was right on time to pick up Maddy an hour later. He looked different without his clipboard and production company ID hanging around his neck. Less . . . jerkish.

"I'm going to ace this class," she said to her brother, then put her earphones in and dropped down on a stately leather chair in the main room with *To Kill a Mockingbird*.

"I can see this went well," he said. "I'm surprised." He pulled out two twenties and a ten and handed the bills to her. "Thanks."

Well, at least he didn't try to get out of paying, as Patrick had warned he might.

"We're headed to Harbor Heaven, Maddy's favorite restaurant, for dinner. You could come, if you're free. She seems to like you."

Bea wasn't a cynical person in general, but she couldn't help thinking that Tyler had only invited her so he could steer the conversation back to *To Kill a Mockingbird* and get Maddy an extra hour of free tutoring. "I have a date with Patrick, but thanks."

He made his trademark move of rolling his eyes. "I hope you're not pinning your hopes on him. I'm telling you, he's a notorious womanizer."

"He seems great to me."

"Right. He probably promised your biological mother a speaking role, right?"

"He doesn't even know which extra is my biological mother."

"You know why? Because he doesn't care. You're just some pretty young thing to him. Just be careful. That's all I'm saying."

Now it was Bea's turn to roll her eyes. Patrick had spent a lot of time showing Bea he did care, by listening. "Thanks for the unsolicited advice." She walked over to Maddy and tapped on her shoulder. Maddy removed one earbud. "Remember, read two chapters every night this week. We'll meet again next Wednesday. Promise you'll do the reading?"

"I promise, I promise. The Trevi Fountain is waiting for me."

Bea liked Maddy Echols and there was no way she'd let her fail the class. She hoped like hell that Tyler's bribe of Italy and the Trevi Fountain wasn't all hot air and that he'd actually take her.

When she got back to her room at the inn, Bea slid the shell aside, picked up the piece of paper with Timothy Macintosh's contact information, and stared at it.

Maddy's words came back to her. *I can't imagine not wanting my birth mother in my life, especially if she's nice. You're so lucky.*

Bea didn't know how lucky she'd be when it

came to her birth father. He'd denied being her father twenty-two years ago. He'd walked away from Veronica completely. Veronica had never heard from him the entire time she'd been at Hope Home.

Maybe he'd really believed what he'd told Veronica. That he wasn't the father, that he couldn't be. Maybe he wasn't a bad guy.

Bea picked up the shell and put it to her ear. "Should I call him? Right now?"

The whoosh in her ear told her nothing. It was like a Magic 8 Ball saying Ask Again Later.

She could pick up the phone right now and call. Just as she'd done with Veronica. But she'd had the advantage of knowing Veronica wanted to be contacted. Timothy Macintosh truly was a stranger. And given the way he had walked away from Veronica, he likely would not be open to hearing from Bea at all.

She stared out the window, at the stars, at the treetops. This was something she had to do, had to finish.

She took a sheet of Three Captains' Inn stationery and wrote:

Dear Mr. Macintosh,
I hope you won't find this letter terribly intrusive. My name is Bea Crane, and I'm the biological daughter of Veronica Russo, who has named you as my biological

father. I was born on October 12, 1991, in Boothbay Harbor. I understand from Veronica that you denied being the father of her baby, and I understand that you might not be my biological father. I am writing because I'm here in Boothbay Harbor, and have recently met Veronica for the first time, after having found out, also very recently, that I was adopted. I'm interested in meeting you, if you're open to it, and would be open to taking a DNA test, if you'd like to go that route. I'd love to know about my biological father's family background. That's all I'm interested in, by the way—I just want to assure you of that.

Thank you,
Bea Crane

She addressed the envelope and headed out to the mailbox on the corner of Main Street, watching the letter disappear down the chute.

Chapter 20

VERONICA

Veronica spent Saturday in her kitchen, surrounded by flour and butter and sugar and baskets of fruit. She was on her twelfth client pie of the day, this last one a Key lime Confidence Pie for her neighbor Frieda, who was nervous about applying to nursing programs for a second career. As Veronica grated lime zest into her mixing bowl, atop the condensed milk, egg yolks, and Key lime juice, she tried to summon up her own confidence—to call Bea. To call Nick. She hadn't heard from him since Monday night. Not a word since he and his daughter had left her house after the pie class. She'd been so sure he'd stop by or call—something—but he hadn't. Maybe she'd been reading more into their blossoming . . . friendship than was really there. Or perhaps there was some fallout from his taking Leigh to her class when her grandparents were up in arms about it. She couldn't stop thinking about him, though, which had her Amore and Hope Pies come out perfectly the past several days.

Her phone rang, and she wiped her sticky fingers and grabbed the receiver, her fingers crossed that it was Bea. She hadn't heard from Bea since Monday night either, when Bea had called to ask for Timothy's contact information. Five days. Had she called Timothy? Had he denied being her father? Or was she sitting across a table from him in a restaurant right now?

"Hello, Veronica speaking."

Silence for a moment. And then, "Veronica, it's Timothy. Macintosh."

Veronica dropped the receiver and grabbed for it. Jesus Christ. Her heart was pounding, and her lips felt dry.

"Veronica?" he said. "Are you there?"

She took a deep breath. "I'm here." She didn't have to wonder how he'd tracked her down; her number and address were listed in the telephone directory.

"I received a letter yesterday from someone named Bea Crane. Is it true? Am I the father? And I mean without a shadow of a doubt?"

She sat down at the table, trying to get over the shock of hearing his voice. "I was a virgin when I started dating you, Timothy. You were the only guy I slept with until I was nineteen, as a matter of fact."

She heard his own intake of breath. "You're sure. You're absolutely sure."

"I'm sure. As sure now as I was then."

He was quiet for a few seconds. "She wrote me a letter. She said she'd be willing to take a DNA test if I wanted to go that route. I suppose I should, just for legal purposes."

Veronica could hear the worry in his voice, the fear. It was much the same voice it had been at sixteen, if a bit deeper. "She's twenty-two years old and was legally adopted as a newborn. You have no legal obligation to her, Timothy, if that's your concern."

"This is just so crazy, so sudden. She says she wants to meet me, to know about her biological father's family and medical history."

"She's a lovely person, Timothy. I can assure you of that."

"I just don't know," he said. "I've kept track of the time. When . . . the baby would turn eighteen. I wondered if I'd get a call."

Veronica stood up and paced as much as the phone cord would allow. "So you did wonder if you were the father?"

"Well, I've always known it was possible. To be honest, I've been thinking about it a lot lately. My wife says it's haunting me. Especially because I saw you recently, about six months ago. My wife and I were visiting friends of hers, and as we walked past a diner I saw you. I don't come to Boothbay much since my parents moved out a long time ago. I almost fainted when I saw you— it was just so unexpected. I'd heard you moved down south."

"I moved back to town a year ago."

"My wife thinks I should have settled the answer of whether or not I really fathered your baby a long time ago. For the last few years, she's been telling me to call you and ask you straight out, after all these years. But every time I picked up the phone, I put it down. Not even a month ago, Beth handed me the phone and begged me to call you and just find out once and for all instead of letting it eat at me like this."

Veronica froze.

Beth. Her client who'd ordered the Cast-Out Pie.

The kind of pie that would get someone off someone's mind . . .

The question. That was what Beth wanted to cast out of his heart.

I'm not the one who has to cast someone out. It's someone else who has to get someone out of his goddamned head.

Beth, who never did pay her, was Timothy's wife.

"I have always been kind of haunted about it," Timothy said. "Not knowing if it was true, if I treated you terribly and had been wrong. I've never known the truth. I never wanted to know."

She blocked the image of him, standing there in the brick alleyway the last time she'd seen him. His expression, the anger as she'd told him, shaking and crying, that she was pregnant. "I think when you see Bea, if you agree to meet with her, you'll know once and for all that she's your daughter. She has your hair, your smile. There's just something in her expression that's all you."

"God," Timothy said. "I'm sorry, Veronica. I'm sorry."

He started sobbing, and then there seemed to be someone in the background talking to him, and then he said he had to go and hung up.

Veronica sat in her kitchen for over an hour, the call from Timothy echoing in her head. She glanced at the unfinished pie. She'd have to throw it away and start over, not that she could tonight. Confidence was something Veronica was lacking in right now, about Bea. About how this would go between her and Timothy.

She picked up the phone and pressed in Nick's number and told him about the phone call.

"Come over," he said. "Leigh's been asleep since eight forty-five. Bring your pie ingredients if you want. I'll help you bake."

Twenty minutes later, she sat at Nick's kitchen table, sipping a glass of wine as he stood a foot away, making a Confidence Pie. The sight of him, barefoot and in a blue T-shirt and jeans, separating egg yolks, grating the lime zest, made her want to stand up and kiss him.

"You okay?" he asked, whisking the ingredients.

"I'll be okay. It was just so . . . strange talking to Timothy."

"I'll bet. Sounds like he finally accepted the truth, though."

"Thanks for inviting me over," she said. "I needed this."

He sat down beside her and took her hand and held it. When he looked at her, she wondered if he was going to kiss her—and then he did.

She was about to wrap her arms around his neck and kiss him back with everything inside her, but the doorbell rang.

"Talk about bad timing," he said. "Hold that thought," he added with a smile at her.

When he went to the door, she heard the voices of a man and a woman, the woman saying something about Leigh's watch, which she'd left at their house, then the woman saying, "What's that I smell? Lime juice? Are you drinking?"

"I'm making a pie," Nick said, his voice weary. "Thanks for bringing back Leigh's watch. I'll tell her you brought it back."

A woman, in her early sixties, with a silver-blond bob, burst into the kitchen. She stared at Veronica. "It's you, isn't it. That pie lady. Leigh described you to a T," she added with disdain. She turned to Nick, furious. "And now you have women over? When Leigh's asleep in her room?"

"Gertie, first of all, Veronica and I are baking a pie, not having sex in the living room."

A tall, thin man, also in his early sixties, came into the kitchen. "Don't be crude, Nick."

"You two listen right now," Nick said. "I'm not going to live this way. Not a moment longer. I

352

love Leigh with all my heart—you know that. I'm doing my best—and yes, my best is good enough. I'm sorry that Vanessa died. Things might not have been working out between us, but I loved her, I cared about her. And now you're fighting me on being a parent to Leigh when I'm the only one she has left? Be her grandparents—I've never taken that away from you. Have I ever tried to limit the time she spends with you?" He turned around, his hand shaking on the counter.

"I'll go," Veronica said. "I think the three of you need to talk."

She slipped out the kitchen door.

Veronica stayed up as long as she could, hoping Nick would call and tell her how he and Leigh's grandparents had left things, but by one o'clock he hadn't called, and she must have fallen asleep soon after. She could still feel the imprint of his lips on hers, feel that beautiful urge to kiss him back. She wondered what would have happened had his daughter's grandparents not burst into the kitchen.

Nick was the past and present in one, and she had a serious thing for him. She couldn't help smiling when for the third time in twelve hours, she whisked together egg yolks, condensed milk, Key lime juice, and zest for Frieda's Confidence Pie. She felt it, felt the little opening inside her heart. She liked Nick DeMarco and, from that one kiss last night, she knew he liked her too. A lightness that she hadn't felt in years settled around her, inside her.

My heart is open to Bea. My heart is open to Nick.

This time, she got the pie in the oven.

Just as she closed the oven door, the phone rang and Veronica grabbed it.

Penelope Von Blun.

"I wanted you to know I did what you said," Penelope told her. "I prayed over three salted caramel cheesecake Hope Pies that our prospective birth mother would listen, that she'd believe everything I was saying, and then I called her and asked if I could talk to her, just me and her, and she said yes. I told her that I'd been trying to impress her, to be what she wanted, so I toned down my look and tried to look more church-going or something. I told her what I thought about before I'd drift off to sleep, sometimes thinking so much, wishing so hard that I couldn't get to sleep at all. I told her what her baby would mean to me, why I thought I would be a good mother. I told her everything. And I think she started to like me."

"I'm very glad to hear that, Penelope." Veronica was starting to like her too.

They hung up, and Veronica flashed to an image of herself at sixteen and pregnant, at Hope Home, at group counseling, in private therapy with the very nice social worker who came once a week to meet with each girl. When she'd first arrived at Hope Home, she'd refused to say much at all, but slowly, week by week, she began opening up. She thought of those girls there today, thought of all they were going through, all they needed to say. Maybe, with her experience, she could be a help to those girls.

An hour later, Veronica delivered her pie to Frieda, wished her well with the nursing school applications, and then drove to Hope Home before she could change her mind.

Veronica pulled open Hope Home's screen door and smiled at the woman at the front desk, same place it was decades ago. "My name is Veronica Russo. I lived here twenty-two years ago when I was sixteen and pregnant. Hope Home did me a world of good, and I'd like to volunteer here in whatever capacity you might need."

The woman smiled and stood up and extended her hand. "We can use all the experienced help we can get. Let's sit down and you can tell me about yourself and fill out some forms. We'll have to check your background and references, of course. When would you be able to start? A volunteer flaked out on me and I was counting on her help at our free-talk period this weekend."

Veronica sat. "I'd like to start as soon as I can."

● ● ●

As Veronica sat on a chair in the extras holding tent late Monday afternoon, her thoughts once again went to Nick, who still hadn't called. All day she'd tried to put it out of her mind. He was probably dealing with Leigh's grandparents. Perhaps they'd spent the weekend together, as a family, and were ironing things out.

One kiss doesn't obligate him to you, she reminded herself as she headed home and prepared her island counter for her students, once again having no idea if two of those students wouldn't be coming.

At a few minutes before six, June and Isabel arrived with June's son, and then Penelope arrived, looking like her old self—a good thing. The jewelry was back. The makeup. The real Penelope. And like her look, her smile was very real. "Things are looking good," Penelope said. "I'm hopeful again."

Veronica barely had time to talk to Penelope because the doorbell rang, and a shot of pure happiness burst inside her. She opened the door— but Nick and Leigh weren't alone. Leigh's grandmother was there too. Nick introduced them, officially.

As Nick and Leigh stepped in and chatted with the other students, Leigh's grandmother said, "I wanted to apologize for how I acted the other night. That wasn't fair of me."

That was a turnaround. "Stay for class?" Veronica asked.

The woman seemed pleased by the invitation. "None of those strange pies? I'm not a fan of that mumbo-jumbo."

"Just good old strawberry rhubarb tonight," Veronica said.

"Then I'd love to stay."

As Leigh led her grandmother into the kitchen, Nick whispered in Veronica's ear, "Took me the last two days, but I got through."

Veronica smiled. She felt like something was getting through to her too.

On Tuesday morning, Veronica heard from Patrick Ool's assistant that the extras for the diner scene wouldn't be needed until two o'clock, so she called the director of Hope Home and asked if she could come earlier. A group session was set for ten. Veronica drove out to Hope Home, turning onto the long dirt road with its canopy of trees. When the white farmhouse with its hanging sign and porch swing came into view, Veronica saw herself sitting on that swing, scared, worried, fearful for how she'd feel after she had the baby and gave her up, and she remembered the counselor sitting down beside her and just holding her, letting her cry. That was exactly what Veronica wanted to do for the girls here. Listen. Be a shoulder.

She parked in the lot, near the very spot where she had given birth in an ambulance. She sat there and watched the few girls who were walking around the yard. They looked so young and vulnerable, though one or two had a tough edge to their expressions, to their makeup. Just before ten o'clock, she headed up the three steps and pulled open the screen door. A woman she didn't recognize sat at the desk.

"You must be Veronica," she said, standing up. "I'm Larissa Dennis, head counselor here at Hope Home. You're just in time to join Group."

The director appeared, welcomed Veronica, and sat down at the desk, and Veronica followed Larissa into the large room that faced the backyard. There were ten huge purple beanbags in a circle, and some rocking chairs. The room was just as it had been twenty-two years ago. Painted a very pale blue, with inspirational posters on the walls.

As the clock struck ten, girls began coming in and sitting down on the beanbags and chairs. One very pregnant girl chose the recliner. Many of them had anxiety balls in their hands.

"Morning, girls," Larissa said. "We have a new volunteer joining us for group every week. Veronica Russo lived here at Hope Home twenty-two years ago as a sixteen-year-old. She'll be helping guide discussions and just generally being of support and service. Turns out Veronica is a master pie baker, so she'll be in the kitchen when she's not needed. Anyone who wants to learn to make a few different kinds of pie, meet in the kitchen at eleven."

There were a bunch of "Me!"s, which made Veronica smile.

"I'm craving pumpkin pie so bad," a red-haired girl on a beanbag said.

"Key lime."

"Chocolate cream."

"Anything but apple pie. Too boring."

Veronica smiled. "How about one of each?"

The girls cheered. Pie had a way of making people happy. Even—especially, maybe—pregnant teenagers.

"Any consensus of topic today?" Larissa asked the group.

"Since someone's here who used to live here, can we just ask her questions?"

Larissa looked at Veronica. "Okay with an impromptu Q&A?"

"Ask away," Veronica told the girls. "Just say your name first so I can get to know who's who." She glanced around, glad she didn't know the name of the girl Penelope had her hopes pinned on. That gave the girl some anonymity.

"I'm Allison. Did you regret giving up your baby?" a girl with poker-straight blond hair asked.

No easy pitches here, Veronica realized. "To be very honest, no, Allison. I had a total lack of support. From my family, from the baby's father. I was alone. And very scared. Giving up the baby felt like the right thing to do."

"Did the kid ever try to find you?" another girl asked. "Oh, I'm Kim."

"Yes," Veronica said. "Very recently too. I'd left my contact information with the adoption agency and the Maine State Adoption Reunion Registry."

"It must be weird when the kid you think you'll never see again suddenly comes back into your life," another girl said.

"It brings up a lot of old memories, that's for sure."

"Remember that blond chick who came by a couple of weeks ago, the one who said she was born here in the parking lot?" Kim said to another girl who had serious attitude in her blue eyes. She looked angry and conflicted, and Veronica made a mental note to be available to talk to her during the pie tasting. Some girls needed to ease into asking the questions they most wanted answers to. "She was trying to decide if she wanted to contact her birth mother."

Veronica froze. They were talking about Bea. No doubt about it. Bea had said she'd come here.

"I felt bad for her," Allison said.

"Omigod, Jen, remember how you threw your turkey sandwich at her for making Kim cry?"

"Not my proudest moment, but I was so pissed at her for not knowing how she felt. How could you not know how you feel? She shouldn't have come here."

It killed Veronica to think of Bea, who seemed not to have a mean bone in her body, getting yelled at, getting a sandwich thrown at her. Bea must have felt awful.

"Everything is a learning opportunity," Larissa said.

"I'm going to be very, very honest," Veronica said. "I think that girl you're talking about is my birth daughter. Long, blond hair? Brown eyes? Tall?"

"Omigod, yes," Jen said.

Veronica nodded. "We did finally meet and I'm so glad."

"I like knowing that someday my baby will try to find me," Kim said. "I know you don't, Jen, but twenty years from now, you might feel totally differently."

"Doubt it," Jen said. She turned to Veronica. "So what now? You're suddenly all mother-daughter?"

"We're working on just getting to know each other."

Jen glanced around at the other girls, then back at Veronica. "Can I ask you questions about your family? My mother hates my guts for embarrassing her. Apparently, everyone knows and she had to quit her country club."

"My family wasn't supportive. Some families are. I had friends here whose mothers and fathers would visit a few times a week. It made me feel awful, but it made me want to find my own happiness, you know?"

"So what did you do?"

"I decided what I wanted for myself. To travel, see the country."

"I want to move to California. The second I'm eighteen, I'm out of Maine," Jen said.

"What about the father," Allison asked. "Is he still in the picture?"

"No," Veronica said. "He told me it couldn't possibly be his baby. And I never saw him again. I think he was scared to death and used his fear to turn on me."

"God," Kim said, glancing at a girl with long, brown hair who looked to be around five or six months pregnant. "That's like Jordan, Lizzie."

"Thanks for reminding me," Lizzie said. "I'm trying to totally forget he ever existed."

"Did you?" Jen asked Veronica. "Forget he existed?"

"No. But I tried also." She glanced at Lizzie. "It got better, though. I pushed a lot of it out of my mind, willed myself to forget. But I'll tell you something. It's important to deal with your feelings, let them out, cry if you feel like crying, ask questions if you have them. If I could go back and change something, you know what it would be?"

They all stared at her.

"I would have opened up more to people. Told them what I'd been through. Talked about it. I wouldn't have hidden it. I wouldn't have thought it was something to be ashamed of. I would have talked about how scary it all was."

"Well, Jen never shuts up," Kim said, "so she won't have that problem."

Jen threw her squeezy ball at Kim, and everyone laughed.

The girls continued to ask questions and Veronica was as honest as she could be without instilling any real fear or worry. She liked being here, liked listening, liked talking to them.

"You were wonderful," Larissa said as she walked Veronica to the kitchen, where Veronica would bake three pies and give a lesson to whoever wanted to learn the fine art of pie baking.

"Thank you. I used to be one of them. So it was easy." As she was about to go into the kitchen, she turned back. "Oh, Larissa. I heard there was a reporter writing an article on Hope Home. If you have her contact info, I'd like to talk to her."

I would have opened up more to people. Told them what I'd been through. Talked about it. I wouldn't have hidden it.

Now she'd take her own advice.

The moment Veronica arrived home, she called Gemma, who wanted to talk to her right away. They'd be meeting here in a few hours. As

Veronica headed into her living room to tidy up for the interview, she suddenly thought of cherries.

Cherries, with their beautiful deep red color, their burst of sweet and tart flavor, the way they'd always reminded her of tiny hearts, especially when there were two on a stem.

And even though she'd made quite a few pies at Hope Home this morning, she had one more pie in her.

A cherry pie. Henceforth known as Colin Firth Pie.

Veronica went into her kitchen, her head clear, her heart warm.

Chapter 21
GEMMA

Late Tuesday night, close to midnight, Gemma left Veronica Russo's house with a bag containing two boxed pies, one fudge and one lime. The streets were still teeming a bit with Fourth of July tourists even though the Fourth had come and gone, the decks of restaurants jutting out on piers still lit up and full of people. She couldn't wait to get back to the inn and finish her article. Veronica's story, all she'd shared, had moved Gemma to the point of tears more than once. Now her article would come a beautiful full circle.

She crept into the inn, worried about waking anyone up, but the newlyweds in the Osprey Room were right behind her, waving an unopened bottle of Champagne and asking Gemma if she thought Isabel would mind if they raided the refrigerator for some of that incredible pie she had available every day. The couple was clueless but sweet, so Gemma gave them the fudge pie Veronica had sent her home with, keeping the Key lime Confidence Pie for herself.

As she headed upstairs and passed Bea's door, she was so tempted to knock and tell Bea everything Veronica had said, but of course, she wouldn't. *All these years, twenty-two years, I thought I was running away from my past. I thought I'd come back to Boothbay Harbor to face that past. But it turns out my past—the pregnancy, reactions from my family, from the baby's father, all that paled in comparison to what I was really running from: how much I loved that baby girl I held for two minutes against my chest. How much I love her now, even though I barely know her. You can love someone without knowing them much, did you know that? I fought against it all these years. But not anymore. Regardless of whether my birth daughter wants me in her life or not. I'll always love her.*

Maybe that was what maternal instincts were all about, Gemma thought, unsettled in a good way by all Veronica had told her. She slipped on her noise-canceling headphones to block out the laughter coming from the newlyweds' room and got to work, her fingers flying over the keyboard of her laptop as she worked on the long middle of her article, the personal stories: a birth mother reuniting with the daughter she'd given up for adoption. A teenage girl determined her baby be raised by a wealthy couple, then discovers that money alone wouldn't satisfy her—only a loving heart would. A birth mother, now remarried with children, who'd never told her husband of the baby she'd given up for adoption seventeen years earlier. Two women, now in their sixties, who'd been pregnant teenagers back when Hope Home had first opened fifty years ago, had shared their stories with Gemma by telephone and Skype, stories that had made Gemma cry. A lot had changed in fifty years. And a lot had not. Gemma wrote until her eyes started to water from exhaustion.

At just after two in the morning, the article was done. She sat back, expecting to feel sad, bereft that it was over, but all she felt was proud—and never so sure she was doing what she was born to do.

One of the women she'd interviewed, a prospective adoptive mother, had used exactly that phrase. *I feel like I was born to be a mother, but I'm not sure it'll ever happen . . .*

You're so lucky, she remembered another interviewee, fifteen-year-old pregnant Hope Home resident Chloe Martin, saying to her when Gemma had revealed that she was pregnant.

When would she ever figure this out? she wondered. What if she never did? How was she supposed to go home this week to a life she couldn't imagine? If only she had a solid job as a reporter, she could be both—a reporter and a mother. A working mother, like so many other women. But without a job, without even a lead— and she'd applied online for nine staff reporting jobs since she'd been in Maine—she would go home and slowly morph into Alexander's mother and sister, this article just her last beautiful hurrah.

• • •

In the morning, with the sun shining bright into her window, Gemma woke up from a strange dream in which she couldn't get her baby out of a baby carrier on her chest, but the baby wasn't an infant; she had a woman's face and looked scarily like Gemma's mother. Gemma sat up, trying to shake the remnants of the dream from her memory. That wasn't even one she wanted to look up in the dream dictionary.

She supposed it meant she worried she'd be like her mother. Or that she was carrying her worries about being a good mother and it was all tied into her own feelings about her mother. Maybe a lot of both, she knew.

She lifted up her tank top and put her hands on her belly, still only slightly beginning to round. "Hey, little one," she said, tears stinging her eyes. "If you're listening, I want you to know that I will love you. The minute I meet you, I'll love you. How could I not? That is not even a question. I'm just missing some synapse, some switch that'll get turned on when you're born. I think I'll feel like Veronica Russo does—that I always loved you. Even if I didn't know it."

A note was slipped under her door, and Gemma got out of bed to pick it up:

Today's breakfast special is crepes—chocolate and/or strawberry! xo Bea

Bea was such a sweetheart. Right now, she

knew Bea was unsure how she'd proceed with Veronica, what she and her birth mother were to each other, how—and if—to forge a relationship going forward. But with Bea's big heart and how alone she was, and Veronica's strength of hope, Gemma had a good feeling they'd work it out.

She reached over onto her dresser for her laptop and proofread her article, just under three thousand words, proofed it again, then sent it by e-mail to Claire at the *Gazette*.

She wasn't in the mood to eat breakfast with her fellow noisy guests, so she skipped the crepes and headed out to Harbor View Coffee for a decaf iced mocha and a scone, then took a long walk around the pretty side streets of the harbor. She'd miss this place. She'd have to go home by week's end; she had no other reason to be here. There was talk that Colin Firth was coming to town on Saturday to film his scenes, but there'd been rumors before and not a sign of him. She wasn't getting an interview with Colin Firth. It was time to go home and face her future.

As she walked down Meadow Lane, she watched a father push his toddler on a tire swing hung on an old oak tree in the front yard of their house, and she smiled at them, imagining Alexander doing the same thing. This was Alexander's dream, she realized, to be doing exactly that. Her husband's dream. All she'd been thinking about these past few weeks was her own dream, and maybe now that one dream had gone belly up, it was time to dream another one, as Meryl Streep had said in the movie *Heartburn*, an old favorite of Gemma's. Dream another dream. She was going to have a baby. It was time to accept that wholeheartedly. If it turned out she didn't have maternal instincts, well, then she'd learn how to be a mother.

Her head and heart a bit more settled, Gemma was about to turn back to the inn to call Alexander and let him know she'd sent in her article when she noticed the cutest house a few doors down. The yellow craftsman had a widow's walk and a quaint porch with a rocking chair, and between the sweet scene with the tire swing and that rocking chair, Gemma could almost see herself sitting on that porch, rocking her baby back and forth. Becoming someone new, someone she didn't know but could grow into.

She touched her hands to her belly. A little over a week ago, she'd been on a hospital cot, wondering if it was over before it had begun for her, before it had a chance to begin.

She took a picture of the house, making sure to get in the widow's walk and the porch, and texted it to Alexander: *A: maybe you could find something like this for the three of us in Dobbs Ferry. I love the widow's walk—and a porch with a swing is a must. xxG*

In a few minutes he texted back: *I'm thrilled, but are you telling me that my meddling mother actually changed your mind? Sorry she got on you. She told me about it, and I told her she had to back off.*

Wasn't your mother. It was me. I want to do the right thing for us, for the three of us. I love you, G.

Facts faced.

By the next morning, Gemma still hadn't called Alexander to tell him she'd finished the article, that she was coming home . . . soon. She lay on her bed, her hands on her stomach, *Your Pregnancy This Week* next to her. She'd had dinner last night with June and let it all come out, and even June had said that for all she knew, Gemma could love suburban life. After all, she loved Boothbay Harbor, a tiny town.

But Boothbay Harbor was different. Boothbay Harbor had always been a saving grace, a harbor in itself to Gemma, the place her father had taken her for a month every summer after her parents' divorce. She'd always been happy in Boothbay, the vibrant coastal town a constant ray of sunshine. She had old friends here, wonderful memories. And she loved the old wooden piers and boats in the bay, the cobblestone and brick streets lined with one-of-a-kind shops and every imaginable cuisine. She'd talk to Alexander about vacationing here next summer. Maybe every summer.

Her e-mail pinged and Gemma went to her

laptop, hoping it was from Claire, who'd say she loved the article and had another story for Gemma, not that Gemma would do that to Alexander, as much as she'd want to.

It was from Claire:

Gemma, your piece was beyond fabulous! My boss loved it. He wants you on staff—that's how impressed he was. I'm prepared to offer you a full-time job as a senior reporter, covering human interest and your own column, with full under-standing that you will take maternity beginning late December . . .

Gemma burst into tears. A job offer. One she couldn't accept.

She imagined herself living here in this sweet small town she adored, working on stories like Hope Home, having her own Sunday column. Spending time with old summer friends who'd blossom into everyday friends. Making new friends, good friends, like Bea. Watching her belly grow, month by month, and spending weekends decorating the nursery in a house like that old yellow craftsman, a house she could live in, breathe in, become a mother in. Coming home after work to Alexander, where they'd learn to be parents together.

Living three hundred miles away from her mother-in-law.

For all that, she'd leave New York City in a heartbeat.

The offer was almost cruel, considering she couldn't call Claire and scream *"Yes!"* at the top of her lungs, which was what she wanted to do. So instead she called Alexander. "Claire—knowing I'm pregnant—offered me a full-time job as a senior reporter with my own Sunday column. At a decent salary too, well, not by New York standards, of course. I wish I could take the job. Why can't any of the New York City papers I sent my résumé and clips to see in me what she sees?"

"Gemma, you're a great reporter and a great writer. Between the economy and newspapers shutting down, you're caught in the crossfire. But you had a great last assignment, and now you'll come home and embrace your new life."

"I know, I know," she said.

"And listen, I've been thinking. If it's Dobbs Ferry in particular that bothers you, we don't have to move so close to my family."

That was something, at least. "I guess that would help." But she knew he was thinking a town over, not a county away. "I'll drive down Saturday morning, okay?" she said, unable to keep the tears out of her voice. "I have some great people to say good-bye to up here."

"I'll see you Saturday night, then. Listen, sweetheart, you're going to love your new life. It's our next step."

If only Gemma could believe it.

Chapter 22

BEA

Bea stood in front of 26 Birch Lane in Wiscasset, a fifteen-minute drive from Boothbay Harbor, her finger poised to ring the doorbell. In moments she would meet Timothy Macintosh, her biological father. She closed her eyes for a second and summoned up the advice Patrick had given her today at lunch—to remember that Timothy had called her back, invited her to his home. Timothy had sounded like a kind enough person on the phone, if a bit hesitant. He'd explained that half of him truly had believed he wasn't the father of Veronica Russo's baby, while the other half worried all these years that he was. That had been weighing on him a long, long time, and he was looking forward to facing the truth once and for all.

She rang the bell.

There was a simultaneous gasp when the door opened. He was twenty-two years older than the boy in the photograph, but he looked so much like her. Very tall, with thick, wavy blond hair. His eyes were hazel, not brown like hers, but there was something so similar about their faces. The shape maybe. Something in the expression, the way they smiled.

"I don't think you'll need that DNA test after all," the blond woman standing slightly behind him said.

Timothy had his hand over his mouth. "It's very nice to meet you," he said, holding the door open for her to step in. "This is my wife, Beth. Our daughter is out with friends, but maybe you can meet her another time, after we've sat down with her to tell her about you, of course."

"I'd like that," Bea said.

Bea had to cut her time short with the Macintoshes at four, since she had to meet Maddy for their tutoring appointment at five. Yesterday, Tyler had called to switch tutoring days from Wednesday to Thursday, since their grandparents had come to visit, but keeping the first meeting with Timothy to an hour and a half seemed about right anyway. Both Timothy and Beth were very formal and awkward with Bea, but she'd chalked that up to nerves. They were kind, bending over backward to share stories about Timothy's family, whose ancestors came from Scotland. Bea jotted down what Timothy had said about his family's medical history, an uncle with agoraphobia, a grandmother who'd died of ovarian cancer, a bit of depression here and there, but overall, strong, hearty folk. Timothy's mother had been a secretary, and his father in construction, like Bea's own father, and both Macintoshes seemed to love hearing about Bea's childhood. Timothy and Beth had been married for seventeen years, and given how they'd sat with their arms entwined the majority of their afternoon with Bea, it appeared they were very close, that Beth was something of a rock for him. They were planning to tell their daughter about Bea that night, and Timothy promised he'd call about getting together again in the future.

She'd left Wiscasset with a lightened heart and drove back to Boothbay Harbor, but once again, Maddy was late for their tutoring session. Bea was right on time at five o'clock, but the crew trailer, where they'd arranged to meet this time instead of the library, was empty. The plan had been to meet up there and then go find a quiet spot a good distance away, under a shady tree, and talk more about the essay question for *To Kill a Mockingbird*. Bea had reread the first half of the novel since last week and found so many beautiful lines and passages that reminded her of the quote Maddy had chosen to write about. The reading, the tutoring—all of it made Bea surer than ever that she was meant to be a teacher.

There weren't too many people hanging out by the crew trailers; a crowd was lined up by the craft services tent. Maddy, though, was nowhere to be found. After their terrific session the other day, she was sure Maddy wouldn't try to ditch her tutoring session.

Bea went outside and glanced around. No sign of Maddy.

Ah, wait. A flash of her long, dark hair and unmistakable laughter came from in front of a trailer that was parked by a fence. What was she doing squished over there? Bea headed over and heard giggling. Maddy was with a boy, clearly. And her make-out session was about to be broken up for her tutoring session.

"Maddy, you're—"

She wasn't with a boy. She was with a man.

Patrick Ool.

"What the—" Bea began, almost unable to believe what she was seeing.

Patrick's face turned red. He jumped away from Maddy, and his expression changed, as though he'd already formed the lie he was about to spew.

"She's sixteen!" Bea screamed at him.

He looked faux shocked. "What? She told me she was nineteen."

"It's true, I did," Maddy said.

Bea felt sick to her stomach. She shot him a look of disgust, then turned to Maddy. "Maddy, it's time for our session. Let's go. Now. And you," she said to Patrick, "you can go to hell."

"I thought she was nineteen!" he said. "And sorry, Bea, but maybe if you weren't such a prude. I mean, how many times have we gone out now?"

Bea stopped, turned around, and punched Patrick Ool in the stomach as hard as she could.

She heard Maddy gasp and Patrick mutter "crazy bitch" before she grabbed Maddy's hand and marched her away.

"So by that 'prude' comment, does that mean you guys were seeing each other?" Maddy asked, glancing sheepishly at Bea as they headed past the barricades to a quiet area that Bea had picked out.

"Were, yeah."

"Sorry. I didn't know. He was flirting with me and told me he had to kiss me or he'd die. He's so cute, so I went for it."

Bea shook her head in disgust. "You told him you're nineteen?"

"He asked how old I was, so I lied. He said, 'Yeah right,' though. I'm really sorry, Bea."

Bea could feel steam coming out of her ears. She stopped and turned away from Maddy, giving herself a minute to calm down. Even if Patrick the prick had believed she was nineteen, he knew she was Tyler's sister. And he obviously had it out for the guy. She kicked at a rock, then resumed walking. "And he started making out with you anyway. Scum. Maddy, you have to be careful of men like that. Especially on film sets. Stick to boys your own age, okay? Please?"

"Okay, my brother lectures me enough. Can you save it for tutoring?"

She gently yanked Maddy's hair. "Your brother seems to care about you a lot, Maddy. Appreciate it. I have no one."

"Why not?"

"Because sometimes I'm an idiot about who I choose to spend my time with. Your brother told me Patrick was a womanizing jerk, and I didn't believe him."

"Tyler never lies. It's pathological. I could have told you that."

Bea had a feeling that Tyler Echols hadn't hit up Maddy's birth mother for money, that Patrick had lied about that to make sure Bea didn't listen to Tyler's assessment of him. Patrick had gone out of his way to undermine Tyler—probably because Tyler wasn't a jerk.

Bea stopped under a shady tree and spread out the blanket she'd brought in her tote bag. "Sit," she said to Maddy. "Let's get cracking. We'll forget about bad men and focus on good men. Like Atticus Finch."

While Maddy took forever to get out her book and notebook, all Bea could think about was how blind she'd been. And she owed Tyler an apology.

The second tutoring session had gone as well as the first. Maddy had read the chapters, was able to discuss the text and relate two passages back to the essay quote on her own. With Bea's nudging, Maddy had found three more in the first six chapters alone. Bea loved this—guiding Maddy through careful questions that would lead her to make connections, watching her face light up. Maddy had progressed from calling the book "To Kill a Boring Bird" to proudly explaining what she thought the real title meant.

"Hey," came Tyler's voice.

Maddy couldn't close her book fast enough at the sight of her brother. Bea was hoping by their next session, Maddy would be so into the book she'd want to keep talking about it.

"Can we talk privately for a minute?" Bea asked him.

"Don't tell me you're quitting," Tyler said. "She yammered in my ear on the way over earlier about people named Scout and Jem and Atticus and Boo."

Bea smiled. "Nope, not quitting." As Maddy's earbuds went in, Bea led Tyler away several feet and relayed the sorry story about coming upon Patrick kissing Maddy, that he'd sworn up and down that Maddy had told him she was nineteen.

Tyler was steaming mad and let out a string of muttered curses.

"I owe you an apology, Tyler. He's pure scum and I didn't see it. How are people such effortless liars?"

"Years of being around certain kinds of actors have rubbed off on the jerk. I was an idiot for bringing Maddy here. But it's not often we're filming in her backyard, so I wanted to do something for her to cheer her up."

"Because of how upset she's been over what happened with her birth mother?"

He nodded.

"I owe you another apology. Patrick told me I should be wary of you and make sure you paid me for tutoring Maddy because you'd hit up your sister's birth mother for money. He said he overheard you talking to another PA."

"What an ass," he said, shaking his head. "It was the other way around. Her birth mother hit me up for money. I said I didn't have any to give, which was true. Maddy wrote to her again six months ago, but the letter came back return to sender. Maybe that's for the best, for Maddy."

"Yeah, it probably is. I'm glad she has you. I wish I had an older brother looking out for me."

"I've been looking out for you," Tyler said. "You just didn't know it."

She smiled. "Guess so."

"Can you keep an eye on Maddy for a few minutes? I'm going to go have a talk with Patrick. And by talk, I mean I'm going to punch his lights out."

"Before you get yourself fired, rest assured, I already punched him in the stomach."

"I'll make sure to aim higher, then. His nose maybe. Or much lower, perhaps, with a solid kick."

Bea laughed, and for a second they were both silent.

"So maybe you'll have dinner with us tonight?" he asked.

"I thought you didn't like me."

"Well, you thought wrong, again." He smiled at her, maybe for the first time since she'd known him.

For a minute there, over sesame chicken and fried dumplings, Bea thought Maddy might bolt out of the restaurant.

"You know what happens when you mess with men like Patrick *Tool?*" Tyler had said, pointing a chopstick at his sister. "When you go too far with any guy? You can end up pregnant, Maddy. And then you'll have some very unfun choices to make."

"Not listening," Maddy said, covering her ears.

He pulled her hands away. "I'm dead serious," he said. "Denise was fifteen when you were born."

"Okay," she snapped. "I get it. It was just kissing. Kissing."

"And you were surrounded by trailers and inns. Very easy access to closed doors."

"Can I eat my dumplings before they get cold?" Maddy shouted.

"When I know you're listening," he said. "Really listening."

"God, I am. I hear you."

Bea sent Tyler a smile across the booth. She

didn't know Maddy very well, but Bea would put money on the odds that she was listening.

They tried to split the last dumpling in three, which sent it flying off the table and made Maddy laugh. By the time they were cracking open their fortune cookies, Bea wished they'd just sat down so she could spend another hour with these two. Tyler was smart and funny and serious and kind, and Maddy was on the immature side but had a lovable center.

Bea read her fortune: "You can never be certain of success, but you can be certain of failure if you never try."

Wasn't that the truth. Bea slipped it in her pocket.

"What did you get?" she asked Maddy.

"A smile is your personal welcome mat." Maddy rolled her eyes and grinned like a maniac. "How's that?" She took a nibble of her cookie. "What's yours say, Tyler?"

Tyler cracked his open and pulled out the fortune. "An inch of time is an inch of gold." He raised an eyebrow, then popped half the cookie in his mouth.

"Let's ask for new fortunes," Maddy said. "Only Bea got a good one."

"You get what you get and you don't get upset," Tyler singsonged, tapping Maddy's hand with her unused chopstick. "Remember how Dad always used to say that?"

The famous eye roll was back. "He still does. And anyway, doesn't that totally contradict Bea's good fortune? If what you get sucks, you should get upset."

Bea laughed. Maddy would be just fine with age and wisdom.

When they walked back to Main Street, where Tyler's car was parked, Maddy got in and put in her earbuds.

"Can I drop you home?" he asked.

"Nah, the inn's just right up the hill."

He glanced up the twisty road, then back at Bea. "So maybe we could do something sometime?"

"Definitely."

He smiled. "I'll call you tomorrow then."

He squeezed her hand and looked at her, then got in the car. As Bea headed up Harbor Hill Road, she glanced back, watching until the taillights were out of view. She had no idea where she'd be living in a couple of weeks. And Tyler would be traveling the world, working on films. But that didn't mean they couldn't be friends. Maybe even more.

On her way to the inn, Bea pulled out her phone and called Veronica.

"Would you like to get together soon? This past week, I was thinking that I wasn't sure I had anything left to ask you, anything more to tell you, but I was . . . running a bit scared, I think.

Overwhelmed. And it turns out I have a lot to tell you."

"Oh, I know all about that," Veronica said. "And I have a lot to tell you too. How about tomorrow night at seven at my house? I'll make you lasagna and you can help me bake a pie."

"I'll be there," Bea said, thinking that Cora Crane would like Veronica Russo a lot.

Chapter 23
VERONICA

It was so strange to be holding her order pad, wearing her typical uniform of jeans, white button-down shirt, and Best Little Diner in Boothbay apron, when there were three large cameras, microphones, and huge lights in every direction inside the diner. So many people stood on the sidelines. Veronica glanced out the window at the crowd of people behind a barricade across the street and was startled to see that nudge, Hugh Fledge, waving his arms at her over his head like a lunatic and blowing a kiss at her with a huge goofy smile. She hoped he was as harmless as he seemed—a pest who wouldn't give up but wasn't . . . unhinged. She'd talk to Nick about what she could do to get Fledge off her back.

For this scene, Veronica was the counter waitress. The new second assistant director, Joe Something (apparently Patrick Ool had been reassigned to equipment and wouldn't be working with extras; rumor had it he'd been caught canoodling with a minor), told her she had wisdom, kindness, and Maine in her face, and he wanted her front and center.

Veronica wondered about the rumors about Patrick and worried for Bea, but perhaps it was part of all that Bea wanted to tell her. That and how her meeting had gone with Timothy.

I really do care about her, Veronica realized as Joe Something went over the blocking—where actors stood for the scene—with one of the actors. *I tried so damned hard not to let her in, but she bulldozed her way.* Veronica smiled at the thought of petite, young Bea steamrolling her, Ms. Supposedly Tough.

The assistant director blew a whistle that he wore around his neck, which was his annoying way of getting everyone's attention. Good, time to shoot—not that Colin Firth was filming today. Rumor had it that he was coming to town tomorrow, but if Veronica had a penny for every time . . . And besides, the fact that she wanted to get this scene over with so she could go to Gray's Grocery and buy the ingredients for lasagna told her that her heart wasn't so much in being an extra anymore. Bea was coming to dinner tonight; her heart was in that.

Each table in the diner was full of extras, and the counter was half full; Veronica got a good chuckle at the "typical Maine diner customer": there was the crusty old man reading a newspaper and having the fried haddock and fries. Three teenage girls who looked like they stepped out of an L.L.Bean catalog. The reserved middle-aged woman in twin set and pearls, whose instructions were to dab her lips twice while eating her apple pie—one of Veronica's. A dad and his young son, with an adult and child-size fishing pole leaning against the wall next to them. Two twenty-something hipster types with a map of Maine spread out in front of them. And Veronica behind the counter with her coffeepot.

All her counter needed was Colin Firth. She got her fix of seeing his handsome face by watching his films; over the past two weeks, she'd seen ten more of his movies—and had watched *Love Actually* twice more, since it made her so damned happy.

And so damned sappy. Veronica Russo, sappy. That was a wonder.

But she'd let go of the fantasy of Mr. Darcy. He was a character, an idea. A very good idea, but an idea. And Colin Firth, despite how much Veronica loved him, was an actor on screen. Nick DeMarco, on the other hand, was six foot two inches of reality, and she was ready for him. When she'd made her Colin Firth Pie the other night, it wasn't Mr. Darcy she'd been thinking about as she stirred her cherries and sugar and vanilla. And it wasn't Colin Firth she'd imagined as she'd eaten every last bite of a slice. She'd only thought of Nick.

The actors got into place, and Veronica gave the set her full attention. In this scene, the female lead and her fiancé were having an argument that involved her dumping a lobster roll on his head and storming out. They'd rehearsed the scene with an empty plate four times and had shot it twice today with the real thing, which meant hour-long breaks to wash the lobster bits out of Christopher Cade's hair and change his shirt. Apparently, wardrobe had thirty of the same blue dress shirts at the ready.

As they waited for the sound guy to attend to whatever was the problem, Veronica relaxed behind the counter and decided that after dinner tonight, she'd teach Bea how to make one of her Happiness Pies. One of her own favorites: fudge.

Veronica had the lasagna in the oven and was mincing garlic for the Italian bread when her phone rang. Please don't be Bea canceling, she'd prayed.

But it was Beth Macintosh.

"I wanted to apologize to you for how I acted," Beth said. "Timothy had always been torn up about whether or not he'd fathered your child, but ever since he saw you through the diner window several months ago, it's all he'd talk about. Did I? Was I? What if? It got to the point where our marriage was strained. Then one day, friends of mine in town mentioned your name—not even knowing your connection to Tim—and your elixir pies, and I thought I'd kill two birds with one stone, as they say."

"So maybe the pie worked in a roundabout way, after all," Veronica said.

Beth was quiet for a second, but then laughed. "I guess I owe you fifteen bucks."

"That one's on me."

"Thank you," Beth said. And then she hung up—once and for all, Veronica knew.

Over Veronica's delicious—if she did say so herself—lasagna, garlic bread, and a crisp green salad, Bea told Veronica about meeting Timothy and Beth.

"It was a bit awkward," Bea said, lifting up a gooey forkful of lasagna. "I think he's still uncomfortable with the whole thing, but Beth said they'd tell their daughter about me and would like to get together again."

"I'm glad you found him. You've settled something, and gave him an answer to a question he couldn't let go of."

Bea lifted her glass of iced tea and clinked Veronica's.

As they ate, Veronica told Bea that she'd sat down to an interview with Gemma Hendricks and poured out her life story, and Bea told Veronica all about Patrick Ool and why he'd gotten reassigned to equipment.

"Good Lord," Veronica said, shocked to hear the news. "You just can't tell with some people. I never would have pegged him for a creep."

Bea smiled and reached for a piece of garlic bread. "That makes me feel better because neither did I."

"So . . . are you and Tyler dating now, if I can ask?"

"Of course you can ask. But I'm over dating for now. I like him, that's all I know. Considering I hated his guts a week ago, I think I'll just take this one super slow. The cast and crew are heading to London to shoot for a week. And sometime soon, I guess I'll be heading back to Boston to look for teaching jobs."

Oh. Veronica should have known she'd be heading back to Boston. But she figured Bea would stick around for the summer, at least. "You have family there?"

"There's no one, actually. Just me."

"And me," Veronica dared to say.

Bea looked at her. "And you."

Maybe that was too much for Veronica to have said. She changed the subject. "You're so lucky you know what you want to do. I never really knew. Sometimes I dream about opening up my own little pie diner. But that's just that—a dream."

"A diner of pies? That sounds incredible. And since your pie is the best anyone's ever had, you should open your own place. Who wouldn't swarm a pie diner all day?"

Veronica did have a lot of money socked away. Maybe she'd look into it. Huh. Veronica Russo, business owner. Owning her own place instead of serving. Staking her own claim. She liked the sound of that.

Bea took a bite of lasagna. "I thought maybe you wanted to be an actress or involved with films. Because you became an extra."

"Oh, I only did that to get a glimpse of Mr. Darcy in the flesh. Colin Firth. He's my secret heartthrob."

Bea laughed. "I love his accent." She did an imitation of him that Veronica recognized from *Bridget Jones's Diary.* "You know what's funny? Tyler ended up being a bit like Mr. Darcy. I thought he was the biggest jerk. Turns out, he's pretty wonderful."

"I think I might have a Mr. Darcy too," Veronica said, unable to hide her smile. "He was never a jerk, though—he's just all the good things about Darcy. Honest and honorable, trustworthy, a man of conviction. And drop-dead gorgeous. And you know what, Bea? I'm ready to get back to my life. But not to waitressing. I'll make tomorrow my last day as an extra and spend tomorrow night scouting out possible sites in town for a pie diner. There's a place on Main I noticed the other day. It needs work, but just standing there, I could see my blackboard of ten different kinds of pies, Happiness Pies and elixirs."

It seemed fitting that her last day at the diner would be during the filming of a Colin Firth movie. She wondered if he was really going to show up tomorrow. But Veronica wouldn't hold her breath. If he was there, great. If not, well, Veronica had already found what she'd been looking for: her heart to blast wide open, finally. And it had.

Bea smiled. "I'll be first in line at that pie diner."

"So . . . maybe you could apply for teaching jobs up here in Maine," Veronica said.

From the smile Bea gave her, Veronica could see that the open invitation to Veronica's life had been received. "You mean just stay in Maine?"

"Sure. You have a place to stay. A job in the meantime. And you know that my door is always open."

Bea came around the table and hugged Veronica, and she hugged her back. They lingered that way, neither wanting to pull away so fast. "Maybe I will stay, then."

"Yoo-hoo, everyone," a man's singsong voice called from outside, "Colin Firth just passed me on the street!"

"What the heck?" Veronica said, peering out the window. There was someone out there. A tall, skinny man holding a can stood at the far end of the driveway. She headed to the living room window for a closer look and saw the nudge who wouldn't stop asking her out, Hugh Fledge.

He'd been behind all the fake Colin Firth

sightings? Sending people racing around, hoping to get a glimpse of the actor? What a pest!

He shook the can in his hand and aimed it at the far end of her driveway. Oh, no. That wasn't beer. It was spray paint. She was about to run out and confront him, then realized she could bring in the heavy hitters: aka the police. She grabbed her phone and called Nick.

"That drunken fool who keeps asking me out—Hugh Fledge—is waving a can of what looks like spray paint on my driveway."

"I'll be right there," Nick said. "I'm patrolling nearby. Wait for me—don't confront him."

But Fledge was now spraying on her driveway—with black spray paint. He'd gotten as far as *B I*.

No big wonder what letter was next.

She opened the front door and shouted at him. "I've called the police. You'd better stop. Now."

"Go out with me and I will, Va-va-voomica," he said, shaking his hips at her and continuing with the *T*.

"You realize this is harassment of every kind," she said. "You're going to get arrested."

He was wiggling his finger at her in a "come get me" sickening way. She'd march over and try some tae kwon do that she'd once learned, but she had no idea what he was capable of, and Bea could get caught in the crossfire. Just as he was about to spray again, she ran over and knocked the can out of his hand. He was wobbling, she realized. Drunk fool.

Nick arrived in his squad car and rushed over to Fledge. "Veronica, you should have waited for me."

"I didn't want him to finish," she said.

He smiled, then glanced over at Bea in the doorway. "I'm glad to see you have company."

"We're baking a chocolate fudge Happiness Pie later."

"Maybe you could teach me Saturday night. After dinner at Grill 207?"

Now it was her turn to smile. "I'd like that."

He looked at Veronica, his dark eyes full of so many things. "Pick you up at seven." He gave her hand a brief squeeze, then secured Fledge in the back of the squad car, who'd gotten in a kick at Nick's shin. The kick would ensure an even longer stay in jail.

"We could scrub that *B I* away while the coffee perks," Bea said.

As Veronica worked on the *B,* and Bea on the *I,* all she could think about was that she had met Bea in a driveway for the first time, and now here they were, together again for a new beginning.

Chapter 24

GEMMA

The parlor was crowded for Movie Night at the Three Captains' Inn. The Colin Firth fan club, three women wearing their "Happiness Is Colin Firth" T-shirts, had checked back into the inn since the town was buzzing that the actor was due to arrive in town tomorrow to shoot a scene at the Best Little Diner in Boothbay. The guests from the Seashell and Bluebird Rooms were scattered around the parlor, including two husbands, and according to Isabel, men rarely came to Movie Night, since shoot-'em-ups were rare on the marquee. June was handing out cute bags of popcorn that her son had decorated for the event, and Isabel was handing out slices of Veronica Russo's pies.

Bea and Veronica were waiting on the big sofa and had saved Gemma a seat. Veronica had brought over three pies for the occasion, and Gemma helped herself to a slice of chocolate fudge pie, since she'd missed out on the one she'd given the newlyweds the other night. The two of them were snuggled up on a beanbag, feeding each other the key lime, their arms entwined. Gemma remembered when she and Alexander used to do sickeningly lovey-dovey stuff like that, and she smiled. She missed Alexander. If she had to go home and face her future, at least she was going home to him.

"Everyone ready for *Girl with a Pearl Earring*?" Isabel asked.

Girl with a Pearl Earring. Gemma flashed back to one of her earliest dates with Alexander, at the Metropolitan Museum of Art, when they were twenty-three and didn't have much money, and they'd looked through postcards of art for their bulletin boards at work. Alex had bought her two Vermeers, *A Maid Asleep* and *Girl with a Pearl Earring*, and she'd always loved both, but especially the "girl's" haunting face, her eyes, that one beautiful pearl earring. She still had those postcards, but now it was in her big box of stuff from when she'd had to clean out her desk at *New York Weekly*. Suddenly she wished Alexander were here, sitting next to her, holding her hand.

Tomorrow, she thought, the warring feelings settling down some.

The lights went off and the movie began, and Gemma was transported to the seventeenth-century Dutch republic, as a poor teenage maid named Griet, played by Scarlett Johansson, slowly dares to assist and model for the master of the house, the reclusive painter Johannes Vermeer, who has a very jealous, pregnant wife.

Between the exquisite period detail and the

intensity of Colin Firth's performance, Gemma was riveted to the screen, as was everyone else.

"The longing between them!" June said as the lights were turned back on. "Aside from how beautiful the movie was, the photography, the absolute longing that was captured between Griet and Vermeer almost made me uncomfortable."

"Because it couldn't be and because their connection was so special," Bea said.

"Did Colin Firth look incredibly hot with that longish hair or what?" one of the members of the Colin Firth fan club said. "All those smoldering gazes!" She fanned herself.

There was general agreement on that.

The discussion continued for a while, some saying the movie didn't have enough action, but Gemma thought it was beautiful—and very sad—as it was. The newlyweds left for their room, giving each other exaggerated haunting gazes à la Griet and Vermeer, and Gemma had to smile. The Colin Firth fan club insisted that Colin Firth would be here tomorrow; someone who knew someone who knew someone had gotten word to one of them that he was arriving in the morning to film scenes in the diner, but Veronica, beset by the fan club for details and information, swore on a stack of imaginary Bibles that even she—and the assistant director—couldn't say for sure if he'd be there.

Gemma smiled at how important she'd thought

an interview with him would be. And it would be important to editors who'd relish a story on him, especially from the perspective Gemma had in mind of a travel piece. But now all she wanted was to go home and see her husband, feel his arms around her, and slowly morph into the new Gemma—mother to be, a role that she would put her heart and soul into, whether it was incredibly difficult for her or not. She was ready to go home, wherever that home turned out to be. She'd make her new life work for her, somehow, someway.

Slowly, the room began clearing out. Bea and Veronica left for Harbor View Coffee, and Gemma helped Isabel and June clean up the pie crumbs and pieces of popcorn from between sofa cushions and from the floor. And then it was time to go, up to her room, for her last night of sleep as the old Gemma, intrepid reporter.

Someone knocked on the front door of the inn, and Isabel wondered out loud if she'd missed getting ready for a late arrival as she headed to the door, but when she returned, there was Alexander.

Gemma stared at him. "Alex? What on earth?"

"You think I'd let my beloved pregnant wife drive seven hours hunched over the wheel of our little Miata?" he said. "I flew up to drive you home tomorrow morning."

He was wonderful that way. "Thank you." She hugged him, breathing in the scent of him, the security of him. Sometimes it felt very, very good.

She couldn't believe he was really here, standing a foot in front of her, looking a bit tired, his sandy-blond hair mussed, but otherwise absolutely wonderful.

"Let's go for a walk," he said. "Show me that yellow house you texted me a picture of. I want to see what you have in mind. I want you to be happy."

She knew he did. Holding hands, they walked out into the warm July night, a beautiful breeze lifting the ends of Gemma's hair. They walked down to Main Street, then turned onto Meadow Lane. "That's it," she said, pointing to the craftsman she loved with the widow's walk and porch swing.

He looked at it, then turned back to her. "I've been doing a lot of thinking the past couple of days. I think you should accept the job offer from the *Gazette*, Gemma."

She stared at him, her stomach dropping. "Are you saying you want to split up?"

"Are you nuts?" he asked. "Of course not."

"Well, Dobbs Ferry, New York, is a long commute to Boothbay Harbor, Maine."

"True, but this isn't," he said, pointing at the yellow bungalow.

"What?"

"I told you that somehow we'd find a way to make this work for both of us," he said. "And here's what I came up with. We have a lot of money socked away. I can take off a few years if we're careful, if we live here in Boothbay instead of New York, and if you're the breadwinner, supporting us with your full-time job."

Her mouth dropped open. "You're going to be a stay-at-home father?"

"Why not? I could use an extended break from my job. When Gemma Jr. starts preschool, I'll go back to work. But for these three years, we'll cut expenses. We'll get three times for our apartment what I'll pay for a house here. My parents won't be thrilled we're moving so far away, but it's an hour-and-a-half plane ride from New York. You'll be a working mother, and I'll be the stay-at-home dad. We'll both change diapers."

Gemma's eyes filled with tears. "I am the luckiest person on earth."

"We both are.

EPILOGUE

In the morning, both Bea and Gemma were invited to the movie set, thanks to Tyler and Veronica, and the special passes around their necks helped them navigate through the crowds behind barricades lining Main Street. But when they arrived at the Best Little Diner in Boothbay, they learned the shoot was delayed for three hours—and no one was confirming if Colin Firth was on set or not.

The extras were dismissed until two o'clock, so Veronica led Bea and Gemma out the back door to the coffee bar that had been set up behind the diner, along with trailers and equipment Veronica wouldn't have thought could possibly fit back here.

"Hey, everyone, it's Colin Firth!" a man's voice called out.

Gemma rolled her eyes. "I love how no one's even bothering to look. We've all had enough of the loser who called wolf."

"Loser who called hunk, you mean," Bea said.

Veronica stopped short. "Wait a minute. The guy who kept shouting out fake Colin Firth sightings is in jail."

The three of them quickly looked to the right, and there, walking quickly into a trailer parked in a wide alleyway, was Colin Firth himself, wearing jeans and green Wellingtons.

Veronica's mouth dropped open, then she burst into a grin. "Okay, I said I'd live if I didn't see him, but to be honest, those five seconds were worth everything. Still, all I really want right now? To go scouting out locations for my pie diner with Bea."

Gemma smiled. "I know exactly what you mean. A few days ago, I'd have been busting down that trailer door to get an interview with him. But now all I want to do is go house hunting with my husband, right here in Boothbay Harbor."

"I still can't believe you're moving here," Bea said. "I'll see you at Movie Night at the inn some Fridays, at least?"

Gemma slung an arm around her. "Definitely. And, Veronica, hurry up and open that pie diner because I'll be craving your fudge pie throughout this pregnancy."

"Bea and I might have made you a fudge pie last night, after we left Movie Night," Veronica said with a smile. "It's in the fridge at the inn, with your name on it. It's for everything you've done for Hope Home and for us. I can't wait until the article comes out."

Gemma gave Veronica a quick hug, but they were bumped apart by some women jockeying for position to see inside the diner.

Bea glanced at the trailer Colin Firth had darted into, now surrounded by a huge crowd of people behind a barricade as police officers tried to keep some order. *I saw him for you, Mama,* she said silently up to the sky.

Then Bea, Veronica, and Gemma headed away from the set as more shouts rang out that it really was him this time.

A Note About
Veronica's Elixir Pies

No recipes are included with this novel for the very good reason that Veronica's special elixir pies, whether her chocolate caramel cream Amore Pie or her Key lime Confidence Pie, are about you—not the ingredients. Use any recipe you'd like for peanut butter coconut pie or blueberry pie, for example, and while you're gently rolling out the piecrust or mixing your sugar and butter and chocolate, think of what you'd wish for and then think some more while you're savoring the finished pie. Or, if you're pressed for time, just go buy a pie from your favorite bakery and wish away while you're enjoying every last bite of a slice. Your wishes just might come true.

Amore Pie: chocolate caramel cream pie
Spirit Pie: shoofly pie
Feel Better Pie: blueberry pie
Confidence Pie: Key lime pie
Cast-Out Pie: peanut butter coconut pie
Hope Pie: salted caramel cheesecake pie
Happiness Pie: your favorite kind

Acknowledgments

Once again, there aren't enough thanks in the world for me to express how grateful I am to my literary agent, Alexis Hurley of InkWell Management. Best of the best. And to my editor, the wonderful Karen Kosztolnyik of Simon & Schuster's Gallery Books, thank you for helping me find the real story. To everyone at Gallery for the incredible support—Louse Burke, Jen Bergstrom, Heather Hunt, and the tireless Kristin Dwyer. A huge thank-you to every writer's secret weapon—an amazing writer friend: Lee Nichols Naftali, I owe you big, especially from three thousand miles away now.

I will never forget watching the BBC miniseries of *Pride and Prejudice* back in the mid '90s and saying to myself "Who *is* that?" when Colin Firth appeared on screen. I've been captivated by him ever since. Thank you, Mr. Firth, for your fifty-plus roles, for making us swoon, for making us believe and care, for transporting us—the joy of movies.

Readers Group Guide

One summer. Three women. A quaint seaside town. And Colin Firth—maybe.

Bea Crane is spending a monotonous post-college summer building Mt. Vesuvius burgers at Boston's Crazy Burger when she gets a life-changing letter—from her late mother. The letter tells Bea that the parents who left her orphaned weren't actually her birth parents. After contacting her adoption agency, Bea gets a name and a number for her birth mother. With nothing to lose but her job as a burger maven, Bea packs her bags and heads to Boothbay Harbor to find her birth mother: Veronica Russo.

Rumor has it that Veronica Russo's pies can solve any problem. During the day, Veronica works as a waitress at The Best Little Diner in Boothbay Harbor, but when the waitressing day is over, Veronica moonlights as a maker of magical pies. But in spite of being able to make her customers' wishes come true, Veronica can't stop dreaming about the baby girl that she gave up for adoption as a teenager. But when she receives an unexpected voicemail from her daughter, it seems that Veronica's life might be on the brink of changing.

After Gemma Hendricks loses her high-powered

job as a New York City journalist, it seems that she doesn't have any ground to stand on against her adoring husband, who wants nothing more than to settle into life as a happy, suburban couple—preferably in the house next to Gemma's mother-in-law. When Gemma discovers that she's expecting a baby, she does the only rational thing that she can think of to escape her seemingly inevitable future as a soccer mom—she runs away to her best friend's Boothbay Harbor inn for plates of pie, long nights of girl talk, and maybe a couple Colin Firth movie marathons.

None of the women realize how much one summer will change their lives. But as Gemma scoops an unexpected newspaper story, Veronica gets cast in a Colin Firth movie shooting in Boothbay, and Bea meets a hot young assistant director, it seems that the summer in Boothbay just might be full of surprises that none of them could have anticipated. And through the wild ride of the summer, each woman learns some valuable lessons—about her dreams, relationships, and the hope that we all hold of someday meeting a Colin Firth.

1. In the opening chapter, Bea learns that she's adopted via a heartfelt letter from her deceased adoptive mother, Cora. What was your response to this revelation—or, as Bea later refers to it, this "lie of omission"—

especially considering the fact that it comes in the form of a letter? How did you feel about Bea's levelheaded reaction—did you expect her to be angrier or feel a greater sense of betrayal? Have you ever had to deliver news or make a confession so groundbreaking or potentially upsetting that you did so in writing rather than face-to-face?

2. Veronica says that her special "elixir pies" are simply regular pies with "some prayers and wishes and hopes baked in" (p. 207), but some locals seem to think that they wield more power than just "the spark of hope in their names" (p. 208). In your opinion, are the pies truly elixirs—adding a magical realism twist to the otherwise realistic novel—or do they simply give customers just enough added hope or confidence to take control of their own destinies in some way?

3. The themes of identity and a sense of belonging are inherent in each of the three heroines' stories. When Bea finds out that she's adopted, Tommy insists: "Your entire life has been a lie" (p. 16), but Bea disagrees. What are the building blocks of each woman's identity, if not her biological makeup, her familial lineage? From where do you derive your own sense of self?

4. Veronica still seems to be battling her reputation as the "high school slut" who got knocked up at sixteen, thanks to snide remarks from the seemingly snobby Penelope Von Blun and from her own sense of shame at how her family and friends reacted to the news back when she was a teenager. Can you relate to Veronica's inability to shake her old reputation, to move on from a formative event that—while far in the past—still affects her in the present?

5. When Gemma first arrives at the Three Captains' Inn, she finds herself relating to Bridget Jones more than she'd like to admit while viewing the inaugural film of the inn's Colin Firth movie month. Is there a particular film or cinematic heroine whom you related to, or have related to in the past? If so, did seeing a version of your own struggles play out on screen help you deal with them in any way?

6. Mona, Alex's mother, could easily be a fundamentally unsympathetic character given the extent to which she intervenes in Gemma and Alex's lives—think of the scene in which she calls Gemma, saying accusatorily, "Think of the baby if your own husband doesn't matter to you." (p. 325). Can you

understand where she's coming from, or do you see her as a villain of sorts?

7. Were you surprised to discover who Beth, the woman who'd ordered the Cast-Out Pie for "someone else who has to get someone out of his goddamned head" (p. 350), really was? What does this tell you about the real impact that Veronica's pregnancy had—and continues to have—on Bea's birth father's life?

8. The importance of female relationships—whether they're friendships or mother-daughter bonds—is a theme that resonates strongly throughout this novel. In light of this, what do you think of Veronica's grandmother's words of wisdom, which stress putting oneself first, always: "People will come and go from your life for all kinds of acceptable and crappy reasons, so you've got to be your own best friend, know who you are, and never let anyone tell you you're something you know you're not" (p. 87). Which of the three heroines in this novel, if any, best follows this advice?

9. As Gemma tries to make peace with her impending motherhood, she reflects: "Mother-hood wasn't about who gave birth to you, who adopted you, who raised you. It was

about love, commitment, responsibility. It was about being there. About wanting to be there" (p. 167). What do you think about this definition of motherhood? How does it apply to both Bea's story and Gemma's?

10. What do you think of Alex's ultimate offer at the end? What do you see as his turning point, if he has one?

11. At the novel's end, all three heroines decide to begin the next chapter in their lives in Boothbay Harbor, the charming coastal Maine town that feels like a central character in and of itself. Gemma says of the town: "Boothbay Harbor had always been a saving grace, a harbor in itself . . . She'd always been happy in Boothbay, the vibrant coastal town a constant ray of sunshine. She had old friends here, wonderful memories. And she loved the old wooden piers and boats in the bay, the cobblestone and brick streets lined with one-of-a-kind shops and every imaginable cuisine" (p. 371). Is there a town, city, region, or any other landmark (perhaps a favorite hiking trail or café) that you consider a "harbor"—a place to which you attribute feelings of security and happiness, a place that holds treasured memories?

12. When Veronica tells Nick DeMarco that the delicious pie he's tasted is just a "plain old Happiness Pie," Nick responds: "Nothing plain or old about happiness" (p. 267). What do you think about this statement? Do we undervalue the beauty of general contentedness? What defines happiness in the lives of Gemma, Bea, and Veronica?

13. Each heroine ultimately finds her happy ending in Boothbay Harbor, but unlike in a Colin Firth romantic comedy, these women's happy endings don't necessarily involve men—they find fulfillment in other ways: familial bonds, career moves, a sense of belonging. Which woman's trajectory did you find the most relatable and why? The most enjoyable?

ENHANCE YOUR BOOK CLUB

Take a cooking or baking class together! Veronica teaches a pie-making class to locals in Boothbay Harbor. Look up local cooking classes in your region and sign up with your book club members!

Cast the film! If this novel were adapted into a movie (a Colin Firth movie, perhaps?), who would play which character?

Host a Colin Firth movie night! Following book club, screen your favorite Colin Firth film!

Bake your own elixir pie to serve to your book club members! What kind of hopes, wishes, or sentiments would you bake into your own version of Veronica's special elixir pies?

Make it a double feature! Read *Finding Colin Firth* in tandem with Mia March's hit debut novel, *The Meryl Streep Movie Club*! This novel, set in the same charming seaside town, features several characters you'll recognize from *Finding Colin Firth*.

Center Point Large Print
600 Brooks Road / PO Box 1
Thorndike ME 04986-0001 USA

(207) 568-3717

US & Canada:
1 800 929-9108
www.centerpointlargeprint.com